D1465459

The Casting of Mr O'Shaughnessy

THE CASTING OF MR O'SHAUGHNESSY

EAMON DELANEY

BLOOMSBURY

First published 1995

Copyright © 1995 by Eamon Delaney

The moral right of the author has been asserted

Bloomsbury Publishing Plc, 2 Soho Square, London W1V 6HB

A CIP catalogue record for this book is available
from the British Library

ISBN 0 7475 2002 X

Typeset in Great Britain by Hewer Text Composition Services, Edinburgh
Printed in Great Britain by Clays Ltd, St Ives plc

Chapter 1

Commission

This is a gruesome story. One fine morning recently in Cambridge, final mathematics students assembled with hushed nervousness in the Great Senate Hall to sit their tripos examination. One student – presumably with a heart less palpitating than his surrounding colleagues – sat at his numbered desk, quietly sharpened his pencils and, pushing a pencil into each of his two nostrils, put his head forward and proceeded to hammer the pencils against the desk and up, up into his head and towards his brain. He died noisily in an obscene amount of blood amidst many upturned desks and chairs.

There are easier ways to go, but then, if you've had a disturbed and painful life, you may as well die in a disturbed and painful way. Let the world clean you up, having messed you about. This is the attitude of the people who now jump naked from those fine gleaming buildings of New York to ensure that when they reach the sidewalk they will also – the flesh being weak, as the Christians say – reach the fifth floor. If I ever had the guts (excuse the pun) to end it all, I would choose a more sedate, a more civilized method of exit: cover my body in mustard, a quart of whiskey flung back hungrily, or – the doctor used to inform me this would work (and he has more than an incidental interest in these things) – stand underneath a steaming hot shower and very slowly keep on increasing the temperature. Your body will adapt to the heat at each scorching interval, your blood will be far from cold-blooded (despite your murderous state of mind) and presently you will stand there red-raw and yet quite cooked (like a stove lobster) and resembling one of those puffy-pink middle-aged joggers who plod the paths of suburbia. Finally your

1

body will lose the control of your mind, your heart will beat faster and faster in the searing heat and then suddenly say – like that self-same sad and sweaty jogger – 'Enough'. And stop. But the shower wouldn't and since – excepting American newly-weds and rugby players – people do not generally disturb each other in showers, when eventually encountered, your body would be as clean, soft and rosy-hued as a baby's bottom or that elderly jogger's tenderised scrotum. Unfortunately, your body would by then be as much use to you as our jogging friend's genitals, as dry as the walnuts they resemble. And as useful, the father of Michael Collins notwithstanding.

I mention all this because, like my former doctor, I have a more than incidental interest in death – the death, to be precise, of that dry old walnut Cornelius O'Shaughnessy. You have no doubt heard much about Mr O'Shaughnessy. You have probably heard too much about Mr O'Shaughnessy and his long and illustrious career and are quite tired of opening the morning paper and seeing his wizened eighty-nine-year-old face caught in open-mouthed pontification about the law, freedom and the Republic, and his personal contribution to each. How many times has his curriculum vitae been paraded before us – how he manned a window in Boland's Mills during the 1916 Rising; how he wiped out ('engaged' I think they call it) a lorry-load of Black and Tans as a young volunteer in 1920; how he went to London for the Treaty negotiations as Collins's bodyguard and courier and told his great leader on the way back that the signing of it was 'a sorry thing'; how he eventually shelved the gun and founded a political party in 1940, entered parliament and, eventually, government, as a bleak-faced minister in the inter-party government of the bleak late forties. You've seen those cabinet photographs – the assembled mournful faces sitting around a bare polished table and looking at the camera with all the listlessness and eye-sagging lethargy of their isolationist, emigrationist, post-war state. An Irish emergency. And in among those grim and grainy faces are the gaunt high cheekbones and pursed lips of the Minister for External Affairs, Mr Cornelius O'Shaughnessy, TD.

The initials BL should also be added, for by the close of the dark thirties – 1937 to be precise, the same year he resigned as Chief of Staff of the IRA – O'Shaughnessy has been called to the Bar as a sharp and learned practitioner, plying his trade with duplicitous quiet in the Four Courts, the very building in which in 1922 he sandbagged the windows and defied the fledgling, Treaty-signed

2

Free State government, setting in motion that charming episode of fraternal blood-letting known as the Civil War. As if to bolster, to sandbag the irony, the clients of Mr O'Shaughnessy, BL, both then and now are invariably a long line of violent Republicans as defiant as their wizened, humped but steely-eyed advocate once was in his day.

The baffled smiles flickering across the faces of these sullen bombers as they are freed on a bizarre technicality is testimony to Mr O'Shaughnessy's considerable legal skill. It is in fact through the law, and particularly international law, that Mr O'Shaughnessy has elevated himself into an esteemed and famous statesman. Small 's', please; he's hardly the States man. But he is what the Americans call a commentator, a wise old hand consulted on for his shaky but 'experienced' opinions delivered from the side of his mottled mouth in a deliberative, quavering and thus all the more sage-like voice. Mr O'Shaughnessy has had a feverishly active retirement, chairing inquiries into Middle Eastern atrocities, sitting on multilateral legal commissions, overseeing the UN-fostered independence of some new slice of African statehood, patron of this, vice-president of that, protesting outside the American Embassy, lecturing, writing and setting out into endless student-debating theatres steered by the warm strong hands of reverential adolescents who hear approximately eight sentences of his long, whispered, guttural speech and applaud vigorously. Up on your feet, lads, for the Grand Old Man of Irish Republicanism.

The pinnacle of Mr O'Shaughnessy's career (many careers indeed for this speckled chameleon) was receiving the Nobel Peace Prize. Strange perhaps for a man with such a militant past, but then Menachem Begin also climbed those Stockholm steps just as disinclined as Mr O'Shaughnessy to repent of his explosive career. No doubt behind the twin television screens of his spectacles, Mr Begin was even then, as he mounted the Nobel steps, visualising the effect of phosphorous flames on Lebanese children, sad that it could be. Subtle, stealthy Mr O'Shaughnessy had none of these direct-hit crudities. Indeed so subtle, so simperingly successful was the man that he soon added the Lenin Peace Prize (the other one) to his collection of war medals. And so off he padded to Moscow (how could his weary-warrior shuffle not impress these nodding Politburo veterans) where he gave a long, ponderous acceptance speech about peaceful co-existence, the world and humankind, that was applauded woodenly throughout with admirable precision. At

3

intervals, his lips would pucker silently to re-emphasise a global truth (and give the interpreter a chance to catch up) and the banked semi-circles of Soviet heads would clap knowledgeably, foreheads frowning in accompaniment.

In the honoured tradition of Irish politics, operating in a perpetual ideological void, Mr O'Shaughnessy has been all things to all men. In the cloak of a Republican, he has been socialist and conservative simultaneously. And that's Republican without the larger, small 'r' sense of the word which allows a plurality of views and the liberty of the individual. No siree, the Church saw to that. During his long career, Mr O'Shaughnessy has not so much evaded the main issues of the day as absorbed them, talked his way inside and surrounded himself with its ifs and buts ('We must look at this issue from all angles'). 'Radical' is an epithet often applied to the man, a dubious way of saying that he is outspoken and makes regular – oh how regular – well-timed denunciations of large parts of the social system or the establishment, if that description can be given to a consensus that regards itself as transitory and uncovered, developing. O'Shaughnessy hits out at nebulous enemies like 'bureaucracy', 'the fat cats', 'the intelligentsia', 'the slave instinct' (i.e. 'Brit-lovers') and that hoary old monster, 'the media'.

His most regular invective is reserved for his successors: today's politicians. Incompetent, lacking backbone, losing touch with the common values, plastic men manipulated by public relations. These modern politicians accept humbly and even echo the descriptions heaped upon them from the angry saint, this Augustine of the Republic. In the Sunday papers, they are photographed smiling, beefy-faced and expectant, gathered around the precious antique, keeping him warm. Or else Mr O'Shaughnessy is caught in his mid-*seanachaí* pose, being listened to with deferential radiance, a mixture of grandiose poise and strategic informality. Of course, later on, when Mr O'Shaughnessy has been wheeled away and long tucked up in his Clonskeagh bed, and the modern political faces are feeding on closing-time pints and thus beaming more sincerely, Mr O'Shaughnessy will not be quite as worshipped. Disparaging remarks will be made about 'old grandad' and 'his interfering holiness' and of how he could be 'a right tool sometimes'. One TD will inevitably draw matters to a close by draining his glass – Adam's apple yo-yoing away – and with a smack of the lips wonder when the old whore is going to kick the bucket. Guffawed laughter

4

will ensue followed by a counselling voice saying, 'Ah, lads, lads, give it over.'

Guffaws aside, the modern politicians revere the man and to honour officially his upcoming ninetieth birthday and the Seventieth Anniversary of the Rising in which he and his father had taken part, the Government proposed to erect a statue of Mr O'Shaughnessy in St Stephen's Green in Dublin. After consultation with the subject, who modestly agreed with the proposal despite his dislike of the proposer, An Taoiseach made the announcement when he gave the oration at the Annual Michael Collins Commemoration Ceremony in Beal na mBláth, a venue that gave credence to those sly suggestions that the idea was not unmotivated by An Taoiseach's own desire to win himself back in with old-style Republicans, after the image corruption of too many Anglo-Irish summits. This it did, to an extent, and there was relief that 1916, which used to be celebrated with gusto until the 'Northern business' soured the rituals, hadn't been completely forgotten.

However, a degree of controversy greeted the decision. Were there not enough statues in Stephen's Green? Why couldn't such a project be built out of private initiative rather than public funding? Why should one man (especially this man) be honoured for an event that subsumed the individual, just because he's one of its last surviving participants? (The implication here being that they should honour someone who wasn't crafty enough to survive it, such as perhaps The O'Rahilly, Sheehy Skeffington or any of the many unknown civilians who got in the way.) But the most persistent question, related to this and enquired of initially with immense delicacy, but, as it was left unanswered, asked with increasing stridency, was, why didn't they wait until the man was perhaps . . . deceased, passed away, no longer with us or, as the gentleman TD with the salivating jaws would put it, had 'kicked the bucket'.

The Taoiseach fluttered his hands and dismissed these sensitive reservations with admirable brusqueness. The statue would be made now because Mr O'Shaughnessy's ninetieth birthday coincided with the Seventieth Anniversary of the Rising. Because Mr O'Shaughnessy's father died in that Rising. ('Mine didn't, thankfully,' he added, 'but we owe it to both of them.') Because, as a historian, the Taoiseach understood better than anyone how important it was to retrieve the 1916 tradition from the hands of its unworthy hijackers and no better way to do this than for the

State to honour one of the Rising's last living participants. As an economist meanwhile the Taoiseach needed to get back to the more present business of his sums or our sums, or our children's sums. So after he'd finished fluttering his hands and answering questions on his proposals, he'd leave in his wake government spokesmen who would call journalists to the Dáil lobby or the bar counters of surrounding hotels to explain to them that the statue was being put up now because, as well as everything else, there could be an election and you couldn't trust the other shower with the memory of a man who put de Valera out of office after sixteen years. They had a long list of their own people to put up. As for St Stephen's Green, there were no statues or busts on its west side and it would be fitting to have O'Shaughnessy erected facing Iveagh House, headquarters of the Department of Foreign Affairs, his old ministry when its affairs were 'External' and the world was a place we could do without.

And the fact that O'Shaughnessy was, well, still alive? Nothing wrong with it. People have had statues made of them while they were still in their prime and, let's face it, is O'Shaughnessy? Spokesman leans over and clinks ice: You know, Jim (you old Pol Corr, you), people say that the T. is of less than a green hue about this 1916 stuff (O'Shaughnessy himself used to say it until . . . well, until recently), but I'll tell you, by the time he gets this commitment unveiled people like O'Shaughnessy himself will be of a less than green hue. With his health (from what I hear) and with the rate the man we appointed to do the job is working at, I'd say old Cornelius will be feeding the green before he gets there and giving up the last of his acids to the rich Glasnevin clay. Do you get me?

It is in fact regrettable that O'Shaughnessy won't have been able to see the unveiling of his own statue, but there you are. His funeral would have been a great display of trumpets, banners, guns and flags, teams of priests and a who's who of funeral-goers. The toothy, pregnant-bellied TD who has long awaited the 'kicking of the bucket' would now at this high pharaoh – passing moment – take his place in the cortège, his fingers assembled neatly behind his black Abercrombie coat, thoughts assembled with dignity beneath his corpulent face. At the last post, the serried ranks of mourners would go silent and gaze down wistfully at their black shoes, stealing an occasional glance at the high fluttering tricolour and wondering how much longer the ceremony will go on for.

A further flutter, confined to artistic circles, greeted the announcement that the commission for the statue was not going to be open to competition. There wasn't time and besides the Government didn't see the need for it, not for a contract such as this. The Minister of State for Arts and Culture at the Department of An Taoiseach was instructed to set up a 1916 O'Shaughnessy Commemoration Committee, chaired by himself and comprising four unknown civil servants as advisers. After one month's deliberations and two meetings, the committee decided to award the commission to Mr Robert Wycherley, 4 Marks Lane, Westland Row, Dublin 2, with whom I have worked for the last year and a half as a sculptor's assistant.

The announcement of this decision created some confusion, because the terms of his contract were for 'an artistic work to the honour of Mr O'Shaughnessy and the Easter Rising of 1916'. The Minister made clear to the media and concerned philistines that the understanding was that this meant a statue. It was a statue that had been discussed in the Dáil, it was a statue that was privately deemed unseemly to erect while Mr O'Shaughnessy was still with us, it was a statue that he had given his consent to. A statue it would be. Mr Wycherley went a roundabout way to agreeing to this but that's further downstream. For the moment however, classicists and old boy Republicans alike were suspicious. Mr Wycherley was a modern artist and they didn't know about that modern art. Sure he did stuff that the critics and fellows on the *Late, Late Show* might tell you is progressive and visually exciting and imaginative but we just want a statue of old Con with the eyes still in his head. We're all into that avant-garde, abstract business. That's progressive and long may it continue, but save it for the galleries, boys.

Underlying this suspicion of Mr Wycherley's artistic temperament was an unspoken one about his cultural temperament. The two do not go hand in hand or at least if they do in the minds of the old boys suspicious of Wycherley it's in the unfortunately more artistically ambiguous sense of the irresponsibly surreal. Sure, he was asked to do a statue, but a statue that looks like what? They remember his sculpture in honour of the late Archbishop O'Mahony of Cork, God rest his soul. It was a large upright piece of abstract minimalism that resembled a phallic bicycle pump, entitled *Mission*. Mr Wycherley, not being a Catholic, was suspected of having an elaborate joke, at the expense, financial and spiritual, of those who were.

No one really cares about an artist's religion. In fact, he's assumed to have none. Nor about his class, which is supposed to be '-less', or at least artisan and unclassifiable. The Wycherleys of Kilkenny had long ago sold off their Unionist sympathies with the family silver. Some of them Gaelic Leagued it with an enthusiasm that embarrassed their tenants, since the poor old latter were beating better English into their kids so that they could go away and come back with the money to buy out the damn Wycherleys. That was all in the past and what a quaint past it was, but this present descendant, this bicycle-pump bloke, aroused uneasy feelings. It wasn't that he might have hidden loyalties, it was that he appeared to have none. None. And that upset the *fáinne*-polishing patriots, the old boys, the men who were 'out' with O'Shaughnessy at some stage of the game. This was a special job. It was the first Republican-related statue in Dublin for some time. It could be the last if the revisionists kept going the way they were. In short, it was a great opportunity and the traditionalists weren't sure that Mr Wycherley was the appropriate man for the job.

Who was? They weren't sure. They'd have liked a solid con-ventionalist, a fellow for 'likenesses'. It was a pity old Broe wasn't still alive; Ned Broe with his concrete raincoat and a bandolier you could strike matches off. *There* were statues that didn't fall down in a storm. What the traditionalists wanted of Wycherley was a rifle and cocked shoulder, middle-distance-gazing ditch-Cuchúlainn with lots of noble folds in his bronze clothes. Nothing that would frighten the kids but, you know, something that would give you a start if you came round the trees with a few on you. They wanted a commitment, a reverence, a lovingness between the artist and his piece of an intensity that Michelangelo couldn't have worked up for his marbled young men. Debonair Wycherley was suspect, a bit ironic. His blood didn't stir for his subject (even if, as things turned out, O'Shaughnessy's blood stirred for him and they got on quite well together). His great-great-grandfather was Unionist MP for Kilkenny; not that that has anything to do with anything but you know what we mean.

Having pottered around his dusty studio for eighteen months I can testify that some of these suspicions were not unfounded. Tall, thin and bald with the cotton-white remains of his hair hanging over his denim collar, Wycherley (sixty-four) saw himself as a gentlemanly mocker, a man with a laconic, well-worn amusement at the world and what he would plumly call its 'foibles'. He walked languorously around the studio checking on the activities of his assistants, a knowledgeable, almost sarcastic grin on his supposedly aristocratic face. This intimidated us into nervous respect for the man until, after about six months of working in his desultory, chaotic, though not unproductive studio, we saw that he was, beyond the light smiles and pithy asides, an embittered man tired of and yet unable to throw off the tweedy eccentricity expected of him and his displaced class. He was tired of the hack work, the horses for courses, the busts for nouveau dining-rooms, the 'something' that won't clash with the ashtray on the boardroom table. This is what he now felt his career would end up with. His own work, his actual creativity, had long ago petered out. It hadn't been up to much, he recognised that. He had long ago been confronted by the limits of his imagination or at least of the lack of substitute hands, discipline and thought-through to do more than another bronze dog for a Foxrock garden. He was embittered. Believe me, he was very embittered until O'Shaughnessy freed him.

I thought I was going to have permanence, he told me over a bottle of whiskey one night. When I was coming through the Metropolitan College of Art with all the rest of them in the forties I thought I was going to have an effect, make changes, do something special. I thought I was going to have permanence, dammit. But now, Jesus, now, I sometimes think I've ended up with little more effect than someone like Forbes who snaps at my heels. (Forbes was one of the artists who wanted the O'Shaughnessy commission and having failed to get the Minister of State, his fellow Sligoman, to deliver on some alleged nod and wink to him, he naturally enough criticised the way the commission was awarded.) Is it to his unmemorable level that I'll sink when we both pass on, when we all pass on, and the annals of Irish art are written for our period? I'm not going to have a lasting impact. Shane, I'm not going to have any fucking permanence. That was his reiterated complaint to me that night and to himself, I'm sure, on every other night. Oh, but he was going to have permanence. The procreative curse aside, in the summer of '86, he certainly was. The O'Shaughnessy contract was going to be, like the old historians used to say, 'what it should have been'. It was going to be the last great commission of his career. All the bitterness, the bile, all the mad thoughts were going to be burned, purged from his mind and mould. Years of waiting, years of waiting, as Pearse would say . . . he was going to give it his best shot and I was there to help him.

Of course that hadn't been decided yet and nothing was said in the studio. Nothing could be said. At least not until he had taken us aside,

9

Tess and me, his two youngest assistants, who confidently expected to be working with him on the O'Shaughnessy job, and told us that we were 'in'. Well, of course we were 'in', who else would be? You see, in that dusty, barn-like studio with its wooden veranda and its cluttered, high-walled courtyard, Bob Wycherley had been a bit of a father to us, a good and benevolent master, who separated us from what he called, in his more drunken moments, 'the rest of his staff' – mere craftsmen, hewers (pronounced 'whores') of wood and plaster and drawers of water . . . he often got them mixed up. Very mixed up. He only had two other staff and we suspected that sometimes under the influence he pretended to think he was back in the sixties when he had twice that number. He was also mistaken in belittling the rest of what staff he had. Murphy, the welder and handyman, and Ramsey, the oven-stoker, were far more effective to his studio than we were but then they weren't young and carefree and joining him for drinks and indulgent and even respectful of his sour oddities. In fact, they ignored him. Ramsey, because he lived in a world of his own; the studio, basically, and his little fishes. Murphy, because he thought Wycherley was a poser, but not necessarily not up to something. He was never to know how right he was.

It took a long time before Wycherley said anything too much about the O'Shaughnessy job. We'd go to the Windjammer with him for a few drinks after work on a Thursday and a Friday and he'd sit there and he'd talk about everything else under the sun but he wouldn't mention the big job, the commission that people still wrote to the papers about. If we mentioned it, which we inevitably did (time was moving on), he would raise his long white hand and say, 'In time. All in good time.' It wasn't just the issue of who was going to work on the project; we all were at some stage. It was the issue of the project itself. No plans appeared to have been made, no maquette models mounted, no drawings, no skeletal structures strung up for the first fleshy wax to be applied, no drawings or photos that we could see. And true to my past, I scoured his office in the loft for Tessa's benefit.

Neither was there any discussion on how he was going to respond to the challenge of doing a conventional statue in a modern context. He wasn't going to be drawn on that one. No, siree. A journalist from the *Irish Times* rang up wanting to do a piece on how the O'Shaughnessy statue was progressing but sorry, chum, there was no progress to do a piece on. This was late May and the statue was to be unveiled in August. Precisely, on or around the 12th, the old boy's birthday. The Minister of State was getting worried and got his civil servants to get on to Wycherley, but Wycherley wouldn't talk to them. Proper order. Why should he talk to an Assistant Principal in the Department of An Taoiseach about how 'his thoughts' on Mr O'Shaughnessy's statue were 'coming along'? Tell them to stuff it, he said, grandly. I'm an artist. Tell them that; I'm an artist not a sculpture and it's a sculpture not a statue. (The civil servants used to ring wondering could they speak to the sculpture, Mr O'Shaughnessy. If you could, maties, you must have a bloody great gift for talking to the inanimate!)

And inanimate he remained on the subject. 'In time. All in good time.' I thought Wycherley was running it close but, as it turned out he was doing fine. He had given himself lots of time and a perfect alibi. It was a drizzly evening, drizzly after another hot day, and as per usual we were sitting in the back snug of the Windjammer, around the corner from the studio at the end of Lombard Street, as it goes to the river. It was very much a local pub, frequented in the early evening by busmen and people who still, or used to, work in the docks or for the gas company. We didn't mix and kept to the back snug behind the pimpled glass. Wycherley would order by standing up and putting his fingers over the partition. We let him do this all night. On the wages he was paying us, we weren't going to join him, at least not on the paying front. When his fingers finished wiggling, he would resume his seat, an ash-heavy cigarette in his other hand. He smoked a lot. Up to three packets of Player's Navy Cut a day. It was one of the pleasures he most enjoyed and I should know because such was the tradition of our trinity that in the snug in the Windjammer, Tessa always got to sit on his left and I on his smoke-drifting right. To watch him was a sensuous act if you had strong nostrils. He smoked the way he walked, seductively closing heavy-lidded eyes to pull exquisitely on his cigarette, the fumes uncoiling from his wide mouth as he held out and quietly pondered on the burning tip, arranging his next utterance. It would come, the drinks would come and, rising to pay, the ash would flake down his tan tweed jacket and worsted trousers, generally worn with a violently coloured shirt – pink, yellow or lime; or all three – unbuttoned to reveal in fibrous form the white hair that bushed across his eyebrows and hung down over his collar from halfway up the back of his bird-like skull. In a curious exchange of gender habit – or supposed gender habit; we sculptor's assistants get to see and put our subjects in all sorts of shapes – Wycherley would sit most

11

womanly, with his long legs crossed, one foot nodding contentedly, whereas bold-eyed Tess, the stylish parody of a tomboy in suede waistcoat, white T-shirt and faded denims cut at the knees, sat with hips apart, chin in hand and front teeth biting her nether lip as she listened, that lip reddening, to Wycherley revealing, at last, some of his plans.

He flicked his ash. It was going to be an interesting reversal of the received role of realism. Ah. A lot of alliteration there, Bob, but what else? The idea was that he would portray Mr O'Shaughnessy in the form of a conventional image that would reflect his life and career and yet be representative in an abstract way of the larger ideas about Irish history. Tessa's brown eyes opened but his closed to inhale deeply. It will be figurative? she asked. Of course. Sounds interesting. It is. Tess was excited. She smiled and took a gulp of beer. Will he be pleased by it? I don't know, said Wycherley and he looked at me out of the corner of his eye. What, eh, is the conventional image you, eh, had in mind? I asked, casually, on cue. Wycherley's long white hand brushed away some blue smoke that was hanging about. I can't really go into that until I show you the plans. And when would that be? asked Tess hopefully. Soon, he said. Really soon, or like . . . soon in a few weeks' time? Wycherley was not pleased by this intemperate question and he looked at his pupils from beneath his white brows with a schoolmaster's disapproval. Why are you so impatient? he asked, folding his arms and putting his chin up haughtily. Are you not glad to be involved? Oh, we are, said Tess, we are. And we were, dear comrades, we were. I even bought him two drinks before the night was out, just to clinch the deal.

Tess was happy but picture how I felt. I'd been plugging into this guy since I was ten years old. 1974: that was the year I first read about Michael Collins and his Squad and of how they liquidated about eighteen British agents in their beds one fine Sunday morning in 1920. Lofty, our history teacher, told us about it. He would put great relish into telling the story. Of how they were all nearly caught the night before, sitting around a dinner table in Vaughan's Hotel. (You'd think they'd have the celebratory dinner afterwards, he said with a little laugh, and the boys would look at him nonplussed.) 'Oh, the next morning, they got up, I'd say' – and he looked out the window – 'very early.' Yes, very early. That was definite. Some of them got mass. The others, presumably, did without. They headed for their various locations, 'automatics bulky in their pockets'. That was the great phrase: hurrying along in their raincoats with 'automatics bulky in their pockets'. Nothing was spared from hereon. They brushed past doormen, servants and wives and 'headed' for the bedrooms. Men 'reached for their hidden revolvers', as if this was a sly thing to do. 'They were riddled,' said Lofty with a flick of the head. Riddled. There was blood everywhere. Men were hanging out of windows with blood all over them. Pillows were burst open by the shots. 'Women were screaming,' he said and flicked his head again, as if to say, what would you expect. Collins's men composed themselves and left. Interestingly enough, he said, without a trace of irony (we were children, after all), one of those men is going to win a big peace prize this year. Does anyone know what it is? It's the Nobel Peace Prize.

The rest of the day's events, the revenge of the British at Croke Park when they fired into the crowds, and in Dublin Castle when two prisoners were tortured and shot, were delivered in a more sombre tone. The cries of McKee and Clancy were heard in the night-time street, cries now not heard, and erased from the recorded history like the rest of Lofty's colour. But it was high drama for us and after it maths and civic instruction were a crashing bore. That summer, that hot summer of the World Cup in Germany, I read all I was able on Michael Collins. I read slowly and what I couldn't take in, which was a lot, I went back to Lofty to explain in the hope that rather than elucidate the boring evolution of Collins's politics and his differences with de Valera on the Treaty, he would tell me more stories about fellows hanging out of windows and burst pillows.

He did, too. He told me about Collins dropping through a skylight to escape the British or riding around on a bicycle unnoticed or running into a cinema and forcing them to show a fundraising newsreel for the Republican loans, even though he had a price on his head. Not that anyone needed forcing, Lofty would stress. He told me too about the incredible loyalty men had to Collins. Not just the members of his Squad, the Twelve Apostles as they were known, but brigade lieutenants and 'column' leaders and officers and soldiers and politicians up and down the land. So loyal were they, so trusting in his judgement and ability, that at the time of the Treaty when the country was splitting in two (there was no mention of the other split, the Northern split; that didn't come into Lofty's narrative), many men, many great men, said, when Collins signed the Treaty, 'What's good enough for Mick Collins is good enough for me.' Mind you, not all of them, said

Lofty after a pause. One man, that fellow I told you about who's still alive and is going to win the big prize (in my innocence, I thought the issues were related. In my maturity, I think the issues are related). Well, that fellow was in Collins's Squad, he was one of the Apostles. But he didn't support the Treaty and in fact when Collins returned from London after signing it, this fellow told him on the gangplank (the gangplank was an addition I always regretted losing in after-editions), when Collins asked him, 'What did you think?' he said, 'I think it is a sorry business.' A sorry business. And the poor leader hadn't even set foot on land. For ever after I wanted to know who this fellow was.

For Tess too this would be a contact of great moment. She has been here two years and got to the studio on the pull of her mother who knew people who knew Wycherley and didn't want to see her daughter at a loose end when she returned from Europe. Not that she wasn't qualified. She had done one year in the National College of Art and Design before she left the country and in terms of informal education – courses, books, five weeks at the Dublin Art Foundry and a methodical survey of the continent's museums: Etruscan to modern, terracotta to steel – she had more experience than I had, whose lone achievement in the visual arts was some lurid death threats I sent to the Fathers in Artane, complete with diagrams.

I'm surprised Tess has stayed in the studio so long because there isn't a huge opportunity to pursue one's own creative ideas there, unless your ideas are as criminal as mine and then you get the opportunity of a lifetime. But I know and hope hers aren't and so I'm surprised. Also she doesn't stick around places long and, like me, she likes to wander. Her first move wasn't an option. She was expensively expelled from Alexandra College for smoking dope in the classroom at lunchtime. Not that she's naturally a dope smoker. She's not. But when the teacher came in, hers was the hand the joint was in. Smoking gun. O'Shaughnessy knows the story. She sat her Leaving Certificate in the Leeson Street Institute and went into the pre-diploma year in art college, but after a year of smoking a few more joints, drinking in the Clock and building installations with suedehead visionaries in black leathers and decadent sneers, she decided to quit the college and head for the continent. Two girls came with her, India-bound jewellery makers from Galway, and on the strength of hard-neck, forged Inter Rail cards and the sort of reckless charm that drives easily led Latins bananas, they reached the glorious city of Istanbul where – hug, hug – they separated and the Galway girls got ready to head through about three war-torn countries to get their beads and muslin.

Tess though, she stayed, and on the strength of her damn posh accent she cajoled a job teaching young Turks English. Eventually the gruelling tasks of trying to arm these potential immigrants with a lucrative tongue ('We want to speak as Americans') proved too much for impulsive Tess and soon she was back in immigrant-ridden Germany working first in a gherkin-canning factory and then as a sort of ambiguous waitress in the dubious mini-Manhattan of inner Frankfurt. Come September, it was the clinical rusticity of Bordeaux, among the rest of the world's young travellers. I can see her now, standing to take a rest amid the dusty vines, her big chest heaving, her cheeks red and bunched as she tosses back her then abundant ponytail to smile perspiringly at the farmer's wife. But art beckoned again and nursing a desire to satisfy the creative urge that played havoc with her heart and sensibility, or something to that effect, she returned to Dublin and, through an acquaintance of her mother's, was taken on as a temporary sculptor's assistant in the studio of Robert Wycherley. (I'm temporary, too. All is temporary in Wycho's life, including the lives of his subjects.)

The mother, you see, is something of an artiste herself; a former stage actress still doing the occasional 'suitable' role to supplement her considerable half of the divorce settlement she made in London with Tessa's father, James F. Masterson, a successful minerals speculator now living in Navan, Co. Meath, close to the mining communities he owns so much of. Tessa lived with her mother and younger sister, in a big-windowed house on Strand Road, Sandymount, facing the beach and protected from the salty winds of the bay by a jungle of roses, shrubs, and blood-red rhododendrons quite ludicrously overgrown.

After our chat with Wycherley in the Windjammer we made our way along Strand Road. Disentangling the hungry briars from my jacket, I followed Tess up to the front door. She had it opened quickly and we stepped into the warm and slightly brandified air of the hallway.

'Tessa, petal, how are you?' asked stately Mama gliding in from the living-room in a long blue dress.

'And Shane . . . how is Shane?'

Mother was in high spirits, the cause presumably of the sudden drop in daughter's. Shedding her jacket with the backwards shrug of a disgruntled coal miner, she told Mother that we'd been confirmed for the O'Shaughnessy contract.

Mother's hands went up in silent benediction.

'Why, that's wonderful,' she said. 'Tessa, dear, what did I tell you?' And she told us what she told us before. That, of course, Rob Wycherley would want, would need us helping him, that it would be a great experience, that it would be a unique experience, that the subject was still alive and well and (this tickled me) that it would 'set Tess up'.

Taking vigorous cognisance of this advice and fighting off demands that we change our 'wringing clothes', we were guided purringly into the log-fired sitting-room to be introduced, again ('You know each other . . .'), to Angus Fitzgerald, an elfish Abbey actor famed for his ecclesiastical roles and a benign, precious pomposity that has become impossible to distinguish from the roles he plays.

'Yes, we know each other,' said Tess curtly but Mr Fitzgerald saw no curtness and smiling delicately he allowed his bony hand to flutter up and grasp ours with slow but firm assured pressing.

In his other hand he fondled a bulbous brandy glass, lolling it expertly by the heat of the fire. An awkward pause. On Mrs Masterson's sudden suggestion that we must be starved we gladly vacated the living-room and adjourned to the kitchen for something to eat and later on, at around 2 a.m., as Tess showed me into the absent sister's bedroom where I would stay the night, we could still hear from the warm sitting-room below the hollow halting laugh of the still very much alive Mr Fitzgerald.

It's not over yet. A new day hasn't dawned. Not by a long shot. Collins slept better when he could hear the stirring of horses in the stable near Devlin's. He took fright after passing one night in a strange house because the birds didn't sing outside his window at dawn, or so Frank O'Connor tells us in his hagiography of the man. Have we reason to doubt him? Collins was a hunted man and he had work to do. Here I am in a strange room myself and I've no desire to go to sleep just yet. I slept here once before and a few times on the sofa downstairs where Fitzgerald is now probably trying to move in on the mother. I can hear her laughter from here, collusive or abusive I'm not sure, but he seems to think it's funny. What does Tess think? Shuts herself off. Used to it.

Doesn't have the imagination I have, which is a good thing. She's had parents. They're split now but she's had them. I haven't. She knows the story. It's a nice bedroom this, looking out on the sea. Tess is just below in what was the dining-room during Father's time, when guests were entertained. She was up here then but she moved down for more room (canvases, paints, shop-window dummies, etc.) and Jessica, the younger sister, moved in.

Jessica turned teen recently and had the place decorated for her communion. It was theme decorating to the limit: a simple and not unattractive motif of a tiny red-and-green two-petal flower on a white background repeated all over the room, on the wallpaper, the lampshade, the picture frame, the curtains, the duvet, the pillowcase, and even, I suspect, her soft young skin if she lay in bed too long. The dresser, happily, she left as it was, scrubbed blond wood and neatly filled up with her books and trinkets: delf dogs, school medals, dayglo pencils and a miniature treasure chest filled not with pearls and rings but with badges and stickers collected at the RDS Spring Show.

On the wall, Blu-Tacked to avoid marking the flowers, were posters of pre-pubescent dogs and pop stars and a big map of greater Dublin. The first time I saw this map I was reminded of the one we used to have on our dormitory wall in Artane and how we used to think Dublin looked like an old woman. It was lying in our beds during the plentiful idle time that that institution gave us that set it off. Don't you think that the Head of Howth is like an ould one's head? said the Twist one evening when we were all looking at the map and lying on our beds smoking rolled butts of toilet paper. And it was true. It was just like an old woman's head with the Baily lighthouse at the end of her nose and Doldrum Bay in her mouth. Have a look yourself. Sutton, where my girlfriend lives, is the back of her neck. A pain in the neck. Kilbarrack is her chest, with the walkway to Bull Island emerging from her nipple. Clontarf was her belly, Sandymount her hips and her feet reached Dalkey Hill. Where the Liffey emerged would have been – and here I want to stress that there were no adolescent titters but only a matter-of-fact observance – her fanny. It would, said the Twist, holding his loo-roll roach between thumb and index finger, be going in as far as Butt Bridge which would signal the beginning of the inner folds and then on as far as Island Bridge, 'twisting and turning', he reminded us, which would be the, eh, womb.

This was very exciting stuff for us on a hot day. We looked at the map and swallowed hard and didn't think to question the Twist's knowledge of women we didn't know and city we hadn't seen.

Isn't it a funny thing though, I said, going back to the Head and recovering myself, that where the Summit of Howth is is exactly where the eye should be. But we can't see it from here and so we could regard Ireland's Eye, just to the north there, as her eye plucked from her head. There was silence for a moment. Ah, ever the poet, said the Twist, not unkindly, and they were impressed. They were very impressed.

That was a long time ago. I took a look out the window at the night-blue sea. This is some job I've got on O'Shaughnessy. Green light tonight. Look at the red lights on Howth. The sooner it's over the better. He'll be on my mind now until the job is finished. I have to think of him as an idea, not as a living person. It's easier that way. Think professionally: of objects, of shapes, of wax and bronze. Rationalise, distance yourself, as you get closer. And yet as you get detached, immerse yourself. Get stuck in. Summon all the anarchic energy and to-the-end demented creativity you've ever mustered, the boldness honed and self-fed over a lifetime. If anyone can do it, I can. The danger was always that I'd dare myself too far. But who's holding me back? Embrace the danger. Free the spirit.

Enough of this; I opened the window. Ah, the smell of the sea! Its timeless, draughty brine, brought up on a breeze cool and balmy on my face. The drizzle has stopped but between here and Dun Laoghaire pier it must be still drizzling somewhere because its fairy lights are twinkling and not staying still. The slates are wet below me. There's a boat crossing the bay and there's Sutton, away over there. That's where Niamh lives, the girl I'm supposed to be going out with except she's away in Paris at the moment working as a waitress. She's a third-year medical student and she works the summers for the fees. Paris is an unusual choice; they usually go to London or the States. New York, Massachusetts, Cape Cod. They usually go back there too, a lot of them, because work is scarce here. Promises unfulfilled. Did O'Shaughnessy think that we would always be exporting people? I expect he did, behind all the rhetoric. Flags and emblems haven't changed economic realities. To be honest, things haven't been the best between Niamh and me and I'd be surprised if they lasted another year. Her being away is a handy break, a break to avoid a break.

I had a look down to see if Tessa's light was still on. It wasn't. It was out. It was time to join her and go to bed myself. I kicked off my shoes and clothes and got in under the polka-dot duvet. With the lights out, you can hear the sea from here. Sounds travel better

18

in the dark. O'Shaughnessy will tell you that, or any of the men he trained in the hills of the Wicklow darkness. He'll tell you that and then he'll grin. I've seen him do it in interviews. After all these years don't take me too seriously. His humour could undermine us, but in fact he doesn't have much. What emerges is cunning and self-serving and not without an element of rehearsal.

When Mellowes and the rest of my friends hear I've been finally confirmed for this commission, they'll get great crack out of it. Of course, they'll never know the crack I'll get out of it, literally, but for most of the job they'll be so tickled that someone like me, who like them has had an exorbitant interest in the affairs of the men of O'Shaughnessy's generation, should get so close to creating something to their memory and to the memory of their most illustrious member. They were tickled when I told them I might be into it. They'll be even more tickled when they hear it's true. I don't tell them everything, of course, but I give them hints. They're my sort of close friends but you don't tell anyone everything. I never did. It was part of my learning.

The next morning there was quite a surprise for us pushed through the rusty post slot of the Mastersons' front door – a slightly rain-rippled envelope addressed to Ms Tessa Masterson, Artist. Inside was a letter typed on very light, almost scarious paper. Thin-skinned paper but thick-skinned words:

> We understand you propose to assist in constructing a state-sponsored statue to the retired Republican terrorist, Cornelius O'Shaughnessy. We believe that yet another statue of a violent Fenian is an unwanted imposition on any populace and we would strongly advise you to reconsider working on such a monstrosity, or face the consequences.
>
> AVNS

'This is outrageous,' proclaimed a bathrobed Mrs Masterson, reading the letter for about the sixtieth time and pushing toast and marmalade slices out of the way to concentrate.

'Are you sure, quite sure, that this is not some stupid joke by one of your college friends?' she persisted in asking her pyjama-clad daughter.

'Oh for Christ's sake, Mother. Do you think my unhealthy, exam-condemned friends are going to trek all the way out here in the rain, in the middle of the bloody night, to deliver this distinctly unfunny letter?'

'Yes. Actually,' replied Mother primly. 'They might have been coming back from a beach party or taking a break from study – how do you know . . .'

'A beach party? In the drizzle?'

'God knows, these days. Shane, what do you think?'

'Well, like I said, it doesn't look like a joke. It looks authentic. I mean, it could be anybody. There are lots of people who don't like O'Shaughnessy. We saw that when the commission was first announced. Mind you, this is quite extreme . . . but then you don't write poison letters and make them sound mild.'

I looked at Tess. She was chewing her nether lip again but she didn't look too worried.

'Oh, it's probably some crank who has a grudge against O'Shaughnessy,' I said. 'Someone whose father got ditched in the Civil War or more seriously lost a seat to O'Shaughnessy in the forties.'

Mrs Masterson flapped her hand dismissively. She didn't like talk of politics and violence except in Yeatsian terms.

'No, no. Not at all,' she said and her divorcee's ringless hand brushed away my lightly meant theories with the last of the toast crumbs. 'This is the work of an organisation. Obviously the work of a group or society. It reads "we", you see,' she pointed out to my apparently manifest stupidity. 'AVNS is four initials, you see.' I looked at her vacantly. 'It's definitely not a crank . . . giving the police his full initials.'

'A schizophrenic maybe. . . Andy Vincent and Noel Smith,' ventured Tess, callously upsetting her mother's convinced reasoning.

'You're hilarious, Tess,' said Margaret, looking at her. 'I can see you're taking this as seriously as you do everything else.' Tess lolled her tongue and concentrated on crushing an eggshell to dust. 'And you, Shane, if I might say so. You don't seem to be taking this very seriously.'

'I am,' I protested. 'But I've seen these sort of letters before. People are always writing letters or making phone calls and pretending to be the IRA or the UDA or the ABC. It's dodgy because if some of those people caught you, you'd be in trouble, but it's easily done. Anyone could have written that letter. It doesn't even look professional. Look at it – it's battered out on a rackety typewriter. I refuse to be intimidated by something like that.'

20

'No one's being intimidated,' said Mrs Masterson.

'I have a few enemies,' Tess put in. 'And so does Robert. He has loads.'

'And what about the fact that this was delivered the night he asked you to be involved in the O'Shaughnessy project?'

'Coincidence,' I said.

'And that they have our address?'

'Easily got,' said Tess. 'I mean, they've had plenty of time to do research on us.'

'Exactly. If they were serious about this they would have started months ago.'

Mrs Masterson pursed her lips and looked at us both. Started months ago. Who would have left it this late to write a letter like this against O'Shaughnessy's statue? Tough language; it didn't look jokey. Some old codger who's nursed a lifelong hatred of the IRA. A retired British army officer, maybe, who got Tessa's name from the article the *Sunday Independent* did about us a few months back, when the commission was being first discussed. The article gave Tessa's background. It didn't give mine, thank God. Or could it be someone imitating a retired British army officer? I thought of my own friends and their gift for historical mimicry. They can put it to cruel use, but not this cruel, surely. No, not to Tess. To me maybe, but not to Tess. Mellowes is always at it, writing over-the-top anti-divorce letters to the *Irish Times*, applying to the British Ministry of Defence for an Auxiliaries' pension, inviting the neighbourhood to an Opus Dei 'whip-round'. Actually, this is just the sort of letter he and I would write. Curious.

'Well, if it is an organisation,' said Margaret, reading it again, 'they're violent, obviously, or pretending to be, and anti-Republican. The language sounds very Unionist, I must say. It has an Ulster ring to it – words like "consequences" and "imposition". And of course, the Presbyterian declarativeness of "We believe" . . .'

I looked at Tess. She was watching her mother and chewing a pyjama sleeve.

'Stop that,' said her mother, slapping her lightly.

'Are you trying to scare us?' protested Tess.

'Well, they are very upset up there,' her mother reminded her.

'Upset with us, because of this Anglo-Irish Agreement and everything else.'

21

'There's no reason to take it out on O'Shaughnessy,' I said, half laughing.

'Or us,' said Tess.

'No . . . but he's the sort of figure in the South that symbolises . . . something they vehemently oppose.'

'Ah, Mother,' said Tess.

'No . . . no . . .' insisted Mother. 'It would be one way of getting back at the Irish Government. Maybe they've friends down here.'

'It would be a mighty strange way,' I said, laughing, though the prospect was hardly one to relish.

'Should we show it to the police?' asked Tess.

'I think you should show it to Mr Wycherley first.'

Sitting behind the bruised oak desk in the attic office he called his oratory, weathered Wycherley had a different theory as to the culprit. The letter didn't surprise him, he said, and he took it in his nicotined fingers and perused again its contents with mild disdain.

'Yes, without a doubt,' he told us softly, releasing two tusks of nostrilised smoke. 'It's him. It's the work of Samuel Forbes. A sad pathetic product of a jealous mind not yet come to terms with its creative deficiency . . .'

'Samuel Forbes?' cried Tess.

'There was always a danger that it would come to this,' Wycherley calmly explained. 'That at the end of his career, denied the last closing commission that he assumed was his, his pathological jealousy would bring him into the era of the criminal make-believe. I had heard that he was not well, that he was attending sessions in St John of Gods, that he was drinking heavily and dreaming up wild schemes to revenge himself upon me . . . but, quite honestly, I didn't think it had come to this. He excels the standards of even the Dublin art pit. Feuds go on, people are shafted, maligned and libelled but this . . .' He held the membrane-thin sheet in his trembling hand. 'This is quite sad. Sad but audacious. How dare he!'

'But how can you be so sure?'

'But . . .'

'It's him, all right. The language of an Ulster Loyalist is just the sort of duplicitous tongue in which this sawdust geriatric classicist would write poison-pen letters,' continued Wycherley with gruff invective, blue fumes issuing dragon-like as he spoke. 'He's so sly he can't come straight out with it.'

22

'But why would he write to me?' asked Tess.

'Because he's so sly he can't write straight to me. He has to get at my soft underbelly.'

'Mmm,' said Tess, smiling. 'But listen . . .'

'Of course, you haven't been home yet?' he said to me.

'No.'

'He wouldn't know where you live.'

'He could find out.'

'That's right, of course. You share some of the same watering holes,' he said slyly.

'But, Robert, please,' insisted Tess. 'You can't just assume . . .'

'Not true. The city's a village,' I protested. 'You go to the same places . . .'

'Excuse me!' he said to Tess sharply. 'I know what I'm talking about. I have suffered the Dublin art world for many years. I know its characters and its capabilities. I know Sam Forbes like I know a recurring toothache or a bad boil on the backside, and I know the sorts of tricks he gets up to. I didn't know he would go as far as this but then he hasn't been a well man recently and not getting the O'Shaughnessy commission has sent him cuckoo altogether. You know that. You saw the comments he made in that *Sunday Press* article. He's been blabbering revenge against me at umpteen bar counters. Eccentric revenge, I believe, the sort of half-cracked plans that have him cackling to himself and into his drink. He's not supposed to drink with the medicines he's on but who can stop him?'

Wycherley tweaked his nose.

'He's been up to this sort of stuff for years. At one time, he was going around saying that I was stealing my own sculptures so that I could get the extra work of replacing them. That Presbyterian memorial in Wexford; he was so annoyed that I was doing that – oh, because he is, I think, Presbyterian and memorials are his game – that he started spreading rumours that some local sectarian strand of the IRA were against the memorial and were going to get at the sculptor. Can you imagine? People just laughed, but it's not so funny all of the time. It's been going on now for some time, since 1964 at least. It's not funny because over the years he's been losing more and more of his marbles and there's always the possibility his madness may get dangerous . . . Who else would have written this letter? Don't you think that anyone who was this upset at the prospect of another IRA statue – and it's not an IRA statue – would have spoken up before now? Where was this AVNS last year when the project was first announced? There were objections then. Why weren't these among them?' said Wycherley, and he held up the see-through paper.

'Well . . .'

'And what a way to voice your opposition – why not a statement, or a secret news conference or public gesture of some sort? Rather than' – he dropped the feather-light letter with derision – 'a sneaky letter to one of my staff.'

'So you've no doubt it was Forbes,' pressed Tess.

'Oh, I could always be wrong,' he granted. 'But as sure as I know Forbes and as sure as I know the patterns of his mad mind – which these days I'll admit I increasingly don't – this letter was his handiwork. Yes, I'm sure of it, this sad, little letter' – he tapped it lightly with his finger – 'was penned by his arthritic hand for no other purpose than the sheer maliciousness of upsetting work on a commission that he could never have hoped to have gained for himself.'

'Eh, why . . . why do you think he wouldn't have written something like this when the commission was awarded, when he knew he was not going to get it?'

'Because he was boiling up to it,' said Wycherley sternly. 'He hasn't been well lately and he's been boiling up to it. Brooding and scheming and finally summoning up the courage.' He sneered down at the letter and shook his head. 'But we've to put it behind us. We're not to give him one more minute of the attention he doesn't deserve. There are nurses to look after him. We've got a lot of work to do in the next few weeks and we can't afford to be put off in our plans by a cheap stunt like this. Now come on, let's dally no further,' he declared and he rose from his desk with an abruptness that surprised us.

'Are you not going to go to the police?' asked Tess.

'What for?'

'For safety's sake.'

'I'll do whatever is necessary for safety's sake.'

With which he took the letter, folded it and put it away and led us back down the spiral staircase into the main workshop. Tess and I looked at each other. She shrugged but she didn't seem too worried and that was the main thing. For the rest of us it might be a different story.

On one knee on the workshop floor, goggled Murphy, the welder, was applying a blue flame to a mermaid's back, finishing the curvaceous surface for the nymph's placement in the fountain of a Malahide garden. It was derivative stuff, the sort of work Wycherley tried to avoid doing and Forbes tried to get, though each claimed the opposite of each other. The nymph's sisters were yet to be bronzed; as Torremolinos-bound typists might say, and hope for the same degree of what Bob calls permanence. Their fragile wax bodies had been encased in sturdy pebbled plaster and placed in the shoulder-high oven. Inside that hot ember-glowing little room, fed routinely with shovelled coke, the fish-tailed maidens would eventually melt away, leaving nothing inside the burnt plaster mould but the air-filled space of what the Greeks used to call their souls – the shells of themselves.

I followed Wycherley out into the yard.

'Do you really believe Forbes wrote that letter?' I asked him.

'Yes,' he replied, looking at me shrewdly. 'I do. Actually, I do. I know what he's like, Shane. He's capable of anything.'

'I don't know. I think it's someone with a political grudge.'

'You know . . . maybe you're right.' He put his hands to his mouth and spoke through them. 'Anything's possible but we're going to have to forget about it, Shane. We can't let it upset our plans.'

'Of course,' I said. 'Of course . . . Mind you.'

He looked at me.

'It's an uncanny sort of interruption, though . . . all things considered; the letter, the gist of it.'

'I'm trying not to think about it, Shane, but . . . yes, yes, it is. But then when you think about O'Shaughnessy's life and all he's been up to, it's not really. I'm sure he has lots of enemies, lots of them, and that's where I think Forbes thinks he can fit himself in.'

'Maybe.'

'Go on. Get out of here.'

Since there was little on hand for the afternoon except the melting away of those mythic ladies, Wycherley had agreed to give me the rest of the day off. Tomorrow we would discuss the melting away of that other mythic character, Cornelius O'Shaughnessy.

Chapter 2

A Statue Considered

July afternoon, lovely sunshine after last night's drizzle. I'm going to put that letter out of my mind. Sour intrusion into our neat and cheerful plans for O'Shaughnessy. Forbes. A man must be ill if he has to stoop to that kind of tactic. He has been low of late and not getting the O'Shaughnessy commission was a big blow. What Wycherley didn't mention was that Forbes had more or less been promised it. Informally, by the Minister himself. It was a reckless indiscretion, like so many a politician can make when his good will carries him away. They come from the same constituency and Forbes had been at a function in the Sligo Arms Hotel that the Minister was attending. They got talking after the ceremonies. This was only two weeks after the Taoiseach had made his announcement at Beal na mBláth so naturally the conversation turned to the contract for the job. It was late at night, drinks had gone down, an election was coming up, and the Minister of State saw the 'Sligoman gets contract' headlines in the *Champion*, perhaps. Anyway, Forbes was being persistent and he managed to extract some sort of commitment that, wink, wink, the Minister would see him right.

As it turned out the Minister didn't see him right and Forbes was livid. He was turned out of the Minister's clinic, hurling abuse, and the Minister was from then on uncontactable, which rapidly became the mental state of poor Forbes himself when he saw his bitter rival Wycherley get the job. He hit the gin heavily and parked himself next to all the other kidney-dialysis machines sitting in Grogan's. Allegedly, he started having delusions and swearing revenge against Wycherley, the Minister, the critics,

26

the Arts Council, the Royal Hibernian Academy and any other institution or individual he had come badly in contact with in the last thirty years. Even the kidney-dialysis machines started having fears for his reason. His sons tried to calm him down and quietly admitted him to a drying-out clinic. But he wouldn't hear of it until he had got even with that 'long line of homosexual misery from Kilkenny', which is a scandalous thing to call anyone. I'm on pills anyway, he told his sons.

The letter? Yes, he has a bitter sense of humour to write something like that. And the childishness. That would be just the sort of pathetically ineffective revenge gesture he'd get up to. An idea sparked on a bar stool and encouraged by some twisted dypso with an undergraduate sense of fun. 'That'll have him shaking in his boots, Samuel.' I can just see it. Well, it hasn't and it won't. How could it? What we're up to would put in the shade anything those guys could come up with even in their whiskey-soured imaginations, and we're not going to be interrupted by them either. No, siree. Ours is a job no one could imagine.

Go to it. Embrace the day. Outside sun much preferable to the cindery heat of the workshop where the ovens are humming most of the time. Ramsey tends them during the night or sometimes Tess or I if we stay over. There's a sleeping bag upstairs in the oratory. I've brought the odd nubile back there after an evening in Tobin's or the clubs. They're very impressed by the sculptures. The workshop was formerly a seed warehouse for the quays and the oratory was the foreman's office. It was also a stable at one stage though the idea that it housed undertakers' horses I find far too convenient to the fact that we have the back yard of Nichol's funeral chapel on one side of us and the graveyard of St Mark's Church on the other. It's also far too convenient to my current state of mind and I think Wycherley was getting it up for me. I doubt if there was ever any connection between them but their proximity gave a black undercurrent to our coded exchange. It had been a stable though, and the tether rings are still visible above the furnace.

The property was attached to one of those big houses on Merrion Square when that square was a noble village green with amber horseshit on the cobblestones and wigged gents tapping their canes and discussing the Renunciation Act with gesticulative vigour. Peruse, please, Maldon's *Prints of Dublin Scenes (1780)*. Peruse them closely the next time you meet them as laminated table mats or time-killing prints along the blue rope of your neighbourhood bank queue, and you'll see, if you squint hard enough, the stocky figure of Bob Wycherley, give or take a few pounds and centuries. Ample-bellied below his tasteful fanlight or condescending with the buxom fruit seller on the corner, you'll see the young Wycherley as he was, perfumed hairpiece astride his healthy head, sturdy-necked with a brass-buttoned chest and bulging calves that fill their stockings to the breeches like export-only oatsacks. Off he goes through the deserted streets of those motionless, ghostly scenes of Maldon's Dublin, the Protestant Toytown, to see how far the pavements have been laid and what sails have been stilled on the riverfront. Will he pass his stables on the way? For this is or could be great-great-grandfather Robert, MP for Kilkenny and owner of 8 Merrion Square, the nearby stables of which were passed down eventually to become the studio of modern Robert's father.

No. 8 incidentally is now an accountant's and advertising agency and was the unsuccessful subject of an interior conservation battle in the sixties when money-swinging speculators were moving in with the nod of a progressive Fianna Fáil government. Students got inside the house and refused to come out. And guess who came down to give interviews and support the occupiers. Yes, none other than the veteran of occupied buildings, Cornelius O'Shaughnessy, who was going through his anti-the-moneyed, mohair-suits stage and wanted to profess his disapproval of the flash little capitalists who, in the name of rugged individualism and 'a wink and a nod to Republicanism', were ripping the town apart in search of a quick mark. An empty shell was left and a preservation order was put on the façade. Oh, in O'Shaughnessy's day, the droll ones would say, a building got destroyed *because* he occupied it, but it was ideals not plaster he was preserving.

A bit of both in Wycherley's case. I remember one evening at dusk walking down Lower Fitzwilliam Street; he stopped our walk to peer wistfully at the long, slender-framed windows of the houses. His lips moved tremulously and his wide, wondrous eyes roved the sunset-golden panes. Then, in a moment of quiet drama one bony hand clawed my shoulder gently (a pass at last?) and the other pointed up at the tall house-front.

'Those high windows,' he said. 'That is what it is all about.'

I remained hushed, the breeze on my cheek, the silver and orange reflections of the setting sun coagulating and fracturing across the thin-ribbed windows.

'That is what what is all about, Robert?' I asked softly, feeling that the moment deserved a first-name intimacy.

'Shane, my dear boy,' he explained, 'those high windows are what our culture, my culture, is all about.'

Make of it what you will. Make of Wycherley what you will. To most the man is wilfully, innately enigmatic, wrapped up in the folds of his over-civilized sensibility, walking like an unperturbed bird through the jostling streets of the city. But well played, Wycherley; well played. In the spring of '86, I got to the core of his enigma. I wouldn't use the word heart for that had been squeezed and hollowed and worn on his sleeve for the wind to whistle through. Ah, droll chap, that Bob; there's a cutting edge to his gloom. Sparks in the forge. But well played, man, well played.

A northbound train trundled above me as I passed under Westland Row bridge. Twelve-thirty and aproned vendors are already selling the evening papers. 'Loyalists prepare for Portadown showdown'. End rhyme there, they've been preparing for these showdowns for years. The 12th is on Saturday and whether they can or can't march through the Catholic part of the town is going to be a test of the Anglo-Irish Agreement. Are they our police or everybody's? Here's a couple of people now who need policing, obstructing my path as they file into St Andrew's for lunchtime mass. They must be hungry. That's it, pay no heed to him who's thirsty; the man at the gate who's looking for the price of a small one. God love him, he can hardly stand up and put his hand out at the same time. The bloodshot eyes are going up and down like slot-machine raspberries hoping to win a bit of short change. Whoops, the unintentional lunge. I don't want that.

Interesting, Oisin used to say, how St Andrew's casts a shadow on the birthplace of Oscar Wilde across the street. A death-bed convert like Casement and O'Flaherty and Mellowes standing up. It's never too late. They won't have to work on O'Shaughnessy, though. He's well back into the fold. Excommunicated twice and as near to it again in the red scare of the thirties, but he's made his peace with God and Rome. Well prepared for a peaceful exit, duckdown pillows and rosary beads entwined through the faithful fingers. Or that's what he thinks.

I took a look at his resting place on my way through the Green.

29

He's not in the fountain-spotted centre but is over on the south side, opposite Iveagh House, headquarters of his former ministry. Nice spot. Between two huge chestnuts. The only other bust or sculpture near by is the head of James Joyce who has been placed facing Newman House but who when viewed from behind looks as if he is strangling himself with a bejewelled hand. Enough. It's time to go home. There could be something there for me.

Harcourt Street. Don't look now but there's an unhealthy-looking poet coming out of No. 36. A great rake of astronauts living in that house. Almost all of them were in my Tuesday dole queue and would be in Tobin's afterwards. This one's called the Foetus but look at him too closely and he's likely to follow you, smiling oddly and flapping his brown corduroy jacket. Take a peek; wet head and monkey-limbed with globular eyes that only half open like those of the sunny lizards. Some time ago, a suspicious guard saw him talking to a sycamore on Hatch Street but he licked his froggy lips and said he was calling a cat.

I don't need to tell you but better people lived on this street once. The big fellow had his HQ at No. 6 but moved to No. 76 when the police and soldiers came raiding. Collins had Detective Hoey shot the next day outside police headquarters in Brunswick Street. In time No. 76 was also given away and in time, the suspect, a spy called Quinlisk, was equally dispatched when he got out of his depth as a double agent in Cork. 'In time' was the great phrase in the history books; in time, inevitably, you'll be got. I hope they never get me in time.

The police headquarters is right across the road. All day and all night the cars of the guards, detectives and Special Branch go in and out, bumping over the entrance ramps and saluted by the guards on the gate, tending to the surveillance of suspicious activities and the solution of serious crimes.

When they come off duty you can hear them go in and out of the Harcourt Hotel next door, one of the places they've firmed up for after-hours drinking. Some friends of mine tried to avail of the facility and bravely attempted a secret knock on the locked lounge door. For their neck they were half invited in but they weren't sure about entering. You drink with the law after midnight, you don't know where you might end up. Keep your distance: that's my policy.

Though I share this house with what seems at times to be a hundred other lonely lodgers of different shape, size, colour, my name and that that of Dr Sanjay and Heike and Elke are the only names sellotaped next to the cracked doorbell. The turnover is too great, the desire for anonymity too pronounced on the part of the beleaguered tenants and the cunning landlord for any more names to be freely affixed for public show. How proudly native does the typeset 'Michael Collins' look beside the Indian doctor and the German au pair, not to mention all the other Greeks, Arabs, Africans cooking away in their dingily lit whitewashed rooms with kitsch plastic-bead curtains and foul-smelling carpets trod on by God knows how many different feet since the fifties or whenever it was this house was divided into a hundred human-sized cupboards.

Inside the bare, unfurnished hall I scan the shelf over the meters and peruse the waiting mail – electricity bill for Michael Pigott, Esq., the landlord (or not the landlord, since for tax purposes, he denied to me that he was the landlord and told me he was only the agent. If he's not the landlord then I'm not Michael Collins and so there's no harm in me forging his signature on the rent-allowance form he wouldn't sign). What other mail is here among the dust and anti-divorce leaflets? A small parcel for Constantine Stavrakis, a letter for the Kenyan, a postcard for Mahatma. All these people so far away from home – might as well be orphans like myself. Goodness – two letters for Shane McArdle. Or at least one for Shane and one for his mate Michael the lodger. But no French stamps, no little cockerels or Miss Liberty's. My own little Miss hasn't taken the liberty to write to me. No stamps at all, in fact. These letters have been hand-delivered. My heart is starting to boom a little. Who would drop me a note in my real name here? I recognise the loopy, careful scrawl of Sean Mellowes . . . but the other? Let's find out.

I tread the two short flights of stairs to the dark basement and confront my bent plain door. Before opening one's post one should always wait until one's door is opened, the weak bulb is switched on, a pot of low-pressure, sputtered water is on the grill and one is seated at the small, false-grained table facing the basement street light. Slice the envelope with a Bewley's knife and deftly flick open the page:

Loyala
Bird Avenue
Clonskeagh, D. 6.

Michael, my good sire,
Sensational news. First of all, greetings from my broken studies.
Have you been firmed up to help your boss on the O'Shaughnessy

statue as you said you would be – Tuesday or Wednesday this week? If you have, good. Because my extensive research into the d. of O'Higgins, which you chide me for, has led me into some remarkable revelations, or the potential for the unmasking thereof. Granted the suspicion has moved away from my peace-loving neighbour but I now have it from two reliable sources that in the man's presumably voluminous papers there is a batch specifically on the issue of the O'H. murder and the identities of the assailants.

Skin the Goat had a conversation recently with your friend Tess (?) and she confirmed casually that you would all be meeting O'Shaughnessy regularly from now on. In his house, I assume; he's an old man and not as active on the massage-parlour circuit as he used to be. Shane, I'm not trying to muscle in but this gives us a remarkable opportunity. Contact me as soon as possible. I have plans that you must hear about. Keep it all hush as I know you will and destroy this letter as soon as you've read it.

Invincible in research,
Sean Mellowes

I was waiting for this. I feared it. Mellowes has been trying for years to solve this mystery and now he wants to muscle in on my contact at a time when I am setting up something very delicate and very dangerous. It was inevitable. O'Higgins was shot leaving his house to go to mass on a Sunday morning, 10 July 1927. He had headed up Cross Avenue without taking his bodyguard who had accompanied him on a swim at Blackrock earlier in the morning. As O'Higgins approached Booterstown Avenue, a boy on a bicycle gave a signal to a motor car on the other side of the road. A man came out and started shooting at point-blank range. O'Higgins tried to run for cover to the gate of Sans Souci, another house. His attacker followed shooting and then O'Higgins fell on the footpath; two more men emerged from behind the car and finished him off. Unlike the scene of his father's death, there was no one to tell the gunmen, 'Stop shooting; he is killed; you need not fire again.' They were taking no chances and indeed he lived for five hours with seven bullets in him. Like the killing of his 'political father', Michael Collins, one bullet had entered his head behind his ear and, as with Collins, there was a great debate as to who put it there.

The automatic assumption was the IRA had killed him to get revenge and stir things up and maybe even reactivate the Civil War. There was an outcry but there was no Civil War. The Government pushed through legislation that forced the Opposition either to take up their seats or not contest elections. Dev would have to take the oath to the King that the Civil War was fought over. He pushed the bible away and told the clerk of the Dáil that he was not taking the oath. Then he went through the formality of taking the oath and led his party into the Dáil. Wonderful logic. Clever man. Democracy is saved and Dev's constitutional career moves on smoothly.

Meanwhile, as O'Higgins is being buried, scores of IRA suspects are being interrogated, including O'Shaughnessy. The light falls upon him and he is in fact charged but then he produces what is apparently an incontestable alibi and he is released. Leaf out of your book, O'Shaughnessy, I'll be hoping to get. Gradually all the IRA suspects are released and no one is charged for the killing. The IRA never claim it, either officially or unofficially (as if there was a great difference in 1927) and so the speculation grows over the years and decades. The premises rank as follows:

i. It was the IRA but they were too chicken to admit it.
ii. It was a faction of the IRA that didn't have permission from headquarters and wanted to heat things up.
iii. It was relatives/friends/IRA freelancers of family/families that had men executed by O'Higgins's government.
iv. It was the disgruntled faction that lost out to O'Higgins in the 1926 attempted army coup.
v. It was an inside job done by Free State hardliners (ignoring the fact that O'Higgins was supposed to be the hardest of the hardliners) to force Fianna Fáil into Dáil or force them bloody well out of it and have a massive crack-down on the IRA.
vi. It was British intelligence trying to achieve the same.
vii. It was trigger-happy alcoholics enraged by the drastic changes in the licensing hours.

Solid, stolid Sean had ploughed through all these theories and had dismissed most of them. A book came out last year that came down firmly for number ii and actually named three of the IRA men, but Mellowes is, needless to say, not convinced that that is the full story. He feels certain that there was a big name behind it. There had to be, he says. It was a huge job that could have inflamed the situation and the nod would have had to come from the very top. He feels certain he knows who the big name is. The big name, he says, is still among us. He feels certain he can prove who the big name is before the big name is not among us. And that puts me in a very strange position, as you can imagine. A very strange position. Strangely comforting, in a way, but very strange.

I'm dying here, procrastinating, buying time. I know what's in the other letter there. I'm sure I know but I don't want to open it. Before I touched it, I took off the bubbling pot of water and put Mellowes' letter to the reddened bars. It lights and burns voraciously, gulped in flames. Black ash flakes, as soft as gossamer, floated to the carpet. The other letter was sealed tightly (a wet tongue) and tore jaggedly with a sawing noise when the knife ploughed it. Unfolded, it was crudely typed and quite familiar. Here we go:

You propose to assist Mr Robert Wycherley in constructing for the purposes of public monument a statue of the Republican terrorist, Cornelius O'Shaughnessy. We believe that this statue is unwanted and unnecessary. It is a further insult to people like ourselves, among others, and it will not be unveiled. For your livelihood, as a young man who enjoys life, you should cease working on this project or face the consequences.

In memory of the men who fell in Belgium seventy years ago this month.

Signed
AVNS

What the hell! What men in Belgium? Is Forbes bringing a personal angle to this? Is he pulling on the disguise of some obscure grievance, a cause as lost as his own? I read and reread the letter. Extraordinary.

Or is it? Any old joker could have written it. I could have written it myself. What's this personalised note, *as a young man who enjoys life*? Sure that's got to be Forbes. He bought me drinks on many an occasion. He's always ribbing me about being out and about, enjoying life, having a good time. And telling me to get away from Wycherley who he here names and tells me not *to assist. Insult to people like ourselves* – that's got to be a code for 'we real, representational sculptors'. *Among others* – that's got to mean all the other sorts who will be offended by Wycherley's sculpture to O'Shaughnessy, and as Forbes knows, there are more than a few. And what does that ambiguous phrase *for the purposes of public monument* mean? Sure that must be a sly dig at what they perceive to be Wycherley's attempt at a public statue. In other words, you are going to help him to have a try in constructing a real statue as opposed to an unreal statue. And *constructing*. The very phrase is belittling, conjuring up a picture of a plodding, workman-like attempt, the noisy precariousness of a child trying to do a man's work.

But the Belgium bit is odd. Forbes is not historical. He's a trickster but not historical. Would he put in a bit like that just for a throwaway flourish? He must have. If it's him we're talking about and, for the moment, I'm not prepared to consider anyone else. What men who fell, though? Lots of men fell. The Ulster Unionists are celebrating the Somme this month. The British Legion have had a few services. The papers are full of it. Probably more on that than you'd get for 'our' 1916 and that's a turnaround. They're even thinking of bringing the Legion into a national ceremony on Sunday. Forbes or whoever could have picked up on putting the idea in to throw us and antagonise. Think of the opposite to O'Shaughnessy and you think of the Somme and all that.

And yet if it is not Forbes . . . I read it again a few times and it started to annoy me for some reason. I hated the way it was a different letter to the one Tess got. I hated the thought that someone was experimenting with us, changing the language to cajole and frighten, according to the respective receiver. I hated the thought that someone – it could be Forbes, it could be someone else – was sitting somewhere right now and thinking about me reading this and being frightened. God, that drove me mad. I fright at nothing. And if I did fright at anything it wouldn't be pathetic letters like this. Look at the yoke, badly typed on something close to civil-service toilet paper, the sort of stuff you used to have to use when you visited the National Museum; glassy and sore, with 'Oifig an tSolathair' stamped all over it. The language has changed since this morning. No consistency. The solicitous *We understand* has been dropped. Obviously, the penny did. O'Shaughnessy has come out of retirement; he's just a plain Republican terrorist now. Either he's suddenly still hobbling across the Border in disguise

35

or else these people think that to sculpt him would bring him out of retirement and so they invest his bronze replica with the same inspirational magnetism that the UVF saw and destroyed in Wolfe Tone's statue in the Green. Interesting. Obviously these statues are dangerous things. Unlike these letter-penning cranks, full of sound and fury but as harmless as a park-bench drunk roaring his head off. Or in this case, high-school skunk letting his steam off. The peevish, self-pitying and noisy-neighbour quality of *it is a further insult to people like ourselves*, the childish indignation of *it will not be unveiled*. Stamp your feet while you're at it. And as for the comically condescending *as a young man who enjoys life*, in its infinite suggestiveness it could be a kindly grandfather, an ironic genial priest (come, come now) a lascivious lubricated aunt (come, come, come, now), anyone but a man or spurious organisation intent on seriously hindering my welfare. The exaggerated overreaching attempt at historical authenticity at the end, *the men who fell in Belgium*, is over the top and undermines, tripwires, any credibility it might have had. A silliness more shell-shocked than Forbes. Somme Tommy out there in no man's land is having a gas time. Barbed jokes – I can't take them seriously and I won't. We have an important job to do and we can't allow ourselves to be disturbed by friend or enemy. It's none of their business.

No way. We have a plan to come up with and a false plan to rehearse. There's lots of play-acting ahead and my heart feels cold at the prospect. Can it be carried off? I've seen plenty in this studio and I've seen Wycherley at close hand and he's a crazy enough bastard to go through with what he's planned.

It's worse he's getting, not better. Why only this morning I chanced upon the shirtless employer, his furry chest like a long, lichen-crusted rock, pointing growlingly at himself in the studio mirror. He was making voluptuous, duck-lipped noises and crossing his upright legs like a coy dancing girl. We connected eyes suddenly in the mirror – my heart jumped at his cold penetrative stare in the corner of the glass – and quite abashed, he relaxed and laughed luxuriously. The full frank stare that had a tantalising forbidden quality, tentatively evoked on the first opening of the AVNS letter but more associated with early adolescence – the free, fugitive sensation of first joints, a stolen car, pilfered underwear or a wet delving of the fingers in something warm, slippery and membranous as the mouth of a landed pollock. Ah, but in those steady reflected eyes I also felt a glimpse of his madness. And it was his normal, pacified, how-do-you-do madness, burrowing away like a rabbit that must eventually occasionally surface – it was this that fascinated me. It was this, of course, that first confirmed to me that here was the man who would let me take my life's revenge and realisation, and not baulk at the crunch, but it was also the sort of moment that suggested that having made the commitments we had, from hereon more than our political scruples would be breaking down.

The art itself I had unmotivated, meretricious interest in. A musician, after all, is what Shane McArdle really is. I only became a sculptor's assistant because, accomplished and locally successful as I was, one grows tired of blowing into a saxophone in the smoke-filled clubs, week after week, band after band. Gradually I wearied of standing there, ears plugged, eyes dilating, puffing to be heard above the din of the angry drummers and flaunting guitarists I was playing with. My elbows began to sag, my feet would shift restlessly and my breath came out tired and flatulent: odd noises of a muesli-fed vegetarian sitting at the long end of a Wavin pipe. Of course, because the sax is a holy and sensuous instrument, my emotional listeners in those dark wine clubs and restaurants would applaud this tired disintegration of my enthusiasm as it emerged in a broken sound of soulful tragedy. Long-haired girls would close their eyes and swoon to these apathetic car-ferry noises as if I was playing the very valves of my heart, or indeed my golden horn, which, with indulgent indifference to my reverential onlookers, I was.

So when I met Wycherley at a bar counter in Lincoln Place one wet night and he, impressed by my duplicitious erudition in the visual arts (all names and labels) and, I'd like to think, my winning smile, offered me a job in the studio, I said thank you, and went home to the basement of 59 Harcourt Street, to pack my horn into its purple fur-lined coffin. It was without reluctance but not without sentiment that I packed away my horn. It had not only been a permanent and trusted friend over the years, it had been my livelihood; it and its windy cousins. You see, as a 'rootless orphan' (their words, not mine) I was 'placed' in the care of the Artane Boys' Home, an institution for orphans on the north side of the city run by a grim bunch of Roman jokers known as the Christian Brothers, or 'Fathers' as we called them in some weird pact of unnatural dependency. I was placed in their 'care' at the age of five, by I know not whom and in circumstances I care not to discuss. The home, as we all know, has a famous Boys' Band and it was then that I first played the trumpet, a tiny figure in a blue-and-red cloak, shorts and cap.

Many of you, thousands of you, will have seen me parading round the pitch in Croke Park, fourth or fifth from the back, before and during the interval of most of the important Gaelic football and hurling games of the mid seventies. On the All Ireland Final Day when the seething, crushing cauldron of Croke Park would settle somewhat at the half-time interval and seventy thousand people would stumble out to buy programmes, pee, smoke, chat to a man up there they hadn't seen in years, drink Bovril and soothe their rasping gullets with swigs of hip flasks, then . . . then out of the tunnel we would emerge on to the pitch, blue capes fluttering in the breeze, drums, tambourines, and trumpets striking up. And at this moment, every year, the television commentator would say, 'And here they come, the Artane Boys, playing "The Banks of My Own Lovely . . ."' as if the cavalry had arrived to save the occasion. Despite such sentimental affection, as soon as the players re-emerged to raucous roars for the second half, we were rather unceremoniously bustled off the field, often hurried over the sideline by a shower of half-gnawed apples flung impatiently from the upper recesses of the Cusack Stand.

At the 1974 final between Dublin and Galway you might remember Jimmy the Twist dropping his baton in the centre circle. You might also remember me the following year losing my place in the 'D' after the moment when the band breaks to form the capital letters of the finalists.

Eventually, of course, it was the sentence I had to break free of and in 1980, when an age old enough to survive in the outside world was reached, I walked out of the home dressed in a Premier Dairies jacket and never came back. You could say that to break free from the story was the ultimate objective, not to be achieved until the fiery end. Rory O'Connor was not outside the walls of the Home with twenty men to meet me but I got along OK with the contacts I had. The most important one was the name of a man who ran a bookstall at the Dandelion Market. He was a friend of the Twist's (who was in on my escape) and he gave me a job immediately on the strength of my telling him he was selling certain books (*Parnellism and Crime* – original series, *Lesser Known Annals of the Phoenix Literary Society*) at a fraction of the real price. I worked there happily for one and a half years, or until it was discovered that I had gone back to selling certain books at a fraction of their 'real price', only this time it was to arranged buyers who would buy the books on my behalf for a small fee in the Bailey later on. But the scam couldn't last, and when I got the sack I had to go back to the music; an unhappy interlude I was glad to abandon when art beckoned in the form of a wacky Protestant.

Ms Collins, take a letter:

Sean, *a chara*,

Received two crank's letters this morning relating to Mr O'Shaughnessy. The first from your good self, the other from a man called ANVS who – would you believe this – threatened 'my livelihood' if I worked on the statue. We think we know the lush who penned it. I'll tell you about it anon. Anyway, like Cromwell, I put your letter to the torch. I look forward to hearing more about this information on O'Higgins (you never give up, do you?). I'm wary already but still. I'll be at Loyola on Sat. at eleven but I'll see you in the meantime. As Big Mick would say, 'Prepare,' and unearth some Bacardi for my arrival.

Is mise le meas,
Shane

While sealing the envelope I could hear from Ahmed's room above me the mournful wailing of a young Arabic songstress. Ahmed has racks of these crackly cassettes, their covers displaying Semite nubiles, all pink lips and spidery eyelashes, erupting bare-shouldered from satin dresses. The Tehran mullahs burnt these voluptuous ladies in their thousands, the public piles of melting plastic and vinyl coagulating into fiery pyres that would smoke for weeks. Replaced by Islamic hymns and the grand melodrama of Hussein's death. Killed in the field like Collins. More sword, less sorcery.

Popped next door to empty the golden contents of my bladder and resketch my itinerary for the rest of the day. Meet the good invincible, Oisin, at three-thirty in the One-eyed Docker. Not quite. The One-eyed Docker is a fictitious pub, like telling hangers-on about the 'great session' going on at 51 Haddington Road and they arrive, six-packs under the arm, at the Fifty-One pub. I'm meeting Oisin at the Wolfe Tone in Mary Street. His choice. He works around the corner at the Warehouse, if one could call lying around smoking joints and strumming guitars working.

On my way I'll call into the GPO to post those letters. Michael's first stand for the Republic and he lived to tell the tale.

It quickens the passage of the mail and lightens the load of the postmen to go directly there and not be bothering with these green pillar boxes. 'Is this to be the height of our achievement,' shouted the bitter O'Shaughnessy after the Treaty was signed, 'painting the red boxes green?' And then after the sour laughter had died down, 'Well, we'll paint the land red to undo it!'

Strong stuff. Down below, a good masculine froth of suds had been rattled out of the water so after a few swift shakes of the long fellow – wearing his German helmet; how appropriate, his condolences were with Adolf – I button my fly and stoop to swiftly polish the brogues. No plaster-speckled bohemian loafers for me. Leave that to the unshaven young Wycherleys down from the NCAD with their scruffy overalls, Oxfam coats and Papua New Guinea earrings. I wish to cut an impressive figure in town and will not be mistaken for an artist. Though, I must say, the aesthetic does rise up in me violently when I count my pound notes and I see the blanket-shawled tinker woman they have replaced the graceful, demure, lithe-necked Lady Lavery with. What is the country coming to? Lovely Lavery – she fancied Collins, like myself. Now she's gone. This worm-haired hag is what it's coming to, financially and sexually. And financially I am not coming to much, judging by the homogeneous green look of these crumpled bank notes. No purple tens and not a peep out of WBY who fancied O'Shaughnessy's mother. More colour tomorrow when I get paid and they start making their way over the counters and into the bar tills. But charity begins at home and before I leave the bedsit I take out the sea-green bottle of Jameson and my Papal Visit souvenir mug and fling back two throat-scorching, neck-wriggling medicinal shots. If you could inject this stuff it would be even better.

At the end of the street, I stepped into the perspex phone box to phone Wycherley. 'Emergency calls only', read the digital display. '999,' a fräulein once told me in a Munich youth hostel, clutching her legs and blankets, but that's another story . . . I'll try the next box, love; it ain't an emergency yet.

Come on, come on.

'Bob? Listen. I've got another of those letters . . . I thought I should tell you. It was waiting for me when I got to the flat. What do you think we should do about it?'

40

'What do you mean, what will we do about it? It doesn't say RSVP, does it?'

'Well, in a manner of speaking, it does.'

'What does it say?'

I pulled out the letter and read him the text.

'It's just like Tessa's,' he said.

'More or less, but with a few crucial differences.'

'Yeah, it's even more like Forbes.'

'That's what I kind of thought . . . the bit: "as a young man who enjoys life . . ." Eh . . .' I read it again. 'Yes.'

'The bastard, that's him.'

'Do you think so?'

'Definitely.'

'Really?'

'Well, I mean, Shane . . . I'm as sure as I could be. That's his mock diction, his underhand teasing. He's gradually giving himself away. That's probably the intention. "People like ourselves" – the guff out of him.'

'You know, boss, we should . . . you know, we should be careful all the same. Given what we have to do . . . we should keep our minds open and not draw him in, if it is him.'

'Exactly. Open but not distracted, which is this pathetic creature's objective. Don't tell me about being careful. We have a job on hand and we're not going to be put off it and that's the main thing. That's what's crucial. Leave it with me, I'm going to start making a few discreet, very discreet, enquiries . . .'

'Where?'

'Oh, here and there . . . the places where our paths might cross.'

'Do you want me to bring down the letter?'

'No need. I have the gist of its miserable contents. Jesus . . . this is some joke. Coming at the right time too. A joke and a bloody irritating one.'

'Well, there's a bit of style to it, you have to admit.'

'You would say that. Go on, enjoy the rest of your half-day. I want you in good shape for the rest of the week.'

'So you can put him in good shape for the rest of his life.'

'No boozing or staying up all night.'

Right then, that's that off my mind for a while. I've touched base, as Corny would say when we put him *in situ*. Bob sounds

41

sure but I'm not so sure. But either way it's not something worth worrying about. Not with what we have on our minds.

I crossed the street and went into the Green again, around Lord Ardilaun sitting in his chair. No, that's one thing I'm not into: statues sitting in chairs. Some bright spark had the idea recently of littering the city's parks and traffic islands with statues of the city's 'famous writers' and, worse still, 'famous characters' sitting on benches. The idea was that ordinary folk, children and shoppers – mere mortals, as I'd call them – could sit beside cranky O'Casey or get up on family man Yeats's knee and no doubt colour in his monocle with a robbed Eason's marker. Did you ever hear the like? What the man, a politico, had in mind was something like the George Segal sculptures in New York and Boston, depicting anonymous urban figures sitting on benches reading newspapers or arguing business points, although I think the only comparative bench this chap had in mind was one for himself in the Corpo Chamber.

Anyway, some brighter spark hit back by suggesting that such 'interactive' sculptures with their patronising and plain inaccurate postures (Yeats among the businessmen? Shaw among the ladies?) would never be considered for political or historical figures. Oh no, they must always be above the people, erect and purposeful, their eye on an approaching bus. And, quite right too, is what I say. We couldn't have the bronze Corny philosophically crossing his legs while some copper tinker is swigging wine beside him or Collins sitting spreadeagled the way he's pictured in 1919 at that Croke Park benefit for Republican prisoners, only instead of Dev and Griffith beside him laughing and clutching their canes, he's got some Jack-the-lad and a red-lipped brasser wearing the faces off each other after a bellyful of cider. No way, man. Up he goes and straight up. I like this Green, though, and so will he if and when he gets in here but sad to say that he probably won't have the pleasure. Like Brendan Behan, who said that the sight he most wanted to see was his own funeral, Corny will, of necessity, have to be content with the expectation.

On my way to the Wolfe Tone I got a quick look at the evening papers. Familiar front page – bloody joke of a summer in the North. Loyalists determined to march through the Catholic part of Portadown but Agreement is stopping them. Want to give the finger to the Fenians, their constitutional prerogative. In Dublin, controversy grows over the proposed National Commemoration

Ceremony. Republicans speak out against the presence of the British Legion in the Garden of Remembrance and against the laying of a plaque there to honour Irishmen who died in *all* wars. Now that's very like the language Forbes is talking, or at least the reverse to it. Is that where he got the idea? I wonder . . . let's see. Lt.-Gen. Costelloe said he would not be there and the 1916–21 Club are threatening boycott. Not consulted. Mislead as to nature of ceremony. FF politicians considering being conveniently absent . . .

'However, there is much interest about the position of Mr Cornelius O'Shaughnessy, generally considered a spokesman for the men of 1916–1923. He is understood to be strongly opposed to the idea but is not speaking out due to his desire not to embarrass the Government which has committed itself to another 1916 commemoration, a special statue of Mr O'Shaughnessy himself. The proposal for the statue came on the personal initiative of the Taoiseach, very like the idea for the commemoration ceremony. Mr O'Shaughnessy was not available for comment yesterday. He is at present out of the country attending an anti-imperialist symposium in Paris . . .' Well now, that's interesting, that's very interesting. Have I got coins? I have. I'll give my boss another little tinkle before I hit the Wolfe Tone.

Pulling up his long legs in the Wolfe Tone, 'Jesus,' said Oisin. 'So have you got this letter on you?' I gave him the letter and his black brow tensed. Long white fingers pushed the fallen slices back on to his head.

'Jesus,' he said, reading. 'It sounds like the Reverend Ian.'

'I hope it's equally full of wind.'

'God, it should be; it's almost too wordy to be taken seriously. Wordy and mysterious . . . "the men who fell in Belgium". That's obviously the Ulstermen who died in their thousands seventy years ago this week. Is this guy Forbes a closet Unionist or something?'

'This is his cover. And it's handy that he waited till this week to use it, with the celebrations and documentaries on the Somme and all that. "In memory of the men who fell in Belgium" sounds very plausible and impressive – authoritative – but there are giveaway appeals like "as a young man who enjoys life, you should" . . . more or less, give up working for that old chancer, the constructionist.'

'Why don't you confront him with it?'

'I haven't seen him. I mean, he's hanging out in Grogan's, but I don't want to seek him out. At least not yet. I don't want to give him the pleasure . . .'

'You'll see if he sends some more?'

'Exactly. Tess got one as well.'

'Oh. What did hers say?'

'The same thing. But it was more political. "Republican terrorist" . . . "violent Fenian" . . .'

'Ah, that's someone acting the Orangeman.'

'I think Wycherley is going to have them checked out. He's going to make a few, I hope, discreet enquiries around Forbes's whereabouts. What have people heard him say, etc. It shouldn't be difficult because by closing time these days he's apparently been shouting his head off and Wycherley's name features therein.'

'Mmm.' Oisin pulled at his long nose. 'Well, if it's not this guy Forbes it's probably some old colonel in West Cork who's pissed off, like the rest of us, by the amount of Republican statues we already have to crawl around. No offence to your own noble efforts,' he quickly muttered, the white hand aflutter.

'No . . .'

'Are you going to go to the police?'

'If we receive any more I'd say we might have to.'

'He's a popular guy, O'Shaughnessy, but he's deeply unpopular as well. This sort of thing is to be expected.'

'True.'

'It's funny though, *you* getting something like this and you being into O'Shaughnessy's period and all. I mean, like the rest of us.'

'So are lots of people.'

'I suppose.'

We sipped our pints and I put away the letter.

'I wouldn't say it's anything to worry about,' Oisin said in a tentative way.

'I don't intend to give it any more thought than it deserves.'

'No . . .' he said and he sipped his pint again.

The barman was yawning. A long, heavy, air-the-dentures yawn.

'The other letter I got was from Mellowes.'

'Mad mouldy Mellowes!' said Oisin with relief. 'How is he prospering on the lush plains of Meath?'

'Grand. I had to burn the letter, something I was tempted to do with the other one.'

'My God. Why did you have to burn it?'

44

'Because he instructed me to. The letter referred to his ongoing investigation into the killers of the bold O'Higgins.'

'He's not into O'Shaughnessy again. The man was acquitted twice by Mellowes himself and once by the law.'

'He's on to his papers. Two sources he can't reveal but which are reliable tell him that somewhere in O'Shaughnessy's papers lie the details on the case and the identities of the assailant. It would appear that the details will confirm Mellowes' theory that Harry White's memoirs published last February only tell half the story.'

'Selective revelations. You can't trust a gunman's memoirs. Look at my own Tone and the way he was bowdlerised. What's to say O'Shaughnessy would put the real truth down on paper?'

'We shall have to see. As Chief of Staff he infuriated his officers by documenting things that shouldn't be documented. He can't suppress the lawyer in him. He needs to keep a record for himself, whatever about posterity.'

'Whatever indeed. Discretion being the better part of valour. So what does he want you to do – steal the papers when your subject's back is turned? Quiz him under hypnotism?'

'I don't know,' I said, irritated at Oisin's flippancy. 'Sean assumes I'll be out in O'Shaughnessy's house, which I will at some stage. So take it from there – a few innocent questions, a bit of subterfuge, check the place out. Who knows? Sean said nothing except destroy the letter. So keep the matter close to your chest.'

'Ah,' smiled Oisin, 'the melodramatic touch! A quick glance over one's shoulder. I must say, Shane, with all due respect to Mellowes' previous investigations, this one sounds a bit pie in the sky, a bit ambitious, to say the least.'

'Well, we haven't heard what it's about yet so give the guy a chance.'

'OK, point taken,' conceded Oisin with a humble nod.

'Admittedly, I'm a bar-stool graduate and unserious guesser compared to the wizard of detective scholarship beyond in Bird Avenue. I suppose if he does have a strong lead our lips should be as sealed as a nun's gates. And if I don't hear from him, you'll keep me informed.'

'I'll keep you posted,' I corrected. 'Informed is a superstitious word around these parts.'

'Indeed. A nod is as good as a wink to the blind man in the park, as Dev's aides used to say.'

And he sipped his pint.

Chapter 3

Times Returned

When I arrived at the studio the next morning, things had become a little more serious. After Wycherley put the phone down on me yesterday afternoon, the damn thing started ringing and ringing incessantly. Journalists had received copies of the letters sent to Ms Masterson and Mr McArdle and they wanted to know what was going to be done about them. The police were contacted and so were Government Information Service, who contacted the Department of the Taoiseach who got in touch with the Minister of State who was up in his native Sligo attending the inaugural lecture of the twenty-second International Yeats Summer School ('An Irish Revolution Foresees its Death', by Professor Shawn B. Finkelstein of Asgardia College, Boston).

So Wycherley didn't need to go to the police after all. They came to him. They arrived down in the studio, in an unwashed squad car, to ask about the letters. Before Wycherley knew it, he was confronted by a Detective Sergeant Hurley and two guards walking around his studio. Naturally, Wycherley got a bit panicky. He'd never had guards in his studio before and usually he liked to keep as far away from them as it was possible to be. With their assistance, he tried to contact me at the flat and at a rake of other places, but I couldn't be reached.

So they examined the one letter over an over-friendly cup of tea in the kitchen. (Wycherley wanted to get them out of the sanctity of his studio about which they were far too nosy.) They listened patiently enough to his suspicions of Samuel Forbes, his eccentric and disappointed rival, but naturally they weren't going to make any comments on Wycherley's convinced claims about Forbes's authorship of the letters. Hurley stroked his breast and told him to put it all down in writing and have it brought up to him in Garda Headquarters. Naturally it would be treated in the strictest confidence.

An 'open mind' would be kept on the matter. The letters were anonymous and mysterious and it was impossible to say who was responsible. However, they were not unusual. Poisonous and threatening letters are sent to people all the time and the gardaí regularly have to investigate such matters. Generally the investigations and the letters come to nothing and we would hope that that would be the case in this situation.

O'Shaughnessy is the sort of character about whom people could be expected to write threatening letters, whether in jest or in earnest. However, precisely because of this there is a good deal of sensitivity about the statue 'up above'. Wycherley pointed to the ceiling but he meant the Government. Notwithstanding the Government's commitment to erecting a statue of him, O'Shaughnessy had not been shy to criticise them about this 'mixed' commemoration ceremony that was to take place at the weekend, and this letter seemed to stray into the same territory. Different people perhaps, but the same territory. The Government were a bit 'anxious' about that, said Hurley with a wink and no more.

And because of the sensitivity about the matter in general, and the public interest in it and the need to be safe and vigilant, Hurley was going to arrange, through Pearse Street Station, to have two or three gardaí hang around the neighbourhood over the course of the next week. Wycherley protested that this was unnecessary and attention-seeking and would give Samuel Forbes great satisfaction. Hurley ignored his reference to Forbes and asked Wycherley if he had some objection against being protected. No, said Wycherley, with the eyes of three guards upon him, it's just that . . . You're beginning to sound like O'Shaughnessy, said Hurley with a grin, but a serious grin. We can't get him to accept any sort of protection, at any time. It's the old instinct – you'd think he had something to hide.

'Would you relax,' I told him the next morning.

'Shane, how are we going to work with police outside our front door?'

'Just ignore them. They're not outside our front door. Think of them as being at the end of the street doing traffic duty or neighbourhood walkabout . . . they've no connection with us. They're just part of the urban scenery.'

'"Urban scenery". Listen to him. That's all we need.'

'It hardens you up to have to work under the nose of the police. That's the way Collins used to do it. Right under their bloody noses. Don't be hiding away or acting suspicious. Keep the cops close to you, as close as you possibly can. They can watch you but you can watch them and you can watch them watching you and even more closely and you can develop a sort of a permanent alibi, which is the most useful thing of all.'

'Forbes will be chuffed.'

'That's the other thing, if it's not Samuel Forbes – no, hold on, don't squint – if it's not Sam Forbes, it might be just as well that we do have a cop or two within hollering distance. Seriously, Bob. We've got to think about that. We don't want to be attacked on our flank while we're going for the big one. We might end up being grateful that the police were not a million miles away.'

The palm of Wycherley's long hand rubbed his bald head and he stared at the table.

'Look,' he said, with a sigh. 'I accept that I could be wrong on Forbes, but my feeling is strengthening not weakening. Francis de Paor told me last night at the National Gallery that Forbes had told people that one of the reasons I got the O'Shaughnessy commission was because the Taoiseach's wife admired my work – can you believe that?'

'No.'

'He's a very bitter man, Shane. The story now is that he's so aggrieved at not getting this job and a clutter of other jobs that he says he's going to give up sculpture altogether and turn to writing.'

'That is desperate.'

'Desperate and pathetic. Writing may be therapeutic but there's no need to take it out on us.'

'You think that?'

'Why not? He's out to get me, Shane. He was speaking some very dangerous language in Grogan's recently. He was also, incidentally' – Wycherley lowered an eye – 'in the said hostelry on Tuesday night and left before closing time. A most unusual development. He'd been attacking me before he left. A number of people heard him, reportedly. They couldn't but. The drink was down and the voice was up. It's a pity that the Minister didn't know what kind of person he was dealing with when he let slip, if he let slip, a promise to consider his fellow countryman for the O'Shaughnessy contract at that function in Sligo. He knows Forbes's c.v., and he'd have to, but I don't think he knows how nasty the little classicist has become. Or crafty. Forbes was an actor up there, you know.'

'Yeah, he mentioned that.'

'A terrible actor, apparently. But well able to dress himself up in the language of others.'

'Sure aren't we all. What time will Tess be back at?'

'Very shortly, I'd say. She left just after nine.'

'And what time will the police be . . .?'

'Lunchtime, he said.'

'Well,' I said looking at him frankly, 'there was always going to be the chance that we'd have protection like that.'

'I know.'

'We might as well get used to it, practise being the key to confidence and all that.'

Wycherley made a small smile and said nothing.

'I'll be outside.'

'Get a look at the papers. You haven't seen them yet.'

They were spread out on the kitchen table.

THREATS MADE AGAINST O'SHAUGHNESSY STATUE

The Government's proposed statue of Cornelius O'Shaughnessy, which caused some controversy when it was first announced last August, has become the subject of threatening letters from an organisation known as the AVNS, it emerged yesterday. The letters were addressed to assistants working on the statue and call upon them to stop working on the project 'or face the consequences'. Copies of the letters were sent to newspapers. The letters refer to Mr O'Shaughnessy as a 'violent Fenian' and a 'Republican terrorist' and say his statue is 'unwanted and unnecessary', and 'an insult to people like ourselves', although beyond the initials AVNS nothing is revealed. In its conclusion it states, 'In memory of the men who fell in Belgium seventy years ago this month', presumably referring to those who died on the Western Front in the First World War. The losses suffered by the Ulster Division in that conflict were the subject of marked commemorations in the North earlier this month.

Gardaí are keeping an open mind on the letters and are anxious not to invest them with too much importance. Although the possibility of some form of Unionist involvement cannot be ruled out – the Belgian reference suggests it – the gardaí do not believe the letters are necessarily connected to the ongoing Unionist campaign against the Anglo-Irish Agreement. 'It would be a strange way of doing so, if it was,' said one garda source. Other garda sources described the letters as being more likely from some old Southern Unionist element or from those masquerading as such.

Ironically the letters come at a time when the Government is receiving criticism for honouring those who fell in the two World Wars by having them represented in a national commemoration ceremony in Dublin next weekend. This gesture has been criticised by Republicans – including, it is suggested, in private, Mr O'Shaughnessy – and there is speculation that the letters could have been written with a view to embarrassing the British Legion and others in the run-up to the ceremony. Speculation suggests that such a letter could also provoke Mr O'Shaughnessy into commenting on the ceremony. The Royal British Legion said yesterday it repudiated any connection with the letters and said it regarded them as 'sinister and divisive'. The Minister of State for Arts and Culture would make no comment on the letters and a government spokesman said it was a matter for the guards.

It is very possible that the letters could just be the work of pranksters eager to exploit what controversy there has already been about the O'Shaughnessy statue and about O'Shaughnessy's person and career in general. Mr O'Shaughnessy has not commented on the matter. He is at present on a visit to France. There was no comment either yesterday from Mr Robert Wycherley, the sculptor working on the project. Mr Wycherley was awarded the commission last year when it was announced that a sculpture would be unveiled in Dublin to honour the Seventieth Anniversary of the 1916 Rising and the ninetieth birthday of Mr Cornelius O'Shaughnessy, who fought in the Rising in Boland's Mills. At the time there was criticism from some artists, namely Mr Samuel Forbes of Sligo, that the commission should have been awarded as part of a competition. However, the Government rejected the criticism and stated that in the past Mr Wycherley, and Mr Forbes, have been directly awarded contracts to do monumental work for the State.

Toughen up. I went out into the yard to help Murphy sort a consignment of scrap for melting down. Murphy was officially the welder but since he was also the handyman he fixed drills, coked the ovens, knocked the plaster off casts, singed his hair to pour molten bronze and generally did all the practical constructive things that hapless, helpless Wycherley couldn't (and McArdle wouldn't). In a sense then he was the real artist. Wycherley, the Appreciated Artist, very often merely 'visualised' and stood back from the dust and heat uttering directions. What was Stephen D.'s line? Detached and disinterested like God in the clouds paring his fingernails. That's our Bob with a John Player's in his hand. He would hand down instructions and supervise and by the time a sculpture had finally emerged it would have felt the shaping of up to another four pairs of hands much more (personally? impersonally?) than it would those of its actual, supposed creator. Latch-key sculptor, was how I heard some jealous 'craftsperson' describe him at a Temple Bar opening. But even the biggies do it, especially the biggies: George Segal and Yolima Carrera sending their blueprints into the foundries and then arriving in their big jeeps to collect the casts and lug them away to some black-glass corporate plaza where the people will 'interact' with them in a more personal way than probably their creators ever did.

Not that it's a modern habit. Rodin was the same. A hall full of cautious, aproned attendants on stepladders making the sculpture he 'imagined' while the brim-hatted maestro nodded and smoked his pipe in the background. And yet, the wondrous gallery-walkers of today will stroke the cold bronze cheek of a Rodin and sigh religiously at the fantastic, the classic, the exquisite expressiveness of what Rodin's magic hands could achieve – 'the characteristic curve of that crater-like dimple' – not knowing that some poor Parisian teaboy, an assistant (a Shane McArdle, for God's sake) was responsible for that delightful dimple. And that at the time of its creation the Artist was in la loo sitting in the pose of what he pompously called *The Thinker* and conceptualising his next vision. Today, French loos have no bowls, only those uncomfortable porcelain foot-grips so their squatting artists don't get away with as much.

Murphy. Where is he? His jacket hung from a makeshift sprocket stuck between the limestone bricks of the corner wall. Three wooden tea chests – to take lead, bronze and copper – were set up beside the assorted collection of scrap metal dumped next to the yard door. What a graveyard of durables – candlesticks, mock Tudor tankards, brass nameplates of now deceased solicitors, printer's blocks, clocks' entrails, greenish-lead Greek javelin thrower, severed leg of a felled fountain horse, rusty railings and hundreds of penny coins. Pre-decimal, the big-disc, brown coppers that put sweat in your palms, some with George V, some with a hen and chickens (*Saorstat Eireann*), some with just a hen: Victoria. There's a woman who knew how to commemorate. If we were working for her we'd have the Green to ourselves. Many of her imperial war heroes were cast from the melted cannons of their regiments. Their statues, that is. What will we cast O'Shaughnessy with – the unused bullets of 1916? An explosive mixture. The spent shells of the Squad would be more fitting. The later years left fewer traces. Revolvers only on Booterstown Avenue.

'Hardy man, Shane,' shouted Murphy, emerging through the yard door. 'Chuck what you don't know to the side.'

'Hey, where were you? Come on and give us a hand.'

'I'll give you a kick in the arse if you're not careful,' said Murphy, whipping the plastic cover from a fresh twenty of Major. 'The cheek of the young fellow. Here, you maggot, do you want one of these?'

'You know I don't smoke.'

'Thought you might want to save it for your mother who does.'

'You know I'm an orphan, as well.'

'I do too,' said he, striking a match, 'but I know you're a big fellow and not precious about her memory.'

'Memory? I never met the woman,' I said, sitting on a tea chest beside him.

'That a fact?' said he, exhaling sweet smoke. 'And tell me, did you float out of her fanny like a bubble and she didn't even catch sight of you?'

'What I mean is – '

'Like this,' he declared and he gently pouted smoke rings that rose up and disintegrated into one another.

'I hope I last longer than that.'

'What you mean to say is,' Murphy laboriously corrected, 'you don't *remember* meeting your mother.'

'Whatever,' I agreed, 'but surely you don't remember what might as well not have existed?' Echoing Bob here: no ashes; never was.

Murphy pulled sourly on his cigarette and glanced sideways at me, letting the smoke issue of its own accord. 'What sort of hogwash is that? You've been listening to the Wizard of Odd again.'

'Wycherley is too distracted for philosophies these days.'

'That's where you're wrong,' said Murphy. 'Distractions make more of an Apostle out of him, pottering around the place, muttering bits of wisdom like a doddery old priest.'

'Do you think he's been acting a little strangely lately?'

'This O'Shaughnessy business – with threats and oddballs and peelers outside the gate – it has, let us say, disconcerted the man.'

'But Wycherley has always been a moonwalker,' I said.

'Well, now he's a moontalker. And if you ask me, basket weaving in Dundrum is not far around the corner.'

'What are you talking about?'

'Not the full shilling upstairs,' whispered Murphy, tapping a finger on his right temple.

'That's ridiculous. You're getting carried away.'

'We'll see who's getting carried away,' he sourly suggested and he got up and kicked a few bits of scrap metal.

At that moment, Ramsey came running into the yard waving the *Evening Herald*.

'He's back,' he muttered and he indicated O'Shaughnessy's weasel face staring out at us from the front page.

'Show us!'

'Here – he says it's the English.'

'Hardly a new tune for him,' I said, grabbing the paper. 'Exclusive: M.I.5 responsible for threats – O'Shaughnessy' was the headline.

'Jasus!'

Nobel Peace Prize winner, Cornelius O'Shaughnessy, claimed today that the British Secret Service was out to ruin his controversy-ridden statue. Speaking on his arrival back from Strasbourg this morning, Mr O'Shaughnessy (89), the famous former Minister and IRA Chief of Staff, claimed that threats made against his statue's erection by a mysterious organisation called the AVNS were the work of the dirty tricks section of M.I.5, the British Secret Service.

He also suggested, on being questioned about his attitude to the Government's forthcoming 'mixed' commemoration ceremony, that 'the appeasement of anti-national opinion', of whatever era, and no matter how historically 'unharmful' it might seem, was bound to encourage hostile forces like M.I.5 and give cover for its tracks. However, while appearing strongly to disapprove of the ceremony, Mr O'Shaughnessy didn't confirm whether he would or would not attend Sunday's event. Instead, he dwelt in passionate detail on the revelations that this statue has been the subject of death threats.

'M.I.5 have been determined on revenge since my struggle with them in the twenties,' said Mr O'Shaughnessy, referring to his role in the Squad, Michael Collins's famous unit set up to eliminate British agents in Dublin. The Squad, or the 'Twelve Apostles' as they were also known, destroyed the British Government's notorious 'Cairo Gang' and killed twelve of its agents on Bloody Sunday in November 1921. 'Since those years British intelligence has tried to get its revenge in the most sinister and furtive fashion, involving itself in bloody Republican feuds, penetrating the State's security services and even acquiring short-lived moles in the IRA. I have, of course, been a particular target, given my anti-counter-intelligence activities before and after the war and my subsequent extensive involvement in radical Republican politics. The British were particularly incensed by the reception I received abroad. I have seen at close hand the machinations of their black propaganda but I have seen more than that. I know of countless careers and lives destroyed by their activities. Let me say that remarkable light could be shed on some of the dark deeds in our country's history if all was revealed. By which I mean some shocking assassinations.'

Turn to page 3.

We turned, we turned.

As Minister for External Affairs in 1949, Mr O'Shaughnessy was responsible for the detection and expulsion of Weir and Pratt, two British Secret Service agents who posed as Interpol representatives to gain access to Special Branch files on Republican suspects and the private lives of prominent politicians. On his assumption of office he stated his controversial belief that 'most senior civil servants were British spies'. He made it his task to track down key agents and from 1948–51 he had many State employees relieved of their posts.

For this thirty-year-long campaign, British intelligence was now determined to hit back, claims O'Shaughnessy, by threatening Mr O'Shaughnessy's statue because, says Mr O'Shaughnessy, it would be unseemly, even by M.I.5 standards, to make threats against an eighty-nine-year-old man. To prevent such a Republican monument being erected would be a huge boost to the British Secret Service. It would show they could influence the insidious anti-national campaign trend in public opinion, intimidate the Government and divert its security forces. The latter would be particularly beneficial at the moment, claimed O'Shaughnessy, because it would allow their spies to go on working unhindered. He had it on reliable information that the activities of British intelligence in Ireland, now as active as they were in 1981–82 or in the mid seventies, were in danger of being detected, and our own security forces were said to be close to a breakthrough on their detection. M.I.5 needed to put up a diversion and the AVNS was the suitable, seemingly mad smokescreen to serve the purpose. It also served to achieve one of their long-term private goals, which was revenge on O'Shaughnessy.

Regarding the possibility that a Loyalist group could be involved, O'Shaughnessy said the idea was mistaken. Groups like the UDA were no longer concerned with monuments in Dublin and other smaller groups wouldn't have the resources to be involved. Besides, he had many friends among that community. He had always considered them his fellow Irishmen, he said. The gardaí, meanwhile, are keeping an open mind on the matter and are not prepared to say whether they support the possibility that it may be related to the Unionist campaign against the Anglo-Irish Agreement. 'We receive reports of anonymous letters and threats very frequently so there is nothing particularly unusual about this,' a garda spokesman said.

'This thing's getting out of control,' said Wycherley, looking at the paper. 'The man's a bloody paranoid!'

'They're dramatic claims all right, but not totally implausible,' I said and received a withering look.

'Damn him,' said Wycherley, shaking his head. 'He's blown the thing up out of all proportion. He has us on the front fucking pages!'

'Language, Bob, language,' and he looked at me ruefully.

'No, no, no,' I told him. 'Makes our job easier.'

'You're being way too premature.'

'One thing at a time.'

'I don't agree.'

'Well, I'm in charge,' he said and he lowered his eyes. I said nothing and nodded.

'British intelligence!' He shook his head again at the headline.

'Maybe not British intelligence,' I said gingerly. 'But maybe more than Sam Forbes.'

'Maybe.'

'Shane!' Ramsey put his head through the curtain. 'Telephone!'

'If it's a journalist, no comment,' warned Wycherley.

'Of course,' I said, and I skipped out to the hall.

'Hello?'

'The Eagle has landed.'

'Jasus, Sean, how are you?' It was Mellowes.

'Grand, grand. Grand men make grand claims. Listen, I've got news.'

'What sort of news?'

'It may be bullshit, right, but I'm passing it on to you. I just got a call from the M.M. – our Craig Gardner friend . . .'

'Jasus, *he* would have to get involved. Any political intrigue – '

'No, listen, *Listen*. He was talking to our friend, Finbar Harrington, Dáil hopeful and Parnellite scholar, at a Fine Gael constituency meeting last night and Harrington told him, very much on the QT, that he had it from informed law library sources who these people are – or at least some clue as to who they are.'

'Who? Jasus, who?'

'Well, it's not straightforward. You see, basically, all that Harrington gave M.M. – all that Harrington said he received from his Bar library sources – are a series of riddles, or sort of cryptic clues – no more than that.'

'Of course. Wouldn't you know it.'

'Well, do you want to hear them?'

'Yeah . . . yeah, go on. I might as well.'

'Well, first of all, they're not M.I.5.'

'We gathered that.'

'What is this "limited liability"?'

'Unlimited culpability might be more like it. Anyway, the clue to their identity is that – now bear with me, this might sound strange – their "sentimental heart" rose in the South-east, but their "political heart" is set in Dublin and was broken in Westminister.'

My God.

'What is this – charades? "Sentimental heart" – what the fuck does all that mean?'

'Well, do you want to know what I think it is?'

'What do you think it is?' I said wearily.

'I think it's some Southern ex-Unionists,' he declared confidently.

'What?'

'Their heart was ultimately broken by Westminister when they were abandoned into the Free State; it set in Dublin when their fortunes declined, and it rose in the South-east because that is where they cemented their power – Kilkenny and all that planters' hinterland. Think of the letter: "the men who fell in Belgium seventy years ago this month". These are precisely the people who get the most pissed off by more and more statues of Fenian gunmen. What do you think?"

'I think you can draw any kind of deductions.'

'You don't think you should mention this to the police?'

'No, Sean.' Jesus. 'No way. Come on – these are bloody riddles that have come allegedly from the Bar library through Finbar Harrington and Mr Conspiracy himself, M.M. I can't go to Detective Hurley with these sort of fanciful rumours. It's bad enough that he had to deal with O'Shaughnessy's lurid claims. Jesus Christ. Hearts bleeding, setting and rising – I'm not going to be sucked in on this one. We've enough on our plate.'

'Fair enough,' said Mellowes, a tiny bit hurt. 'But I just thought I'd tell you . . .'

'Oh no, Jasus, thanks. You did right. Thanks a lot. And, I mean, try and find out some more, as much as you can. I can't approach Harrington directly – I won't – or M.M., but if you glean any more, by all means do. Please.'

Wycherley was calling me.

'OK, I'm being called here. I'd better head.'

'OK,' said Mellowes, 'I'll keep my ears open. Oh, and listen, I'll talk to you about the other business the next time.'

'What business?'

'You know – revolvers in Booterstown.' His voice dropped, even more conspiratorial.

'Oh yes. Kevin O'Higgins! God, Sean, I don't know about that – '

'What do you mean?'

'I don't know, I don't know . . . I mean, with all this shit . . . listen, we'll talk about it.'

'Today is the anniversary, you know.' He became suddenly wistful, remote.

'What anniversary?' Wycherley wanted me.

'Of the incident, of his falling . . . fifty-nine years ago.'

'Oh really? Right, of course. "Hot July day". That's right.' July the 1st: I wouldn't have remembered.

'I'll talk to you about it again,' he said suddenly, with what sounded like a catch in his voice. My God.

'Eh, right. And thanks a lot, Sean. I'll think about your clues and theory.' I promised him and I did.

'Be careful.'

'Always.'

When I went inside Wycherley didn't want me at all, he just wanted me off the phone so Hurley could call through. But we had some talking to do and he put my arms in plaster to pass the time.

Harcourt Street. When I opened the door of No. 59, I gave a little start on seeing a bumper delivery of post awaiting me on the table. Some for Michael Collins and some for Shane McArdle. Jesus, why does it scare me when I see that name in print. It's not a new thing, I've always had it. Someone's cooking exotic meat upstairs. Lamb or something. Jesus, Mohange, you should have gone for that. Dublin in the early sixties: sure no one would know the difference. I'd have joined you with a bottle of vino. Tasty typists. I'd try anything once. Anything, so long as my nerve holds. Relax, Shane. A letter, a note and a parcel; I never get parcels. I fear the worst here. Very odd. It's wrapped in brown paper with just my name on the front. I took the lot downstairs, opened the door and before anything could be opened, made sure. I had a pot of water on the grill.

My heart was beating. It always does of course, but now it was beating audibly and – a handy metaphor near by – the boiling saucepan soon erupted, gurgled and was quieted. I took out a fresh jar of instant coffee and tapped out a staccato tattoo on its sealed drumskin – the prelude to the deliciously loud crack of the spoon splitting it open like an empty skull. There's an apocryphal story, and I stress 'story' because it doesn't at all fit the man's character, that O'Shaughnessy once warned an alleged informer during a fruitless interrogation that if he didn't talk soon he'd make a *bodhrán* out of his bollocks and 'then maybe we'd get a few tunes out of you'. An amended version concerns a more decorous part of the unfortunate man's anatomy but I still can't see O'Shaughnessy in the thick of it. He was far too sophisticated to get coarse or up-front in an interrogation ('debriefing', he called it) and he had no great taste for the Irish music. A cup of steaming coffee in my hand, I opened the folder note. It was what I expected it to be:

Michael,
Bluehair and I came in to land at your pad.
See you later,
Jimmy C.
PS. Will you help me paint some cows on Suffolk Street?

Space Cadets! It's well for some, signing on at the Apollo Centre in Tara Street. And I risking life and limb to see O'Shaughnessy remembered, troubles they haven't even heard about yet. Cinders' cows on Suffolk Street. Two Tuesdays ago, after midnight, I scurried out into the street, armed with cardboard cut-out stencils and spray-paint canisters, to help him paint neat trails of cows' hooves along sections of Grafton Street. The dayglo red-and-yellow hooves would begin at a drain and end abruptly at a manhole cover. From afar, a policeman observed our nocturnal mischief but kept his distance. Now Jimmy plans to paint whole cows along the middle of Suffolk and Wicklow Streets. Before that, it was photocopying and colouring ten-pound notes and sticking them high up on building-site hoardings. And people did jump up to get them! Raven-haired Cinders, effortless romantic painter in Oxfam suits and thinly filled T-shirts; he's determined to get a rise out of the people.

Do I think I can talk away the tension? By telling stories I'm postponing the action, a trait of my countrymen my heroes dispelled. OK, so here goes: I started ripping the brown paper off the parcel. My heartbeat quickened. I saw, first, newsprint and then I saw it was a copy of the *Irish Times* and then I saw it was a copy of yesterday's *Irish Times* and then – by Oisin's doodles on the margin – I saw it was *my copy* of yesterday's *Irish Times*. Jesus Christ, the paper I stole in Eason's. I held it up and a note slipped out: a poem, would you believe.

This is a paper you might own
left by yourself in the Wolfe Tone
Miss the *Times* you miss part of the day
miss our warning you'll end up in clay.

As a young man you like a drink
If you value your life this should make you think
Stay close to home and don't go far
Stop for a jar in the Good Times bar
For on his hill no blood did spill
Moonlight's a man who keeps the peace
He's also a man who keeps his word.

And can't end-rhyme, the bastard. What the fuck is this? In God's
name! Am I to take this seriously? Same paper, same rackety
typewriter, same old twisted language. But this is a new game
– a poem, forsooth, a poem! One half of me reverted back
immediately to Forbes as our subject, for this certainly looked
like something worked out over a bar counter. But then when
I read it again it seemed too fluid and menacing for someone as
ineffectual and basically decent as Forbes. No, this guy means
business. This guy has a point he wants to get across. He is
prepared to follow me across town and watch me go into pubs
and pick up my newspaper after I leave. This guy's into frightening
people and I don't like it but, the funny thing is, I dislike it a lot
more than it frightens me. The more I see of my enemy, the more
I read of his letters and poems, with their silly code words and
spooky imagery and gutless anonymity, the more I feel up to
these people. I can handle these people and their childish pranks,
their hit-and-run letters, their melodramatic poems of warning. I
mean, look at this! Look at all the playful ambiguities and awful
puns and hidden meanings that might not be meanings. The idea
of course is that as well as quaking at their warning you also rack
your brains over who they are and what they want and what they
are prepared to do to get it.

On whose hill did blood not spill? Moonlight's? And why is
he a man who keeps the peace when he appears all too ready to
break it? Where is the bar with all the good times and why am
I a young man who likes a drink? Because I'm a young man who
likes a mystery, my friends, and they know it. And they know,
they must know, I'm into things historical and would be mad

keen to unravel these little clues and the little clues they sent via Harrington to our Craig Gardner friend, if those little clues are little clues and not just colourful riddles added by Bar library speculation.

I read the poem through again slowly. It's bad but it's brisk and it's menacing. Or has the appearance of being such. This is the problem. How much is real and how much isn't? How much can we ignore and how much can we afford not to? I think I'll have to report this as soon as possible. Talk to Detective Hurley across the street. We have to be on the safe side and, more importantly, we have to be on the law's side. Forbes, me arse, there's someone else involved in this. I don't see from reading this piece of direful doggerel, how M.I.5 or the Southern ex-Unionists could come into it but I'm sure others would disagree.

God preserve us. I'd better make a few phone calls. Maybe it was time I considered leaving Harcourt Street now that 'they' know where I live. Get a new place to live – that could be a good idea.

Tobin's pub. Pushing the door to enter, the moderate mumble of conversation that rose with the cigarette smoke indicated that the Duke had many customers. In every corner nodded contentedly the wise and wary heads of poets, painters, occasional musicians, solid solicitors, conceptual artists, not yet novelists and the unemployed. The frayed faces of the regulars nonchalantly listened to the amiable air of agreement in their respective circles, only moving to any great effort when they required the attention of Charlie, the head barman, a restless big Galway man not unlike Detective Sergeant Hurley, who ceaselessly wiped tables, pulled pints, grunted genially and barred customers at random. For all the drink that the clientele consumed it could not be said that they partook of food in anything like an equal amount, for they were a sorry sight in physical stature. White, skinny, hard-boned limbs and heads protruded from threadbare fourth-hand suits and moulding jumpers with unappetising regularity.

This evening, however, a more corpulent individual was leaning against the bar: the novelist, Morgan O'Kelly Dillon, non-political pouting toad – despite his reputed descendance from the political dynasty of the same name: John Blake Dillon, the Young Irelander of the eighteen-forties, John Dillon, the last Home Rule leader before Independence, and James Dillon, the feisty parliamentarian. He was also, however, a close friend and accomplice of Finbar

Harrington, our Dáil hopeful and, by happy chance, the author of a long-awaited thesis entitled 'Unfinished Business – the Lost Vision of John Dillon'.

We ribbed him about the title – unfinished thesis and suchlike – and whether it implied that Dillon's vision was a lost one or whether it was just lost on others. But he took it in good form, did Finbar, and he was someone I wouldn't mind meeting at this moment, given that 'broken hearts' speculation he gave to Mellowes. It's not unlikely either that Morgan would have heard of the hearsay, given his voracious appetite for gossip and intrigue.

When I approached, he and his dear friend Sebastian, the tenor, were laconically listening to the story of the evening – the death of Delia Stewart's cat – as relayed by one of its witnesses, the younger Robbie Thunder, astronaut and playwright. *Doleday* was his present lengthy composition, a Beckettian study of eight young men in a pub and, as I'm one of the characters, I anxiously await its finish, if it ever comes. Baby-cheeked but otherwise gaunt, he was an Egon Schiele self-portrait come alive, and pouted as he spoke.

Needless to say, there were no greetings when I arrived nor could the story be interrupted for any human enquiries about how I was. Even the fact that Robbie gave me a bit of quick background appeared to annoy Morgan considerably. He obviously had some good lines prepared for various junctures in the story's later stages and worse than being obliged to be silent for too long he couldn't bear to have his spontaneity hindered.

Thunder's version of the story briefly put: at approximately four-thirty Robbie was walking along Sallymount Avenue, Ranelagh. He heard some hysterical screaming inside the open windows of No. 16. Recognising the address and the voice, he ran through the front garden, up the steps and pushed the ajar front door, and at the end of the hallway, he found Delia Stewart kneeling on the living-room floor, crying out, 'My baby's dead, my baby's dead!' and holding to her cheek the rather crushed, blood-soaked head of a cat run over by a truck.

'It's so unfortunate,' declared Morgan, fixing his spectacles with some sincerity. Cats, a prominent and sinuous presence in his first and second volumes, were a notable exception to his immense and universal cynicism.

'Quite awful,' agreed Sebastian, draining the last whiskey-and-red from his ice-rattling glass. 'And where is the dear girl now?'

'She's gone down to the Bailey to tell the rest of the world about the calamity,' Robbie informed us. 'Do you realise she'd been doing the rounds all evening telling the story of her dead cat. She's very upset. Pouring her heart out to anyone who'll listen.'

'Wearing widows weeds, I believe,' added the tenor with a meaningful rise of the eyebrows.

'So, Mr McArdle,' said Morgan. 'This is a nasty business your maestro is in, and poor old Cornelius O'Shaughnessy chased about by Blunt's leftovers. How are you bearing up?'

'Fine,' I assured him confidently. 'It's just the work of a crank or two.'

'Quite,' grinned Morgan, as if to a child, and he finger-positioned the bridge of his spectacles.

'And these violent threats do not worry you?' asked Sebastian.

'Not really. I haven't seen anything violent occur yet.'

'Very true,' approved Morgan. 'Soldier on. Like the good Cornelius himself, don't you know.' He grinned horribly and lowered his eyes. 'But you don't know who your enemy is, do you?'

'We have some idea,' I said stiffly. 'We're . . . I'm not at liberty to speculate.'

I can't have this discussed here. If he knows about what Harrington heard he'll mention it.

'Not at liberty, that is a shame. No doubt you've had your fill of the matter. Morning, noon and night. Let us hope that as it inevitably does, art will prosper and a statue emerge.'

'Would you have any ideas about who the culprits are, then?' I asked him suddenly. I was sick of his patronising and I thought I'd go for the jugular.

'None,' he said and he put his hand on his heart. 'As you all well know, I enjoy most forms of historical enquiry but I have no appetite for our recent and bloody past. It is all a series of gunshots to my ear. Politics, I leave to those who abuse it. I must confess, however, that the idea of the Ulster Unionists and M.I.5 and the IRA all being responsible at one and the same time sounds no more far-fetched than any other escapade in our nation's annals.'

He waited for us to laugh but only Sebastian tittered.

'But do you know,' he said, turning with matter-of-fact conspiracy to myself, 'that I met your good Mr Wycherley yesterday evening at the Annual Andrew O'Connor Lecture in the National Gallery and we had a little tête-à-tête about the matter . . .'

'You know him?'

'Oh, I know him quite well. Yes, indeed, and we had quite an interesting little discussion about his troubles, which, might I say, do not appear to have affected his form in the slightest. But to the point' – Morgan looked around the bar and I could see what was coming – 'he intimated to me a thought that would sound eccentric to some but that I would find perfectly understandable. And that was' – he paused and looked up the counter and I was glad to see that Robbie was totally unresponsive to this form of theatre and even stood back a step – 'and that was a certain other artistic individual in the town could be making this mischief, an individual who has lost the run of himself recently and has been behaving like a rebuffed schoolboy, and that that individual could be no less a caricature than – Samuel Forbes.'

Damn Wycherley and his mouth.

'Believe me, I readily seconded the possibility. It is a known fact that the man – Forbes, I mean – has a notoriously unbalanced jealousy and that it has, for obvious reasons, reached a tragicomic peak of late.'

Morgan frowned and sipped his Ballygowan.

'Who's Samuel Forbes?' asked Robbie in a bored voice, but Morgan quieted him with a wave of his free hand, as if to say no more of this, I've said too much already, which was as true of him as it was of Wycherley. It's bad enough that Wycherley should confide his opinions so freely but to do so to people like Morgan Dillon, Jesus, help us.

'Ah, Bunter,' said Sebastian to one of their large and loud comrades who had wheezily burst in upon our silenced company.

'Greetings all, greetings all,' he said. 'Has anyone seen Finbar Harrington?'

'I haven't seen the man for over a week,' complained Morgan. 'He threatened he'd be lying low to complete that damn thesis but as you and I know he's been threatening to complete that thesis for the last thirteen years. Now it appears that he has departed our social company for some time, and unless we do something about it we may find him condemned until Christmas to spending each night at home drinking wine and writing history, when you and I, Morgan, are out making it!'

They all laughed, the 'you and Is'; the old debating tricks are creaky but they get them through. Bunter bid a brusque goodbye and ploughed towards the door where he bumped into the fleshless frame of Oisin O'Griofa on its way in. Do I have a surprise for him.

'Here comes your better half,' warned Morgan. 'We'd better revert to the first official language with haste.'

The black-haired frame loomed up, cracking open a Corny-lipped smile. 'My good sire, how are you? Still in one piece, I see, unlike Delia's cat.' A cruel chuckle accompanied the barb intended for Hamilton, who blithely moved aside and spoke quietly and only to Sebastian.

'Your usual sensitivity, Oisin,' remarked the indifferent Robbie.

'Oh, for God's sake, the whole thing is obscene, crying from pub to pub about a bloody cat. The woman is unhinged, with her indulgent display of exhibitionist grief. And what in the name of Jasus is she wearing on her back? A leopardskin coat!'

'A fake leopardskin coat, Oisin,' corrected Robbie.

'Worse still,' grunted Oisin. 'I make no apologies for going "Miaow, miaow" to her earlier on. I think the whole think is grotesque and obscene. A cat! A cat, Shane.'

'You obviously don't understand much about it,' said Morgan.

'I don't,' said Oisin, reaching out to accept his change from Charlie.

'What happened to your glasses, Morgan?'

'Mental fatigue,' he said. 'Comes from too much reading. Something you would know little about.'

'Give me a chance,' replied Oisin. 'You have, after all, a decade's start on me.'

Morgan's inaudible retort was directly, mainly, for Sebastian's ear and they both duly sniggered at its import, giving us the opportunity to beg our leave and move to the other end of Tobin's.

'So, Shane, Shane, listen, O'Shaughnessy thinks the Brits are mixed up in it!'

'Well, to quote Mandy Rice-Davies, he would say that, wouldn't he? But I'm afraid it's got a lot weirder than that.'

'What do you mean?'

I reached into my pocket and gave him the photocopy of the poem. The original was now with Detective Hurley in Harcourt Street. What can I say? He read it again and he read it avidly and, believe me, by the time he was done, he wasn't the cocky fellow he was when he came in. No siree, his white neck swallowed hard and he flicked his greasy black slices back with splayed and aggressive fingers.

'So, they followed us, or they followed you . . . Or someone followed us,' he kept saying, over and over. 'Have you told Mellowes?'

'I left a message with his housemate, the Maynooth Idiot.'

By the close of Tobin's time both of our necks had swallowed hard, and many times, to insure or inure us against anything we might have to deal with later on.

'Two more pints there, Charlie, and two large ones, please. We've a funeral to go to.'

'Ah, that's black talk, boys, that's very black.'

At the front door of McGonagle's nite club in South Anne Street, the next of kin, Jeremy and Eamon, welcomed mourners to the funeral of Fresh, the Thursday-night club they'd been running for two years. Some Betty Boop girls with hula-hoop earrings and polka-dot sockettes passed in before us and a remark was passed about the passing of Delia's cat and wouldn't this have been an appropriate ceremony for the loss.

'It was tragic, most tragic,' said Jeremy in his smoothest *sotto voce* and Eamon's mouth lifted with the slightest indentation of a smile.

He agreed with his partner that times were rough and raising his soft slow voice for my benefit – the squealing of a vodka-distressed female intruded from behind – he said he believed the lorry didn't even stop.

'There you have it,' declared Jeremy, collecting invitations from incoming mourners. 'What more could you expect?' They nodded gravely and we passed on into the dark cavernous tunnel that leads to the dance floor.

Beneath the revolving parti-coloured lights, a scattering of dancers tramped the parquet floor. Alternately blue, green and red, I could see the contorted face of DJ Richard the Lionheart, twisting to Marvin Gaye's 'I Heard it Through the Grapevine'. The poor fellow was killed by his father. My sort of song.

'A bottle,' decided Oisin, with a flick of his chin. 'That grog might be free but it's nothing but fizz and froth.'

'Good man,' I said, and he turned to the lady behind the counter and asked for a bottle of the house red. 'Château de Rocketfuel. We'll paint-strip our insides.'

While he paid the lady and got plastic cups, Jacinta appeared and said something in my ear.

'What?' I shouted. Richard, miffed at the lack of dancers, had turned the sound way up for encouragement and the speakers shook with the volume.

'I said,' she repeated, standing tiptoed and enunciating hotly in my ear, 'that a flat was available. Is it true that you want to leave Harcourt Street in a hurry?'

I nodded, she nodded. We drew closer.

'You can move into Parnell Square. I just moved out and they need about three people urgently.'

Her fingers moved like the legs of can-can girls to indicate a wiggling three, and after further hot-eared conversation it transpired that No. 40 was a four-storey decrepit Georgian house, half renovated and shared by a group of penniless film makers and occasional artists and the odd student like Jacinta. It had a high turnover of tenants and I could join them by moving into one of the big empty rooms upstairs. A more roundabout twist of Jacinta's fingers indicated that it was 'dodgy' but it was very cheap, and, well, if I needed a place urgently. I said I'd take it and knocked my tooth on a bit of broken glass when I went to kiss her for telling me about it. She smiled. It was a pity she wasn't still living there. But, what of it, I'm out of Harcourt Street! Out of their gaze! I turned to tell Oisin the good news but he was gone.

Oh well. Over Jacinta's dearly departed shoulder, I espied a magisterial Tess in the dance area. She was in the company of some angry young men in black polo-necks, a pucker-lipped train of tall Trinity fellows with two days' stubble and nothing to smile about. How well she looks, though, in her clinging black leggings and black halter top, and the incongruous touch, some old fur she picked up in the Iveagh Market. I thought for a moment she had a dead cat on her head. Fond of animals but she wouldn't go that far. How far would she go? Brusquely, I refilled the glasses, sloshing the deadly bullock's blood on to the scuffed counter. The free beer over, people were moving back on to the dance floor and it was wine all the way from now on. How satisfying and amnesiac its acidic, tear-jerking pungency.

'"Oh, stay close to home and don't go far"', I told Tess when she came over. 'That's what I say . . .'

'Oh Shane, stop it. I don't want to hear any more.' She put down Oisin's glass and rubbed a mole on her arm. 'I want to try and enjoy myself tonight.'

'Fair enough,' I agreed slippishly, my words becoming some-what slippery at the edges.

Lovelier in advice and admonishment. Gusty breath, wet mouth.

'Will you?'

'What?' Her creeping fingers moved my glass away.

'Come and dance?'

'No. Better wait for Oisin.' Glass stealthily recovered. 'I'll follow you in a minute.'

'Do.'

'Good sire, you're guzzling ahead of me,' declared the returned Oisin, flicking back his greasy quiff. 'And downed my measure too. Let us have another bottle of that traitor's blood.'

'Where were you?'

'Hey there, more ale for the sires, my buxom wench!' This hearty, if a touch over-boisterous, salutation drew the look of death from the girl behind the counter.

'What did you say?' She sternly stepped up.

'Sorry, excuse me. Talking to a friend. You wouldn't be so good as to bring us a bottle of wine when you're ready, please. Thank you.'

'When I'm ready,' she snapped, trailing away.

'Come here, though, seriously,' I said, trying not to laugh. 'Did you see anyone out there who might be following us around?'

'Nobody. You're staying close and not going far, you see. Your glass, please.' He refilled our cups with the brutal concoction that our sullen barlady had no doubt rummaged the basement for. 'For on his hill no blood did – whoops! – spill. If they're on our tail they've got a long night ahead of them.'

'Tail chasing tail,' I said with a sly smile to myself. 'Get me out of this strait-jacket of a contract.'

'Why aren't you dancing?' Tess suddenly asked, a cute if nosy companion beside her.

'Rheumatism.'

'Yes, you look a little mouldy,' she plumly remarked to a smile from nosy.

'That's right. Going the way of Cornelius.'

'Down the drain,' added Oisin.

'You're slurring your words, Shane.'

'Goot.'

'Are you coming to Risk, ladies?' asked Oisin, draining his glass.

'Too dangerous for us here.'

'We'll follow you,' said Tess. 'It's only one. Keep us a seat. And take it easy, Shane.'

She threw me a mock grimace and eyed me very evenly as I not quite as evenly eased myself off the counter and headed through the tunnel. At the front door I encountered Delia, dressed totally in black except for a string of large amber beads. While Oisin slipped down the steps to the men's – not literally; we weren't that bad – I stood close to the barely moving drained face of black Delia and sympathised with her plight. I offered my condolences and listened, with an attentiveness that surprised me, to a moving and graphic account of death.

'Mario,' she muttered for the eighteenth time. He had to be buried this afternoon – I could see Robbie Thunder patting the final topsoil with Wendy's shovel – but the funeral ceremony proper, and semi-private, was to take place on Sunday. I like propriety in these matters and I thanked her for the invitation. No, she said, she thanked me for the kind consideration shown towards her predicament. Especially when some had jeered, she said ruefully, and to which I made the appropriate sounds of disbelieving condemnation at such childish callousness. Before she hobbled on down the tunnel to the crowded bar and dance floor I made soothing demands for her recovery and I said I would see her on Sunday.

By the wall, the waiting O'Griofa watching my maudlin display with a skeletal grin. Has a beast no feelings?

As the crow stumbles, Risk Inc., our next destination, is no more than fifty yards around the corner from McGonagle's, venue of our wilting funeral. It was down a back lane, among the back entrances of some of the shops and restaurants on Grafton Street, and admittance was by a set of black doors set in a brick wall. A bell is pressed by clubbing hopefuls and Mick or Jodi, the door boys, peer out unseen through a one-way glass panel. Suitably screened, the door is bar-pressed out and callers pass in gratefully and clank down the metal steps to the underground.

Oisin and I troop in and exchange greetings with the boys. They ask about the 'trouble over the statue' but I wave my hand to indicate we won't discuss it.

They laugh and Mick pulls out a baseball bat they have handy and says, 'Any hassle you get from them and they'll get this!'

They keep that there in case the clubbing hopefuls get out of hand and need some of what they came for, and Oisin and I were grateful for the thought. We thanked them, laughing, for they saw we were well on and we headed down the metal steps. How much of my life is spent underground? From cellar to cellar, basement to vault to tomb. Out of Harcourt Street, thank God. I'll be above ground, and law, in Parnell Square.

'What's your sauce?' enquired Oisin sarcastically, there being only wine available.

'What's your price?' I asked, surprised. 'Tell Eithne we want nothing mild, dry or tasteful. A toxic Ribena – something that does the trick.'

'Take a grip, good Shane. You've had much to drink already. I don't want to be holding you over the sink later on, and be bending down to wipe the peas and carrots from your shoes.'

'Too much to drink?' I said indignantly.

'I said "much to drink". I never said "too much to drink".'

A bottle arrived and somehow a note or a card or something got from Oisin's hand to Eithne without me seeing it. 'Here, get your already purple tongue inside that glass.'

Slightly sleepy-eyed with a warm glow suffusing my stomach, I gazed, glazed, before me when I heard my name spoken.

'Mr McArdle.'

'Yes.' I turned around very slowly.

'There's an old friend out here who wants to talk to you,' said a young man in a black shirt. Here we go. White buttons on black shirts; be careful of them.

'Who?'

'Come with me.'

And I did. Time to confront this once and for all, whatever it is.

'Where are we going?' I asked, already following his black shirt back into the dance area. 'The Good Times bar?'

No reply. But I would follow him all right. Time to confront. Once and for all. Whatever it is. My nineteen drinks weigh heavily on my feet but so do my twenty-two years and some of them have been a lot rougher than what this bucko has seen. We crossed the edge of the dance floor. Tess and friends were on their feet, and so was some fat chap who fell earlier. Leave her be, let me handle this.

'There you are,' said blackshirt, pointing me to a corner table around which, with a few friends, sat a familiar face. Relief. My nerves decelerated. It was a pouting toad.

'Mr McArdle – do come and join us,' pleaded the eloquent Mr Harrington, a hoarseness in his fruity voice but a most radiant bulbous sanguinity in his Charles II face.

'Thank you, I don't mind if I do.'

His fleshy gills propelled cigar smoke in my direction, which I discreetly brushed away for fear of nausea.

'And, eh, thanks for the escort, Finbar,' I added, pointing to the retreating blackshirt on his way back to the dance floor to spy, or perhaps even dance, seeing as Finbar's two 'lady companions' went with him.

'Ah, Leslie.' His wet blubberlips opened. 'He was very kind to locate you for me. My eyes are not the best instruments in conditions such as these. He didn't want to rudely disturb your bopping, so he caught you at the bar, I believe.' Another thick blue spume was released from the gelatinous centre of his beard, and the baritone barrister poured me a glass of wine, muttering something about Leslie being an old and new friend of his.

'I didn't know who it was, to be honest; this chap behind me tapping my shoulder . . .'

'You have to be careful.' His hairy chin lifted. 'The – who is it – the AVNS, yes.'

'I want to talk to you about that.'

'Indeed and I should hope so . . . would you care for one of these?'

Mr Harrington pushed across the table a slim box of King Edward cigars.

'No thanks, I don't smoke.'

'But these would do you no harm. Don't breathe them in too deeply and you can savour the fine taste without damaging yourself.'

After an explorative sniff and nail-pinching, the aromatic half-corona was inserted between hungry lips.

'I have a little man in Fox's at the bottom of Grafton Street who keeps a few Caribbean oddities under the counter for me. Rolled on the thighs of beautiful Cuban women, he tells me.' Harrington had a merry chuckle and lit up.

'The cosmopolitan tastes of the lucrative lawyer,' I suggested.

'Not at all,' he said stoutly, puffing out a cloud of slowly

71

entangling smoke with cheeks well bellowed from delivery to judge and jury. 'Those exorbitant sums spoken of in the media – bah, they make me laugh. It is an unseemly business at the best of times.'

And after a derisory chuckle, he filled our glasses – in vain did I try to halt his liberal hand – raised his chin and, peeling a large wet eye, enquired if I had heard what he had told our Craig Gardner friend.

'All that "hearts" business? Yeah, I heard it,' I said, unimpressed.

'What did you hear?' He leaned forward and cupped his ear, confessional style.

Into the cocked ear (the music wasn't that loud but we were getting conspiratorial), I repeated the 'hearts in Waterford, London and Dublin' conundrum that Mellowes had heard from Skin the Goat who had heard it from our C.G. friend who had got it straight from the aspirant's mouth in Dalton's lounge in Donnybrook. The Carolingian head nodded its assent to each aortic item, perhaps surprised that the details were still intact and not chewed out of all distinction. Yes, the AVNS meant business, yes, their 'sentimental heart' was in Waterford. Yes, their 'political heart' was in Dublin. Yes, their 'heart was broken' in Westminster. Yes, that's all I know, said Harrington, and he sat back and puffed complacently.

'What?'

'That's it,' he said and he shrugged and puffed.

'But is there nothing else? What does it all mean?'

'My good man, aren't you happy that I'm trying to solve a mystery for you? Someone came to me with information and I'm trying to use the privilege of my position as a lawyer to find out more. That's why I've told you all this on condition that you did not go to the police with it and I know you're the sort of chap that would stick to something like that. What do the police know about sentimental hearts and the men in Belgium? It's people like you and me who can sort this out.

'Do you know more than you're telling me?'

'I can't say,' he said and he sucked stickily on his King Edward.

'Obviously, I can't say. My livelihood is at the Bar library and you can't expect me to break all bounds of confidentiality. But, I'll be honest with you. I don't know any more than I'm telling you. But I think I may be able to find out more.' He winked and sat back significantly, nodding and puffing.

'Why don't they come out and say who they are, whoever they are?'

'They're playing a game,' he said and he sighed and leaned forward to refill our glasses. 'They're drawing the Government out. They want people to guess who they are.'

'Well, people are certainly guessing.'

'That's true.' He coolly held his half-corona aloft.

'M.I.5.'

'Ah, old tune.'

'Mellowes thinks they're Southern Unionists.'

'What?!' Frank nearly choked on his cigar.

'Well, Southern ex-Unionists, to be exact.'

'Worse still,' he snapped angrily and huffily brushed the cigar ash from his jacket. 'You people! How in God's name did he come up with that?'

I told him Mellowes' finely balanced theory and he listened to me with the most intemperate look on his face. What has him so cantankerous? I know he was into his party leader's 'constitutional crusade' and breaking down barriers but this was ridiculous. His 'hearts' were up for grabs – what did he expect?

'The automatic assumptions are extraordinary,' he said with a condescending sneer. 'I thought the youth, even the youth of Mellowes' unfortunately unexposed background, could show a more mature analysis of what I had managed to extract and pass on to you.'

'You sound like you're taking it personally.'

'Don't be ridiculous.' His prosperous cheeks puffed greedily as he downed his glass in a flourish. I hadn't touched mine. Recovering somewhat and keeping the dark at bay.

'In all honesty, Finbar, you've only yourself to blame . . .'

'Myself to blame! Hear the man – '

'Yes, do hear me – to blame for whatever misunderstanding should arise from the cryptic clues you passed on to us. What do you expect? We're clutching at straws to build up some sort of picture of these people. Seeing as they're too embarrassed to present themselves for what they are and have to rely on places like the grapevine of the law library to get their message through.'

'It has nothing to do with embarrassment. Like I said, I'm sure that's their intention. As far as I can gather, they want to make people *think* themselves into remembering and recognising who they are. They want to make the public relearn their history the way all history should be learned – bit by bit. And, as any psychiatrist will tell you, bit by bit is the only valid process of remembering' – he blew out some cigar smoke – 'for recovering memory.'

'And maybe a psychiatrist would tell me where weird poetry comes in?'

'What do you mean, weird poetry?' he asked and the King Edward left his mouth.

I told him about the poem. I didn't want to show it to him. I still didn't trust this guy a hundred per cent and I think Hurley had a point about keeping some of this stuff close to our chest. But, bit by bit (his own chosen mode of delivery, or theirs), I gave him the gist of the poem. The *Irish Times*, the Wolfe Tone, the Good Times bar, no blood on his hill and all the rest. He nodded shrewdly, taking it all in, and when I finished he shrugged. He sucked on his cigar and shrugged again.

'Well, what do you make of it?'

'More clues, more pieces for the general picture, I'd imagine – '

'Ah, for fuck's sake! What is this, a bloody treasure hunt?'

'Shane, Shane,' he counselled. 'You've got to be patient. Don't let them ruffle you.'

'They don't.'

'Well, don't let them. Play this thing out. It's the Government's problem. I'm sure there's nothing meant personally against you. Or against Wycherley.'

'It's O'Shaughnessy. It's O'Shaughnessy they want to get. Him and his statue. What do they have against O'Shaughnessy?'

'It's not O'Shaughnessy, personally,' explained Harrington. 'It's the fact that the State is honouring yet another militant old Republican. A former IRA Chief of Staff. In this day and age with so much unhealthy violence in our land do we honestly need or want another statue of a man of violence for our children to aspire to and emulate?'

'He's also a man of peace . . .'

'Yeah, sure, and I'll die a Christian socialist with a tax return in my hand. Listen, the statue, or, OK, sculpture as you call it – '

'I hope you call it that when you see it,' I said for a laugh.

'Why?' he said, turning to me suddenly. 'What are you people planning?'

'Nothing. Go on.'

He looked at me with chin raised and closing eyes. You play games and I'll play games.

'Anyway,' he resumed, 'the sculpture is to commemorate O'Shaughnessy the Rebel. The 1916 Rebel, to be exact, and in that sense it will celebrate the tradition of nationalist violence, a noble tradition in many ways but one that surely, Shane, we've had enough of being pushed down our throats. I mean, you can see their point. The cult of violence, the cult of sacrifice and heroic gunmen, has caused and is causing enough damage in our community without us having to give it further commemoration. Regardless of its merits, surely we're moving forward from the celebration of bloodletting. Wouldn't you agree?'

At this hour, in this state, I wasn't up to this sort of argument. I gave an involuntary rise and fall of the shoulders.

'Are there not enough statues there already to encourage future gunmen and bombers and knee-cappers and building-site racketeers? Have we not had enough official commemoration of the "men of action"; glorifying their gory deeds and singing songs to the bravery of their sniping from the hedges?'

Harrington paused to suck on his half-corona, and, far from recovering, I felt once again my head sag heavily with the weight of the wine, the past, the contract, the letters. The lot.

'I'm no pacifist,' he assured me, topping up my hardly touched glass and smoking up my face. 'Far from it. I can see the circumstances in which it is legitimate to use violence for political ends. All governments and states agree, but haven't we had an unhealthy obsession with . . .'

Chapter 4

Out of Harm's Way

I conked out. And it was late the next afternoon before I recovered. No bad thing for, if nothing else, it enabled me to blast the O'Shaughnessy business out of my mind for a couple of long hours and put my consciousness on the giddy edge it required. It seems that at approx. 3.30 a.m. I was dragged out of Risk by Oisin and Robbie Thunder – assisted, I am ashamed to say, by that old neo-parliamentarian toad himself, Finbar Harrington – and brought to Maeliosa O'Farrachain's mouldy flat on King Street where I came to, groggily and in great pain, amidst a gratuitously sunny lunchtime with no curtains nor companion to protect me.

No matter. Nothing had happened on the O'Shaughnessy front – apart from media discussion of his own allegations (no mention of the 'poem' which obviously hadn't been sent to the papers; a curious move) and I spent what remained of the day collaring Murphy to help me move out of Harcourt Street and into Parnell Square. We pulled up outside beloved 59 with a screech, attracting the eyes of one or two guards across the road. Murphy switched on the radio, to check on the 'historical madmen'. But there was no news.

Inside, I quickly took cognisance of my beloved belongings, and like O'Shaughnessy before a 'mission' (or more sinisterly, during one) decided who was to come – and who was to stay. Bits and pieces of clothing I randomly stuffed into a strapless shoulder bag so as to ensure comfortable lining for the contents of my 'drinks' cabinet; a quarterful bottle of Jameson, a half-bottle of Benylin expectorant and assorted other liqueurs such as Lady Esquire boot cleaner, El Blotto nail-varnish remover and a crusty bottle of

Tipp-Ex thinner for all those letters and brain cells I sometimes have to doctor.

A moon-stomping pair of cumbersome Doc Martens were laced together and tied to the buckle of an Aer Lingus carrier bag full of soiled socks, spare tins of St Bernard baked beans and oranges wrapped in ladies' underwear. Or should I say, panties, a more evocative and onomatopoeiac word to describe my reverential relationship with these frayed and fragile articles of brief cotton softness, mementoes warmed and stained in nether secrecy by the curves and openings they so firmly hugged.

Excuse me. Into a roomy cardboard box I tossed a few soup packets, three candles, a pair of salt-and-pepper cellars (National Gallery restaurant) and some knives and forks donated by the Royal Hibernian Academy (Annual Academician Dinner, to which I 'escorted' Wycherley) wrapped in a nice white bathroom towel monogrammed R.H.A. (it had been a long night). These were joined by a neatly folded olive-green canvas army uniform, standard issue Volunteer, 1918, and a near mint-condition 'blue shirt' borrowed from Grandad Mellowes for flattering 'research' purposes. I don't have any uniforms from an earlier period; given the haste with which I left Artane in a Premier Dairies jacket, you'll understand if I didn't have the Corny-like foresight to allow to come with me those dreaded red-and-blue prisoner's rags that I might one day like to parade in for posterity. Future prosecutors and historians may bemoan this fact but sure can't they get the loan of Jimmy the Twist's or a smaller urchin's outfit the way the National Museum got that hat of 'Michael Collins' with the big hole in the back of it? The Turin Shroud syndrome. I hope we don't all turn out to be fakes.

Here I am folding the sheets in which memories and more were lost and found. Reluctant at first to wash them due to my poignant desire at least to sleep with the aromatic ghost of departed Quigley, I finally prevailed two weeks ago when the delicate olfactory tracks left by my blessed's entwined and sticky limbs were cruelly con-fused by the uncoordinated twistings of a tigerish poetess I met in Duke Street. Sated with Verlaine and suchlike lavatorial decadence of the French, acquired through too many idle afternoons spent lounging around the family's abode above Bullock Harbour, the girl was convinced that sheer animalism (sharp teeth and claws) and strong bodily smells (literally, peeling away panties to receive a briny wafting at face-level) were the key to male arousal. How utterly mistaken. Perhaps when one's senses are dulled by a weight of alcohol, but in the middle of clear sober afternoon the appetite flags in the face of such odours and necessitates a playful avoidance of those richly sour areas otherwise a treat.

Is there room for everything? I have a pluralist attitude to luggage, a Tone-type anxiety to leave no one out. No matter how sudden my move to Parnell Square, nothing should be thrown out. Excepting genuine rubbish like old batteries and broken-toed shoes. Gently laid to rest in a shallow wooden beer crate were more treasured possessions. A fist-sized fragment of Nelson's Pillar, blown up in 1966. A shard of Wolfe Tone's chest, grey bronze with a cutting edge, blown up in 1973, and given to me by a commis-chef in the Shelbourne in exchange for a '10-spot' of good Moroccan, purloined through Oisin's dodgy channels. So dodgy a deal in this case that I've avoided the commis ever since; half a hardened Oxo cube hardly being to the favour of him and his drug-taking mates. Tone's lump was joined by four rusty bullet shells found in the Four Courts four years ago when builders were repairing the underside of the dome. For four pints in the Legal Eagle, Finbar Harrington, BL, acquired them from the OPW carpenter in whose extended palm they lubricated. Mr Harrington later kindly gave them to me as a twenty-first birthday present with a half-mocking saluation: 'Until you find a father to give you the key, you'll probably have to find your freedom with these.'

It took us under fifteen minutes to clear my basement cellar. Smelling of the feed of fresh rashers he had just consumed, Mr Mick Pigott, the non-landlord, emerged on to the front steps to watch us, luxuriantly wiping his fingers on his protruding belly. A sort of fidgety anxiety played about his features as he observed our comings and goings – another costly ad in next week's paper, the papers he doesn't read, thank God, and another guileless innocent the week after that. Quick rat's eyes calculated the emergence of luggage, as if I was in danger of making off with his valuable chromeless faucets or fungus-spotted purple-and-pink chintz curtains or a strip of his balding carpet.

'Nice day,' Murphy told him through a smouldering Major, as he lumbered a box into the van.

'That's certainly true,' he boldly declared in a suddenly pompified culchee accent. 'Lovely, no doubt. There's heat in that sun.'

This certainly true statement was accompanied by a sickly smile and a satisfied pink-fingered drumming of his full and gurgling stomach.

'You'll be back, Michael, won't you; to clean the room and leave the keys – and of course to leave a forwarding address so I can send your deposit on to you?'

'I will, of course,' I assured him, skipping back in to go downstairs and lock my empty cell.

We headed over the river for Parnell Square, my new home, where the GPO garrison were brought to surrender in 1916. Young Collins saw the indomitable old Fenian Tom Clarke mistreated by a sadistic English officer and years later had him shot. Clarke was shot within the week. This is where the controversial commemoration ceremony will be held on Sunday – who'll come, who won't come? A ringside seat on history I'll have and more than that before the week is out. No. 38 is Teach Beaslai, home of Collins's biographer. No. 40 is where his biographer comes to life.

Allah be praised. On returning to Harcourt Street to leave my address and ensure that money, I encountered the alleged ex-landlord, Mr Pigott, bent double on the third-floor landing in a posture reminiscent of one of our beef barons in a Middle Eastern mosque.

What's he at? Sniffing Mahatma's doormat? More than his sub-continental feet have applied their fetid odours to your carpet, Mick. Is he peeking under the door? Catching a glimpse of a lassie's ankle. (What sort of well-fed calves are hoofing it across my floorboards? Reared for export – the Mullingar heifers.) He hasn't heard me. Bit deaf, perhaps. Could take him from here. Clock him on the exposed neck with a swift stick, or crack his useless skull with a length of piping. These Winstanleys do the job – hard sharp toes the Clancys had for dancing. Cut close to the bone. (I was so touched to discover Corny wore Winstanleys, a quality national shoe.) Doctor Martens, with their PVC air-pocket soles, are only really good for a solid kicking; a wade-in terraces job, not the sly, quick-killing root. Collins's Squad, according to Vinny Byrne, always wore the slim black brogues. Well polished too. Respectability to their profession. Interesting, because in country picture houses during forties gangster movies, it was a popular habit of the back-row kids to cry out at a crucial moment, 'There's the murderer – the one with the shiny shoes! This was the inevitable giveaway, apparently, during that era's silver screen. Just as well it wasn't the same during the real-life drama of two decades earlier. 'Real-life drama' – how corny the words sound.

The landlord's gigantic backside, streaked with wipes of his rather sticky fingers, quivered as he rooted away at whatever he was doing. Chewing the carpet for afters? Smothered snorts and wheezy sighs suggested it. I decided to give him a start.

'Mecca's the other way.'

He shook like a disturbed hog.

'Oh, it's you,' he declared in a startled way, jumping up busily and brushing the dust from his drumlin paunch.

'It's me indeed, Mr Pigott' I declared boldly. 'Back from the dead.' A jovial sarcastic tone could be indulged now that I was no longer beholden to the man.

'You put the heart across me. I was just – ' He paused to tuck in his shirt flaps (or invent some alibi for his snooping).

'L-listening to the wood lice?' I ventured.

'No, no, no,' he smiled. 'I was testing beneath those doors for draughts. Skirting boards need a bit of fixing. Come on downstairs with me now and we'll fix you up.'

Downstairs, the 'fixing up' involved Pigott fetching a Jacob's biscuit tin from under a bed (his?) and making me out a receipt – finally, a receipt; he wouldn't give me one when I needed it – on the back of a torn section of a Weetabix box. The tin was filled with such pieces of paper for all the tenants and on them primitive accounting methods took note of their tax-evading and legally deniable contributions. These constituted Pigott's records. As Sean Russell told his IRA court martial, 'There were no books to cook.'

'So, Michael, where have you gone to?'

'89 Lower O'Shaughnessy Road,' I told him off the top of my head.

'Where's that?'

'Glasnevin. But I want you to forward the money to a different address . . . for security reasons; a safer post-box. Send it to Michael Collins, c/o Wycherley & Associates, 4 Marks Lane, Lombard Street, Dublin 2. It's my girlfriend's workplace and I won't be around for a while. I'm going on an expedition to India.'

No interest.

'I'll do that so,' he said, concentrating on recrossing his 't's. 'By the way, a friend of yours called just after you left with that man in the van. Sean Mellowes. I told him I didn't know where you'd gone. He said he'd been following you around like a blue-arsed fly. Those were his words. Friendly chap. You're to meet him in the Bailey at six. He said to say he'd made some discovery.'

'I see . . .' Very interesting indeed. 'Listen, Gran will be choking on her fourth Danish; must dash.'

'Goodbye so . . . I'll send that . . . on to you.'

'And I'll send you a card from India,' I cried back.

'God bless,' he grunted, staring at the ground and shutting the door behind me.

Meet Mellowes at six; he's made a discovery. Has he cracked it? He might have. Jesus, he might have. Or else it's the O'Higgins business. But maybe not; he's been around the town after me all day. For once he must have my interests at heart. Six o'clock. I look forward to it. Warm your hands, lads, I love surprises. Six o'clock in the Bailey. But first things first, as Mick would say; let's get the transfer sorted out. And I went across to Police Headquarters to tell them Mick was on the move. Out from under their eyes too.

Now, to certain serious individuals with matted hair, matey male odours and the traditional Volkswagen-through-Clare anxiety (breathe it in – the crack, the air, the sea, the dreary German paperbacks in the boot) to sniff the city in search of poetic reassurance of their chummy knowingness, the Bailey is an unreal pub. Unreal – this from people whose idea of a 'real' pub is some half-deserted O'Casey stage set with sawdust on the floor, no ladies' toilet, a hand-tinted JFK portrait next to the pre-war advertisements for plug tobacco and a ferrety barman eyeing up strange customers from behind a skittles-like row of ornamentalised, disused stout pumps. In such quaintly dreary surroundings, one is supposed to find rewarding company next to some decrepit Corny in a flat cap and threadbare suit out through the gaps of whose yellow fangs comes a barely decipherable stream of colourful abuse about the terrible ills of the present and the wonders of his own embellished past. Wisdom, my eye.

The Bailey they say is too fashionable, too 'in', too young and vacuous and pretentious, not enough broken-toed shoes and down-to-earth dockers about. Nonsense, of course. I warm to the artificiality and dayglo colour of its good-time souls and no better way to dispel Corny's troubles from my mind than by rubbing shoulders with the Bailey's *habitués*: garrulous hairdressers, over-possessed models, underpaid actresses, failure-facing students, karate instructors, solicitors, the odd pouting toad fawning over a doe-eyed deb, brokers getting broker, confident young writers in rimless glasses rummaging golden stubble and the occasional modern musician wasting away inside the racked hides of his black leathers. (As opposed, presumably, to the rickety one-eyed fiddler from Clare.)

Come closing time when the place is packed and smoky and the jostling hoards congregate around the bars upstairs and down, clamouring for more drink as the besieged barmen fire back rapid abuse; and the painted faces begin to melt and the ripe laughter of the luscious beasts in the corner rises to a cackle and the buccaneers, their eyes bulging with lust, close in on their fishnet victims – that is when you'll value it. At such moments the place can be savoured in its full and oozing glory. This is not quite what Corny fought for but the unreality of it, like the unreality of that old soldiers' republic, is something that deserves defending.

During daylight, however, it is a much more peaceful place. I found Mellowes in the far alcove, sitting beneath a commemorative etching of Daniel O'Connell, blindly slurping at the brim of lager froth as his eyes feasted on the lower reaches of an *Evening Press* page. Statue mystery goes on.

'Ah, Mellowes, my man!' I shouted. 'Reading about me as I approach!'

'Shush, you idiot!' he snapped, looking up in disgruntled annoyance. 'Do you want to be heard?'

'But, Sean, I . . .'

'Heard and not seen too, you cunt – where have you been all day? Did you not hear me roaring after your van in Westland Row? And then up I trot to your kip in Harcourt Street – twice – looking for you. Across the town like a blue-arsed fly.'

'Sorry, Mellowes, but we had to look for old Wycherley, just to see how he got on. He had a meeting with the Minister. Besides I had to move house. Get out of the cellar by six.'

'Well, you could have left me directions – I've good news for you.'

'What?'

'I've got it all worked out!' He twiddled all his fingers.

'What – again?'

'Listen – do you want to hear or not?'

'Of course.'

'"Step for a jar in the Good Times bar, For on his hill no blood did spill" – the Good Times bar is on Redmond's Hill! Shane, they're a bunch of Redmondites!'

'What!'

'Work it out – "In memory of the men who fell in Belgium". Redmond's Volunteers died by the score in Belgium – seventy years ago this month. It's them, Shane, not the Unionists! Their political heart is in Dublin – Home Rule. It was broken in Westminster – the refusal to grant Home Rule. Their sentimental heart is where the sun rises, the South-east, Waterford, where Redmond came from. It's as clear as the light of day!'

'Jesus.' I was stunned. 'Do you really think . . .?'

'Of course.' He leaned back confidently. 'Who else could it be? No blood did spill on his hill because, the trenches notwithstanding, *his* was a nationalism of peaceful means.'

He was right. I was flabbergasted; how did we not work it out? Harrington last night – he was practically telling me.

'Fucking hell, how did you find out?'

'Immediately I saw the poem. When the Maynooth Idiot came back from his lectures and passed it in under the bathroom door – I was reading Lord Longford's hagiography of Dev – as quick as I set eyes on it, I knew. When it said. "Don't go far but to the Good Times bar" I knew it was the place near you. I remembered it from Oisin's birthday – I'm surprised he didn't. So I unlocked the door and called the Idiot to pass me in the *Golden Pages* – he couldn't pass it under – I then found the page and there it was: Redmond's Hill. The hump of Parnell's successor! Golgotha of the Home Rulers! The old days of the old party before guns spilt blood.'

'Don't go overboard,' I told him. 'You're spilling your drink.' His enthusiasm was embarrassing.

'Jesus, Shane, I could have spilt my own blood when I think of how we didn't guess who those letter-writers were. The hearts broken and sentimental, the men who fell in Belgium; the desire to keep the peace. It was so obvious. Who else would have opposed the erection of another IRA statue? Who are the lepers of our national history? They must be bulling, Shane. "Cornelius O'Shaughnessy, last godfather of glorified blood-letting, is getting himself put up in our finest green while we, parliamentary democrats, continue to go ignored." Enough is enough, they're saying. Old and obscure as we are, we won't have it. Not this one.'

'But can there be people out there concerned enough to cause this hassle? I mean, do Redmondites still exist?'

'Of course. People have long memories and, besides, non-murderous political methods never go out of fashion.'

'Obviously these people are determined to see John Redmond get his rightful place in history.'

'Or in Stephen's Green.'

'Indeed, no better place to start.'

'I mean . . .' Sean paused. 'They're not a million miles from the sort of ideas we have. Am I not one of those people determined to see Kevin O'Higgins get his rightful place in history? Are you not one of those people determined to see O'Shaughnessy get his rightful place in history?'

'Are you joking?' I grunted. 'The only rightful place I'd like to see O'Shaughnessy get is the rightful place he saw O'Higgins get.'

'Now, now,' cautioned Mellowes. 'Let's cast no stones . . . just yet.'

'No, let's cast bodies instead.'

'Operation Booterstown has yet to roll,' he said with a rueful grin. 'Granted you don't have the passion those Reds or I would have to see our heroes properly redressed, but surely your determination to see bold old O'Shaughnessy up there on a pedestal must have increased the more you've been warned not to commemorate him.'

'Sure, I'm determined more than ever to see him properly commemorated.'

'In glowing bronze?'

'Yes, in glowing bronze.'

'None of that fancy twisted stuff?'

'None of that.'

He smiled and suddenly hopped up off his tool.

'This calls for a celebration,' he beamed, rummaging in his pocket. 'Whiskies.'

'Jameson.'

'Good Southern ex-Unionists', he winked. 'No, don't say it, don't say it.' He held up a fiver. 'I was nearly right. I was close. Indeed you could say that, by Corny's definition, I was as close as damn it.'

84

I smiled and I thought about Wycherley and just as I did the far door bust open and in she came in a breathless hurry.

'Tess, we've cracked it!'

'Congratulations,' she said, holding her heaving chest. 'But things have moved on . . .'

'What do you mean?'

'Which do you want first, the good news or the bad news?'

'How bad is the bad news – the Minister's called it off. O'Shaughnessy's had a stroke? Bob's gone on strike?'

'Robert's fine,' she said between breaths. Her cheeks were red. O'Shaughnessy's cool.'

'Give us the bad news then.'

'Apparently Forbes is thinking of suing him for slander.'

'Shit. How good is the good news?'

'Very good.' And she smiled broadly to prove it.

'They've declared a cease-fire. A cease-fire!' She threw her arms around me. 'Isn't it brilliant, Shane? They've told the Government that as and from 8 p.m. tonight they've called off their campaign, pending further developments.'

'Already?' said Sean, clearly disappointed.

'Why?' I asked, utterly relieved but slightly puzzled.

'I don't know . . .' She dropped her hands and lifted them. 'They said to give the Government time to think about it . . . they said they didn't want to appear overly militant.'

'Where did you hear all this?'

'There's been a statement in the last half-hour. Hurley rang Robert to tell him. It was on the radio as well – all about your man, Redmond, and Home Rule and the First World War.'

'Jesus.' Mellowes and I looked at each other. 'Make those large ones, Sean. Make those bleeding large ones.'

'Here's your friend,' said Tess.

'Who?' I turned around.

'Oisin!'

'I have peace in someone's time,' he shouted, sweeping forward with a piece of paper in his hand. 'I got this on the car radio about ten minutes ago. I had to write as I drove. It's not very neat or detailed but my boys, my boys, my boys' – he slammed it on the bar counter and smoothed its crumples – 'it is the business. It is the bloody business.'

'Another large one, please.'

To All Media:

At this peaceful moment, it is appropriate that the AVNS should now have a chance to reveal itself as the Anti-Violent Nationalist Society, a society opposed to the tradition of violent nationalism in Ireland. It represents something the Irish people have always, secretly and publicly, subscribed to, when they were permitted to acknowledge it, something that is as central to their historical tradition as it is to their political system today; that is, the use of democratic, constitutional means to advance their cause. The Irish people have long seen this democratic tradition as the true benefactor of their past success, be it religious or land reform or the actualities of political power.

However, they have not been let acknowledge and cherish this tradition properly, due to the distortion of history and the imputed efficacy of the methods of violence during those few violent years preceding our country's independence – nominal and partial independence, it should be said, for what was lost was equal to what was gained, as is always the way in times of violence.

The notion has formed that it was the men of violence who were the creators of our modern state. This false notion has not only become the norm but the dominant strand of our nationalism, to the detriment of our constitutional tradition, and has been elevated and celebrated in a near obsessional way in the past fifty years of our country's history. As well as being false and unhealthy in itself, this distortion has led us to the violent tragedy that we see today in Northern Ireland with its competing traditions of political violence. The statue of O'Shaughnessy is a continuation of this trend and an offensive one, coming at a time when some realisation seemed to be breaking through about the dubious merits of this cult of violence. The fact that O'Shaughnessy is to be erected in central Dublin to commemorate 1916 is proof that, far from lessening, this morbid and destructive tradition is still in the ascendant, despite what we believe are the quite contrary and democratic wishes of the Irish people.

We say enough. On behalf of the Irish people, we say enough. It was thus we set out to oppose the proposed statue of O'Shaughnessy, even by the suggestion of violent means if necessary – these being the only methods left to us. However, recognising that we could be led into the trap of the violent methods of those we oppose, we are now calling a cease-fire.

In this period we urge the Government to consider its ill-thought-out plans. We urge them to reconsider the statue of O'Shaughnessy, a former IRA Chief of Staff, and we ask them to consider our demand, a statue of a true Irish patriot: John Redmond, someone who represented what most Irish people would have aspired to in terms of political methods and aims. A man who was our last major non-violent constitutional leader, and led a united Irish party for ten years to the threshold of Home Rule and an eventual independence that would have included more of Ireland than is independent today. A man who gave his ultimate effort, until he was cruelly denied by the antics of violent opportunists at home and by a continental war in which he had invested the whole cause of Ireland in the belief it would gain us Home Rule, a war in which thousands of Irishmen followed his lead and gave their lives in the fields of Belgium. 'That union in the field may lead to union in the home,' he said. 'And that their blood may be the seal that will bring all Ireland together in the Irish nation, and in liberties equal and common to all.'

This man has no honour or commemoration in our capital city, and yet surely at this bitter and divisive hour in our history, as violent now as it was in 1914 or 1918, an honour to him is more necessary than ever. In the words of John Dillon, who spoke over John Redmond's body after it was brought from Kingstown to Wexford, draped with the same Old Irish flag that had lain over the coffin of Charles Stuart Parnell over twenty years before; and that had lain over Willie Redmond's catafalque nine months before, when his young body returned home from the trenches:

Is it too much to hope that the grave we have closed today may cry out with the irresistible voice of his countrymen to take and put into effect the lesson of his life, and to bury for ever the discords and dissension which have been the curse of Ireland throughout the centuries, and consummate the work of John Redmond's life by uniting all Irishmen to work for the good of Ireland?

In this spirit, we ask the Government to consider again the merits of a statue of yet another violent Fenian for children to look up to, and consider instead our humble request for a statue of an Irish hero, officially neglected but dear to the hearts of so many Irish people, a man to whom the children of the future – for the future – could genuinely aspire.

Our request is a humble one but, remember, our determination is very keen. You have a week to consider.

Captain Sunlight

Where was I? Not since the morning after I first escaped from the Artane Fathers and – on the run like Corny – spent the night hidden behind the cold altar of the city's procathedral, can I recollect opening my eyes to such a high ceiling.

Then as now I woke startled by the sudden unfamiliarity of my surroundings, but like Ernie in the hedge or Mick on the sofa of one of the Squad's grandmothers I quickly got my bearings; especially when I saw my lovable belongings stretched out in the morning sun. Light, bright light – it was good to have left Harcourt Street. It was good to be a free man again and above ground. And it was good to be a plotter when people think – poor souls – that you're being plotted against.

The room had been stripped bare, denuded of any former glory. Filigree plaster moulds had been picked out, a grand fireplace removed, lamps pulled, fittings nicked, and now it could be a suitable setting for a bit of minimalist theatre or a trampoline session or a dead-keen sculptor's assistant to plan and hide. But not everything was gone. Along the wall at intervals next to the three windows were three white sinks of stained vitreous enamel; alone in the big room (Magritte, where are you?), they stuck out conspicuously as a reminder of the three bedrooms they once serviced, the pockmarks of partition still visible. How many lonely souls stooped to wash their faces there? Bursting a blood vessel in the process like Arthur Griffith. Why do the deserted domestic items of the past seem 'lonely' when we see them now?

88

An iron from a thatched cottage. A Victorian maid's looking glass. Pearse's pen. They weren't 'lonely' when they were being used.

Why does Griffith seem lonely when we see him now? Because he was isolated at the end and died of a broken heart? Why does his position in the Treaty negotiation seem particularly lonely, a loneliness so poignant you can feel it before he sets out for England? Was it because their position was doomed from the very start and he was going to carry the can and he knew it and they knew it? His life's work was encased in a strait-jacket and if you can't smell blood from a long way off you can smell failure. Not a failure for him, of course. Not at all. A triumph. But when you're not your own man the difference between triumph and failure is more than a form of words.

Let's go. I slip out quietly without disturbing anyone, anxious to be on the road for Clonskeagh. Pulling the door behind me, I just couldn't help chuckling deliciously to myself all of a sudden. A harmless but cunning little titter. All in all, everything was colliding nicely again. It was a bright sunny Saturday morning and I had a new house. I'm safe. The AVNS have revealed themselves. They called a cease-fire. They're who we thought they were: ineffectual, sentimental fools. Their game is up. They're going to call it off. Wycherley will come up with a new plan, and Corny will be cast gloriously. Forbes will get his pittance, someone else will get the blame and we will get the glory.

No time to waste, it'll be done in record time. We'll make August the 12th and no one will believe it. And today – today, today! This beautiful day – why, look at the little children play. Hopscotch, is it? We'll get the ball rolling when we sit down to dinner with O'Shaughnessy. Good old Corny, we'll make sure you're remembered. You owe us one, so out of your crafty filing cabinet, perhaps Mellowes and I will, at long last, find out the full details on who shot Kevin O'Higgins. Invincibles away! There's work to be done.

An involuntary cackle escaped my mouth and I skipped delight-edly up Parnell Square, causing an elderly gent to step anxiously aside, perhaps expecting a meat cleaver between the ears. Crossing the road my merriment was damn near extinguished by a reckless bread van. The saucy old driver honked. Up went my fingers and a colourful stream of abuse issued towards his departing open window. Around the corner, on the other side of Parnell Square, I was gratified to see that the stop for the 11 bus to Clonskeagh was situated directly opposite the gates of the Garden of Remembrance. Corny's old stomping ground. But he won't be stomping in there on Sunday. No siree, nor the Sunday after that nor next year nor the year after.

But this was only one part of the charming configuration the 11 bus formed for Corny, me and death. Because, look at your map or timetable (as reliable a document as the one I'm giving you), and you will notice that the route of the 11 bus runs all the way from Glasnevin to Clonskeagh and back. One terminus is situated outside the gates of the cemetery and the other – you guessed it – is on the Roebuck triangle, a few paces from the old fellow's house. And where do I come in? Well, on its winding way from the great patriot's cemetery in the north to the last patriot's house in the south, the No. 11 stops – where else – outside the gates of the Garden of Remembrance. But on its way back, up the other side of the square, it stops directly outside the door of No. 40. Would you credit it? And all to let on the fellow with a glint in his eye.

I waited. A tall, white-haired gent waited with me, surveying his nails. Across the road, a cranky turnkey was pulling back the grand gates of the memorial garden. Opening up. They must be expecting a visitor. Trundling its disconsolate, even contemptuous way down North Frederick Street, an 11 approached us. Would it even bother stopping? Yes, it veered violently in towards the stop with a sweeping shoosh and a banshee scream of brakes, causing not dissimilar banshee screams from some unfortunate hag who had ventured off the pavement with her hand outstretched. The accordion doors snapped open and, around my legs, a swarm of suddenly appeared children piled on greedily like squealing piglets. The white-haired gent was not quite as agile, a fact which merited a derisory smirk from the gum-chewing driver – a sort of overweight Dan Breen – whose meaty paws impatiently gripped the Sellotaped steering wheel.

We took off with a jolt. Whitehead was knocked into a seat. I held fast to a chrome pole and hauled my way up the littered stairs. My eyes rose to a Rotunda dome that flashed past the window at an extraordinary rate, as Dan hurtled into O'Connell Street hoping to terrorise a few civilians. The piglets were up the front, lapping up the panoramic view as they hopped from seat to seat shouting out the windows. I made my way down the back, as all lads do, though these days I don't carry a black marker to leave my escritoire. I've graduated to more permanent means.

A half-hour later we were out of the city, the driver continuing his reckless journey through the suburbs. Alarmed car-honks greeted Breen's bluster bus as it piled across the junction with Eglinton and Milltown Roads, ignoring the amber lights and screeching the vehicle around the dangerous corner of Clonskeagh Road, denying any access to a van hoping to leave Smurfit Paper Mills. We took the Dodder bridge with a twist but thankfully, from here on, Breen was forced to relent to nature (or at least, road conditions), for it was now all hill until the terminus.

The engine roared to its climb. Like a concrete beacon, the Belfield water tower, high over the roofs of shrubberised suburbia, marked the playing fields of the university. This is a quiet area, especially in the summer. The names of the childless roads bespeak calm anonymity: Whitethorn, Whitebeam, Maple and Wynnsward. Trees, lots of them, and rose petals confettied on the warm bonnets of big glossy cars in the driveways of equally arboreally named homes. Chestnut Lodge, Elm Grove, Cherryfield. All very bushy, and English.

How deliciously incongruous then to see, in the midst of all this – Roebuck House, home of the late Speranza O'Shaughnessy, beauty and great English-hater, and now occupied by her only son. Older, bigger and hidden by higher trees than its surrounding neighbours, one could glimpse bits of the roof visible as we climbed Clonskeagh Hill. Eyes peeled with curiosity, I wiped my near window and waited for us to pass. Of course, in her day – what am I talking about? – in *his* day, none of the surrounding bungalows was built and the house had an extensive stretch of land. She set up the Celtic Dawn Fruit Company and kids would come and pick strawberries and raspberries for jams. Apparently it was great fun. Gentleman Jim's mother did it and remembers going into the house for big teas of cakes and lemonade and the Grande Dame hovering over the chattering children with her berry-stained hands. The money went . . . well, we all know where the money went.

The bus was almost empty now and Breen slowed down to let students off at the stop outside Isaac Butt's old house (a blue plaque was visible but nothing else) and Wynnsward Drive, which, at its gable side, offers a back entrance to the college. Among them was a temporarily displaced commuter-ticket holder who, much to the conductor's disappointment, finally remembered a makeshift book mark and kept his place. In the distance the college's playing fields were dotted with Subbuteo-small footballers and tiny white goalposts. People at play, making noises louder and nearer than their size merited.

The accordion doors hissed closed and Breen pulled out from the last stop before the terminus, in sight at the top of the road. I was the last man on board. We passed Roebuck House. Flashes of tantalising masonry and drawing-room windows were visible through the retreating trees. The narrow driveway seemed tunnelish, underbranched and marked by an ancient succession of dark barks. The gates were open. I would be in there later on.

'Last stop,' roared the conductor as the 11, true to the last, unnecessarily flourished itself into the empty triangle and came to a grinding halt. Nobody was waiting at the terminus and when I descended the stairs Breen had turned off the engine and was sitting staring blandly at the empty bus shelter (all this for nothing?). The conductor had unstrapped himself, lit up a cigarette and stretched out contentedly on a nice seat to peruse the form – be it nubiles or horses – in an English tabloid.

It was midday and I made immediately for Loyola, a hundred paces away, paces increased and complicated by the unexpected harassment of a mangy cur who came yelping out of some old dear's driveway to tackle me on my way down Bird Avenue. The old dear was pottering about in the garden, pruning roses or some such worthless Saturday activity (like hoovering lawns or soaping cars) so I had to be careful about how I handled the irritating creature. I looked into his eyes: small mad marbles of ludicrous anger, popping forward as his head barked away some dog version of domestic dementia (can dogs get neurosis?). The old lady obviously thought it OK for her ragged overgrown rat to terrorise passing civilians and busily doddered into her garage to fetch a watering can, trowel or perhaps a gun. So feigning fear I coaxed the snapping jaws a little closer and then, checking to see that she was still indoors, I let rip with a vicious left foot, a clean sweeping arc such as Corny would have been proud of in his unpatriotic soccer-playing days. The startled woolly skeleton was propelled backwards, whimpering loudly as it hit the iron gates, rolled over white-bellied and skulked away. Old dear emerged suddenly, trowel in hand, and seemed to be crowing something in my direction but I had no time to stop.

Three dogless semi-detached gardens down the iron gates of godless Loyola swung open at a touch. Up the grass-cracked path

I skipped, applying a quick finger to the melodious doorbell and standing to attention. Steaks and O'Higginite stake-outs – I looked forward to it.

After a few seconds, an anonymous human shape appeared behind the door's pimpled glass. Its blurred hand click-clicked with the lock and the door drew back to reveal the tall figure of Greycoat Ryan. He gave a grateful 'Aah' of recognition, muttered for me to come in, gnawed a nether lip and then fell into his customary silence.

'They're in the back room,' he said and then followed me down the corridor.

'Who's that?' a voice shouted from around a doorway. 'McArdle! The free man! Come on in – we were just saying a decade that your cease-fire holds. You know, like the old ones in Hans Place during the Treaty talks.'

Inside the cigarette-polluted back room, smirking Mellowes and a grinning Skin the Goat were sitting around a table littered with half-finished coffee mugs, entrails of the morning's papers (themselves littered with half-finished Corny mugs) and lots of pieces of paper with diagrams on them – the plans, evidently.

'Hello, man,' I greeted. 'Skin, boy. Long time no see.'

He stood to shake; a bony hand grasped mine.

'You've been a busy man I hear and read.'

'I hear the same of you,' I told him.

'What's that?' The other hand was stuffing a crumpled shirt-tail inside his dangling braces.

'Bet you feel better this morning,' declared Mellowes. longer a marked man.'

'Marginally.'

'Sit down, sit down. I'll get you a cup.'

I sat down and got a goo at the diagrams. They were economic graphs not plans for a paperchase.

'Pity you weren't here earlier,' Mellowes called out from the kitchen.

'There was a lengthy discussion about your case on the radio. Professor Dudley Edwards talked about the Redmondites and the First World War and was tomorrow's ceremony enough, going too far, or not far enough? The fellow on the Hill of Howth, you won't be surprised to hear, accused us of having a national amnesia about the Home Rule commitment of thousands who fought in the trenches of Europe and said we had erased them out of our history because of our obsession with the handful of men of 1916, the handful who established the cult of violence with which we're still suffering.'

'He's right.'

Mellowes filled the kettle and plugged it in.

'The Minister was interviewed and reiterated the Government's commitment to seeing the O'Shaughnessy project through. "However," he added, "we would always be prepared to listen to people's views on what is, after all, a public monument."'

'He didn't say anything about artistic views?' Hot from his encounter with Wycherley.

'No,' said Mellowes, 'he was talking about the AVNS though he didn't name them. He said the Government had already gone to a considerable extent to accommodate the views of those who honour different aspects of Ireland's past and this mature and pluralistic attitude was continuing. Tomorrow's shared commemoration ceremony was an obvious example. There was, he admitted, a case to be made for a statue of someone like John Redmond but that case was not to be made by violence and intimidation. The Government would have absolutely no dealings with terrorists or troublemakers.'

'Hear, hear,' smiled the Goat, baring his tobacco-yellow fangs.

'No disrespect, but it was obvious that your affair ranks a pretty low priority compared to the other matters burning up the Government's mind. Like today's Twelfth and how the Agreement survives it.'

'ay it remain so,' I said. 'We've burning matters of our own.'

'The old boy himself was on, interviewed at his home. Oh, last night's revelations were no surprise to him. Not at all. He always suspected that certain elements of the old Parliamentary Party, corrupted as they were by Westminster, were sympathetic to the aims of M.I.5 and wanted to see the Republican Movement destroyed. Low and dirty work, he said. Those who weren't naturally into it could, at any rate, be bought, blackmailed or intimidated into co-operating. No problem – they were as good as English themselves.'

'Jesus, really?' The kettle spumed noisily as the Goat hopped to it.

'Oh yeah. And when the incredulous interviewer interrupted him with, "But, Mr O'Shaughnessy, this is all a long time ago,"

Corny spluttered his indignant awareness of how long ago it was but that these people's descendants were often well prepared to carry on such nefarious activities. That was one reason why British intelligence retained such a good network in Ireland, even unto the present day. Apart from its straight political and material advantages the motive of revenge was a very powerful one. Both M.I.5 and the old traitorous Parliamentarians, in whatever guise or offspring, were well disposed to taking belated revenge on the Republican Movement that did them down. "Revenge", he kept saying. "Remember how strong the motive of revenge is in our history!" Shane, I seriously think the old boy is losing a marble or two. Senile dementia. Sad, I know, but at least it makes things easier for us if he's suspiciously listening to the sound of his own heartbeat. You should have an interesting time this evening, if this morning's paranoid rantings are anything to go by.'

'Thanks,' I said, taking a cup. 'Between Corny and Wycherley it should be one of the great "delusions of persecution" sessions.'

'Oh,' said Mellowes, raising a hand, 'that reminds me – your boss was contacted by the programme but was "unavailable for comment".'

'Lying low?'

'Probably hungover,' I said evasively.

'But,' continued Mellowes, his raised hand becoming a finger, 'he had let it be known that "whatever the results of any negotiations or talks the Government might enter into with other parties, he, as the commissioned sculptor, would have the O'Shaughnessy piece, as he put it, completed in time for its unveiling on O'Shaughnessy's ninetieth birthday, as was originally planned. Shane, that's less than a month away! You told me he'd only started on it this week.'

'No,' I said, unruffled. 'I said he'd only formally and finally asked Tess and me to be involved this week. I mean, he's made all the plans and preparations. Of course he has. They're the hard part. The finish is a cinch.'

'What, the casting and all?'

'Just that.'

'In under a month?'

'No problem. Quicker even, if we had to.'

'You might have to,' said the Goat under his breath and Greycoat laughed.

'Everything's under control,' I said and I gulped my coffee.

The mug had a blue lion painted on it. Mellowes' birth sign. And Corny's. His ninetieth – deadline for a dead lion. Good one, Shane. Now let's see you perform.

'Milk?' offered Mellowes. They were watching me, seeing if I was under stress. Sean was looking at my cupped hands. For casting burns, I suppose. The process fascinates him. It fascinates most people. Long may it continue to fascinate them and they stay knowing little about it.

'Meat, please, too,' I said putting down the milk. 'I'm starving.'

'Ah, the tribulations. Don't worry. I'll be throwing those steaks on in a minute. But first I'd like you to run your spare eye over these.'

His broad hands shuffled the papers.

'These, I take it, are the plans?'

'They are indeed.'

With eagerness, Mellowes pushed a butt-laden copper ashtray ('Souvenir of Rhodesia') from under my offended nose and slid the cryptic drawings around for inspection. They appeared to be of quartered squares and lined rectangles.

'What are they? Designs for a new Ludo board?'

'No, you fool, they're the floor plans of Roebuck House.'

'Ah, snakes and ladders.'

'Or Haunted House,' grinned the Skin.

'You mean Cluedo,' said Mellowes. 'We're trying to solve a murder.'

'Or cause one,' I said cryptically. 'Are these really the plans of his house?'

'They are.'

'Good work, men,' I said, quite taken aback by their foresight in plotting the house's interior so well and in such detail, and by the degree of research they'd done to back it up. They'd even met big Joe Moran, the journalist and former student agitator, who'd interviewed the old boy. One sheet had the division of the ground floor where Corny spent most of his time, and another had the furniture arrangement of the living-room, where Corny, retreating from unnecessary space with the necessary years, spent almost all of that time, hovering between desk and armchair. That was when he wasn't out attending meetings and addressing rallies, or being beetled about in his chocolate Volkswagen.

Downstairs was actually a combination of front and back rooms

96

with the high interconnecting doors left permanently open and two large windows giving on to the gardens on either side. Across the hall, the dining-room was only used on special occasions (lucky us) and the kitchen was the preserve of the big housekeeper who came in, morning and evening.

Less was known about upstairs. One half was taken up by the giant bedroom that belonged to mother and that has been kept as a shrine to her ever since. People have spoken about its huge four-poster bed and four alcove windows looking on to the back garden and filling the room with sunshine. Two (or three) smaller bedrooms adjoined this room. One was the one that he slept in, if a man of such energy can ever be described as sleeping. It was important that this narrow room was sandwiched between Mother's former abode and another small bedroom, believed to store books, because the further he was away from midnight stirrings around his house the better for our safety.

A crucial feature, Joe told us, was the main staircase, since it was vital for us to know Corny's line of sight as he moved up and down. (We didn't want to be surprised by the relic descending in his night shirt.) He even took into account the implications of two gilt-framed mirrors hung at opposite ends of the staircase, just in case one of those Cornelian corneas, on their sleepy return to the bedroom, caught the reflection of some lunar-blue shadow moving through the downstairs hall with a bunch of files under its arm. Joe seemed to have an uncanny knowledge of the house's interior, for a man who only visited it about four or five times. With relish, he told us the height of the bookshelves, the colour of the lampshades, the faulty cistern in the upstairs bathroom and even, God forbid, the ominous creak on the eighth step upwards (memorable to any man, perhaps, whose gargantuan footfall would cause the tightest board to groan for mercy).

Sitting in an unmolested corner of Bewley's and deep into their third 'interrogative' session with Joe (a misnomer since no interrogation was necessary for Joe to spout forth a veri-table wall-to-wall description of Corny's demesne), Mellowes and Greycoat, who took notes, began to get the impression that Joe was being somewhat imaginative in his recollection of Roebuck House. They reminded themselves that Joe had been there to research a Mercier Press paperback called *Some Memories of Old Rebels*, a handy-sized anthology of amplified anecdotes that he planned to ghost-write with the same panache as he brought to Dinny Stapleton's *Flying Columns, Fleeing Canons.*

Once the subject of Corny's files was gingerly broached by Mellowes, Joe's eyes twinkled with immodest conspiracy and he proceeded to describe, in great detail, the location and arrangement of what he called 'the O'Shaughnessy Papers'. Secret hiding places were collusively hinted at for the 'classified stuff' beneath floorboards, under beds, inside 'something that rocked' – a chair? a horse? Corny himself? – and the inevitable chimney.

'But the heavy stuff,' he whispered, between hearty sucks of coffee, 'was down below where the black stuff comes from.'

Further disinterested proddings revealed this to be the coal bunker.

'Ah,' obliged Mellowes, weary of the black stuff he'd been drinking all afternoon and the surfeit of useful, if dubious, information it accompanied.

However, we were soon to appreciate how accurate and very useful some of his information turned out to be. Subsequent checking by Mellowes, mostly under cover of night (this was before the threats), but also when Corny left for his morning walk or was motored off for the daily book launch/protest/appearance at the Bar (Greycoat serving as lookout), revealed that, among other things, all visible life did appear to take place in the downstairs living-room, that the curtains were left undrawn in the other rooms (except the mother's), that Corny was very often not there but simply, as of old, 'out' and, whether he was or wasn't, there was next to no security apart from the two gardaí who stood outside the house last Thursday morning before Corny asked them to leave. Mellowes, to his joy, couldn't even find the tell-tale metal box of a standard suburban burglar alarm.

It was this fact, among others, that led Sean to give new credence to Joe's remarkable claim that, in terms of old files, records and papers, the 'heavy stuff' *was* down below in the coal bunker. For if the house's general security seemed surprisingly lax – deviceless, thin-paned windows, dog-scratched back door, dog deceased – its coal bunker looked notoriously secure, once you pushed away the long grass and took the five steps down to its underground doorway. Hewn of sturdy old wood with metallic reinforcements, it had one of those big black Kilmainham Jail keyholes, button-shaped like Munch's screaming head and just begging for the iron version of a key that some people; other people, get in plastic for their twenty-first birthday. Or for the freedom of the city, a subject that Corny should currently know much about.

But there were other compelling reasons for Mellowes to believe that this conspicuously secure coal bunker might contain more than mere coal. In 1982, Dermot Gilhenny submitted his seminal work, 'The Declaration of the Government of Ireland Act, 1949'. As well as having access to his papers, Dermot had vigorously interviewed the old declarer himself on the subject. So Mellowes vigorously interviewed Dermot on the subject of the old declarer's house and, more specifically (but discreetly) his papers.

Dermot's young bearded focus being reverentially stuck on his subject, he remembered little of the house's furnitures or trappings, never mind in what order the old boy's papers were kept. Except he did remember, and it struck him as odd at the time, that in order to fetch certain vital cabinet memos, O'Shaughnessy would excuse himself and leave the house. Just up and left, out the back door. After a few minutes, he would totter back, slightly windswept (this was October), clutching, with splayed fingers, the relevant files. Did you ever notice, Mellowes slyly enquired, as an ambitious long shot, that any of the documents had, by any chance, a sort of black dust on them? No, frowned the perplexed Dermot, he couldn't recollect any black dust.

But Sharon Travers ('Mother and Child Scheme, 1953–54: The Afterbirth', MA 1982) did recollect 'the dote, Mr O'Shaughnessy', telling her over a cup of après-discussion tea that while he had no qualms about opening certain of his Mother and Child era papers to those 'academically interested' (i.e. politically motivated liberals, sod off), he felt a little different about documents relating to his 'underground days' (i.e. IRA after the Civil War) and in fact kept them well locked up in the basement. As if they were prisoners, says you.

The interesting thing here is not that Corny still had a charming weakness for dashing ladies come to enquire of his dashing past and still felt the urge to tell them where his sins or secrets might lie. This shouldn't surprise us. What should was that when Sharon, politely snooping around the kitchen while Mrs Williams, the cook, prepared Corny's lunch, innocently enquired if she kept her wonderful vegetable supply in the basement, Mrs Williams cooed, 'Oh no, love. There is no basement.'

'All of this,' declared Mellowes, gathering his bits of papers, 'is enough to convince me that despite all these maps and diagrams we're probably going to have to get inside that dark little coal hole to find what we're looking for.'

'The O'Higgins killing,' said Skin the Goat. 'You can be sure he won't leave that lying on the kitchen table.'

'In other words,' continued Mellowes, in language that disturbed me, 'we can reef through the gaff high and low, rip the arse off the rocking chair, burst open the safe, if you wish, but, in the final analysis, I reckon the O'Higgins details, if they exist, are tucked safely between coal bags in the bloody vault.'

'Hold on,' I said. 'This sounds like a full-scale break-in.'

'Well, what did you expect – that we were going to spirit the documents out? For, Jasus' sake, we knew that we were going to have to get into some part of the building – '

'Well, yes, maybe, to look around. But I never thought we were going to ransack the place!'

'Ransack, my arse!' he declared. 'We're not the Black and Tans. We were only ever going to tiptoe around, make a few enquiries. Excavation, historical research.'

'For future generations,' nodded the Goat.

'Besides, what I'm trying to tell you is that we might just as well skip the house and go straight for the coalshed. And taking a look in the man's coalshed is hardly a crime, is it?'

'Well, actually, considering the current climate with Corny all over the papers and cops running around trying to make sure that no one messes with him or his statue, I'd say it's probably a massive crime.'

'We've picked a fine time to trespass on the man's property. Threats against his statue, people out to get him – do you realise if we're found hanging around that garden we'll be hauled off and on the front pages tomorrow? "AVNS nabbed – assassination attempt on O'Shaughnessy failed".'

'Don't be silly.'

'Silly? And how would I look? "Threatened sculptor's assistant gets curious revenge – man to make statue wrote letters to stop it".'

It doesn't bear thinking about.

'You're being ridiculous,' said Mellowes.

'Listen, up until he got rid of them, there were guards trailing that guy's every movement.'

'He's had that all his life . . .'

'Yeah, but now he's their baby and they have to look after him. Half the country is watching the news in case anything happens to its greatest living patriot.'

'Complete exaggeration – '

'Nutters could come up his driveway at any hour, and now, in the lull, we decide to come in their stead.'

'You're completely over-reacting,' said Mellowes. 'There's a cease-fire on. A lull, as you call it. Besides, we'll be in and out in a jiffy. No one will see us. The guards are gone, banished, finito, and the housekeeper will be away. The place will be deserted tomorrow and we can do it then.'

'Tomorrow – what time tomorrow?'

'Tomorrow night. He's going to a dinner in Athlone for the honour of Judge Hanrahan and it's unlikely he'll come back before Monday morning.'

'Yeah, I remember Wycherley saying something about having dinner with him on Saturday because he was going to be away on Sunday evening.'

'It's a shame, in a way, that he won't go to the ceremony tomorrow because it would have given us tomorrow morning to play around with as well.'

'Too risky,' said the Goat.

'True,' said Mellowes, 'but it'd have given us time – '

'And, how, pray,' said I, 'to ask the as yet unasked question, do we get into the impregnable coalshed? Corny-style – with eighteen pounds of gelignite?'

'No,' said Mellowes firmly. 'We'll have to get the key, which is where you come in.'

'Oh.'

All eyes turned on me.

'Shane.' Mellowes looked at me closely and took a deep breath. 'You're going to dinner with him tonight. You'll be close to him. You're risking your life to make his statue. You'll be drinking his port, chuckling at his witticisms, attending to his proprieties, generally buttering him up. It could be a long night. It probably will be a long night. Somehow during that long night you've got to find out (a)' – he put up a finger – 'if he does indeed keep documents in the coalshed and (b)' – another finger – 'if he does, where does he keep the key.'

'That's a tall bleeding order!'

101

'Shane.' He stretched out his hand to still me. 'Can I flatter you for a moment?'

'You can try.' His face was intensely serious.

'Shane, you're a skilful, sly, devious and duplicitous operator. Just like Corny himself.'

'Charming.'

'You're the best. I've seen you get people to offer up their innermost secrets, to tell you their bank-account numbers, their grandmothers' infidelities, their grandfathers' atrocities. Why did they call you Andrew's Liver Salts in Artane? Listen to me, man, you'll be in your element tonight. You know Corny's life story like you know your own. Better, in fact, because you've a fair idea who his parents were . . .'

I smiled and he smiled. If anyone else said it . . .

'You know almost every rank, office, gun, he held. From Boland's Mills to CND. You know his period – all his periods. 1912 to 1932 to just about the present day. Inside out. You know his contours as well as you know those of Collins and about his parents there was no question. If a man can still sow at seventy-five he doesn't keep quiet about it.'

'I'm not sure about that.'

'Listen to me,' he said and I stopped smiling. 'Corny's ninety and he's almost as lively. Almost, right. Get Tess to do a bit of fluttering while you're working the seams. He likes being charmed. He loves it! He'll be eating out of your paw. Soften him up. Ask all the right questions. Fawn and be firm. Be flatteringly familiar with all his thoughts and actions. Reverential, even awed, in the presence of such living history. Find the vein and work it. Remind him of obscure instances that no one else would. Steer clear of the obvious – the Rising, the Civil War, the IRA, Cumann na Poblachta. Don't even mention the Mother and Child Scheme, and don't overdo it on the Trojan mother.'

Mellowes drew breath and nodded his head.

'Humbly suggest just how wonderful it would be to see some of those old IRA directives – "Does he have any? Really? Where?" Tess and you would just love to see some. Make sure Tess is near by batting her eyelids at the exciting tales of this wonderful old man. He's a sucker for a bit of skirt. Young skirt, especially. If you pile it on as good as I know you can, by the end of the night, with the wine in his veins and the mist in his eyes, he should be up and shaking for those dusty old files. Any old files – all you have to do is see where he gets the key from. Of course, undoubtedly in such a situation, you'd probably be called upon to escort the old gentleman out into the black night and down into his coal bunker. That'd give you a good look at what he has stashed away down there.'

'And what if the old gentleman decides not to show his guests any deep-vaulted files in the middle of the night?'

'Shane, you've got to try. Stranger ruses have worked before. Think of what we've done. We've been through so much together. We can pull this one off. You can pull this one off. You're on safe ground. Yes, you're taking a risk but look at your privileged position. He's within your risk. He may be wily but he's ninety. His artistic memory is in your hands. You're a historian, a fan, you could be his biographer, you're making his statue. He'll love you, Shane, he'll love you.'

'You've got it in you, man,' added the Goat.

'You want me to steal the key, don't you?'

'Borrow it,' said Mellowes. 'When he puts it back, drop your hand when his hump's turned.'

'He'll notice it's gone.'

'He'll think he's mislaid it. It'll only be gone for a day or two. He won't be thinking about it. He'll be up to high dough with the dinner, whether he should go to the ceremony, and how he should handle the AVNS and M.I.5, and how he should prepare for his extradition case opening in the courts on Tuesday. He won't miss it. And if he notices it's mislaid, what's he to think – his charming dinner guests took it?'

'Maybe. He could think back to how he was coaxed to open up the cellar by that smooth-tongued bastard – '

'Who is risking his life to build his statue. Come off it.'

'If he's in the courts on Tuesday why don't we look for the key then? He's in the studio Wednesday, so it'll have to be before then.'

'Shane,' said Mellowes wearily. 'I don't think the key's going to be in a Waterford goblet or hanging on a hook by the sink. If it is, great. Because, hopefully, you'll be sussing out the whole place throughout the night, and will spot it. Remember, any pretext or excuse to leave the room and go mosey around, use it. As I know you will. But I'd say that key's well buried. And I think your best bet is to stick with him and, using all the forces of persuasion you can muster, try and get him to inadvertently show you where he keeps the thing . . . besides, on Tuesday, you'll be leaving it back.'

'Back?'

'Well, I'll do it if you don't. Putting it back's the easy part.' I live near by. I see all his movements and it'd be no problem to me.'

This offer threw me aback and if it was a tactic, it was a clever one.

'Tonight's your night though, Shane. You're going to have the opportunity and there's never going to be another opportunity like it. Are you going to take it? Are you going to try? Are you going to be the old bold Shane we always knew, or are you going to turn it down?'

'It's a long shot.'

'Weren't they all long shots, Shane? Getting McEoin out of jail, getting Dev out of Lincoln Jail, getting O'Shaughnessy out of Mountjoy Jail, getting the Brits out of Ireland, getting the country out of bondage. Weren't they all long shots, Shane? Every one of them. The First Dáil, the War of Independence, the Rising, Emmet, Tone. Are you going to snatch the opportunity, however slight?'

'You can do it!' urged the Goat.

'Think of O'Higgins's memory and the dash of his mentor Collins. Think of all the huge risks he was prepared to take so that you and I could sit here, free. Have you a fraction of Big Mick's daring?'

'I'll try.'

Chapter 5

A Dinner to Savour

At 4.45 p.m. I came down Clonskeagh Road from Loyola and, as arranged, met Wycherley and Tess sitting on the railings of Isaac Butt's house. Like birds of prey they were both quietly looking across the road at the dark trees surrounding Roebuck House and, to my irritation, appeared to be less than well dressed for the Great Patriot's dinner table: Tess decked out in a floppy brown suede jacket and ranch-hand Levis, and Wycherley, almost Aids-thin, elongated out of a grey turtle-neck shirt and soot-black mohair suit from the Lemass era. They didn't see me so I dived into a suburban garden, crossed a low fence (Butt's windows were open so someone must live in there after all) and crept up behind them.

Pushing a broken twig into the back of Tessa's neck, I shouted, 'Stop your statue or I'll cut your throat!'

'Shane!' yelped Tess, springing from the wall.

Wycherley cringed with disgust and made a cutting remark about the nation letting its orphans on the loose. His red-eyed face was the pallor of unsalted butter and he appeared to be holding his stomach; hangover or the psychosomatic tension of the big job.

'You look like you're going to a funeral, there, Bob.'

'Hush, Shane,' said Tess. 'He's in a fragile state.'

'And I'll put you in one if you're not careful,' he grumbled.

'Come, come, let's have a cease-fire. It's all the rage.'

'It won't be what we'll be doing,' he said with determination.

'No?'

'No. The unveiling ceremony has to be on his ninetieth birthday and I want what we've been forced to do finished a week before that.'

'That's very tight.'

'The whole project depends on it,' he said impatiently. 'It has to be done. After what happened yesterday there's no question about it. Our reputation depends on it. Yours as well as mine. And the Government's. I gave them a commitment.'

'All according to plan.'

'That's right,' he said softly and he avoided looking at me.

We watched Wycherley. He looked weary, tired of the whole affair. He expressed his disappointment, and annoyance, at the Government's outright rejection of his first proposal: a sort of half-open box, symbolising the Rising. The philistines, he said; any abstraction was beyond them. Don't worry, they would get the super-realism they were looking for. The whole project had caused him nothing but grief, from beginning to end. He wanted to see the back of it. Now it's reported that Forbes was thinking of suing him which was ridiculous. Out of order. Even if he did perhaps over-hastily blame Forbes for the early threats and was now prepared to acknowledge that there was probably more than a spurned sculptor behind the AVNS, it still did not justify going to court over what were merely word-of-mouth allegations. Slander was one of the city's liberties – couldn't he handle the cut and thrust? Look at all the people the media and politicians and experts on the street slandered by linking them with the AVNS. Would the UDA be taking action, or M.I.5, or the South African Security Service (suspected because of Corny's anti-apartheid activities)?

He would give as much time to the Forbes court case as he had given to the AVNS 'threats' that caused it, which was very little. The campaign of the faceless and, for all we know, personless Captain Moonlight had got far too much notice. Redmondites, my eye. They had done – Wycherley looked around here as a woman had entered an adjoining garden – they had done, he said in a lowered voice, nothing except write a few letters and now they were pompously calling a cease-fire! Pending further developments! Well, cease-fire or not, Wycherley would go on with the job. Same as always. He would see a memorial of O'Shaughnessy erected in St Stephen's Green on his birthday, regardless of the stymieing efforts of Forbes, Redmondites or the commemoration committee. OK?

'OK,' we answered.

'No problem,' said I, touching his arm.

'Thank you,' he said and a soft grateful smile played about his lips and twinkling bloodshot eyes. 'Thank you so much.'

Dishevelled and drained as he was, a proud craggy glamour emanated from his wax and cotton features during this touching if slightly embarrassing moment of suffused affection. We, his adopted, had seen him through thick and thin, and we would see him through to the end.

'Come on.' He touched my elbow and we rose from Butt's wall.

'Let us go and see the man we're to encase in bronze.'

A clear grass verge sided the slipway from the kerb to his gates. On two granite pillars, small signs read respectively, 'Roebuck' and 'House'. We passed in and crunched up the short curve of gravelled driveway. Trees surrounded us on all sides, linking densely above our heads to give the effect of a tunnel through which sparkling fingers of sunlight managed to penetrate. Up from between years of broken twigs entangled in the thorned undergrowth, shot bright yellow dandelions. Suddenly, the driveway parted, the trees thinned and the house grew in our vision. The first thing that struck me (previously accounted for by Joe and other visitors) was what appeared to be a large outside garage, wooden and gable-shaped like a cricket clubhouse or a gospel hall. Could this be where Corny went to fetch the files among the coal? Outside its barn doors the chocolate-brown Volkswagen sat squatting in the sunlight, a goggle-eyed bulbous little beetle, toy-like and incongruously innocent, considering its owner. He drove it himself until recently, but now the daughter takes the wheel.

A swathe of round-pebbled grey gravel semi-circled the front of the house and our heavily scrunching soles signalled an approach that our mute tongues certainly didn't. It was very quiet. The greying whitewashed house bore little sign of internal life. The upstairs windows were veiled as was, further up, a loft skylight. The spacious downstairs windows, however, had their velvet curtain folds pulled back and belted at the waist and as we mounted the first of the seven stone steps to the blue front door, I caught an intriguing glimpse of bookshelves, oil paintings and mantelpiece within.

We stood before the front door. Wycherley, out of po-lite habit, wiped his wrinkled George Webbs on the doormat, and rearranged the remaining bits of his hair with tremulous fingers.

Tess, fidgeting with the last walnut button left on her jacket, smiled and said to me, 'Shane, there's no bell.'

In other words, they were waiting for me to knock. Me – the silver-fingered Corny of the squad, whose gentle knock, knock, knock brings them out. I lifted the heavy head of his Anna Livia knocker and far from gentle was its resounding clack–clack! The whole door (house? bed? Corny?) shook with the iron thuds. We waited. Footsteps approached. Fairly fast ones for an old man. Was he already trying to impress us? A tiny telescopic spyhole eyed us and, for a laugh, I put my fingertip over it, blotting out the old boy's world. Wycherley, far from laughing, knocked my arm down.

Jesus – just in time, for the door pulled swiftly back to reveal, not the old man we expected, but a wondrous young creature in a black sleeveless dress, whose wonderful wet wound of a welcome mouth asked us something I can't remember – well, I can, actually (it was, more or less, 'Who are you?'). But the apparition of this radiant creature – with big soft Bambi eyes and a tangled wreath of Rossetti hair, of my own height (age? generation? political import?) took me by pleasant surprise. What, pray, is such a splendid creature doing treading, or should I say, daintily toe-kissing, the floors of Corny's abode this soft Saturday afternoon? His granddaughter? If so, I'm a Provo tomorrow. His mistress? If so, I'm a reincarnated Black and Tan come to kill the cradle-snatcher.

'Oh, I am sorry!' she flustered, when Wycherley explained who we were.

'Mr Wycherley and company – of course. Do come in!'

A bare arm ushered us into the hall.

We had nothing to offer the coat-and-hat stand, already over-burdened with galoshes, worn slippers, walking sticks, Homburgs and about fifty hanging coats (his victims at a rough count) and so, coatless and awkward, we stood around waiting for the poor dear to finish relocking the door. In fact, poor Vanessa (she introduced herself while she was on her knees – like so many of Corny's victims) had to work squeakily the rust-tough bottom bolt up and down, to get it across and into its stubborn ring. With the vigour of the yanking effort that ample woolwork of tendril hair shook loose around her head like an unravelled tea cosy. And, just as unseemly, but even more becoming, her straining dress gradually worked its way up a here-and-there freckle-speckled full-white thigh, closely followed, as you can imagine, by my beady eye.

'Do you want a hand?' asked Tess, casting an accusatory glance at her gentlemen companions.

'No thanks,' came a strained voice. 'I've just got it – there!'

'Goodness me,' declared Vanessa, rising to her feet with a flush of colour and smoothing her dress. 'You can never be too careful about security these days. Especially the last few days. Mr O'Shaughnessy has been very laid back about it, but I think it is terrible. How anyone would want to terrorise an old man about things that happened seventy years ago – isn't it just terrible?'

'Shocking,' I said, measuring the concern in those green doe-eyes. Stone the bleeding crows – his mistress at ninety? Couldn't be.

'Do you have a police watch on your premises, Mr Wycherley?'

'Not since last night and the so-called cease-fire,' replied abrupt Mr Wycherley, brazenly looking about the place. 'Quite honestly, I share Mr O'Shaughnessy's laid-back attitude. I've taken little notice of the whole business. Cranks through and through. Shall we go in here?'

'Oh . . . eh.' Vanessa's little face fell. 'Why, yes. Yes, do,' she cried, nervously slipping behind us. 'Do go on into the living-room. Mrs Williams will bring you in some tea. Sit down, please.'

On seeing Mr Wycherley proprietorially head for the fireside leather armchair, Vanessa bashfully bounced forward (she does skip!) to clear from its squashed cushions a heap of books and journals, and on seeing Mr Wycherley agreeably ease into the leather she retreated from the room smiling apologetically. For what? Skipping? The books for being there? Who knows, but our vigilant, taciturn and probably weird presence didn't help. She was off to fetch the man himself, perhaps waking him from an early slumber.

'Nice girl,' ventured Tess after the door shut.

'Yes, very,' snapped Wycherley, glumly peering into the empty grate.

'Sorry I spoke.'

'You will be, the place is probably bugged. Shane! Sit down out of that, and stop snooping around the man's house.'

'I'm just looking at his bookshelves,' I protested, already up and about and, I have to admit, absolutely enthralled by the room's shelves and trappings.

'Tess, dear, you wouldn't fetch me a glass of water from the kitchen?'

The 'living area' was very much as Joe described it. It was a hybrid of two rooms – a front living-room in which we three had quietly sat before Tess left and I began scouring, and an attached drawing-room – the two successfully de-partitioned in the middle the way Corny would wish the country was, with two big bright windows at either end.

Though the walls were crowded with paintings and pictures of the dead Corny knew, it was very obviously a 'living area': his last retreat. Unwashed tea cups and crumbed plates were discreetly stuck in between the neat piles of papers, journals and files that grew Manhattan-like from polished tables. Let's hope our quarry – the tell-tale papers – is downstairs and not up here or we'll never find them and let's hope Joe comes up with a better description of what they're sheathed in. At the foot of one of the many bookcases that reached to the ceiling was a line of shiny shoes, a heap of recent newspapers and a glass vat of what looked like homemade wine but could have been diluted blood (take it easy, Shane). In a corner there was, indeed, a row of those big pin-stripe suits he swims around in. They were hanging on a rail and they looked amazing. A fully open wardrobe! I'd have shown them to Bob if he wasn't busy fighting a hangover and reading some notes.

'What are you looking for?' Wycherley called, wiping Solpadeine from his mouth and getting a fag out.

'A skeleton,' I said and there was a titter.

'Shane,' scolded Tess, almost presciently but then laughing herself.

'Good evening,' announced Mr O'Shaughnessy, and the laughter stopped like that (I click my fingers).

'Oh, good . . . good evening,' we all murmured, stunned by the silence of his entry.

His shut the door gently, coughed and came over to shake hands. Hushed, we rose to greet him, and he tottered towards us, smiling wanly with those wet lizard's eyes of his bulging out of a grey-skinned skull. It was a shock to realise how old he was, and looked, seen in the flesh. One forgot because of the high public profile, the speeches, the court cases, the activist politics, that this was one of the oldest of the old fighters, a man who defended Boland's Mills with Dev, only four years his senior.

We warmly shook. I could feel the bones moving within, reasserting the great O'Shaughnessy, a hand that has killed many a bad and fine man. I'm finally in his company. He'll soon be in theirs.

Loose-fingered Wycherley appeared to receive the withered paw less warmly, perhaps afraid he might pull off some of the flesh he hoped to sculpt, a tactile reminder of his own mortality.

'You must forgive my delay,' croaked Mr O'Shaughnessy in that familiar coffee-percolator voice. 'I was in the shower.'

The shower?

'The shower?' said Tess, speaking for all of us. Sure a shower would kill him. Or would it? He was fast on his feet and he swung around.

'For a wash, young lady. And who are you?'

'Oh,' she said, a bit flustered, and stepping forward while a waxen claw patted her to sit. 'Tessa Masterson's my name. I'm so glad to be working on – '

'Yes, I know your mother,' he interrupted and clutching her hand for safety he plopped down beside her, his little shoes rising as he landed. Black Winstanleys, I noted with secret satisfaction. My shoes!

'She was a wonderful actress in her day,' he expanded, leaning back and roving his pink-rimmed eyeballs across the three of us. On 'actress' I noted the furious French phlegm gargling its way up his turkey-throttled throat.

'But she's still an actress now,' Tess gently pointed out. It was a sore point with the family.

'Yes,' he said softly and paused, crossing his thin legs. He was moving around inside one of those greatly oversized pin-stripe suits, this one of thick navy wool, worn over a wrinkled white shirt and a floppy yellow tie. Oisin would have loved it. I loved it. Him. Now. I could see what Sharon Travers saw. He was a dapper little dote, as cute as a rat in an overcoat. Preserved, he'd make a lovely sculpture.

'McArdle, is it?'

'It is,' I said, but you don't know *my* mother.

'McArdle . . . Shane,' he said to himself, a fact which made me nervous.

'Shane is a fine name. There's not enough Shanes around.'

'One is enough,' muttered Wycherley.

'I am grateful to you,' he announced, after another awkward pause, 'for your patience.'

'Nonsense,' said Wycherley. 'You were only a few minutes.'

'I mean,' he explained, 'for sticking to the commission to do my statue. Despite all these threats and trouble the Minister tells me that you have no intention of pulling out. I am most grateful. You must have suffered a great deal of distress from this' – he gesticulated vaguely, and prematurely, towards the fireplace – 'this absurd mischief . . . fomented trouble. Never did I think a memorial to me would come to this' – hand flapping loosely at the grate – 'though, now that it has, it doesn't surprise me.'

'I can assure you, Mr O'Shaughnessy,' declared Wycherley with confidence, 'we were never too alarmed. How could we take any of this AVNS business too seriously? Cranks from beginning to end, and quite honestly – '

'Be careful,' interrupted O'Shaughnessy, the fleshy lid of one round eye rising ponderously. 'Be careful.'

The now customary pause followed. We waited in the intimidating silence. Not a sound. Only the noise of O'Shaughnessy's gums engaging in a bout of lubricious saliva-swallowing.

'The British,' he said, licking one lip and linking his hands.

'Oh,' said Wycherley.

'I see their hand in this.' He nodded, and on cue, a right hand once again floppily gesticulated to the fireplace. 'The whole thing smacks of amateurs, masquerading as historically concerned politicals. Redmondites, they call themselves! In 1986!' He coughed energetically, shaking inside the oversized suit, and brought up tears. 'How could such people be still around, threatening to blow up statues, or those gifted enough to make them.'

Wycherley nodded.

'It is all too much to believe.'

It certainly is.

'Too fantastic for this day and age.'

'Very true,' I judiciously interjected.

'The AVNS.' He spat the initials out with great sarcasm. 'Running around with their contemptible little letters, calling me a retired terrorist – how dare they!' he said raising his voice, and veins. 'Do they expect to be taken seriously? Behaving like that? I tell you, the whole thing's a charade!'

We waited quietly for the exertions of an all too audible

phlegmatic cough to subside, after which Corny steadied his twitching legs with a palm on each kneeball and proceeded to tell us about who was really behind 'the recent stunts'.

'The British,' he said, tightening his jaw, 'are out to get me. It's a very personal thing. Since the twenties and later, into the forties . . . the thirties. And beyond. I had no option then but to order the disposal of some of their most notorious agents. The story's well known . . . but there are other parts of it as yet unwritten.'

Yes, we're working in it, as the man said.

'They – the British Secret Service – have been determined on revenge ever since. There are other reasons for their continuous vendetta against me – but I can't go into them.'

He suddenly and quite abstractedly looked towards myself which, as you can imagine, unnerved me a bit.

'Will you make it for my birthday?'

I'll bring the balloons.

'Will I be erected, I mean.'

'Oh . . . eh, yes. Definitely,' said Wycherley with almost brutal emphasis. 'I mean, if we work to schedule and there are no major hitches. Everything's set. I have the material, the manpower, the full facilities. Obviously, my studio will be fully given over to the rapid and effective completion of the project. The final execution, you see, is a very quick process.'

'Sound ominous,' smiled Cornelius. 'What does it entail?'

'Well,' smiled Wycherley, leaving his cup down, 'it is known as the lost-wax process of bronze-casting. I would have, say, a wax figure of you – the effigy of the sculpture, if you like – and I would put it inside an oven. Under intense heat, the wax figure would melt away leaving its mould in plaster, an empty space directly representative of what has now disappeared. The next stage is for molten metal to be poured into the mould. It cools and hardens and when the mould is broken, you have a bronze replica of your earlier wax figure.'

'Most interesting,' said O'Shaughnessy, recrossing his legs. 'And thus a statue is born, so to speak.'

'Exactly, and a wax figure disappears,' grinned Wycherley, softly fondling his chin. I looked at Tess. She was smiling. She thought she knew it all.

'The process is thousands of years old. The ancient Egyptians perfected the technique. They would take birds, animals, even the bodies of people, coat them in wax and then burn them inside moulds so that the shell cavities remained for gold and silver replicas to be cast from.'

'So you have your plans all worked out?'

'That's correct,' said Wycherley. 'I take it the Minister told you this morning about the proposals I submitted to the commemoration committee yesterday.'

'Well,' sighed Corny, 'all he said was that it will be a standing lifesize bronze figure on a limestone plinth, which was enough to make me very happy because, if you'll excuse my ignorance, and please, do not take offence' – a frail hand landed on Tessa's knee – 'I am an old man and I do not understand everything about modern art and modern sculpture. Frankly, I didn't know what you'd come up with. I thought you would want to do a very abstract, sort of avant-garde piece of sculpture which would be beyond my comprehension and, I would venture, above the heads of most ordinary people.'

'Not at all,' assured Wycherley. 'I understand my brief. This is a government monument of a public figure for a public park on a public occasion. The nature of the memorial requires a certain gravity of conventionality, the standard orthodox methods of . . .'

Wycherley waffled on about the state-paid portrait artist bit and the responsibility of the imagination in treating history. I couldn't have done better myself. This wasn't selling out, this was selling. And he was now about to propose the ultimate in consultation between the artist and subject. He had told Tess about it earlier on and she was very surprised. And very excited – she thought it was a marvellous idea. Not a new one, of course, but one that in this case would have obvious advantages: that Corny should participate in the making of his own statue.

'What? Would you go away out of that,' laughed O'Shaughnessy, flapping his hands dismissively. 'Sure I'm too old to be trekking around a hot studio. Is it carrying bags of plaster you want me for? Would you stop that, Mr Wycherley.' His little contracted chest shook with amusement inside the big jacket.

'Quite seriously,' continued Wycherley, 'if I am to get a faithful depiction of you – your height, your features, your build – if I am to capture your whole figure and frame exactly, I really would need to get some plaster reliefs of some of the more important parts of your body.'

'Well,' quipped Corny, nudging Tess and winking at me, 'the

114

most important part of a man is his face and the best plaster relief of that will be the death mask!'

To our slight unease, he tittered and tapped his shoes. The subject of death seemed to warm him up.

'That's another day's work,' said Wycherley, watching O'Shaughnessy's merriment with close satisfaction. 'But I really would be most obliged if you could participate in even a small way in my preparation for your statue. You'd enjoy it. It would be quite an experience. Nothing painful. Just a few mould impressions. It would help me tremendously. After all, we want as accurate and recognisable a representation of you as possible – correct?'

'Well, yes,' he agreed, 'without being vain. Yes, that would be the ideal.'

'So what better way to ensure accuracy than from doing real physical impressions in plaster of your limbs and features?'

'I suppose . . .'

'And, as an artist, I believe there is nothing more wonderful than having the subject participate with the creator in the actual creation of its own image. You would essentially be a part of the making of your own artistic vision – an exciting prospect in modern sculpture.'

'That's a bit above my head.'

'Well, then, quite honestly, the practical reality of the situation requires that you get involved, because without such help I may, I just may not be able to meet the deadline of August the 12th, for the unveiling on your birthday.'

'Oh,' uttered the near ninety-year-old lips. 'Well – I don't know . . . thinking about it . . . I don't see why not.'

Wycherley smiled.

'It could be interesting. What . . . what exactly am I required to do?'

'Lend us your body for an afternoon. That's all. So that we can take plaster casts of what one might call your component parts. Very simple. You'd be no more than an hour or two in the studio. And we'd look after you very well. Isn't that right, Tess?'

'What? Oh yes, of course . . . of course.'

Corny smiled and nodded.

'Ah, you're very good,' came the croaky whisper and a set of dun-spotted fingers gently gripped her knee. 'You're all very good,' he slowly amplified, twinkling happy anticipatory eyes at the three of us. 'Sure, of course, I'll help out. It's no skin off my back – I hope!'

He slapped a knee (his own this time) and rocked with laughter, proud of the quip. We obligingly followed suit, all yo-ho-hoing with such exaggerated laughter that in an uncanny representation of his own entrance earlier we didn't notice the sudden arrival of a body into the room. Mrs Williams stood by the door wiping raw-red knuckles on her apron.

'The roast is on!' she shouted loudly. Compensation, if needed, for her mouse-like entrance. 'It'll not be ten minutes more. Would you care to come and start?'

'Thank you very much, Betty,' Cornelius replied tetchily, calming her down and visibly irked by the rude interruption of his merriment. Or by the strain of seventeen years of yelling.

'All right, then, shall we pass to the other side?' suggested Cornelius, hands on knee-caps, preparing to rise.

'Of what?' I asked.

'Of the house,' he said stiffly. 'What did you think?'

'Oh yes, of course,' I replied, raising a nervous laugh, and getting to my feet accompanied by Wycherley and Tess noisy with apologetic amusement. But for some odd reason, I had the impression that it was me O'Shaughnessy's big eyes were fixed upon as he came up from the sofa assisted on either side by Betty's big bicep and Tessa's tensed forearm, respectively.

A few moments' confusion ensued as Corny tried to distract Betty's attention away from Mr Wycherley's 'bad turn' – 'Are you weak at all on your legs?' she asked the wrong man – and on to his own desire to have the television turned on for the six o'clock news. He wanted to see the news before we began. So while the alleged ex-hangover protested his Solpadeine-revived health and busy Betty suspiciously sniffed his empty glass, Tess offered, as a good turn, to switch the TV on, if it could be found.

'Unfortunately, the thing is moved around at night,' Corny told us, making it sound like a vampire's coffin.

So as not to disturb the great visionary who is usually working until late downstairs, Ms Singleton (Vanessa – where is she?) took the TV set upstairs to watch the last programmes before going to bed. So she sleeps here! Saucy rat, vampire's slave; I'll have to get to the bottom of this.

Meanwhile, guess who was sent upstairs to fetch the 'thing'? The TV, that is. Able at least to do a valuable reconnaissance

on the way, this able-bodied youth was sent hurrying – 'Quick,'
cawed Corny, 'it's just turning six' – and duly took the stairs
three at a time. Mellowes was right about the mirrors, wrong
about the steps (they all creaked. Well, every three foot-springs
up). At the top of the stairs, the TV was, disappointingly, waiting
for me. Disappointingly, because I was hoping it would be inside
her room, and if the vampire's slave was there, I've have to knock
and disturb her languorous things as she reclined, prostrate and
sheet-entwined, sucking a finger over some book on the Civil
War. And if she wasn't, I might have a chance to snoop, quietly
sift through letters, trinkets, dried petals, distended stockings, and
look under the bed for a pair of his overturned shoes. Collins in
metropolitan headquarters, he always took a memento.

But all the doors were closed on the upper landing and besides,
I, and what I carried, were wanted pronto downstairs if Corny
was to catch his news headlines. I lifted the great bulk of a 'thing'
and some 'thing' it was; *c.* 1968 Bush with white knobs, false
oak-grain sidings and aquarium-thick glass, and together we
thudded down the now individually creaking steps. The 'thing'
blocked my view as I went and I had to rely on memory to retrace
my steps around banister and hallway. How fortunate then that
just as Mrs Williams, to whom he was giving cooking instructions,
was retreating out of the room backwards, Wycherley caught sight
of a big glass box with legs, entering behind her.

'Yes, rare to medium rare – Oy! Watch the TV!' came the cry
to the puzzled woman.

She stopped and so did I. A nasty accident was avoided.
Relieved, and without letting me drop the thing, she took my
roasting order. Rare and not too much meat. I wasn't hungry.

'Oh, are you ill, as well?' she started.

'Over here, over here!'

Stooping, Corny scuttled ahead to point out its resting place;
precariously upon twin piles of files. Before it was out of my
arms and perched he had the thing plugged in and coming alive
(trying to electrocute me?). The fuzzy picture composed itself into
the last dongs of the Angelus. A still Raphael: Mother and Child
Scheme. Not a murmur of a prayer out of Corny. Wycherley,
strangely content, lit up a fetched cigarette, and relaxed, crossing
long legs. The dramatic signature of the news came on and we
had pictures of blood running down a policeman's head. It had
been a hot Twelfth. Rioting all over the North. Orange parades

117

deteriorate into savage pitched battles with the RUC. The situation at Portadown as bad as feared when Orangemen refused the 'right' to march through the Catholic part of the town. Loyalists attack the police for 'upholding' the Anglo-Irish Agreement. Like a drunk's eye, the camera wobbles and shakes close to the clattering of nailed clubs, bricks, running and screaming at the crash barriers and then the precise, paused 'jump, jump' of plastic bullets after the powerful orange of petrol bombs exploding on armoured vehicles.

We waited for the violence to die down, to tail off, as we got into the programme and the items lessened in importance. Then, hopefully, the stern newscaster will tell us the latest on the 'O'Shaughnessy statue' affair. I watch Corny. He folds his huge sleeved arms and blankly watches the flickering screen, waiting for the scenes of present violence to pass.

But they don't pass. From the Tunnel in Portadown we go to Belfast, to Derry, to Armagh and across the sundered Province. Charred vehicles, policemen's families burnt out, rocket attack on RUC station, two punishment knee-cappings in West Belfast, funeral of Catholic building worker shot on building site and man charged for the killing of part-time UDR man shot dead on his milk round in South Fermanagh. O'Shaughnessy watches all this without saying a word. This evening's news is so packed with incident that there is no room for an update on his story. The fate of his statue, and the state of the 'so-called AVNS cease-fire', as the media so-call it, are irrelevant this evening. Compared to the heat and death in the North, the story of a threatened as yet unbuilt statue is a peripheral, almost comical distraction, a parochial madcap affair peopled by remote oddballs, sour cranks and the central figure of the tediously legendary war hero, Cornelius O'Shaughnessy, still with us and popping up everywhere.

'Will it ever stop?' Tess wondered to the room, shaking her head ruefully.

Cornelius said nothing and, realising as we did that his story was not about to appear, he rose from the armchair and abruptly switched off the set.

'Let us pass over and eat.'

Obediently we rose again and trooped after his lordship. 'Folly the leader one be one' the Republicans used to say about Dev, follying him into the field and then, what was left of them, into the lobbies, since a great many of them had follyed him into a maze that only he could escape from. A few too follyed Corny and have since gone to ground.

A set table awaited us in the dining-room. On the walls were more paintings, framed photographs, scrolls of honour. Over the fireplace hung a Seamus O'Sullivan portrait of Mother as a young, very young woman; a radiant little creature wrapped in fun scarves and dark brackish oils, her innocent, surprise-eyed face peering out with fearful wonder. The Republican demagogue had yet to emerge. Beneath the portrait stood, with hand on mantelpiece, another radiant little creature – Ms Singleton, she's back! – who in an uncanny enlivenment of the painted lady above her, peered at our approach with the same fearful wonder. At me, in particular, she glanced as if she could read my very thoughts.

No surprise then that the poor dear blushed when Corny introduced us. Hand squeezing clammy hand, her pollock-soft mouth bubbled my name: 'Ah, Shane.' I'll give you 'Ah', I grinned with internal cunning. Rather devilishly, I thought. In fact, rather stupidly. But with an equally silly grin, Corny muttered something about how you two should get to know each other! What's this? I thought. Fancy himself as a matchmaker? Plotting to pawn me off on his granddaughter/grand ex-mistress and recompense his guilt through youth. Plot ahead, my fragile friend.

'Succulent as a suckling pig!' Mrs Williams roared modestly as she carried her, as yet untasted, roast beef out of the kitchen and towards the table. The joint was parked with ceremony between Corny and Vanessa, there to be presumably distributed. To my disappointment it was already carved, a service I had been planning to volunteer. But it was a fine hunk of cooked carcass, sitting steamily in an oily pool of warm blood and showing through its sawed slices the requested bits of red rare, pinkish medium-rare and crustily well done. I watched Corny placidly observe Mrs Williams fork the dripping slices on to Vanessa's plate, and I felt hungry again. But Corny was passing on the meat, would you believe, as, of course, was Tessa, a fact which considerably displeased the cook. Vegetables were doled out: vegetarians first. We sat obediently. Once again the big lady's dextrous skills were impressively displayed as she went from shoulder to shoulder scooping Brussels sprouts, diced carrots and buttered peas out of the segments of two porcelain half-moons. The depositing of each portion was punctuated by two sharp cracks on each plate, ostensibly to free the spoon of clinging vegetables but probably

119

also an aggressive reminder of our collective impotence regarding the meat. Needless to say no amount of grateful remonstration could prevent huge heaps of unwanted vegetables being shovelled on to us – 'Not at all! Not at all! You'll need every bit you can get. Look at that fellow (this to me), he's like Bingo on a bad day.'

'Oh, but, please, I couldn't eat all that!' whined Ms Singleton, trying to stay Mrs Williams's hand with her tender arm and very nearly getting a crack of the spoon across the knuckles.

'Let's commence,' Corny curtly announced, perhaps a little embarrassed by his housekeeper's homespun wit. Even a rebel, especially a famous, Frenchified, bohemian-mothered one of Corny's credentials, could feel mildly let down by such a display of unsubtle if well-meant humour.

But she soon returned with two bottles of wine, both red, both uncorked, and with the same glass Corny tasted both and greedily nodded assent.

'Thank you, Betty. Could you bring up three more. Shane, young man, would you do us the honours?'

Up rose the young man to circle the table and fill the fools' glasses, a bottle in each hand.

'Red or redder?' I asked Tess.

'The one in your right.'

'Oh, good choice. Say when.'

'Now!' Her hand shot out.

'Sorry, my hand is heavy. Mr Wycherley, both, I suppose?'

'Just fill the glass,' he grunted. Gladly, O Master. To the brim.

'Mr O'Shaughnessy?'

He waved me on. 'Vanessa before me.'

'Of course. Sorry, I forgot myself. Vanessa, pet, what's your sauce?'

A little embarrassed, she pointed to the Étranger '85.

'There you go now,' I said. 'That'll put colour in your cheeks.' With which it already appeared. 'Mr O'Shaughnessy . . .' A bit late, perhaps, in your case.

'The Château Ypres,' he said in a crisp tone.

His was poured more gently. That lizard's eye watched my hand as I watched the back of his, mottled and claw-like, ready to pounce. But from up here, he looks helpless. Shrunken head, its wax-frail skin moulting. Familiarise, build yourself up –

'Enough, enough . . .' The hand rose and trembled me to stop.

120

I gave myself a good big glass and sat down, leaving the bottles in the middle.

'That's a fine wine,' said Wycherley.

'Yes, I've some nice ones,' said Corny with obvious pride. 'I keep a cellar.'

He keeps a cellar?

'Small and modest but very useful.'

'Oh.'

So he keeps a cellar. Mellowes, where are you?

'Here?' asked Wycherley, his interest perking up.

'Oh yes,' crowed Corny. 'Very valuable Bordeaux my mother brought back from France. Some, would you believe, with the years just after the Great War upon them.'

Bottled blood of the battlefields. Corny guzzling them down.

'Goodness,' sighed Wycherley. And I his *sommelier*.

'From cell to cellar then. Eh?'

'I'm sorry.' He strained forward, touching his near ear.

'Oh, nothing,' I muttered. 'I was just asking Vanessa for the salt cellar.'

'Ahhh . . .' Corny tossed his chin. Mashed carrots within.

Wycherley gave me a severe look, munching like a sheep, but Vanessa, God bless her, passed the salt on cue and smirking as he chewed, shot me a lovely quick languorous wink. There's hope yet. I can see she likes a bit of slagging, especially at your man's expense. Well, no better man, Shane, and no better occasion.

Across the table, though, it was serious business. Tess was fawning to the charms of the old codger and gazed into his face with polite shut-mouth crewing and glazed eyes. Some witticism was being exchanged and you could see she was taking in all the lines and contours as he leaned forward for emphasis. The skull beneath the skin. When he spoke his mouth opened like a goldfish retching for air between the words. Or does that make any sense?

'I think it's time for . . .' Wycherley lifted his glass, suggesting we do likewise.

A toast! I'll do this. This is my chance.

'Let me,' I said. 'I want to toast Mr O'Shaughnessy.'

Wycherley looked at me with surprise. 'OK,' he said after a pause. 'Go ahead. You're a man of more words than I am.'

'Thank you. Comes from having less years. Are we all ready? OK.' I cleared my throat. They all waited. How do you propose a toast? Here goes. 'Well, first let me say how wonderful it is to be here, sitting and eating at the table of a man who in many ways is synonymous with the recent history of our country.'

'Here, here,' grunted Wycherley. Corny made the suitable self-deprecatory noises of embarrassed modesty.

'I am sure,' I continued, 'that it is a proud honour for us all to sit here with this great and legendary man – a man who has been at the forefront of the climactic events in the formation and evolution of this state.'

Corny coughed and coyly shook his head.

'And, most of all, it is a special personal privilege to know that it falls to us to ensure that he is properly commemorated in a most physical way here in his own city. We will ensure that you stand proudly in bronze on a pedestal in St Stephen's Green.'

'Here, here,' said Wycherley, with *gravitas*, and the rest of them unctuously smiled at the beaming statue-to-be.

'This toast then is to the early and successful completion of our statue of Cornelius O'Shaughnessy. Come hell or high water, come Redmondites or British agents, come violent anti-nationalists, begrudgers, or cranks of any kind, come the vagaries of the commemoration committees – '

Wycherley looked at me sternly.

'Or the jealousies of mere court sculptors – '

Wycherley looked at me even more sternly.

'We will ensure that our statue – your statue, host – will be unveiled by the 12th of August, your ninetieth birthday. By that stage, I'm sure you will have been well toasted, and let me assure you, it is a great honour to be involved in the process.'

'Very true,' declared Wycherley and they all concurred happily, clinking glasses. I had done a good job. Corny, the old rogue, sat granny-like, wringing his hands and simpering bashfully.

'That was very nice,' he said, husky with emotion. Doubtless the man receives such adulatory toasts everywhere he goes but perhaps, coming from a historically minded young man, reverentially working on his statue in the face of the most awful threats, it strikes a more touching chord in the old boy's heart. I want to get in there. I want to get those files and papers.

'I must say,' enthused Corny, appearing to struggle for the words. 'It is . . . a great pleasure to be working . . . with you all. Mr Wycherley . . . Tessa . . . Shane.' He nodded gratefully to each of us, and we nodded gratefully back. A sudden bony claw sprung up on Vanessa's elbow. 'And you, my dear . . . in another regard.'

We all murmured our thanks. I knocked a fresh glass back.

'But to have my statue completed in four weeks – that is extraordinary. It can be done?'

'With your co-operation,' said Wycherley, tensely eyeing him.

'Oh yes. Yes, I see. Of course! I look forward to that.'

'So do we. More wine?'

'Eh? Oh yes. Yes, please.' Nimble-fingered Bob topped up the glasses, host first.

Tessa said, 'Please,' but I thought she looked ever so slightly suspicious. It was the first time I had seen her look suspicious and it was worrying. What was wrong – my toast and Wycherley's enthusiasm?

'Well, God bless you then, if you can make that deadline,' said Corny, sniffing his glass.

'Don't you worry,' replied Wycherley. 'We will. Won't we, Tess?'

'Absolutely!' said Tess and she smiled. Good girl, Tess.

We all sipped our glasses in quiet thoughtfulness. The wine was going down, that's for sure. We were on to our sixth bottle. Pity the food was being partaken of more modestly but then we were given heaps of the stuff. A crowded plate awaited me. Diced carrots and buttered peas: green and orange – the troublesome colours of our land. Squares and spheres. Incompatible. With me, for starters. Eat the meat first and then go from there. Vanessa, I noticed, was faring better, fairly demolishing the Brussels sprouts with those clean white incisors. Snap, snap. Marks on my chest.

'I said I thought it had a fine body,' said Bob. Speaking not of my own thoughts but of the wine.

'Oh, very good,' replied Corny. 'Most assuredly.'

'Yes, a good firm body,' I chimed in, pretending to have a clue. Not fooling Bob though, who gave me the black look of utter unamusement.

'What about yourself then, Tess?' asked Corny, tapping her on the forearm and ignoring the raised voices. 'How did you come to work with Mr Wycherley? You told me earlier you had worked in Istanbul.'

'Yes, that was about two years ago. I wanted . . .'

Tess then proceeded into her own little life story which you

123

already know. Interesting, yes, but we've heard it. Corny's we've heard many times, but there are still unlit corners. One is below this house, holding, hopefully, the secrets of Kevin O'Higgins's death. It will take many more gold-medal bottles, fulsome tributes and warmly exchanged anecdotes by the fire before I can perhaps surreptitiously probe my searchlight in and around that dark corner again.

But in the meantime I thought a bit of reconnaissance was in order. I did need a leak. Four glasses of wine, two Bacardis and a cup of tea were converting. I stood up quietly and begged leave, to go to –

'It's upstairs,' croaked Corny, interrupting his flow, if one could call the noise of a coffee percolator going backwards a 'flow'.

'Thank you.' I creaked across the carpeted dining-room and passed beneath the watchful eyes of Mother. Half the picture's glass was gilded by the evening sunlight, a purified dying sunlight which had lost its heat and yet, as it goes down, edges the lace curtains and the walnut sideboard with a phosphorescence of burning gold.

In the hallway, not a sound. Good. Can do without Mrs Williams. Stealthily, I gripped the banister and crept up the stairs. No matter how soft the tread, it was as I earlier expected when carrying the TV set, and every third step creaked. What strange arrangement is this? Are there coded signals involved for a friendly approach? At the top of the stairs all the doors were still closed. Could take a chance, but I wouldn't want to disturb Mrs Williams. Jesus, I'd love to snoop; the mother's quarters, kept untouched. The good man's bed, if and when he sleeps here. But there's no time. Too risky.

I turned a porcelain white knob on the door in front of me, murderer-style. The bathroom. In one corner squatted an ancient Victorian-footed bath, rust-stained at the stopper chain, with a sunflower-shaped shower overhead. No curtains: he must be nursed. Black-and-white chessboard tiles ran the length of the bath wall around the bath tub and around the mirror above the washstand basin. The white surface enamel was lined by thousands of threadline cracks, barely visible unless you went up close. Like an old painting or a middle-aged woman's skin. On the sink's side a towel rack had recently been reinforced and fitted with ribbed rubber, presumably for lowering and rising from the toilet bowl alongside, and a corresponding hand-hold was bracketed to the wall opposite. Poor fellow. It's all ahead of you, Shane. Half a century away but ahead of you.

Built into the wall above the toilet, a many-shelved wooden cabinet, displaying the toiletries of a man who was once himself left on the shelf of a wooden cabinet. A stickler for details I took it all in as I stood there, loosening Dev from his hammock and stretching him out for release. No need to, he was stiffening up already. Weather and wine puts muscle on a man.

Corny's cabinet contained some envious surprises in among the expected facecloths, hand lotions, pill bottles, cotton wool, bandages and cut-throat razors (bits of his former battle kit, no doubt). Keeping an eye on Dev's aim below (he told the boys in Boland's, Shoot anything in uniform, and Jesus, he was right. I'm a sucker for a uniform. Schools mostly but even a bloody traffic lady gets me going). I picked up a twisted tube of Fiacla toothpaste, reclining like a headless Henry Moore next to a multicoloured bunch of toothbrushes standing in a jar. 'We're squeezing the IRA like toothpaste,' boasted Roy Mason, but what has Corny got to do with toothpaste these days? He has no teeth, surely? I mean, real ones. Where are his false gums, his denture tablets, or the tell-tale salt-stained glass? Further evidence that Vanessa resides? I rattled indecorously through the cabinet's contents in search of feminine traces – cold cream, eye pencil, hairclip, anything. I even examined the surface of the sink and then, when Dev was finished and popped back in his tent, scoured the bath for any strand of stray hair longer than two inches and darker than Connemara grey (that's ash-grey to you and him) that just might have stuck sinuously to the enamel, when the water went down and the young lady got out. A sight I'd love to . . . no such luck. Nothing.

I gave Dev's head a vigorous shake before popping him back in. With difficulty. He was fairly stiff, tingling for a rub. In search of the River Ganges. What consolation for now? Vanessa, the lubricious lovely – if I could find a stray pair of her discarded panties, soft and mildly odorous, I could keep the long fellow happy. Wrap him in a perfumed shroud, lay him gently to rest. Wine's going straight through me. Very nice, too. Must get stuck in. I wonder where Corny's cellar is? It must be near the coal bunker. I could tell him it's my birthday tomorrow and I wouldn't mind an old bottle of Château de Anything, – 19 de Any Year. Or that I'm going to a funeral where a casket is obligatory. He likes me, I think. Appreciated the toast, excellently delivered – and very taken by my defence of Collins's memory and, of course, the defence of his own against artistic interpretation and constitutional subversion.

I was very taken too when he mentioned my performance in front of the Collins Movie Monitoring Committee – taken aback. He misses nothing! Not a trick. To think that the great O'Shaughnessy knows that I made a four-minute speech last April in a back room of Buswell's Hotel, protesting at a Hollywood plan to portray our Michael as some womanising Sancho Panza. And that Major Vinny Byrne told him! The two remaining members of the Squad discussing me? The Apostles once divided by civil war come together to discuss the Orphan McArdle. So legends do communicate. Old and grey and full of sleep but nodding by their fires they keep tabs on an awful lot of what's going on. Eyes and ears all over the place. We'd better be careful, Mellowes and I, invincibles all. If one wrong mouth gets wind of the fact that Corny has hot papers on some big deaths, and that we're after them, I could be in some very serious trouble. It wouldn't just be the end of Operation Booterstown, it'd be the end. My career, my livelihood gone. My bloody safety would be threatened, and this time for real. No letters, no times of grace. God knows who wants the O'Higgins killing kept quiet. It could all get a little dangerous and, if word escaped, Corny might decide to burn the damn files and take his secret to the grave. Deny history.

I'll stay no more and get out of here. The door shut behind me with an accusatory creak, echoed by the alternating squeak and groan of each step on the way down. On the penultimate step I came face to face with my own roguish reflection in the hall mirror. Vivid, unabashed, surprisingly murderous. The hallway was quiet. Empty. Noises in the kitchen. Mrs Williams banging pots. All's clear. Entry by stage left. I composed my features and assuming the suitable look of humility I turned the handle and burst in swiftly, the door clicking shut behind me with busy purpose. But no such casual air could disguise my noted absence. The four faces looked up and watched me approach the table. I nodded at Wycherley, smiled at Vanessa and sat down.

'We were wondering what had become of you,' said Corny, munching carrots to himself. 'Thought maybe you'd fallen down a hole or something.'

'Not quite,' I smiled, shifting in my seat.

'The wine cellar,' suggested Wycherley, himself lowering back a generous glass. Indeed, quite a bit of wine had been lowered since I left. The same couldn't be said for the food, however.

'I'm sorry if. I was gone long,' I explained, reaching for the bottle. Tess smiled and obligingly pushed me over a new glass. 'I was actually admiring your back garden, Mr O'Shaughnessy, from the upstairs window.'

'What upstairs window?'

'The . . . eh . . . bathroom window.'

'But it's locked.'

'The bathroom window? It's not, no.' What am I saying? It must be locked.

He looked at me and I hid my nose in the glass.

'It's slightly ajar,' I relented. 'You can sort of see out of it.'

Much as I can see out of this glass, slightly a'jarred.

'Strange, that,' he sniffed. 'Must have Betty check it out. I keep all my windows closed, you'll notice.'

'Notice,' I said, gulping my last mouthful.

'Security. Particularly these days. But also my health. Doesn't do a man at my age any good to have all sorts of weather coming in the windows. Enough of a lungful on my morning walk, when I'm all wrapped up. I find wine is a better medicine. For all of us. Shane, rise up there and do the rounds again. I've had Betty bring up two more. Is there anyone for more meat?'

'Please,' they said. Takers still. That surprises me.

While Corny's gnarled hands forked fresh slices on to the passed-over plates of Wycherley and Vanessa (bit of a horse, this girl, her plate cleaner than anyone's), I obediently circled the table, sloshing out healthy glassfuls of Cornelian medicine.

'Vanessa?'

'You say when,' she said coolly, baring her big white teeth.

Indeed, you lovely lively. I just might.

'You missed some good stuff,' whispered Tess, meaning conversation, not wine.

'Steady your hand there, Shane, or you'll never pour metal in my studio.'

'Beg your pardon, Bob, I've seen you siphon silver with the shivers of DTs.'

'And have you ever seen me fluff a cast? Ever?'

'Not that I recollect, no. But I've yet to – '

'You'll get your chance, my boy. You'll pour on Mr O'Shaughnessy's statue.' Mr O'Shaughnessy smiled at this. 'But discipline those hands of yours – we don't want him holed with air bubbles.'

'Aerated like a chocolate bar,' laughed Corny. 'It's a sensitive operation, I take it?' He pursed his lips with enquiry.

'Very. Pinpoint accuracy under intense conditions. We have to move almost intuitively and at great speed.'

'Sounds a little bit like an ambush,' he laughed. The wine's certainly warming him up. 'Shane, how would your shaking hand be with a gun in it?'

What a question.

'Eh . . . I'm not sure. It takes practice, I suppose.'

'Not much time for practice in '16 or '20, when you are those same fresh years and called up to volunteer for your country. You're thrown a Lee Enfield and told to get cracking. In the thick of it, before you've had the fine leisure to practise.'

'You were that young?' asked Tess.

'Younger,' said Corny grimly and he sat back. 'I was an officer in the IRB at fourteen. We were kids. We had to grow up quickly. In our company of the Dublin Brigade there were very few of us who were beyond our teens. But killing men puts years on you. A lot of years on you, I can tell you. Of course, some of us never made it through to feel those extra years . . .' He looked into his wine glass, swishing its maroon fluid by the stem. The twilight sun caught it and danced ruby lights over the tablecloth.

'Are there any of you left?' asked Tess. 'I mean, of your brigade.'

'Not many. Very few from the War of Independence, fewer still from the Rising. Mind you, there's a lot that I wouldn't know, up and down the country, but the last five or six years alone have taken a great many of my former comrades. By the end of this decade almost all of us will have gone.'

Tess, with her pulp lip extended, looked a little sad. Everyone went quiet. Too quiet. The sun was going down and we watched Corny swirl his wine with knotted fingers.

'Except me, of course,' he suddenly grinned. 'Who's already lived to be ninety.'

Relieved, we joined in and laughed softly as he sipped from his risen glass, eyes twinkling.

'Aaah . . .' sighed Tess and tilted her head. She was clearly touched.

'Ninety,' repeated Corny. 'Give or take a month.'

128

'Give us that month,' Wycherley put in with jovial confidence, 'and we'll see you live for even longer. We'll see you properly honoured on your ninetieth birthday. The greatest honour a man could have – '

'Is to die for his country,' interrupted Corny, raising his finger.

'Of . . . of course . . . but I . . . I . . .' Wycherley was struggling, ambushed.

'Don't forget that,' said Corny, and his lizard's head jawed forward to emphasise.

'Yes, of course.'

'Because it is a selfless thing, an impersonal thing, and, we must admit, a statue isn't.'

'Absolutely. But what I meant was,' explained Wycherley, getting firm with him, 'that in another context, in the context of the personal and the material, it would be difficult to find a greater honour, or present, if you like, for a man on his ninetieth birthday than having a statue of himself erected in St Stephen's Green.'

'Very true,' he nodded sagely, 'and I am most appreciative.'

'And isn't it,' pressed Wycherley, 'better than any of your comrades have received?'

Jesus C, Bob's like an uncle giving out presents.

'Perhaps.'

'They must be pleased, all the same.'

'They are, of course.' He put down his glass. 'Those who've let bygones be bygones.'

'Oh.' Wycherley was surprised. 'Even now? Surely you all see eye to eye now?'

'My eye, we see eye to eye,' he said and I nearly laughed. But you dare not laugh.

'Even after sixty years?'

'Especially after sixty years.'

He looked morosely at the bottles of wine.

'And there are personal experiences that you don't forget. Ever. I won't forget rolling up Rory O'Connor's mattress after they woke him before dawn and took him from our cell to be shot, without warning, without trial. As a reprisal for something someone else did. Shot, because the so-called Government wanted to make an example of a man from each province.' He looked at his glass. 'Some example they left us.'

129

He looked at Tess sternly and then, checking himself, at his glass again.

'Some example,' he said and puckered his lips towards the brim of the glass.

O'Connor's mattress. O'Higgins, his best man, was the last to sign his death warrant but in signing it, he was signing his own. The fateful cycles. And by the less exalted cycles of conversation the table-talk turns very much in my direction again. O'Higgins could be raised here. But it turns so closely it's too near for me to deal with and somehow, against our host's flesh-and-blood experience, my curiosity seems academic and shabby. Brazen, even.

The table was quiet and the sun went down with a last glint on the cutlery being crossed on plates.

'There was good and bad on both sides,' I ventured calmly and they looked at me.

'Yes, Shane,' said Corny, clutching his napkin. 'There is always good and bad on both sides – according to the history books. But what matters is what happened.'

'I can imagine,' I said and I could. 'All the old comrades you would have met tomorrow – I mean, if it was just your own ceremony and not "mixed" and you were going to it, would you be on talking terms with all of them?'

'I don't want to talk about that ceremony,' he said. 'I have strong views on this de-nationalisation of our past and the way this government has taken the liberty to go about it. But they are sticking to their guns on my statue so I'm grateful to them and I don't want to be drawn into controversy about it in public. The ceremony is wrong. It's wrong for all sides. It's the sort of pluralism that pleases no one and it is so insidiously corruptive of our national spirit. But to your question: yes, I believe I would get on with most of my old colleagues I would meet at a more ideal ceremony.'

'Do you harbour any bitterness?'

'Against those fellows?' he said, meaning the Redmondites. Or, as he saw them, the British Legion.

'No, against your old adversaries?'

'You work for peace now, don't you?' Tess needlessly butted in.

'For many years now.' He dabbed his lips with his napkin.

'Peace throughout the world,' I necessarily added.

'I try,' he said, smoothing his napkin upon the table. 'Whenever

130

people are oppressed and suffering I try to help. To undo things.'

'In Ireland too?'

'Of course,' he said. 'The situation in the Six Counties is intolerable.'

'For the Protestant people as well, of course. Would you try to help them?'

He gave me a cold eye as he coughed fiercely into his rumpled napkin.

'It is difficult,' he said, hoarse, with a tear in his eye, 'to help people who bring suffering upon themselves. Are we all finished?'

'Yes,' said Tess eagerly. 'That was lovely.'

'Very nice.'

'We must thank Mrs Williams,' said Wycherley, folding and refolding his napkin. 'The beef was excellent.'

'Ah, Mrs Williams!' In she burst, with remarkable, or I suppose, unremarkable timing. Probably primed like a Shelbourne hare.

'Well now.' Knuckles on hips, she surveyed our plates. 'You all seem to have done surprisingly well. Let's see . . . Mr Wycherley there, your bad turn, I see, has gone with your dinner. And Mr O'Shaughnessy' (whose plate was a colourful mess) 'oh, Mr O'Shaughnessy loves his spuds, so he does. And Vanessa, dear, you've certainly put down a healthy bit. Yes, and wine too. Let's hope it stays down. Young Tessa, the vegetarian, you've done justice to your name.' She stooped closer. 'One, two, three – only five peas left! Good girl.' I'm in trouble, here it comes. 'Mr Shane – look at him! Do you not like good Irish country vegetables?' I do, I do. 'Have you no appetite at all?' I ate all the bloody meat. 'Are you on hunger strike or what?' No, ma'am, that's more our host's game. 'Well, honestly, I don't know. Little wonder there's hardly a pick on you.'

'Betty, you wouldn't light a fire inside?' asked Corny, confirming what Joe had told us.

'Fire?' she repeated as if she'd been asked to kill someone.

'Please,' he pleaded. 'I know it's mid-July and exceptionally mild and all that but it'd be nice to sit around a fire after dinner. Besides, sun's going down and it might get a bit nippy later on.' He winked at Tess. 'For a man my age.'

'Oh, fair enough,' grunted Betty, now sounding exasperated with the old as well as the young.

'Oh, and you wouldn't bring us up two more bottles and put them by the fire?'

'Goodness,' she frowned, 'have you not had enough already?'

'Just two more will do nicely. A special occasion, Betty. These fine people are going to sculpt a statue of me. Think of it, it's very special. How many famous people could sit down in advance and discuss a statue of themselves with its creator? A public statue, mind; discount all those vulgar vanities the Victorians went in for, stuck up in public places to celebrate some chappy who paid for the railings. Or their modern equivalent: the busts of modern moguls erected in their gardens or in the swanky corridors of their endowed schools and God knows what sort of educational institutions I've seen in America. Expensive codology. How many of those follows have had their statues commissioned by their own state? Tell me that now. That's very special. To have your own statue put up by your own country, by popular consent, and to celebrate the very revolution that established your own country's path to independence. Tell me that now.' Corny was glowing. 'A real statue, I will modestly contend, is one erected for and on behalf of the people.'

Wycherley, the real statue-maker, just grinned.

'It's a wonderful honour for you,' grunted Betty, unfolding her arms, 'and, the Lord knows, you deserve it. It's the least the Government could do. There's little enough tribute paid these days to the men that freed this country.'

'And women,' Vanessa piped in.

'Them too.'

'It's not fashionable, you see,' said Corny, fondling a sarcastic lower lip. 'The revisionists have done their work. We're all deluded romantics now: extremists. Or – what was it – "retired terrorists". Out of touch, they say. I'll tell you who's out of touch. We're made game of as vainglorious poets or ignorant common gunmen. Out of touch, I ask you! It seems we couldn't see what they, wise modern historians, could see coming. Wonderful gift – to be retrospectively far-seeing.'

I liked this and I joined the hum of quiet amusement it engendered. But Corny was matter of fact. Brisk. When he got going on this topic, the years just fell away.

'We forced the British out at the point of a gun. That's the fact any historian must start with. Or finish with. It had to be done, and it was. The people celebrated. End of story. Well, not quite the

132

end.' He looked at his hands. 'But then, you see, that was nearly seventy years ago and now some feel we're at a distance enough to mock. Pessimists like to mock. They tell us that Pearse wore women's clothes, that Constance Markevicz kept a roomful of skulls. After mythologising Collins, now they're demythologising him, trying to find him with women. Or men. The latter the better. Oh, we're a great people sometimes for picking holes in things presented to us as sacred.'

'Like each other,' I ventured.

'Exactly,' grumbled Corny, 'pure character-assassination.' But I'd been thinking of the real thing.

'People are afraid to stand up for their past, they think of us as . . . as . . . as assassins,' he shouted and a spit was rummaging in that lower jaw.

'The attitude is, even if it had to be done, it was dirty work so let's not dwell on it. Too much like the present business. Well, God knows, they dwelled on it in big style twenty years ago. You couldn't stop them talking about the flying columns, Macroom, Kilmichael, the men of the West, the raids and rallies. They were putting up memorials with great gusto, and then suddenly' – Corny tried to click his feeble fingers for emphasis but only a powdery rub sounded – 'they stopped, or were told to stop singing all those songs. Roddy McCorley was dead, and to be forgotten. The powers-to-be told people to forget. Forget! In 1966, Kevin Barry was to be sung from the rooftops. Ten years later he was to be swung from the rooftops!'

Rather indelicate analogy. Is he trying to shock us?

'His song was banned from public broadcasting. Can you imagine it? And this time by an Irish government. Because, to be honest, I don't know which is worse – to destroy a man's life or to destroy his memory.'

I put it to him that many a man's life is destroyed just to preserve his memory.

Dodgy one, this. Corny, grim-lipped, was thinking about it.

'All the more reason, then, that they should be properly honoured,' he said, with the confidence of one who will be.

'Do you think John Redmond should be properly honoured? Putting out of your mind for the moment all the AVNS nonsense.'

'He has been properly honoured.'

'But he's been virtually forgotten about.'

'Exactly,' said Corny, 'but he got great press this week. That's for sure.'

'No, but I mean apart from all that ballyhoo, you hardly hear tell of him.'

'What do you want – parades down O'Connell Street? A Redmond summer school beyond in Waterford? Isn't he in the history books, in his proper place? Who is John Redmond? He was a minor figure at a major time, and he's become more minor with the passing of time.'

Something that could be said for all of us.

'He was of the same era,' I ventured.

'Not at all. By my time, he was finished.'

'But wasn't he the leader of the Irish Parliamentary Party when you were in Boland's Mills?'

'Maybe. But when he came out of those mills he wasn't going to be leader for too much longer. No sir, his days were numbered. Ours were beginning. A different era.'

Era, my eye, I felt like saying. You had to be executed first. Or your father had to be.

'In 1916 Redmond was tired, very tired. His party was spent. All constitutional means of gaining any meaningful independence had failed. By their democracy we couldn't even get Home Rule and, at that, Redmond's home rule was a sorry substitute for self-government. Westminster was a waste of time. As I see it, it was always a waste of time but some were prepared to take stepping stones to freedom. Parnell raised the spectre of native unrest at home to force concessions from the Government but by the time I was a teen that game was already futile, and wholly unsatisfactory to people who wanted freedom, pure and simple. They wanted repossession of their country, not the honourable right to collect taxes for the crown.'

Redmond faded from the table and, through another quiet lull, we all fell to finishing our apple tart. Silver spoons scraped plates made golden by the setting sun. Wonderful moment, I thought, as the suffused tawny glow coated milk jug, table top, salt-and-pepper cellars and – ah, my russet lovely! – the downy ripe cheek of sated Vanessa. She's thinking. They're all thinking. Do I look as wistful as that when I'm stilled by this talk of the past, and of great men beaten down? By the wine, the old dusty-bottled wine, laid low and up from the vault.

Betty came and and approached the table. Even she seemed

mindful of the moment, and after finishing our apple tart we were all encouraged to come and sit by the fire inside to have our coffees. Corny dropped his huge napkin and led the way.

'Make yourselves comfortable,' said Betty and she headed for the kitchen with a rub of her hands.

'Great. Thank you,' we said and we all settled into the front room again.

Corny sighed. 'She never brings up enough coal.' He looked at the fire. 'Used to briquettes, you see, and thinks coal is something that takes a long time to burn.'

'Coke maybe but not coal,' said Wycherley with a wink at me.

'I'll have to get some more,' said the old man, looking around grimly. 'I like to keep a fire down here after I've gone to bed. Keeps the warmth in the place.'

'I do the same myself,' said Wycherley. 'I have to.'

'One more bucket is all we need.' Corny looked towards the door.

'I'll go out for you,' I gallantly offered.

'Ah no.' Corny flapped his hand. 'That's not fair. You're a guest.'

'No, I'd be glad to,' I insisted. 'It'll be no problem. I could do with a stretch.'

'Sure he carries sacks of the stuff,' said Wycherley and the girls were laughing.

'Come on,' I said and I got to my feet unsteadily. 'Give me the bucket.'

'Are you sure?'

'Certain.'

I took the noisy bucket and he gave me a steady look. 'You'll get the key off Betty. I think she's in the kitchen.'

'Great,' I said and I blinked a silly smile at them all, slumped or curled in their various seats. 'I'll be back in a second.'

'Don't get lost.'

I went out the door and down the hall to the kitchen. My face looked flushed and bold in the hallway mirror. This is it.

'That's the lad,' crowed Betty, a growth of suds on her hands. 'That's the kind of guests we like. Put your hand in my pocket there and you'll get the key.'

With a patient smile and the stealth of a Grafton Street dipper,

I wiggled my fingers inside the kangaroo pouch of her kitchen smock.

'Which one is?'

'The big one, love. The big one.'

'This?' In among the jangling, I felt a heavy iron key on a single hoop.

'That's the fellow. Now, do you know where you've to go to? Out that door, down the steps and it's below the grass on your left. A small black door. It's dark inside the cellar so you'd want to take that flashlamp on the shelf there.'

'Great.'

I grabbed hold of the bucket and the flashlamp and went out into the night. What an evening. I looked at the clear white moon and I nearly chuckled going down the steps. Ah, the cool clean air; drink it in. And the fragrance of mown grass and the pine trees at the gable. When will we see them again? Jesus, soon, maybe. I'm in giddy form but I'm a trier. I need air. It's too high inside and I'll be glad to get out of it.

My feet bounced on the lawn, padded as if they were treading artificial grass or a series of plastic doormats. It's this crew-cut they give the grass, trimmed around the moat to take the imprints of intruders. Hee, hee. I went down the four steps and there was the black cellar door. Deep breath. I put the big key in its big hole and turned and the door opened inwards with – what else – a creak. Cool darkness and the smell of must and old furniture and coal. I switched on the flashlamp and caught bits of benches, suitcases and the curved red brickwork of the ceiling, leaking mortar like cake icing.

The wooden coal box was at the bottom of the cellar. I went in quickly and shovelled the bucket full. What else is in here? Jesus, don't ask. I wasn't going to look around. No way. I had one object in mind and it wasn't in here. Not yet. I pulled up the full bucket and crunched my way out. The door locked, I went up the steps and headed back for the kitchen.

'Good man yourself,' shouted Betty, chucking scraps of our dinner from one plate to another. Her dog Bingo's breakfast, lunch and tea.

'Not a bother,' I huffed and I gave her a broad wink. It was a big kitchen. Pots and pans and jars of fruit. The mother's legacy, the Movement's takings. Crates of potatoes stood by the door, as pink as an Irishman in Greece.

'That's great. You're very good,' said the relaxed Corny as I came into the room and they all agreed with him. 'Just chuck some of it on while you're standing.'

Buoyed up by my trip outside I flung the bucket rather vigorously and half the can went in to smother the thing.

'Ooops . . . ooops,' said Corny. 'That's quite enough.'

'Sorry,' I said and I put the bucket down with a clatter. 'I'm a bit – loose.' I gave Vanessa a sly wink.

'I'll just wash my hands,' I said and I headed for the door.

Right. Now to put my reading into action. I headed up the stairs – creak, dunk, dunk; creak, dunk, dunk – kneed open the bathroom door, knocked the light switch on with the ball of my thumb. We wouldn't want to leave fingerprints, now would we? The door heeled shut; the first thing I grabbed was the fattest bar of soap, a thick pink block of Palmolive in the shell holder of the bath. That'll do the trick. I turned on the hot-water tap and let it run until it was close to scalding. Under the cold tap, with a separate bar of Pears (that old colonial dished out with the bibles of Queen Vic) I washed the coal from my hands. When the steam rose from the other stream I took the pink soap between my fingertip and probed it in under the hot water for a few minutes. It heated nicely. I drew it out, felt it. Getting soft but not soft enough. A few minutes more. I waited. This is the business. If this works I'll be made. My name will be in the books. I'll be a wizard. All will come together in a great set piece. I drew the soap out again and pressed it with my finger. Yes, it's soft. It's soft enough. I think. I pulled out the key, heated it under the tap and pressed it very hard into the soap. It was going in. Slowly, but it was going in. With one thumb on each end of the heated metal, I pressed as hard as I could until it was pushed right in, further in than the depth of its own breadth. Right in. That's it. Lovely. That's enough.

One hard knock of the soap bar on its clear side and the key loosened and fell out on the other, the way you'd knock a man on the neck for his dentures. I took the soap, dried it, wrapped it in a pink stretch of double-strength loo roll and placed it carefully in my pocket. Phew. I could feel the beads of sweat on my forehead. Under pressure, under pressure, your whole life after '16 was under pressure, Michael. How did you get through? You didn't.

When I washed my face and the key and dried both I was ready to go back downstairs. Make haste: taps off, door shut, light off and down the stairs of dignity. Dunk, dunk, creak. Dunk, dunk, creak. I exhaled heavily, slowly but heavily. It felt as if a whole

137

burden had been moved from my shoulder. Not removed, but moved. Wine's sobering off. The lads will love me for this. It can't be said I haven't tried. Tried at least. I gave myself a wink in the mirror. Damn it, I give everyone else a wink, I might as well give myself one.

Betty took the key with gratitude and, with what looked like a croppie's ankle bone in her hand, she told me that young people should make themselves useful around the house for otherwise they'd lose touch with – I'm losing touch with my host I told her with a raised finger; I'd better go in. But sprawled about the room, they were too busy listening to Corny's 'busy schedule' – he had just told them how early he rises, how late he sets – to notice my windy return.

'You've great energy, Mr O'Shaughnessy,' said Tessa, lying back and looking at him with awe.

'Ah, not at all,' he said with an impish grin. 'Not as much energy as I'd like to have – with all the things I have to do.'

'You never stop, do you?'

'Never say never,' he said with a chuckle. 'But . . . no, not if I can help it, I don't.'

'You've certainly been busy lately,' said Wycherley.

'I wish I didn't have to be,' he said with a wry lift of the chin towards the fire. 'Have to be. Vigilance . . . you have to be . . . have to be vigilant.'

He looked at the fire and so did they but I couldn't take my eyes off him. He's tired now, but how tired is he? How long more will he go on, is the question? But Bob was leaving nothing to chance and made rumblings that we should be going.

'Oh, no, you don't have to,' protested Corny, but he didn't protest too much. He was clearly getting tired and Wycherley insisted.

'OK,' declared Corny, and he made to put his shaky hands on his knees. 'Well, thank you so much for coming.'

'Not at all,' protested Wycherley. 'It was our pleasure and it was a great honour for you to have us.'

'It was wonderful,' said Tess.

'Thank you for the toast, Shane,' he said and his thin lips pursed a generous smile.

'God, well, it was a true honour,' I told him. 'I never thought I'd get the chance to do that. I really didn't. That was my great honour of the evening, and for it I am truly grateful. It's been a wonderful evening, Mr O'Shaughnessy. I'll have stories to tell my kids if they ever come home from Birmingham.'

He nodded his head contentedly. 'It's nice to know that there are young people like yourself who are still very interested in the period.'

'Oh, I am,' I assured him.

'It was a very important time. It was what created our state and formed the nation. More than that, it created us and made us what we are.'

Cart before the horse. 'Oh, I know that.'

'I know you do,' he whispered and he smiled softly. 'And your defence of Collins in front of that movie committee shows that you have the courage of your interest.'

'Thank you,' I replied and the girls smiled proudly at me: there you are. 'Well, let me tell you,' I said, 'that tonight has fired my interest. I had read all the stories but it's another experience altogether to hear them, my goodness, from the lips of one of the chief participants.'

'You can never hear all the stories,' he said sagely.

'Oh, I'm sure,' I stuttered and I saw the fire in his shoe.

The rest of them collected their hands and tidied their hair.

'Well, I hope I might see you all again in here,' he said and when he rose from his chairs the two girls grabbed an arm each to steady him.

'That would be very nice. Thank you very much,' said Wycherley, stretching his back. 'And I hope we'll see you down in the studio early in the week.'

'Yes . . . yes, why not,' agreed Corny, his trout-spotted fingers lying atop Tessa's.

'I'll be in touch to make arrangements,' Wycherley told him.

We all went out to the hall. I brought up the rear. If I didn't have a bar of soap in my pocket I'd be half tempted to slip one of these wine bottles going to waste by the fire. I saluted the father instead and watched Vanessa smooth the back of her skirt.

Out in the hall they were discussing how late it was.

'Yes, but it's Saturday night,' said Tess.

'Saturday night's all right for fighting,' added Vanessa with her eyebrows arched. I see, thought me. Bit of the devil still then, are we?

'Tessa, thank you,' said Corny and he took her aside for a cuddle. Well, for a chat but it looked more like a cuddle to me.

'We're going back into town, Vanessa,' I said, making my own move. 'Do you want to come with us?'

'No . . . eh . . . I'll stay here.'

'We might even go for a late drink, if you'd fancy that.'

'Eh, no, I'll, eh . . . I'll stay here. There's a spare room . . . and . . .' Her Pre-Raphaelite face fell a little – was that a blush or the colour of the wine and the fire? 'You know – it'd be no problem.'

'I'm heading towards the Pink Elephant myself if you'd fancy a drink or a dance even.'

'I think the girl wants to stay here,' said Bob with firmness.

'Oh, eh, right. Of course. Relax there, Bob,' I hissed through gritted teeth. 'The Arts Club won't close till three.'

'There's your coat, Mr Wycherley,' said Vanessa, as if hastening us on our way.

'Have we got everything?'

Vanessa was on her knees again opening the door, a gorgeous little figure tugging at the lock. This time it wasn't a brown thigh her hem was riding but my very heart.

I shook hands with O'Shaughnessy. He gripped me so firmly that the flesh on his hand did a forty-degree turn.

'Lovely. It really was.'

Wycherley's hand was shook and Tess was kissed warmly. Again.

'Great to have you.'

Vanessa pulled the door open and came back to do the farewells. With clumsy determination I converted her light peck to a prolonged clutch and buried my nose and mouth in the underside of that gold-grain cloud of tendrils. Was that her breath on my neck? It was. She must be gasping for air.

'I hope I might see you again,' I whispered when I let her go.

'I hope so too,' she said and she stood back and swallowed hard. Rosy apple cheeks and Cranach eyes. Yes she is: she's my type.

'Be careful,' said Vanessa as we went down the steps. I looked back and she looked stunning, clutching her two-tone dress in the night air, the green going a weird, vertiginous shimmer in the moonlight and her Rossetti hair burning at the edges from the light of the door.

'Watch out for Redmondites,' she said with a shameful giggle.

Wycherley smiled and looked at Corny.

'I'm sure everything will be resolved.'

'I'm sure it will,' said Corny.

140

His figure was standing in the doorway, a small and angular being against the yellow light of the hall. A boy in his grandad's suit.

'Good-night, now.'

'Good-night.'

We opened the doors of the taxi. A small argument developed because Tess wanted to walk around the corner to her friends, the Kaminskis, rather than take a lift from us. The Kaminskis were very close by, on Bird Avenue, about a hundred yards down from Mellowes' place, Loyola, but it was ludicrous for her to be walking this part of the neighbourhood at this time of the night. Moonlight and the boys are probably beyond the far wall there, taking notes. She accepted our anguished concern and we dropped her off.

'Thanks for a fantastic evening,' she told Bob and she leaned back to kiss the two of us goodbye. The door shut. Margaret Kaminski's dogs ran out to meet her, half grumpy, half joyous. I know how they felt.

'We're going to the Arts Club on Fitzwilliam Street,' Wycherley told the taxi man. 'And then to the – what was it – the Pink Elephant, I believe.'

The taxi man nodded and spun the steering wheel.

'Well, I think that went very well,' said Wycherley and he nudged me and smiled.

'That went very well,' I said but with an even more secret smile.

'Do you think he'll come then?'

'He'll come.'

Wycherley asked the taxi man if he'd heard anything on the news about the O'Shaughnessy statue, or tomorrow's ceremony or the Proclamation. Without even apologising, the taxi man pointed to his battered tape deck and said he wasn't listening to the radio. He was playing tapes. Self-improvement tapes. That junk the Americans produce to improve your 'self-assertiveness' and teach you how to use conglomerate boardroom techniques on your dogs and children. You're not going to believe this but the one he had in at the moment was 'Leadership Secrets of Genghis Khan'. I laughed quietly and Wycherley laughed and I looked in the mirror to make sure he didn't see us. Dangling from the mirror was one of those Magic Tree air fresheners and a plastic skeleton that glowed in the dark.

'He was tricky, all the same,' said Wycherley when his giggles subsided.

'He was very tricky,' I agreed.

Chapter 6

A Curious Proposal

Outside the doors of the Pink Elephant there was the customary huddle of unfortunates seeking to gain entry and as I shouldered my way through I heard, with some sympathy, their pleading and cajoling. Very respectable gathering they were too, but in the pitiless eye of the tuxedoed doorman inside they might as well have been starving spalpeens outside a yeoman's soup kitchen. No-hopers. You have to drink here almost every night. Then, no matter what you look like – shaven, scarred or legless – once they have your face you are gladly welcomed in to avail of their services and do further damage to yourself. I got to the front and gave Robbie the nod through the glass panel. The door clanked open.

'Sound, man, Shane. In you come.'

'Thanks, Robbie.'

'Hey, Shane!' cried a voice in the crush. 'Can you get me in?'

But sadly the door shut behind me and that was the end of my 'friend's' imploring cry.

'Busy tonight, Robbie?'

'Busy enough. Warm weather brings out the flies.'

'Did Oisín O'Farrachain come in?'

'He's down below. Could be upstairs but – '

'Thanks. I'll try below.'

Down the wide spiral staircase I went, heading for the noisy din of the underground bar and dance floor, while above my head, going up, I caught sight of two long pairs of sleek-stockinged legs, moving with languorous unison on high-spiked heels. I stopped to watch them step around and over me, and such was my charged condition, I could have sworn, as I saw their gartered stocking tops recede into the flicker-lit darkness, that I heard a nylon swishing accompany the soft rubbing of warm white thighs just inside the hem of their leather skirts. Oh me, alas! Warm weather brings out the flies all right. And the luscious beasts. And here's one big bluebottle who wouldn't mind the uncomplicated company of such splendidly limbed creatures for an hour or six. Aroused and disgruntled I carried on down the steps. Standing by the door into the dance floor I found Maeliosa O'Falcarra nursing a pint over the tropical-fish tank with its pink, plastic-looking real fish. He looked like a Killybegs trawler hand with battered tweed jacket, pirate's neckscarf and a Holofernes curtain of golden rat-tails tossed back as a greeting.

'I'm getting some air,' he muttered.

'Bad in there?'

'Stuffed.'

'Gandhi's funeral, eh? Is Oisin in there?'

'At the bar, I think. He's been looking for you.'

'I'll brave it so. See you in a while.'

'Good luck.' A limp hand flapped and fell and he went back to his pint. I began pushing through the crowd and immediately met a channel of people coming the other way.

'How's Shane?' barked a rough voice behind me. It was Rod the Jeep, one of the buccaneers, in a black vest and bulging muscles.

'Good man, you're still on the streets. Hopefully now those crackpots will stick to history and leave you alone. How did it feel being followed? The old man has to go everywhere with two guards when he's home, even to the beach. Oops, watch me glass! Listen, Shane, see you later.'

'See you later, Rod.' Rod's father was a judge.

At the counter I caught sight of Lord Fertilizer and the Earl of Charleville drinking champagne. They raised the bottle when they saw me. Good to know people were behind me.

Right behind me at the moment. A handy hazard, as I discovered with the next person I was about to be channelled into. Spunky Swords, I owed him £20 for a ball ticket. It was long, long overdue. The ball had been at Christmas.

'Listen, Shane,' he began shouting from a few feet away, obviously anticipating that by the time he finished we'd be behind each other. 'Hate to mention it but, you know, if you

143

could get us that money. It'd be for the Penny Dinners, as you know. All for charity. Be much obliged.'

'Would you believe I actually have it at home. How can I get it to you?' I rarely see the man.

'Send it by post,' he shouted, already half past me.

'Cheque or money order?'

'Cheque, cheque!' he grimaced painfully. Someone was standing on his foot. I let him move on.

More heads came between us and then I shouted, 'But where to?'

He shouted something, but, what a pity, I just couldn't catch the address.

Then I heard a shout. Oisin and Mellowes were at the other end of the horse-shoe bar, grinning and raising their black glasses. Pleased as punch. They must be sure of my success. So was I. I could feel it in my pocket and, like a coin-rich confirmation boy, I just had to dip my hand in my pocket and feel again, upon explorative fingertips, the waxy texture of my treasure, my retirement pink soap bar, wrapped in its protective shroud of double-strength loo roll.

'Our man on a mission returns!' hailed a perspiring and excited Oisin, as they drew me in beside them.

'Gentlemen, gentlemen, I've got something good to show you.'

'As good as what they've got, I hope,' laughed Oisin. 'How does it feel being worth less than the birth certificate of the nation?'

'Eh?'

'Or the death warrant of those who stand in its way?' said Mellowes.

'Don't be cryptic, Sean. It's not his death warrant any more,' he said, patting me on the back. I hadn't a clue what he was talking about. 'That bit of paper has saved you, Shane. Cease-fire or not. Better they should hold that lifeless document to ransom against the statue than hold your lively self.'

'What?'

'He hasn't heard, Sean.'

'He hasn't heard.'

'Jesus, Shane. Have you come straight from O'Shaughnessy's house?'

'As straight as a dodgy taxi ride, yes.'

They looked at each other again.

'That means Corny mustn't know.'

'Know what?'

'The 1916 Proclamation was stolen!'

'Stolen? From where?'

'From the Civic Museum in South William Street. It happened this afternoon.'

'We thought you would have heard. Jesus, is no one telling O'Shaughnessy what's happening because of his bleeding statue?'

'I heard nothing.'

'They discovered it gone this evening. A chap went upstairs, got his mate to absorb the attendants in the next room and unscrewed the Proclamation in its glass case off the wall. They carried it out in one of these black zip-up portfolio cases. Later they phoned RTE and said that if Corny goes up, it goes up – in smoke. Isn't that a brilliant stunt?'

'Remarkable,' I said and it was.

'And it gets you off the hook,' said Mellowes, handing me a pint.

'Here, drink back and celebrate.'

'I'm off the hook anyway,' I said, clinking glasses. 'There's a cease-fire on. Or at least there was – does this not break their agreement?'

'They claim it doesn't,' explained Oisin. 'In the statement reported on RTE, Captain Moonlight, that dubious non-person, stated that "the remove", as he put it, did not constitute a breaking of the cease-fire "agreement" as it involved no injury nor threat of injury to life and limb – they being men of peace and all that – but merely involved the "borrowing" of the Proclamation for the purposes of "historical rectification". Confident lot, aren't they?'

'Certainly are. How is the Government taking it?'

'There's been no comment,' said Mellowes. 'Sure the news only came through at about ten o'clock. The attendants apparently locked up without noticing the Proclamation gone, which says something for our attendants. Or for our Proclamation. The former, I hope. Oh, I bet they'd notice if a fireman's helmet or a Lord Mayor's foot-scraper was missing. What's the Proclamation doing in a civic museum anyway? In among all that municipal crap: tobacco signs, tram tickets and all the other market-stall *memorabilia* of the now demolished city.'

'Maybe because the only ones who heeded the Proclamation's call to arms were in the city.'

'Don't get dirty. We were never forewarned.'

'Sorry, gents – can I intrude with the present day here and ask a few questions? The AVNS rang RTE, correct?'

'OK, listen,' said Oisin. 'They rang RTE and gave a full report. "Two-man operation," they said. One distracts the somnambulant attendant in so-called charge, the other turns a few screws and off they trot with Pearse and Co.'s handiwork in their portfolio. Obviously upset that their own handiwork had gone unnoticed, especially given their smart timing in aiming for a tea-time ballyhoo on the eve of the controversial commemoration ceremony, just in time for the six o'clock news and a weekend's embarrassment for the Government, they decide to embarrass as well the lowly attendants who failed to raise the alarm and the resultant publicity, by releasing the full details of the operation. I mean, you would be annoyed if you stole the nation's most precious document – its birth cert., as Oisin calls it – and nobody noticed until Monday afternoon, if even then. Mind you, given the views of these neo-Redmondites they should be heartened by this less than vigilant concern for the supposedly sacrosant Scroll of Revolutionary Republicanism. Indeed, they have illustrated a point that contradicts their claims about our unbalanced history. I fear that the black space they left on that wall is all too commensurate with a great blank space in the national memory and that it is only the historical likes of you and me, gentlemen, who care for such things any more.'

I looked at the froth in my glass and thought sadly of O'Shaughnessy. He's asleep now. Oisin is right – who cares for such things now? Who cares for O'Shaughnessy's statue, or for his memory, or for his welfare? Who cares for his fireside stories, as worn and shiny as old coins that they might be? Apart from myself, and Mellowes, and Oisin maybe, and people like us.

'So how was O'Shaughnessy?'

'Great. I've stories to tell.'

'Yeah, well start telling,' said Mellowes. 'Any luck on the one we're here to hear? We haven't asked you directly yet because we're assuming there has been.'

'He has a wine cellar – did you know that?'

'He has a coal cellar too. Come on, Shane, cut the crap. Did you do the business or not?'

'What business?' I enquired bashfully. Keep him on tenterhooks.

'You didn't. I knew it,' he said but he didn't. 'I knew you couldn't pull it off.'

'I had a long, liquid-enhanced conversation with him about many strange and colourful matters of his and our history,' I ponderously began.

'He didn't. I'm telling you.'

'But each time I gingerly approached the topic of O'Higgins, I was shot down as brusquely as the subject of the very story I was trying to raise.'

Oisin smiled. Mellowes didn't.

'He got most upset by the mention of O'Higgins and, particularly, the subject of O'Higgins's assassination.'

'His murder, you mean.'

'Semantics, Sean. One man's meat is another man's murder, as the vegetarians say. By the way, I learned tonight that O'Shaughnessy is a vegetarian. Interesting, isn't it? In fact, I learned quite a few interesting facts tonight about the man.'

'But not the most interesting of all,' grumbled Sean.

'Oh, I wouldn't say that,' I nonchalantly replied. I was enjoying myself.

'Come on, follow me,' I told them. 'Smack, watch these pints, will you?'

The barman nodded.

'Where are we off to?'

'The bathroom.'

'The bathroom?'

I didn't answer but merely led them across the floor to the mercifully near black door in the corner. Pausing to allow a gaggle of respruced girleens to pass out before us, we stepped into a Kafkaesque choice of two more doors. No signs here. Familiarity was expected. The right door led to the gents', certain of whom were blithely peeing on their shoes and drying their unwashed hands under cinder-scented air blasters when we entered. After a number of seconds, we adjusted our eyes to the savage brightness of the mirror-multiplied chamber, and without further ado – the boys were getting restless – I dug my hand into my pocket, pulled out my tissue-wrapped precious pink baby, and with a slow sly grin, placed him gently upon the dry formica.

'It's a bar of soap,' said Mellowes after a blank pause.

I indicated with a mute nod of the head that he was correct but, with my hand, invited him to step forward and examine.

147

Very gingerly he did so and the disdainful claw of his thumb and forefinger peeled back the straggly tissue-covering.

'It's a bar of soap with a hole in it.'

'Ah, but what sort of a hole? Pick it up and examine it.'

He looked at me shrewdly and then, disdainfully, with a sort of sceptical effeminacy, he picked up the disrobed bar of O'Shaughnessy-pink soap as if it were in danger of exploding.

'It's – ' He looked up excitedly. 'It's the shape of the key. Is this – ?'

'It is,' I calmly confirmed. 'The key to the coal bunker.'

'Show us.' Oisin lunged forward.

'Merciful hour!' exclaimed Mellowes, peering aghast at the key-reliefed soap.

'Show us!'

They both examined the now tenderly held soap, turning it and even holding it up to the light.

'Shane, how did you do this?'

'He sent me out to get some coal,' I modestly began. 'I must have made an impression because out of his own pocket he trusted me with the key. So, with my customary quick thinking, I snatched a remembered bar of soap, and made another impression, only this one's more practical. This one I can make a cast from.'

'But . . . but won't the metal melt it?'

'Not at all,' I laughed. 'You don't understand. I'll use wax and plaster.'

'Brilliant.'

'The way Collins did,' I slipped in.

'Collins?' They both looked up.

'That's right!' cried Mellowes, remembering. 'His Lincoln trick to spring the long fellow out of jail. Why did I not – which makes your wizardry all the more brilliant. Shane!' He was becoming ecstatic. 'This is actually fantastic. You are truly miming history. You are acting out the methods of your mentor – to find out . . . who killed his protégé. It's a perfect story!'

'He's a genius.'

'Shane, you're a bloody genius!'

'You've done it. You've done it perfectly. It couldn't be any more perfect. We're on our way!'

'We're on our way!' cried Oisin. 'We're on our way. By Christ, we're on our way.'

With which they suddenly grabbed an arm of mine each and

proceeded to wheel me around in a sort of distracted reel, gleefully taking up one of Oisin's instantly inspired moronic refrains:

We have the key to Corny's shed,
We have the key to Corny's shed.

Around and around we danced on the wet tiles and, as I spun, to and fro, squashed between the humming beats of my fellow invincibles, and listening to their lusty chanting, I thought for a moment: What would Corny think if he saw me now? I mean, what would the old boy think if he walked in; what would he think if he knew that less than half an hour after leaving his effusive hospitality, his prize guest, his querulous young admirer, was now in the underground bathroom of a city night club making the man he was allowed close to the subject of a macabre dance ritual? Poor fellow, after all he did for us tonight. Would he excuse such youthful exuberance on the grounds that he and the Apostles, in their day, occasionally trotted around the tiles of Vaughan's Hotel with the name of the next police inspector on their lips? But before I could wonder any further, the dance was broken up as Mellowes, shouting 'Woah!', sprang forward and snatched a bar of soap (our bar of soap!) out of the hands of a man about to wash.

'What the fu – ?' stuttered the offended washer. It was a close one. The faucet was running and two or three slippery rubs of those muscular hands would have ruined everything. As it was, it looked like they were going to ruin Mellowes, who duly got the message and stepped back, profusely explaining that the soap was our own, that we had left it there by accident, that (look, look) hadn't he seen us dancing (No answer. 'The dancing's outside,' said another voice behind us), that (look, look) it had the relief of a key in it. A key we wanted – wink, wink.

We were lucky that the gentleman had a marked criminal aspect about him (I thought I spotted a coal-blue borstal spot below his left eye) for not only did he look, comprehend and let his fists unclench, but after a few 'You're bleeding lucky's he took the soap to peruse and admire its fragile key-shaped cavity, without even bothering to ask who was its unlucky owner and what were they about to lose. We thanked him for his co-operation, retrieved our imperilled soap bar and beat a hasty retreat.

'You risked your life in there,' I told a clearly shaken Mellowes as we pushed each other through the throng.

149

'I had to. You risked enough to get the thing in the first place. Let's not talk about it. Let's get a drink.'

'Yes, let's. How's our skirmishing funds, Oisin?'

'Not enough for the celebration required by tonight's events. A close shave deserves a stiff drink; a Lincoln imitation deserves two.'

'I've to take it easy. I've to cast this thing tomorrow.'

'Let's all take it easy,' said Mellowes. 'This excitement is wearing me down.'

Having said which, we still had no hesitation in ordering a round of double tequila slammers as soon as we reached the bar. We had to celebrate. Aided by the spirit of Collins and the nerve and cunning of McArdle, we had acquired against all odds the ghost of the key to Corny's coal cellar. We had, with the cajolery of the same, retrieved, against dodgier odds, the endangered same from the grasp of an angry ex-borstal boy. Yes, all was well. The soap was safe, Mellowes was safe and I was safer than ever with the AVNS concentrating on the harassment of manuscripts, instead of people, to further their ends. But, best of all, I had accompanied my master to the table of O'Shaughnessy and, in between bolstering my nerve by behaving with a recklessness that bordered on the tactical, I had seen my master come away from that table with the commitment from O'Shaughnessy that he had always wanted. Yes, it was a high moment. It had been a great night and there would be many more. Bump! Slap and fizzzle! Feel the bubbles rising through your system. Tequila slammers – you can't beat them. Aerated like a chocolate bar was what the man said, and all the other things he said were about to be retold. For all that was on my mind now, in my happy relaxed state, was to gather the ears of my invincibles around me and get stuck into telling them what 'the man himself' was like. What did he wear, say, eat, do? How did he, in both senses, look?

But I took my time. Scrupulous narrator that I am, I was not going to blurt out all the best bits in an excited gush. I had to set the scene. So – while Oisin ordered three more pints – I had the Roebuck table reset, the spuds recooked and Corny himself had to go off stage and silently 'burst' in again in that dramatic first appearance he made before us in the living-room. Betty, God love her, was summoned up and given a swagger more listless than she perhaps deserved. Vanessa, because she disinclined my invitation to come into town, was not quite as pretty as she looked when first encountered. I felt I was entitled to a little indulgence in my new-found role of fireside confidant to the fearless fighter so I wanted to establish precisely the ambience and avuncular atmosphere in which the two of us – I, young, informed; he, needing no introduction – hit it off so warmly on our first meeting. But no sooner had I got into the juicy part of the story but who comes looming in our direction but that inveterate night-club animal and sometime historian, Finbar Harrington.

'Shit,' whispered Mellowes.

'Say nothing.'

'Well, well, well,' he said, holding safely aloft a smouldering half-corona between his effeminately distended fingers. 'If things don't get more and more extraordinary each time I see you. Yesterday, a cease-fire. Today, the Proclamation – what will it be next?'

I made a suggestion but he couldn't hear it, and, with a general flicking of the cigar, he indicated that we might step out into the lobby where there was a lot less noise. I readily agreed and encouraged the boys to take their drinks. I had things to say to this guy.

'So what were you saying?' he asked, putting his drink up on the fish tank where Maeliosa's had been.

'You asked what would it be next,' I repeated. 'And I said I didn't know; what had your friends thought of.'

'My friends?' His head turned around with popped eyes. 'Come, come, McArdle. Just because I predicted the aims and motives of this movement with a degree of accuracy.'

'Predicted, my eye!' I said and the boys flinched. 'You could have written that cease-fire statement. In fact you probably did write it when you went home from Risk that night, having given me a bellyful of it as a rehearsal. Discussing 'the undervalued legacy of men like Redmond' as if the same idea wasn't going to pop up the next day as the central tenet of this nutty campaign – what do you take me for?'

'A friend to begin with so let's not be extravagant in our accusations. Or you might find yourself following your unfortunate employer into the slander courts.'

'Ah, would you ever f – '

'Now, Shane. Please.' His hand went up. 'Let's be calm and reasonable. We're all sane and lucid men here. I admit that I know some of the people close to, even connected with, the AVNS, as they style themselves. This is a small city. That is inevitable. I will also readily acknowledge that there is an element of coincidence between their historical sympathies and mine.'

'Oh, so you know who was writing poisonous letters to me, threatening to destroy my life and livelihood if I didn't ask my about-to-be-ex-boss for a P45 but friend that you are, you decided not to mention it to me. Even though you gladly discussed the whole business with me, and what a terrible trauma it must be to go around with a target on your back because some cunt doesn't like the Government's choice in statues. Good man, Finbar, I knew I could rely on you.'

'You're being quite unfair. Did I not pass on, through Sean here, some important information about what those people were about? Probably the only information you got on them? Did I not make sure to tell you that you were safe? That the AVNS "meant business" with the Government but didn't want to harm any individuals. I told you all these things, Shane, even though they were given to me in confidence at the law library.'

'Riddles!' I said. 'You passed on riddles. Why didn't you just come clean instead of spouting stupid riddles? As a civilian, you were obliged to go to the police. As a friend, so-called, you could have come and told me about why my life was in danger and from who.'

'I came and told you that your life was in danger, didn't I?'

'You gave me riddles, Finbar! Bloody hearts in Westminster and in Waterford. You could have at least told me that Redmond was involved. But you didn't. You had these jokey riddles passed on, as if it was all a big game and you were the bearded cipher running to and fro.'

'I ran nowhere, Mr McArdle. You're being rude and derogatory. And quite ungrateful. Believe me, I've saved you a lot more trouble than you'd imagine.'

'Oh, like, "Lads, don't petrol-bomb your man, McArdle's, flat – he's a nice old set of the Parnellism and Crime series, bound in pigskin, that I'd like to borrow some time."'

The boys snorted.

'You're not being at all funny.'

'No, this isn't really a laughing matter, is it? What if I told you I was going to save you from a bit of trouble.'

'Oh?'

'Well, Detective Sergeant Hurley might be interested to know that a member of the law library – a breed he hates more than Provies and diplomats – was withholding information on the AVNS case. Oh, that's right, Garda Hurley; he says he has what Cohn in *The Great Gatsby* calls 'connections'. That a fact, says the well-read Hurley. And then you'd be well read, me bucko. It's OK to have as clients people who make death threats and steal historical documents but as friends, Finbar? What would the Bar Council say? A puff of smoke and the Prince of Advocacy becomes a punctured toad – ah, Finbar.'

'You're going for blood, McArdle. You'd want to be very careful.'

'I've been very careful all week, Finbar. And I'm getting mighty tired of it.'

'Well, keep your guard up, Shane, because if the police are dragged into this in a way different to the context in which they're already involved, life could get very nasty. Do we understand each other?'

'Are you threatening me?'

'Who's threatening who? I think we've had enough threatening in this episode. Let's, you and I, rational we that we are, co-operate and understand each other on this matter. I am close enough to others close enough to the AVNS to be of some assistance to you in your predicament.'

'A bit late for that. There's a cease-fire on.'

'Cease-fires don't last for ever, Shane. And cease-fires are times for talking. For making contact, you could say. Establishing lines of communication and all that.'

'What are you getting at?'

He sucked hard and quickly.

'Why don't you come and meet somebody not unconnected with our temporary adversaries.'

'And get measured for my own funeral? Come off it – it'd be like Collins meeting Crozier for a stroll in the Phoenix.'

'Collins went to London. Precisely because there was a cease-fire on.'

'Yeah, and came home with his death warrant. Who is this somebody and why should I meet him?'

'He's a harmless old man associated with the AVNS – '

'Everybody seems to be "associated". Why don't we meet the real thing? Captain Moonlight, or his cronies.'

'Because Captain Moonlight is not a real thing, boys. He's an

153

idea. I'm surprised none of you bright scholars got this, but then given your obsession with just a couple of years you can't be expected to remember the basics of the last century or the next one. Cast your minds back. 1882. Parnell said that, if the British imprisoned him, Captain Moonlight would take over. The mob. Better negotiation than the whiteboy's knife at the window. Wouldn't you agree?'

I looked at Mellowes and Oisin.

'Oh, so I'm to negotiate now?'

'Talk to this old man. You'll gain by it. He's perfectly safe and so are you. He just wants to discuss the statues.'

'Statue*s*?'

'The threatened one of O'Shaughnessy and the sought-for one of Redmond.'

'The other way around, you mean. Look, I'm not being a party to any deals. What mandate have – ?'

'No deal, just talk. They believe they can talk to you. They know you're a history man – that's why they sent you those poems and riddles, as you call them. They were testing you. They think that if they can explain their position to anyone they can explain it to you. You are the key man to whatever hopes of an arrangement or settlement there are. Through contact with you, this whole unseemly situation might be resolved. See yourself as an emissary.'

I did. It felt dubious but I must say I kind of liked the idea.

'What do you think, lads?'

'Up to yourself,' said Mellowes. Oisin agreed.

'The police would freak,' I told them.

'The police wouldn't know. The police are not to know. No one is to know beyond you three, me and them. Don't tell Wycherley, don't tell Hurley.'

'Which constitutes a bad half of town already. Where am I to meet this man and when?'

'Tomorrow afternoon.'

'I've a cat's funeral tomorrow afternoon.'

'You've a what?' Eyes popped.

'A cat's funeral. And then I've got to go to Clonskeagh.'

'You're not going up to . . .?'

'No. I'm going to the house of Mellowes here' – I winked – 'for a game of chess.'

'Listen, are you serious about this, or what?'

'I'm serious. I've some casting to do tomorrow morning but then I can meet this man afterwards, around lunchtime. The cat can wait. It's worth missing a cat's funeral if you've the chance to postpone your own.'

The boys snorted again.

'Where can I meet this man and when?'

'At twelve-thirty in the lobby of the Belvedere Hotel on the corner of North Great Georges Street. Do you know the place – it has a blue plaque to John Dillon on the outside wall. Don't snicker – these people are nothing if not consistent. Pity the same can't be said for others.'

'Hold on, North Great Georges Street – that's right beside Parnell Square. The ceremony will be going on.'

'These people are also not afraid to dice with danger. They don't scare easily, you should be warned.'

'Neither does the Government so if they've any stunts planned – '

'Oh, that's rubbish. I don't know where that started from – well, I do, actually. But for goodness sake, this ceremony is a vast improvement as far as the AVNS are concerned. Unfortunately, it's not vast enough and they distrust it precisely because they see it as a way that the Government can fob off their demands for real historical recognition. They want a statute, not a couple of tunes.'

'Don't we all. Listen, who's the statue I'm meeting?'

'The gentleman you're meeting is called Mr Samuelson. You can't miss him. He'll be wearing a grey trilby, a watch-chain, and he should have a tipped cane at his side.'

'To help him make his point, or to help him make his way?' I said and the boys laughed. 'Come here, how will this Mr Samuelson know who I am? I could send along a smack-happy bum boy from Burgh Quay in my stead and then tip off the guards and have them both arrested. Sunday afternoon in a hotel lobby – they'd be as near as caught in the raw.'

'That would be your style all right, McArdle. And such is our history. *Et tu*, Healy. The man with the dirtiest sheets does the informing. But don't worry, this Mr Samuelson will recognise you. It seems he's seen you before.'

'Oh, where?'

'No idea. Be nice to him, and I'm sure he'll be nice to you. You should have no problems. I hear you're a great hand at chatting up the old men on your days off. So long, gentlemen.' He curtsied, tipped his ash, and with head and cigar held high, he stepped inside and slipped back into the throng, leaving us to the disentangling remains of his blue cigar smoke.

'Well, that was something.'

'The bastard! He knows I met O'Shaughnessy.'

'So what?'

'"On your days off", the cunt said. He was probably snooping around the garden, rustling in the bushes. I thought I heard a toad belch that time I went out for coal.'

'Fanciful. You're getting paranoid, Shane. Forget it. You handled him very well.'

'Yes, very,' agreed Oisin. 'You fairly stuck it to the cunt. He knows now we have our sights on him. Him and his little sidelong games.'

'Do you think I should go and meet this guy?'

'Definitely,' said Mellowes. 'It's worth a look. For God's sake, you're finally going to see one of the faces behind the letters.'

And perhaps behind bars, I thought.

'And unintimidating faces they sound too, Shane,' said Oisin. 'It'd put your mind at ease to see the old codgers for what they are.'

'Exactly!'

'Hold on,' I said. 'These aren't the Salvation Army we're talking about. Returned newspapers, menacing letters. They kidnapped the Proclamation today. Why not the more valuable me tomorrow?'

'A debatable point,' acknowledged Mellowes. 'But you're going there to debate. There's a cease-fire on. He's right about that. It's time to talk. You're the one they picked, Shane. And Jesus, unlucky them, because the way you talk, you silver-tongued rat, you'll have them agreeing to an armistice within a half-hour.'

They both laughed and I smiled broadly. I smiled very broadly because what they were suggesting was almost precisely what I had in mind. Almost, but not quite.

'What do you think?'

'Mmm.'

'Go on, man. You pulled it off tonight, you can pull it off tomorrow.'

'Jesus, you got around Corny, you can get around some old codger in a grey trilby and a Dun Laoghaire-pier stick.'

'Go on up there, sure, we'd keep watch outside.'

'I think I'll go,' I declared with a firm smile. 'I think I'll give it a try.'

It was a long shot but it was worth a try.

'Good man, yourself!' said Oisin, clapping me on the back. 'Come on, back to the bar. Celebrations are in order. We've got the key, they've got the Proclamation. But do you know what?'

'What?'

'We've got youth and they've got age.'

'We've got Shane on our side,' said Mellowes, his hand on my shoulder.

'Make them make way there, Sean, so we can get back inside to toast this guy.'

We pushed our way back to the bar but I thought, like Collins when the invitation from Lloyd George came through, that gratifying as the congratulations were, the celebrations were somewhat premature. The hard part was about the begin.

Miraculously I hadn't a head on me when I came to the next morning. The bloody-coloured stuff was usually fierce for giving you the head of a three-days-nailed Christ on a summer's morning after but the mind-concentrating excitement of the previous night's developments and the consequent burning knowledge that I just had to get up and make that key, and then meet that man, and then make our glorious pilgrimage by stealth to Roebuck – all this – plus a keen desire to see what would happen at the commemoration ceremony – helped to keep the hangover I deserved at bay, and had me out of my straw-stuffed bed and on to my bony legs in minutes. Tough day ahead. Two tremendous stunts to pull off as a prelude to the ultimate stunt next week.

It felt early but I hadn't a clue what time it was. I went to the window to check. Four floors below me foreshortened gardaí were nonchalantly walking around the street, placing traffic cones and generally making protective arrangements for the ceremony in the Garden of Remembrance. Typical, I leave Harcourt Street to avoid being in the shadow of these Hurleyites and here they are, milling around my front door on only my second morning here, cordoning off the white-lined parking spaces, putting hoods on the meters as if they were, well, 'for it', and taping off the Garden itself as if it was the scene of a crime. Confident lot; maybe it's about to be. Maybe the Proclamation was only a portent of

157

the real thing to come on Sunday morning and the cease-fire as valid and ineffectual as McNeill's de-mob order. A Redmondite re-enactment of history, the ultimate in an anniversary. Yes, sir, seventy years after the Rising. And I'll get to see it all from my bedroom window and Corny might get to see it from his helicopter, flying in top security, over the roof of the Rotunda, where he originally came to life, and – maybe my mind's not right and I should go back to bed.

I got dressed instead. An awkward business, and one that burnt up valuable time, as Corny might say looking back on how his statue was made. To search for an appropriate working Sunday best, I had to hop barefootedly from magazine cover to bits of carpet to avoid the plaster-dusted floor, an experience more reminiscent of changing in my workplace, not my bedroom. A lost shoe turned up inside the floorboards; it appeared that in last night's haste to undress I had scored a dry-rotted 'hole in one' when I flung it into the dark.

Laces tied, jeans belted, I stood before the mirror to straighten my hair and button up my powder-blue regulation garda shirt. A cheeky gesture, I know, on a day like this, but it was clean and comfortable and I'd enjoy sporting it past the boys below. I was, after all, going on duty myself. A duty as valued and noble in my estimation as protecting a gardenful of Cornys with their sparkling medals from the supposed whims of a few pacificatory constitutionalists with memories of the Great War. I was off to investigate a real crime, not prevent an alleged one.

No time to waste. The planning of a murder to be solved. I opened the stiff window to let in some gorgeous buoyant summer's air and looking straight below I noticed, with a start, that a man in a shirt like mine was looking up at me. A guard. He had heard the creak of the window and was undoubtedly wondering what anyone would be doing up here, on the fourth floor of this old house on a Sunday morning – given that no one is supposed to live on the square. Does he think I'm lying in wait, cleaning my telescopic sight for a *Day of the Jackal* assassination attempt on O'Shaughnessy, if he shows, or the Leader of the Opposition, if he shows, or the President, if he shows on time. Or does your man below think I'm one of his own, on surveillance duty. Maybe he feels he should check. Maybe I should get out of here quickly.

I pulled my door shut and skipped all the way down the wide

staircase to the cool hall, gently passing the second-floor door of my sleeping sub-landlady, into whose purple-dyed fingers I thought even £20 was an extravagance. I think I'll hold out for squatter's rights. Story of my life. Accommodation on sufferance. From the hall I heard bat-like noises in the kitchen; it could be she. I quickly fished out and pushed in my big front door key – which reminds me: do I have? I do. I stepped out into the beautiful day and inhaled; a warm mixture of bus cinders, the Rotunda trees and the salty unseen bay. Listen to the gulls! Beautiful.

Two guards stood at the edge of my footpath, one of them the one who spotted me. I bade them a good morning.

'Good morning. Do you live in there?'

'Yes.'

'How many others live in there?'

'Five others, I think. I just moved in.'

They opened their mouths slowly and nodded.

'What's the story here?' I asked.

'National Commemoration Ceremony in the Garden of Remembrance.'

'Such security.'

'Well, there's been a bit of controversy about it. The business over . . . the O'Shaughnessy statues as well. People could take the opportunity.' They watched me keenly.

'I hear they stole the Proclamation?'

'That's correct.'

They're looking at my shirt.

'Do I know your face from somewhere?' asked the one who saw me. He had a brush moustache.

'I don't think so,' I laughed.

'You didn't use to drink in the Charlotte?'

'No, I did live in Harcourt Street, though.'

'Were you attached to the Terrace?'

'Oh no, I was never in the force.'

'Oh.' He pulled his moustache. 'And yet I know your face from somewhere.' He pulled his moustache again. 'Ah, it'll come to me.'

'Sorry,' I shrugged. 'Anyway, I'd better go. Good luck, now, officers.'

'Good luck.'

Phew! Where he knew me from I did not know but I was glad to get out of Parnell Square. Conway's pub was closed. Good,

159

it's before ten at least. I asked the time of another guard, sitting side-saddle on his Honda. Nine-ten. Excellent. I was keeping better time than I thought but I still didn't want to delay so I resisted the huge temptation to fly into a shop a get a goo at the papers. I can wait, said Corny, I can wait. The Sundays will have full background stories on the whole business. A week's consideration of the week's events. The letters, the cease-fire, the characters. Not to mention the ceremony and the missing Proclamation. Wherefore the statue now? I look bloody forward to it. I'll get them at the studio and have a read between casts.

There's Parnell, wearing his two overcoats in the morning sun. Poor man, he had bad pleurisy towards the end of his days. Caught pleading to the peasants in the driving rain. Ah, but Redmond's death spared him the worst of his own misery. It came weeks before the conscription crisis and the end of the war. Betrayal and failure. His life's work in ruins, his brother dead in Belgium. And the killing was only getting started. How does one die of a broken heart? Medically, physically. Does the organ break or implode in a purple burst – Griffith in the sink? – or does it just peter out under a weight of misery?

So it's O'Connell at one end of the street and Parnell at the other. The two pillars of constitutionalism. What better than to get Redmond in between? God, it wouldn't surprise me if they were looking for the spot where Nelson used to be. It's free at the moment – thanks to an explosion – and thus there'd be a nice irony to his placement thereon.

When I arrived in the studio I nearly burst out laughing to see the wax effigy they'd got up in the corner. The beginnings of O'Shaughnessy's statue, suspended on puppet-like strings from runners on the ceiling. Obviously they'd done a lot of work since yesterday morning, but without hands or feet and only the beginnings, or end, of a wax-blackened head, it still looked like something that walked in from a hot day in Hiroshima. Seeing it really put me in the mood to do a bit of waxing of my own and when I cornered Ramsey – brewing up for Corny's backbone – he agreed to throw my little key man in the oven as soon as the present was made (present for a girlfriend, twenty-first, key to life etc – this was my ruse).

So without further ado, I mooched in on one of his hot cauldrons of lugubriously bubbling wax and, checking to make sure no one was creeping up behind me, I took out the magic soap bar, undressed it of its perforated winding cloth and placed it on top of an upended brick. The key's impression was still beautifully intact, a crisp outline in luminous pink. Using a soft brush, I greased it very carefully with oil. Now for the wax. Dipping an eggcup I drew out a suitable amount and slowly, evenly, spilled the brown substance into the space where the key had been. While it was still pliable, I finger-pressed it tightly into the key's outline and then, tearing the skin off what was drying in the tin, I quickly scooped out another glutinous eggful and packed it into the cavity. When it dried, a hot knife scraped what was unwanted off the top of the soap. One gentle but firm knock of the soap bar's back on the brick and – hey presto! – what falls out but a perfectly presentable replica of Corny's coalshed key.

All it needs now are the required four strips for arms and legs, cleanly cut from a lump of limp wax and very, very carefully heat-stuck on to the key's fragile torso. Ramsey said he would do the rest – the mould and timing – and urged me to go out in the sun and read the papers, which I did without further prompting. Likes to be left alone, the busybody.

'PROCLAMATION STOLEN IN LATEST STATUE SAGA TWIST', spun the *Sunday Press*, with the sub-headline 'Minister says security not slackening'.

'GOVERNMENT WON'T GIVE IN TO 1916 BLACKMAIL', assured the *Sunday Independent* in an ambiguous compound, enhanced, I felt, by a photo of, not Corny, but baby-faced Redmond, *c.* 1918, in his undertaker's hat and white breast handkerchief.

'SECURITY ALERT FOR CEREMONY AFTER MUSEUM THEFT', read the *Sunday Tribune* with the words 'Gone missing', over a photo of the bare wall in the museum where the Proclamation *used* to be. Dark screw-sockets, like the four points of a withdrawn cross, marked the skin-white space that the old scroll had kept untanned.

By Our Reporters
Museum officials have blamed government cutbacks in the public sector for the circumstances that led to the removal yesterday of the 1916 Proclamation from the Dublin Civic Museum. The POA claim that economic rationalisation by the Government has led to reduced staffing and a deterioration in security at state buildings, making a theft such as yesterday's as easy as

the AVNS claimed it to be in a boastful statement they issued last night.

The theft is the latest in a series of activities carried out to pressurise the Government into not erecting its planned statue of the Republican statesman, Cornelius O'Shaughnessy, and comes despite a self-declared cease-fire by the organisation on Friday evening. The cease-fire still holds, claim the AVNS, as they have only 'borrowed' the Proclamation.

In a statement to RTE yesterday evening, the self-styled Anti-Violent Nationalist Society claimed that their 'borrowing' of the framed document was done at 5.30 p.m. while the attention of the attendants was diverted. The document would not be returned, they said, until the Government conceded, or at least is prepared to negotiate on their demands that their proposed 1916 memorial to Cornelius O'Shaughnessy be replaced by a statue of the Home Rule statesman, John Redmond, to commemorate instead the Seventieth Anniversary of the Battle of the Somme and the sacrifice of Irish nationalists in World War I. The AVNS rejected suggestions that it should be pleased by today's shared commemoration ceremony and said that the sharing was basically between the Old IRA and the British Legion, neither of which had anything to do with them. Though today's ceremony was an advance on the traditional exclusivist obsession with the Old IRA, it did nothing to honour Redmond's Volunteers for what they were: constitutional Irish nationalists who paved the way to independence and got no credit for it. The AVNS wanted this tradition to be honoured in its own right.

The Government, however, said they would enter into no negotiations with an anonymous fringe group which had taken the law into its own hands, and promised to press ahead with their commemorative statue of Mr O'Shaughnessy, due for unveiling in August. The Minister of State for Arts and Culture, Mr Nolan, condemned the theft as childish and self-defeating and said that those who claim a desire to see a statue of John Redmond erected in Dublin are doing themselves or their cause no service by such reckless and futile stunts as threatening letters or stealing parts of the country's heritage. Even if the Government were disposed towards erecting some sort of memorial or statue to John Redmond they would now find it difficult to do so. Blackmail and intimidation would achieve nothing, Mr Nolan said. 'And it was a pity that those who called themselves Redmondites didn't realise

162

what a dishonour it was to the man in whose name and for whose memory they claimed to be doing these things.' He revealed that his grandfather .was a strong Redmondite and was one of those instrumental in reuniting the Irish Parliamentary Party in 1900 after the Party split.

Meanwhile, despite the AVNS's description as ludicrous government claims that some attempt could be made to disrupt today's controversial commemoration ceremony in the Garden of Remembrance, security has been stepped up and special garda patrols will be posted around the Parnell Square area of the city throughout the day. Because of the nature of the 'shared' ceremony, gardaí anticipate strong protests from Republican groups as well but it is felt that something more disruptive could be attempted by the AVNS. Opposition parties last night criticised the Government's decision to lift its security watches on various locations following the self-imposed cease-fire by the AVNS on Friday night. However, a spokesman for the gardaí said that the reduction in these special garda postings had nothing to do with any cease-fire but was done in deference to the wishes of those upon whose homes and premises round-the-clock watches had been placed. A Department of Justice spokesman said that a conscious decision was taken to have a more discreet security presence at locations deemed to require such.

Opposition parties generally have not praised the Government's handling of the affair. Mr Raphael McAnally TD, the Fianna Fáil spokesperson of Justice, said that, to many people, the Government was being made a laughing stock by a tiny anonymous band of what he could only describe as articulate troublemakers, and people were beginning to question just how serious the Government was in apprehending this gang or even in finding out who they were. Indeed some people might be forgiven, at this stage, for wondering about the very commitment of the current government to the commemoration of the 1916 Rising, on this, its Seventieth Anniversary, and the artistic celebration of its greatest living participant, Mr Cornelius O'Shaughnessy, on his ninetieth birthday.

'It is nothing short of scandalous,' said Mr McAnally, 'that in such an illustrious year the Government should allow a group calling itself the Anti-Violent Nationalist Society to go around unhindered, making a mockery of the State's proceedings and endangering what was to be one of its lasting tributes to a man who has served his country without fail since he first took up arms in its painful birth throes. Such a mockery was symptomatic of the general deterioration in the way we treated our past, a process assisted by the weakness of the present government and the misguided way in which it was trying to revise our national commemoration ceremony. A government which stumbled into the fiasco of today's 'new' ceremony, involving as it does the introduction of the British Legion into the Garden of Remembrance, can hardly be trusted with commemorating the event for which that garden was built, and it will be interesting to see if Mr O'Shaughnessy, the man whose memory of participation in that event the Government was entrusted with commemorating, will be prepared to come along and join the British Legion in what was the Garden of Irish Freedom.'

The man at the centre of the controversy, Mr Cornelius O'Shaughnessy, was not available for comment last night. However, speaking on the *Saturday Live* programme on RTE radio yesterday morning, Mr O'Shaughnessy repeated his allegations that elements of the British Secret Service were involved in the campaign against his statue. Whether or not local people opposed to Mr O'Shaughnessy were being used to assist in this campaign he could not say for certain but he felt sure that a 'dirty tricks' element of M.I.5 were the organising factor behind the campaign. Mr O'Shaughnessy alleged, as he has continuously done for the last few years, that British intelligence operated widely on the island – North and South – and he said the current campaign, however freakish or eccentric it may look, actually serves the purpose of British intelligence very usefully; it brings embarrassment to the 1916 celebrations, and the Government's organising of them, thus discrediting the State's involvement even in the commemoration of Republicanism. It also tests the sincerity of the Government's resolve against 'terrorism' or 'paramilitary threats' – a very important issue for the British.

Finally, Mr O'Shaughnessy said that considering the antiquated old-boy network that still persists in British intelligence, he had no doubt that certain parts of that network felt they had a few 'old scores' to settle with their Irish adversaries. Mr O'Shaughnessy said they had never forgotten his own involvement in the events of the morning of 20 November 1921 and to strike back at his statue was the only cheap, cowardly way they could, all these years later, exact their revenge. Asked if he was annoyed that there had been no official response yet from the Government or the gardaí to his allegations, Mr O'Shaughnessy said not really. He had pointed to British Secret Service dirty tricks before but no one had listened, and yet after the Livingstone case, and more recently the revelations of Holroyd and Wallace, they had all been proved wrong.

Mr O'Shaughnessy's reaction to yesterday's removal of the Proclamation is not yet known. Neither is it known if he will or will not attend today's controversial 'new-style' commemoration ceremony. He is known to have strong opinions about the proposal but it is understood that he may wish to appear less outspoken on the matter in the light of the Government's difficulties regarding his statue. In general, the Government would wish to see a 'playing down' of the controversy over the statue (and the ceremony) and would prefer it if Mr O'Shaughnessy didn't enter too freely into a debate on his own statue and in particular on the identity or merits of those who have opposed it.

Also unavailable for comment last night was the sculptor in the affair, Robert Wycherley, whose original award of the contract caused some controversy when it was announced. He has decided to remain in the background and has declined to talk to reporters about his feelings regarding the AVNS campaign and the direct threats made by AVNS to his studio and staff. However, these threats appear to have receded and garda sources privately concede that neither Mr Wycherley nor his assistants are now in any real danger. Assurances to this effect from the AVNS have been respected and it is now expected that the organisation will concentrate their campaign around 'bargaining' over the Proclamation, a lucrative haul they can only be delighted about, given its embarrassing connotations for the Government in a 1916 Anniversary year.

The phone rang. Ramsey was busy so I dropped the papers to answer it.

'Hello,' I said. 'Wycherley and Sons.'

'Adopting yourself as my son now, are we?'

'Oh, it's you. A bit of OT, Bob. You told us how fast we'd have to move on O'Shaughnessy so I'm getting a bit of practice in. Hey, what do you think of the Proclamation?'

'I don't. I never did and I hope they burn the thing.'

165

'That's a nice attitude. Easy seeing what stock you came from. It's a bit of crack though, isn't it?'

'Yes, it has an element of the grand gesture about it. Now that they have that to wave at the Government, they can leave us alone.'

'Looks like they're doing that. The buck is getting passed around pretty quick.'

'I'd expect that.'

'Security lapse and all the rest – have you been talking to the Minister?'

'I spoke to him about an hour ago. He's going to the ceremony.'

'As Minister for the Arts? Must be to keep Corny happy. What does he think? It's him or the Proclamation now.'

'I'm sure he feels he's worth every line of it. Thank you, by the way, for your service last night. Apart from your dangerous party piece during dessert you were, to my pleasant surprise and relief, quite splendid company throughout. It went very well.'

'Well, that's very nice of you. I wasn't expecting – '

'No, I have to admit, you were very good. You and Tess. You were friendly and helpful, swapping stories and fetching his coal and TV set. Clearly, he was very touched. No matter how publicly fawned upon he appears to be, he's a bit of a lonely old man and I'm sure such a warm gathering of interested young people around his table lifted his spirits no end. You drew him out of himself, not for the last time, I hope.'

'A smooth tongue. Which is why I too looked understandably surprised by the main course.'

'What is it with this O'Higgins chap? O'Shaughnessy almost choked on his spuds when his name came up.'

'I told you before. He's a skeleton in Corny's cupboard. I wanted to rattle it for the crack – to see how he jumped.'

'Yeah, well, less rattling until we've finished our own. We've a job and I don't want to scare him off. Busy days ahead, Shane. Now more than ever, the onus is on us to fulfil this contract quickly. The Minister this morning offered his full support for a fast casting.'

'OK, great. But listen, the papers say no police leads. What's the story? Even a sniff?'

'Nothing that Hurley mentioned. He called me this morning before he headed off for his match.'

'Get off! Where did he call you from – Caherciveen?'

'From his semi-d. in Templeogue. But he and the boys, you see, go for a "big feed" in Wynn's Hotel beforehand. I was to ring him there if anything "came up". He firmly believes something might "come up" today. The Proclamation maybe. Today could be a big day, he said, and I don't think he meant the match. He told me to keep in close contact. Closer contact than we've had up to now. I think he had his arse kicked from above. Told to stop sleeping on the job. The Government want results and the only results he's giving them are the Sunday scores.'

'Poor old Hurley – what can you do when you're chasing ghosts?'

'He'd like to know. If you've any ideas ring Wynn's before 2 p.m. and after that you could ring Information at Croke Park and have him paged.'

'Paged? You're having me on. Out of sixty thousand screaming people?'

'They don't *all* scream, Shane.'

'They do. Every one of them. They screamed at us each year when we added a few bars to a "A Nation Once Again".'

'No doubt you gave them all the two fingers.'

'No, I just waved at them. Like blind Dev in College Green.'

'Well, let's hope Hurley doesn't suffer from the same affliction because if he is paged up there, it'll be silently.'

'What, they send a deaf-and-dumb dwarf up the stands in search of him?'

'Less Dickensian than that, I'm afraid – an electronic message. He'll see his name in lights across one of those moving scoreboards.'

'Really? They have those scanner-vision screens in Croke now? That's a bit of crack. They didn't have them in my day.'

'Well, they do now. Listen, I can't stand talking here all day. Go and get me Ramsey, will you.'

'Right, boss.'

'And, Shane – '

'Yes?'

Be careful, will you.'

'Of course!'

Poor guy, I hope he doesn't lose his nerve. I fetched Ramsey and looked at the clock. Ten-thirty: I have to meet the boys at twelve-thirty. Hurry up, Ramsey, and burn, baby, burn.

When he returned, muttering something about having to change the burn-out period for the McBride piece, I hastened to the phone to check on my invincibles. Fingers in the holes of 69 – Clonskeagh numbers being rude – and 64 and 36: my birthdate and the year of Corny's appointment as Chief of Staff. It began ringing, or rather bleating. Mellowes' phone always gives off that monotonously bass-slow wheep-wheep of the older models, like a wounded snipe or a man with a flu-filled nose trying to clear his head. Mellowes' phone also always rings for a long time before someone deigns to answer it. Come on, you rascals, shake off that drink-doused slumber. The phone rang on – a suffering plea to be left alone. Wheep-wheep.

'Hello.' It was the Maynooth Idiot, a religious student sharing the house.

'Oh, hello. Doing your washing, were you?'

'No, I was upstairs in the – '

'In the shower like Corny, maybe, washing the tonsure.'

'What did?'

'Never mind. Get me the boys, will you. Sean, please, or Oisin.'

'They're not here.'

'Not there?'

'No, they never came home.'

'Never came home?' Must have kipped somewhere else. Unless . . . Hardly. 'Are you certain they never came home? They might have left early.'

'No, I've been up since dawn and Sean's bed is still unmade.'

'What about Oisin? What about the couch?'

'Michelle slept on the couch last night.'

'Ah – even your celibacy's taken a ride.'

'Michelle's a dog.'

'Even better. Starters can't be choosers. Listen, if they come in, tell them Shane rang and for them to ring the studio.'

'OK. Goodbye now.'

'Goodbye.'

So, they didn't come home. That's not like Mellowes, unless an overly oiled Oisin led him astray. It was a big night, what with the soap and everything. Where would they have gone? After the Pink, and then Leeson Street, who can tell? Just so long as they show on time. It wouldn't be like them not to, not on a job like this. Today's the day of Operation Booterstown. Every part of it counts and after all our talk and planning I know they wouldn't fluff a rendezvous by letting the effects of a premature celebration get out of hand. Too cute for that. Too dedicated. Too scared. Mellowes has put a life's work into this. He's set his heart on finding out. When he heard the O'Shaughnessy commission had gone to Wycherley he got so excited and then he quietened down and prepared to work on a way to rope me in. He's set his heart on finding out. We all have, in a way. We're in it together.

They'll be there, all right. The invincibles won't fail. I mean, they put me up to this, the Roebuck House bit and the meeting with Samuelson, so they have to be there. Not true, of course, but let them think it. The two may seem unconnected but my neck goes on the line today for both of them, and the boys know that. They'll be there.

Mind you, it would be funny if they were kidnapped, picked up on Leeson Street by someone who knew what we were up to and was out to stop us. Give us a warning. Or bargain with us, like the AVNS, on rumbling that we were up to something almost as illegal as themselves. It'd be funny all right. Hilarious. Jesus, those bastards better show up.

Ramsey had the oven door open. His big gloved hand clicked it ajar like a cracked safe door. But he was in no hurry to retrieve my baked mould and stood there for a minute looking into the enclosed flames, wary perhaps of their deceptive calm, seductive even, in their soft mingling of burning reds and white-hot embers all glowing in a tumbledown arrangement of phosphorescent heat. How the ashes glow . . . peaceful now after the turmoil, as if the demon that might have leapt out had – to Ramsey's relief – departed.

We waited. The fire settled until it hardly stirred and then Ramsey, in a flurry, did. With the swift dexterity of Mrs Williams fetching a hot potato from a crocodile's mouth, he picked up the long iron tongs and poked into the mouth of the oven. Out, between the jaws of the tongs, came my little mould, baked golden brown and shedding a few sparks. Ramsey dropped it on to the dust and directed me to fetch two pails of water, which I did with what I thought was alacrity until I saw the way he, the older he, moved the mould over to the middle of the floor, stood it upright in a surround of bricks, slid the heavy lid off the barrel furnace – pausing momentarily to refix his protection hood – and then, very, very carefully lifted his tiny pot of molten out of the furnace and brought it over, smoking furiously, to the mould where, without stopping or asking me, damn him, for assistance, he poured the fiery neon-red lumped molten metal into the hole at the top of the mould.

Gasping a little, Ramsey pulled off his hood and told me to wait, meaning for the metal to settle.

'I hope all this business is finished soon,' he said, tidying his gloves away neatly on the shelf and returning with a hammer. He meant the O'Shaughnessy drama.

'Ah, it will be. I'd say the Government will sort something out.'

'I hope so,' he sighed, blinking. 'Because that's a big job we have to do. It'll be a small figure, Wycherley tells me – smaller that I thought – but it'll certainly be a fast cast. The fastest we've ever done.'

'I know, but it'll be a bit of crack. I look forward to it.'

Ramsey nodded with a sort of sour *gravitas* and proceeded to hammer the living daylights out of my mould. What in the name of God was he doing? The thing's hardly cooled. He'll bend my little man, break his legs, distort the cut of the back so he'll never be able to open any bleeding door. But before I'd time to mouth the lamest of protests, he had the thing shorn down to what looked like the last scrap of a bleached dog bone. I know Michelangelo felt the need to free the figure from the marble but at least he took his time about it. From out of the plaster fragments he picked a long chalk lump and held it up to the light. This I took to be my little stick man but it looked more like the abominable snowman, and I seriously wondered if he had the right lump until, watching his busy hands chip, chisel and pick, I noticed, with growing heart, a shape emerge that was not dissimilar to that I had earlier made so hopefully in wax. Rather rough-hewn perhaps and rather frayed around the edges, but it had, nevertheless, the potential of a key, a key with arms and legs, the sort of masonic oddity you might see stitched to an Orangeman's sash.

'It'll make a nice present,' said Ramsey, pouring the rest of the steam on to it. The steam rose again and subsided.

'Present? Oh yes, of course . . . yes, it will.'

He picked it up.

'I was worried we mightn't get the chasing . . . all the detail . . .'

'Have we got – I mean, is it still a key of sorts?'

'Oh, it is, I think . . . we'll have to scrape off all that plaster and then do some filing, careful filing if you want to retain the grooves.'

He twirled the little man between thumb and forefinger.

'Make a nice big necklace, you know. Clean it up and plate it maybe and then put it on a silver chain.'

'Yes, but my girlfriend's not a hippy. I think she'd prefer it on her shelf.'

'Oh yes, of course . . . I was only suggesting . . . em, do you want me to file it for you, finish off the little fellow?'

'Thanks, but you'll get your chance to finish off the little fellow next week.'

'What's that?'

'What I mean is, I'll do it myself. Thanks, Ramsey. Listen, you're ace.'

'No problem. I'll be outside.'

Texture of the legs, my eye. I'll make short work of the texture of the legs. Is Ramsey gone? I looked around. He was. It's eleven. I'd better move quickly. I took the key man over to the workboard and switched on the electric saw. Very, very carefully I put him on his back and slid him in towards the whining blade. Chunk! Off went one leg. Chunk! Off went the other. Clean cuts but a bit deeper than I intended: a millimetre or two into the body of the key.

All it needs now is to take the copper needle I see here handily to my left and dig out the chalk lodged in the stubborn cavities, after which a spot of fine filing is in order (unfiling is what I'll be up to later on, I hope). Rubbed down, I can drop the still rough-surfaced key into a bucket of acid and smugly wait, very pleased altogether with the wizardry of my idea and the way it worked out. A living recreation of something Collins dreamt and executed, here in the palm of my hand. Let's hope Mellowes' side of the plan works out even half as well, and *his* research works.

Chapter 7

Guardian of Remembrance

Marlborough Street. A little tremor when I pass the pro-cathedral. My first night after I escaped from Artane. Also where High Requiem mass was sung over the pale, blood-drained face of Michael Collins. Remains taken here after lying in state in the City Hall for two days and from here borne to Glasnevin in the biggest Dublin funeral since the passing of Parnell. I have been there many times in spirit. On the O'Connell monument, as others were, watching the bier pass by on the gun-carriage that shelled the Four Courts, pulled by six black horses with their heads bowed. Astride a tombstone statue in Glasnevin, I watched Richard Mulcahy give the oration and saw members of the Squad cry as no one had seen them.

When I reached Parnell Street, I turned the corner and there – to my great relief – across the road, were the two boys lounging in the doorway of the Parnell Lounge and wearing Meath hats on their heads. A smart move. They saw me immediately and waved in the typical match-going fashion – 'Here's Jimmy, has he got the hip flask' – and then quickly signalled for me to avert my face as a garda car was coming up Parnell Street in my direction. The place was crawling with cops – in cars, on cycles – all around Parnell Square and its back streets. You could hear their radios crackling a hundred yards away. What the hell possessed Mr Samuelson and his ilk to meet me here? Symbolism, he said. Or derring-do, more like. A trap with one of us about to be betrayed? Him, maybe, the sacrificial lamb offered up by the leaders.

I skipped across the road and the boys emerged from the Parnell doorway to meet me.

'Come on, Meath. Come on!' shouted Oisin, rather unnecessarily. 'Have you got the key?'

'Where the hell were you? I rang Loyola this morning and got only the Idiot.'

'Stop shouting, both of you,' cried Mellowes, touching his forehead. 'I've a head on me that'd kill a brown dog.'

'Well, that's a great way to turn out for the big day! Bloody brilliant preparation – would Collins have gone out to blow temples holding his own? Or spent the night before Bloody Sunday getting skulled into its earliest hours with his Apostles beside him?'

'Well,' said Oisin, with his finger raised, 'Vinny Byrne did say he got holy communion handy enough in Westland Row. Sup of wine, like. Bit of body for a bit of blood.'

'So, how are you feeling, McArdle?' asked Mellowes. 'Your head's as clear as Mick's conscience, I take it?'

'I feel fine.'

'All set?'

'Yep.'

'Nervous?'

'Apprehensive.'

'Don't worry – we're right behind you.'

'That's what worries me.'

'Don't be silly. So it worked then?'

I paused for a moment. 'The key worked, yes.'

They looked at each other and laughed silently. 'Show us,' they said. I hustled back into the Parnell doorway and took out the key. Anxiously they examined it and gave long slow whistles of admiration.

'Excellent!' said Sean. 'Looks a bit rough but – '

'So do you, Sean, but when it comes to the test I think you'll both perform adequately.'

He took the point and smiled boyishly, repositioning the Meath hat on his head.

'OK, so put it away,' he said. 'We'll deal with that door when we come to it. We haven't got much time. Listen, eh – you're up to this, Shane? You're not getting nervous?'

'No. I'm grand.'

They looked at me as if they weren't sure.

'Seriously, I'm fine. I've worked it out and I believe I can handle them. The worst thing they'll throw at me is an old man and a

173

stick. I'm in a hotel, there'll be pre-match drinkers sitting about and lots of cops outside. If anything horrible happens, I can whistle. Where will you be?'

'We're going to sit on the steps of Belvedere College, directly across from the hotel entrance with a view down George's Street. We'll sit there for the duration of your meeting. We'll be wearing these hats. It's cool. It'll look like we're off to the match and we might even get a pint brought out to us from the Tudor Rooms next door. That'll mingle us in nicely and I need the cure.'

'Can you not have orange juice?'

'You'll be having a pint, for God's sake! If you don't, you should. I wouldn't trust old men who invite you to a hotel for a cup of tea.'

'What's this Matt Talbot morality you're giving us, anyway?' complained Oisin. 'You, of all people, who was carried post-Golgotha-like up Grafton Street on Thursday night.'

'Oisin, please . . . a pint will relax you, Shane.'

'A few will transform you – look at how you took on Harrington last night.'

'Right, let's start moving. Slowly now and lots of talking.'

'Always pays to make them wait.'

'Exactly.'

We came out from the back doorway of the Parnell Lounge and started moving up the street.

'What did you think of the papers, my red-eyed friends, or did you not get out of the nurses' beds in time to get a look at them?'

'Predictable,' said Mellowes. 'The media yapping on about precautions, the Opposition yapping on about commitment and security cutbacks. Point-scoring. Sure how was anyone to know the Proclamation of all things was going to get lifted? And this thing of getting out there and finding the culprits without delay. I mean, where are they going to start looking – behind O'Donovan Rossa's tombstone? It's all crap, this concerned-reaction business. If you ask me, none of them gives a tosser's twist what happens to that yellowing scroll. They once had to know it by heart; that's enough to kill anything for most of us.'

'Except the Government.'

'And even they won't lose much sleep if it doesn't show up again. They just want that statue up, and no one harmed and O'Shaughnessy pacified. And I think the AVNS, God love them, might have overestimated the State's concern for its history when they took that thing for ransom. They may find that they illustrated an official blindness to the Irish past in a way different to how they intended when they first set out, i.e. that not only does the country not recognise its pre-war parliamentary tradition, with Redmond its last unfortunate leader, but it also doesn't give a huge toss about the revolutionary tradition now either.'

'Yeah,' said Oisin. 'They should change tack now and issue another statement. Their first one was good. It was a smart, so it was.'

'Like what we'd write,' said Mellowes, with a big sly smile, 'or Corny if he was on the other side. I must say I thought a lot of his comments yesterday. I mean, he must be going crackers now he hears the Proclamation is gone but yesterday he was very cool. His reasons for why M.I.5 are behind all this: to embarrass the Government's involvement in Republican commemorations, to test their attitude to threats or seeming terrorism, to distract attention from other more nefarious activities – I mean, they're fairly credible when you think about it.'

But no one was thinking about it and it was fairly obvious that our minds were on other things – on one thing, which was the meeting at hand.

'How are you feeling, Shane?'

'Grand.'

'Good man.' He clapped my back.

'Still no deals?' He looked at me. 'I mean, if there was something you could say to this Samuelson to fob him off, would you say it? Something like, "Oh I believe, by the by, that the Government have plans for a statue of Redmond in O'Connell Street as soon as you guys are out of the way." Something you wouldn't be quoted on or anything but, you know, would pacify them, cool their ardour.'

'I can't say. I mean, it all depends on what way our discussion goes. I'll have to be careful.'

'Oh fair enough. It's up to you. You're the one going in there. You're the one working on the statue. And no better man than you, Shane, to draw out a man in negotiation or idle chatter.'

'There's the plaque!' said Oisin. It was the blue plaque to John Dillon, high up on the side wall of the hotel. 'Events passed him by – will we?'

'No. Stall up.'

'Don't point!' said Mellowes.

'Relax, for Christ's sake. What more authentic sight could you get than match-day culchees pointing out the blue plaques as they wander through the strange town.'

'Lads, lads,' I broke in. 'Events will pass us by, if we don't get ready.'

'We'll sit down here for a moment,' suggested Mellowes, and we sat on the worn granite steps of No. 20. 'Let him stew in there. Wondering.'

'Twenty-five to,' said Oisin, checking his watch. 'You're grand.'

'I'll go in early,' I said, getting up suddenly. 'Give him a surprise.' I wanted to get on with it and not sit on the steps getting tense.

'OK. Good luck,' said Mellowes and he looked at me. 'You know where we'll be.'

I nodded and looked at them briefly. And then I turned and started walking towards the hotel, slow, self-conscious steps which took me under Dillon's plaque and around the corner to the front steps and the plain glass door of the hotel.

I opened the glass door and went into the lobby. No one about. Not a soul. But the place had a homely, canteenish smell that reminded me of the big dinners we got when the band played around the country, staying at schools and hotels. Mind you, those places had a bit of life in them. This place looks like it hasn't been done up in decades. One eye was shut on a deer's head above the stairplace and a hearse-black grandfather-clock stood stopped, without hands, in a corner. On a table beside it, a stuffed fox was bearing his fangs and protesting at enclosure in a glass box of cardboard rocks and sugary snow. Laminated rail posters from the sixties adorned the walls with headings like 'Tranquillity' and 'Tradition', urging people to discover an Ireland of rusty-haired waifs, oversized hounds and, my God, round towers. What ever happened to round towers? They were everywhere once, from tea-towels to bank ads. A great symbol of cunning and perseverance by the monks, invincibility of the natives, that we used to give a rude phallic quality to when they adorned the backs of our copybooks. Must be out of fashion. Like the other poster, of an orange-and-black train booting through the countryside with the heads of two happy children stuck out the window, breathing it all in. We were never allowed to do that. Didn't I tell you things were different in print.

176

'Can I help you, sir?' asked a woman, deep and unseen, behind an unvarnished desk on the left-hand side.

I walked over. She was sitting in front of an ancient telephone switchboard reading the *News of the World*.

'Are you looking for someone?' she asked over half-glasses. A many-ringed finger kept her place in some English scandal.

'I'm . . . eh, I'm looking for my father.'

'What's his name?'

'Samuelson,' I told her boldly. 'Mr Samuelson.'

'I think he's in the lounge,' she said, examining me carefully and pointing to a narrow corridor that led from her desk to the interior.

'Thank you.'

'Not at all.'

She sat back to her newspaper and I began walking down the corridor. Carpeted, of course, with flock wallpaper made less garish by yellowing. A piano-tinkling instrumental version of 'The Fields of Athenry' was being percolated through a speaker. Through to subdue. Subdue, subdue. My heart was beating heavily now but I had to smile.

At the end of the corridors there was a glass door with 'Lounge' written diagonally across it in gold-leaf letters. I came up to the glass door and looked in. It was a comfortable back room with stools and round tables and a bar at the end, not unlike Tobin's, with lots of glass shelves in front of mirrors, that sixties plastic look that was supposed to suggest cocktails. A barman was polishing glasses. There was hardly anyone in the lounge from what I could see. By an empty grate, two old men were clearing their pipes.

A fat woman in an overcoat was taking tea in the middle of the floor with her morose husband. *Après* mass. In a far alcove, a man was reading a newspaper. 'Proclamation Stolen'. My headline. His nut-brown brogue was jigging, content. Beige socks, tweed trousers and a bouffant of black hair turning grey above the page. *And* a cane, leaning against the arm of the chair. Steel-tipped, leaning there like a complacent corner boy. It's him, the bastard. It's Samuelson.

I sucked my breath in. Very, very slowly and very quickly I opened the door and stepped into the lounge. Softly, with all the delicate treading on eggshells of Corny's confrontation with Detective Watson in the dining-room of the Dolphin or the seamless sound-free descent of Collins on the informers of

177

Glanorgin, I tipped across the room, past the pipecleaners, who paid me no notice, and past the fat lady draining the last of the pot for her husband. In and around the empty stools, I approached the sitting, reading figure – its foot still nodding contentedly away – and landed like a feather on a stool in front of the held newspaper. A hand was let slide into pocket to draw out my trusty gemstone zippo. In the protective shell of my hand – zunk! – it lit up and the flame was lengthened, gloriously lengthened, until it was sufficiently large to be put to the gentleman's newspaper. Once the flame took light and moved towards 'Proclamation' I began to recite softly, 'This is a paper you might own.'

'Eh?' Eyes above the newspaper.

'Left by yourself in the Wolfe Tone.'

'What the – ?' Sees the smoke and panics.

'Do the same to the Proclamation.'

'Ah, Christ Almighty!' Flings down newspaper. Up out of seat.

'And you'll earn yourself the curse of damnation.'

'My God!' Stamps on newspaper.

'The whole damn nation, get it?'

He stamped on the flames and looked at me in terror.

'Are you OK, Mr Samuelson?' The barman rushed over. So did the pipecleaners. He was stamping away.

'What happened?'

'Did you burn yourself?'

'What a terrible thing to – '

'No . . . no. I'm OK,' he said, stepping back from the blackened newspaper. 'I hope your carpet – '

'It's fine, it's fine,' said the barman, picking up the ashes desperately, as if it was his fault.

'What happened?' asked the pipecleaners. None of them looked at me, standing there with hands in pockets.

'I . . . I don't know,' said Samuelson, looking at me ruefully. He was a plummy sort with a pale face and what looked like a greying wig. 'I must have . . . my cigar must have lit the paper.' He looked around.

'It's very dangerous,' said one pipecleaner and the other agreed with him.

'You should stick to pipes,' I suggested.

'He has a point,' said one of the cleaners and I nearly exploded.

178

Samuelson looked at him with intense annoyance and then at me with bewildered vengeance.

'When the cigars seem to be out,' the cleaner prattled on, 'they're often still smoking and – '

'OK, OK, I'm fine,' explained Samuelson and the pipecleaners were urged to go back to their seats.

'Do you want another newspaper?' asked the barman, carrying the remains of the old one away on a silver salver.

'No,' said Samuelson. 'Thank you.'

'OK.'

'Sit down,' said Samuelson when the barman departed.

I sat down. Samuelson tidied his hair and looked around the room.

'What in the name of God was that in aid of?'

'The St Vincent de Paul but it could go to the Save Corny Fund.'

'Tsk, Jesus.' Samuelson shook his head. 'You think that was a great stunt, don't you?'

'I think it was a good one. It was a warning.'

'I heard you were crazy but I didn't think you were that crazy.'

'Now you know. Pull a fast one on us and a lot more will be going up in flames.'

'Two can play at that game.'

'One's got more to lose. In fact, one's got all to lose.'

Samuelson looked at me sourly. He had a sort of slung jaw.

'Did you bring along your protection?' I asked sarcastically.

'You needn't worry. We won't be meeting here.'

He pulled at a gold chain on his tweed waistcoat and out popped a watch for him to flip open and check the time on. Very posh, an old school tie too but with little crowns over the harps. United Services Club, I think, or Trinity Historical. Or RUC, and this thing's as elaborate a set-up as I feared.

'Come on, let's go,' he said, snapping the watch shut and grabbing his cane.

'Where are we off to?'

'Follow me,' he said and he got up out of his seat and grabbed his cane.

I followed him across the lounge. The fat lady stared at him, the man who nearly burnt himself, and the pipecleaners wished us good luck.

'Thank you,' I told him. 'We'll need it.'

But Samuelson said nothing and walked on down the corridor, where some anodyne ivory-tinkler was making aural chewing gum of 'The Boys of Fairhill'. The receptionist looked up when we passed but said nothing; last person to see me alive? A deer with one eye is not a reliable witness. Not once it's lost its head. We crossed the lobby and went up the narrow staircase, as mute as the stuffed fox who seemed to be laughing at us nevertheless.

'We're going upstairs?' I wanted to confirm, as I went upstairs.

Naturally he didn't respond but kept walking, erect and firm, up the rubber-ribbed steps and then down a sparsely lit corridor with bedroom numbers on the doors and a window (on to George's Street?) at the end. But before we got to the window, we turned halfway down the stairs and went up a further set of stairs, rickety and creaking.

'We couldn't have taken the lift,' I said. 'Or is the hunchback at lunch?'

No answer. He kept moving straight ahead of me, up the creaking spiral stairs. At the top we passed a mirror – it was a shock to see how scared I looked – and came out on to another corridor, even more sparsely lit. Just three miserable bulbs throwing out three distinct little pools of fuzzy yellow light like Victorian street lights. Three lights. Bad luck for Parnell and hopefully for his fans.

The bedrooms along this corridor had no numbers on the doors and some of them had no doors and presumably no beds inside from what I could see of their musty interiors. Blinds were drawn and carpets were pulled up and I thought I smelled the decaying flesh of a tied-up Fenian but perhaps I was being fanciful. I was entirely in his hands now. If things got nasty I would have to fight him to get out of here. Who would hear my screams if he had a half-dozen accomplices around the next corner? I'd have to run to a window, break it and shout for the boys.

'Here we are,' he said suddenly and we came to a heavy door at the end of the corridor with '15' on it. What floor was it on? I didn't know but it wasn't the first.

Samuelson was enjoying my nervousness and he smiled at me in a sickly way as he pulled out his keys. The line of the slung jaw lengthened. He fished out, at a leisurely pace, the appropriate key and stuck it into the lock. Whatever's behind this door, I'm in his hands now. Courage of Collins, Shane, and his risks to succeed. The lock was clicked and the door drew softly open to reveal the grim face of Charles Stuart Parnell hanging between two windows. Gilt-framed, in brackish oils, he was sitting on a table with a piece of paper in his hands and looked like he was off to confront someone about the contents.

'Like it?' asked Samuelson, proudly stepping into a room ornate with paintings, *memorabilia* and heavy oak furniture. Sunlight streamed in from what I took to be George's Street. He meant the painting.

'It makes him look like a man of action,' I said. 'Had he just got the vote?'

Samuelson smiled at this and walked around the large round table, running a finger along its finished surface.

I stepped up closely to examine the painting but I couldn't make out any writing on the piece of paper. Just painterly squiggles to represent writing. The painting was a donation from Simon Doyle, Esq., 1890–1975.

'It's an admirable portrait though, isn't it?'

'It'd be even more admirable if others could admire it. What else do you guys have hoarded up here – Grattan's wigs maybe, or Redmond's hunting guns. And the Proclamation – our Proclamation – or is that stuck behind a big rock in Glasnevin cemetery?'

Samuelson shook his head like a prim schoolteacher.

'If you can read and I know you can, you'll see that the painting was a donation. Mr Doyle was a former secretary of the Ivy Day Committee. He was a passionate believer in Parnell and collected many paintings from the era.'

'He wouldn't have shared his enthusiasm with the rest of us?'

'He didn't believe that that enthusiasm was shared and so he wasn't prepared to hand over such a painting to the State,' said Samuelson, pushing his bouffant of hair back. 'Only when Parnell and the parliamentary tradition are properly acknowledged and honoured in our history, should such works be properly donated to the popularity.'

'"Let no man write my epitaph." And what would Mr Doyle have thought of your attempts to rectify that anomaly? What would he have thought of threatening letters and thefts and blackmail?'

'If you mean by that colourful description the articulation of the potential of going beyond parliamentary means to achieve recognition for a just cause, then I don't think he would have been in disagreement. Mr Doyle always said that in our tireless quest to have the missing dimension of Irish nationalism restored to the picture of Irish history, we might have to get a little militant.'

'And bring in Captain Moonlight.'

'And be faced rather with the regrettable possibility of his entrance.'

'I hope there's no regrettable possibility of his entrance today,' I said, walking over to check the glass bookshelves. They were filled with large leather volumes and calfskin Hansards and old *Punch* cartoons of IPP members rising from their seats.

'You're quite safe.'

'And you,' I said, picking up a little print of John Dillon and looking at Samuelson. 'What makes you think I wouldn't have a platoon of police ready to burst in at any moment?'

'Because I trust you not to,' he replied with a quick grin. 'And even if I didn't I could be out of this room in minutes and long before any police or informers could find their ways up here. For, believe me, it can be made a lot more difficult than it looked when we came up here, but not half as difficult as it would be to follow me when I vanish from this room, with plenty of notice.'

'More subterfuge. What is this – trapdoors and secret tunnels?'

'Not at all, not at all,' he said laughing. 'You're being too dramatic. The point is that I would probably have no need to leave this room for I and the room are entirely innocent. There is nothing in here that could be used in evidence for anything other than the once esteemed opinion Irish people had of their parliamentary saviours.'

'Save me this saviours,' I said, replacing the head. 'What am I here for?'

'Would you like to sit down?' he said, taking a seat at one side of the table and indicating the other.

'Don't mind if I – What's this?' The chairs had Meath, Cork, Tipperary carved into their backs.

'Cross-country quiz?' I asked and I pulled out Meath to give them (and me) luck in our match today.

'They were carved by Thomas Olden, God bless him. They symbolise the three seats Parnell held.

'Not literally, I hope.'

'We're not literal people,' said Samuelson sourly. 'As you should know.'

'And I suppose,' I said, getting comfortable and indicating the

182

picture of Parnell, Dillon and Curran sitting in their top hats in Kilmainham Jail, 'those are the three "F"'s?'

'Unfunny,' said Samuelson.

'They were kept in good conditions,' I said, to rile him further. 'Accommodating chaps.'

'Their reputations weren't kept in such good conditions,' said Samuelson harshly.

'But why blame O'Shaughnessy?'

'We don't blame him – he just happens to be the most recent and most excessive example of the glorification of the men of violence, as they then were. Enough is enough. This is the straw that breaks our backs and on it we have decided to pitch our cause. It is the only way.'

I said nothing. We could be arguing like this for hours but thankfully Samuelson came quickly to the point.

'Look, when they, the AVNS – '

'They?'

'Yes, they. I am speaking on their behalf – you don't think they're going to appear in person?'

'Not literally, no.'

'Right . . . well, when they, the AVNS, set out on this campaign they went about it in a somewhat amateurish manner – in a manner that I, for example, wouldn't have agreed with. They are hot-headed individuals, young firebrands, if you like, and I don't think they thought things out. They should have revealed themselves from the very start, straight off, and publicised their grievances. Yes, they should have concentrated their wrath on the O'Shaughnessy statue proposal but they should have said why they opposed it in clear terms, and Redmond's name should have been established in the consciousness from the outset of the campaign. They should also have directed their campaign against the Government, notably the Taoiseach, who gave the commitment to the statue of O'Shaughnessy. You shouldn't have been threatened in the way you were.'

'Glad to hear it.'

'However, the threat to interfere with your work should have been clearly declared and the bottom line should have been that unless a statue of Redmond was erected within a period of eighteen months the O'Shaughnessy statue would be destroyed.'

'But that is the bottom line, isn't it?'

183

'It is now. But it took valuable days of acronyms and teasing communications and phased demands before that position was reached. I fear now that the initiative has been lost to a certain extent and the Government appears to have strengthened its position. To be honest, we, or they – since the decisions were unfortunately all theirs – seriously underestimated the resolve of the Government. We thought they would frighten much more easily. Obviously the letters were something they wouldn't get too worked up about and, let's face it, some of them were downright comical. Anyway, this didn't surprise me but what did surprise me and what certainly surprised the boys in the AVNS was the complete lack of panic the theft of the Proclammation engendered.'

'I could have told you that.'

'We thought that such a theft – symbolising as it would the determination of the AVNS to strike at the very paraphernalia of the historical tradition we seek to demonopolise, in order to gain its proper pluralistic and balanced ends – we thought this would scare the Government into thinking that, my God, these people are determined in their objectives and are pre-pared to raid our museums and steal our beloved artefacts to prove their point. We thought that basically they would be panicked into foreseeing a situation where in fact no monu-ment would be safe from interference, no museum free from anti-Fenian prowlers, and, let's be fantastical, no grave safe from disinterment.'

'Let's be indeed, but they don't think that.'

'No.'

'They don't seem to care.'

'They don't,' said Samuelson, almost sadly.

'But surely this proves that you're wrong about the State being all gooey about its 1916 tradition?'

'Not necessarily. The State, in the form of the present gov-ernment, may not be unduly worried about the fate of the Proclamation or the long cult of militancy surrounding it, but the State, as a historic institution, still offers no room for a balanced history that properly reflects ourselves.'

'So what do you want me to do?'

Samuelson inhaled deeply and stroked his bouffant.

'We think you have an understanding of our position. We think you alone of all people involved in this unfortunate affair have a clear and sympathetic understanding of the quandary we are in. You know your history – '

'Most of it,' I quipped. 'But I don't know me old man.'

'Your country's history,' he said, flapping his hand. 'I mean, you understand our country's historical traditions. You understand how they interact and compete. How one can have prominence in a national consciousness and eclipse another because of the vagaries of retrospect and hindsight.'

'And?'

'Whatever,' said Samuelson, agreeing with me to keep his flow. 'I won't argue. We could argue this all year. The point is that whatever your viewpoint, you understand – you alone, perhaps – understand our position, our aims, our neglect at the hands of those who have created the so-called verities of our public history. That is why the AVNS sent you those letters and that scribbled-upon newspaper. They were testing you out. They were seeing were you really as much a history buff as it appeared to be their fortune to discover. Were you really as interested in modern Irish political history as you appeared to be? Why, if I was an old-style believer – and I mean that in terms of an old-style God and the pre-determined old-style history we seek to oppose – I'd have said it was providential that you were involved in this whole business.'

'I'm more of a wit than a Whig myself, but what makes you think I'm a big history buff? Who told you all this?'

'We've done our research. And obviously Mr Harrington among others has filled us in. We've heard about certain pursuits of yours. Oh, innocent pursuits – the speech you gave to the Collins Movie Monitoring Committee is an example of one.'

'Everybody seems to have heard of that speech.'

'Well, I wouldn't go that far.'

'Well, how far will you go and how far am I to go, to call your guff if not your bluff?'

'The language,' said a bemused Samuelson shaking his head.

'Well, that's what it's all about, isn't it?'

'Debatable . . .'

'That's what I mean.'

'Yes, em . . .' He paused.

'So come on, what and where's my role, as Dev told the boys holding Jacob's.'

Samuelson stroked his chin again and coughed politely.

185

'Basically,' he said, leaning forward, 'we think you can play a crucial role – we think you can be a key to an ingenious resolving of this whole affair.'

'I like the sound of this. Keep talking.'

'What we would like you to do is to go to your boss, Mr Wycherley, and propose a deal to him. You propose to him that the studio approach the Government and tell them that you cannot go on working on the statue, and unless something is done to resolve the current controversy and the tension and strain it is creating in your life, not to mention the threats and publicity you have had to suffer, you will have to review your involvement.'

'If we're in, we're in.'

'Listen to me. Your humble proposal would be for the principle of a statue of John Redmond to be conceded. Not to be erected immediately but maybe next year, or even, at a stretch, the year after that. If your proposal was accepted you would not only have solved the controversy, and brought peace to our lives, you would have ensured that your statue would not be interfered with, you would have got the Government off the hook and – let's not be sanctimonious – our reward to you would be to ensure that when the time came you would do that statue of Redmond.'

'Ingenious indeed.' And it was. 'But our lives aren't under threat. You, or rather they, have withdrawn those threats.'

'It doesn't matter. You're living under an atmosphere of fear and tension. Your lives may be safe, for the moment, but your statues aren't.'

'That's fine,' I said and I had to smile.

'I mean, I am sorry to have to guarantee you this but as long as the AVNS demands go unmet, that statue of O'Shaughnessy will never be safe. In fact you can make that a condition of your demand to the Government: that you're not going to waste time and nervous energy, as well as artistic inspiration,' he added with a little smile, 'on a statue that is going to be destroyed.'

Outside the window, music could be heard. The band was striking up the National Anthem.

'The Government will say it'll be protected.'

'It can never be totally protected. Not for ever.'

It was the shorter version. The presidential salute. The head honcho has arrived.

'But the Government will wonder,' I told him, 'how come we're

186

so frightened now when we weren't in the beginning when your language was even more threatening.'

The music stopped.

'It was building up,' explained Samuelson. 'It's come to a head. Front pages, Proclamation stolen. Dark men take over. You can't handle it any more. I mean, we can have the direct threats reintroduced if it makes things easier.'

'Oh no. Please don't do that.'

More music. A hymn. The beginning of the interdenominational service.

'The fact is that these people – the AVNS – are getting desperate and they are not going to go away and die, I'm telling you. They'll destroy that Proclamation and they'll destroy that statue if it's ever revealed.'

I pushed out my chair and looked at the worn carpet.

'What if it got out that we did a deal to save our statue and get another one?'

'The Lord is my Shepherd'. I used to play that one too.

'It wouldn't . . . why would it? No one need ever know. The Government's not going to reveal the details of how it conceded on the second statue to save the first one – and you're not going to reveal how you threatened to do the opposite.'

I got up off the chair and walked towards the window.

'It would eventually emerge,' I said, opening a red suitcase in my mind. 'These things always do.'

'Well, so what,' said Samuelson and his jaw tightened. 'I mean, what would people say if it did ever emerge? Think about it, why, you could be the toast of the town for sorting out this mess. It could be seen as a stroke of negotiating genius and a cute move on your part. You would be the centre of it all. Sculptor and Co. saves the day. All parties happy. Excepting a few artists who might have felt they deserved a shot at the Redmond job – but all artists feel they're entitled to the commissions others get.'

I looked out the window. Below us, at the top of the street, the boys were sitting on the Belvedere Steps.

'The Government,' I told him, 'are convinced of our commitment to the job. They'd smell a rat and a very big rat if we tried that kind of blackmail on them now. I'm tempted to think they half suspected us of writing those letters at the very beginning.'

Samuelson was bemused at this and blinked his eyes.

187

'What if they said, Right then, back out – we'll find some-one else.'

'They can't do that,' said Samuelson. 'You've got a contract with them.'

'Yeah, but we're the ones breaking it.'

'If you lost that job, we'd issue a statement,' he said, with rising anger. 'We'd issue a statement threatening to kill your replacement.'

'Eh, I see. Thanks,' I said, thinking of Forbes. I looked out the window again. Mellowes was stroking his nose.

'I mean, *they'd* issue a statement,' he said, correcting himself.

I turned to smile at him and he stroked his plume. And then his nose. The music had stopped. Bugle at ease. I continued smiling and went back to my seat.

'It won't work,' I told him, but I was about to convince him that it would.

He looked at me with a deep frown.

'You seem to assume,' I said, pulling out my seat, 'that Mr Wycherley would be receptive to a proposal like this.'

'He'd have to be, otherwise he's going to get nowhere with his statue.'

'Maybe that wouldn't bother him.'

'I believe it would,' said Samuelson with a disquieting grin, 'and I believe he would be the sort of man to try unorthodox means to break a deadlock.'

'So I'd have to convince him and *then* the Government?'

'Convincing one would be as good as convincing the other.'

'Nonsense,' I said brusquely. 'It wouldn't work.'

Samuelson was stung.

'It's the only way,' he said. 'The only *peaceful* way.'

'There could be another way.'

'How?'

I came straight to the point.

'Information is about to come into my hands that if released publicly could cause the Government to abandon its statue of O'Shaughnessy.'

'What sort of information?' Samuelson was very sceptical.

'Information linking O'Shaughnessy to one of the biggest assassinations in the country's history.'

'Who?'

'A government minister.'

'Kevin O'Higgins.'

'Exactly.'

'He was cleared of that sixty years ago.'

'He was cleared of that on the evidence of sixty years ago. However, I am on the verge of getting papers that will explicitly show that O'Shaughnessy planned and was fully involved in the assassination.'

'Where are these papers?'

'Obviously I can't say.'

'But everyone knows who killed him. Their names were in that book that came out last summer. The issue is closed.'

'Well, I'm going to open it up,' I said grimly. 'Because those names were only half the story. They were the stooges, the assistants. The identity of the real head of the operation has never been revealed.'

'The stooges are the people who get caught, Shane,' said Samuelson with a patronising little smile.

'Not necessarily; their names can be stooges to the pages of history.'

What was I saying?

'This sounds like a bit of a story.'

'So did theirs. But, believe me, mine is the sort of story that if revealed would cause severe embarrassment to O'Shaughnessy and to the Government. Severe embarrassment.'

'And when are you going to get these papers?'

'At the weekend.'

'You've seen them?'

'I know they exist.'

'That's different.'

'Trust me,' I told him, smiling broadly. 'I'll have them by the weekend.'

'And what do you plan to do with them?'

'Well,' I said, sitting back. 'If I was to go to the Minister and say that I came across these papers and aren't they very interesting and wouldn't it be sensational if they ever got out – '

'He'd think you were blackmailing him.'

'So what. The fact is that I have, or will have, these documents and I am fully entitled to do what I want with them. I can send them to the papers if I wish, as I'm sure my friends will want me to do. But if I was to withhold them as a favour, then I could reasonably expect him to grant me a favour. A favour not to me

189

personally but a favour which would help us all. And that would be for him to see his way to giving you guys the nod for a statue of Redmond.'

'Rather magnanimous of us, isn't it?'

'Well, you see, I could combine this with what you said to me earlier. I could say, listen, Minister, I'm sick of all this and I think you should give them that statue. Why not? It won't kill us. I'm a bit of a history buff myself, Minister, and I've been reading about Redmond and I think it's right and fitting that there should be a statue of him. Why not, Minister? Just let them know its going to be OK on the QT. Don't announce it or anything, at least not for a few months.'

'And you really think you can just walk into the Minister like that and wave these things under his nose?'

'The Minister and I are like that.' I ballerina-crossed my fingers. 'I have a very informal relationship with him. Since the beginning of this contract we've got on very well. Well, you guys have helped. But he was a bit of a bandsman in his youth and we had a great chat about trumpets and all that.'

Was Samuelson buying all this? He was.

'I could make an appointment to see him, very much on the QT, and as a great favour, you see, I could lead him to the existence of these documents – "I thought you should know, Minister." "Thanks for telling me, son" – and after a bit of chat, I could give him the nudge and wink to do the decent thing and give these boys their statue before any more of this gets out of control.'

Samuelson was watching me closely.

'It's worth a try, isn't it?'

His jawline moved.

'I think it's worth a real try.'

'It combines with our own proposal,' he said.

'Sort of,' I admitted.

He sat back in his seat. 'You wouldn't think of giving or lending those papers to me?'

'No way.'

'Or showing them, even? We don't know they exist.'

'You'll have to take my word for it. I don't know the AVNS exist, for God's sake. I mean, you'll see them in good time. But first I'll have to go to the Minister.'

'When would that be?'

'Wednesday or Thursday. I don't know. I don't want to reveal any more, or else the whole thing will be ruined. And I don't want to be followed or monitored over the next few days. That's very important, right?'

'Of course.'

'So will you give me until next weekend?'

He leaned back again. He's going to be cagey. His jawline widened.

'I don't see why not,' he said. 'There's a cease-fire on until next Friday but I'm sure, for your benefit, we could extend it for a day or two. I'll have to put it to the boys.'

'Well, hold on, sod the boys – do I have your agreement or not?'

Samuelson's nose wrinkled and he exhaled.

'You do.'

'You do represent them?'

'I speak on their behalf. Of course.'

'It's a deal then?'

He looked at me closely. Another hymn commencing. 'Be Thou My Vision.' This one I don't know.

'It's a deal,' he said and his white hand stretched across the table to shake. I didn't expect this but, rather than be like Birkenhead with Collins, I took his hand and shook it limply. He smiled and nodded and I got up out of my chair. It was time to be moving.

'I'll give it my best,' I told him.

'I'm taking a chance,' he said dubiously. 'But then – '

'You were taking one from the very beginning, so shut up.'

'You're a funny lad.'

'You're a strange old man.'

'We're not dissimilar,' he said, smiling, 'in a way.'

'Perhaps.'

'That entrance of yours was something.'

'I wanted to start off on the right note,' I told him and I went back to the window. Boys still there.

'What are you looking at?'

'Just making sure you've no reinforcements called.'

'It'll pass off peacefully.'

'I wouldn't mind catching the end of it.' Mellowes was showing Oisin a piece of paper, pointing to it.

'OK,' came a voice behind me.

'I'll make my own way down – is it safe?'

'It's safe,' he said. 'It's very safe.'

The slung jaw smirked and he pushed his quiff back.

'Thanks,' I said, walking towards the door. I returned his smirk. 'Like I said, I'll do my best.'

He got up and walked towards me. 'No hard feelings.'

'Only statues have hard feelings,' I said.

'Here's a number for you to call if you've got any news – or problems.'

He gave me a bit of paper with a number written on it.

'It has five digits. How can – ?' Every Dublin number has at least six digits, or seven.

'You haven't cracked all our mysteries yet, Shane. Goodbye now.' He stroked his chain and smiled.

'OK', I said, putting the paper away. 'Goodbye.'

With his eyes on my back, I walked towards the door. Hand on the handle, I looked over my shoulder to give him a last glance. He hadn't moved. The sun burnished his hair and darkened his face but I saw the nod he gave me and returned it. For a moment I thought I saw Parnell give me the nod as well but it must have been my heightened state.

Along the deserted corridors I walked, still a bit on edge, but in a much different condition than that I came up in. I nearly felt sad now about the deserted rooms, the doors without numbers and the three yellow bulbs. Sad about Samuelson and his worn carpets and his hopeless cause. Sad about us. Nostalgia for something I never knew. And yet when I passed that mirror on the landing I thought don't feel so sad about them, maybe it's ourselves we should feel sorry for. But I put the thought behind me and looked in no more mirrors. March on, my man, march on.

I came down the stairs, bid goodbye to the receptionist and, before you knew it, I was out of the Belvedere Hotel and standing on its front steps, inhaling the sun. Ah, a breath of fresh air! And the sound of music coming up the street. The closing stages of the ceremony. I felt good all of a sudden. Involved. I had played my part. Done my bit. Shine on me, Mick, I'm about to pull off the ultimate operation. But not just yet. I contained my pleasure and slowly, so as not to arouse suspicion, I turned my head to the right to look over expressionlessly at my two faithful lieutenants sitting on the steps of the college and waiting obediently for any sign of success or failure. They looked like lost boys waiting for their dad outside the hotel. I smiled at them. Puzzled, they smiled back. They were relieved to see me. I was relieved to see them. I signalled to them to stay where they were until I'd passed on down the road, jerking my head to indicate I was going left, to where the music was coming from. To go the other way was to be in danger of Samuelson catching sight of us from that George's Street window. Not that it really mattered but I wanted to be out of his high-up, snooping gaze, among the cops and the citizens, and get a look at all the old boys standing there with their medals. Not all the old boys, of course, and that's why I wanted to get down there.

The boys understood and Mellowes, reseating himself with stalled anticipation, lifted his Meath hat and signalled for me to go ahead. There were by now quite a few Meath, and Kerry, fans hanging about, most of them on their way into the Tudor Rooms and other hostelries for pre-match drinks and dinner and quite oblivious to the commemoration ceremony and the increased security presence around the square. As was I, of course, and with them I mingled, stopping to check my non-existent watch ('When was I to meet Mick and John-Joe?') and showing great interest in the selection of rosettes, scarves, and 'teddybears for the ladies' that some hawker had arranged on the railings on the corner. I even bought an 'Official Programme' from one of his boys, a crew-cut urchin who short-changed me for what turned out to be his own personal product, a single-stapled Xeroxed collection of newspaper cuttings and mistyped prospective teamsheets masquerading as the official Big Match guide. And so I forgave him, for anyone who short-changes the GAA deserves credit and aren't I at the same game with the country's history.

Standing on the corner kerb, gardaí, three of them, examined the hawkers' wares and customers carefully, but mostly they partook in the relaxed atmosphere, exchanging pre-match banter with passing fans and indulging in county put-downs for those wits who told them that their colours weren't represented this year. Wearing the garda colours, Dublin were beaten by Meath in the Leinster final but you can't blame the cops for everything. These stout fellows are as likely to be from Dublin as I am likely to be one of them, notwithstanding my shirt. Which, incidently, went quite unnoticed so Mellowes was wrong in his fears.

He and Oisin didn't dally. When I turned from perusing my programme they were about fifty yards away, bearing towards me with strong strides and determined faces that fake-casually glanced into the sky occasionally, as if to surmise will the rain hold off for the game. If it's one thing we won't make, it's good actors.

Rain had held off since Tuesday and the sun was shining very nicely, bleakly without heat, and the mildest of breezes was coming over from the ceremony. You couldn't actually see the ceremony, given the sunken effect of the Garden and the row of black state cars parked in front of the gates, their drivers leaning in twos against the bonnets watching the ceremony and chatting with some of the half-dozen cops hanging around the front gates and side railings. No slipping away for cups of tea today, I'd say. But to call it a security alert was a misnomer. A significantly increased number of police was posted around the north side of the square, rerouting traffic up Granby Row and binocular-watching the top windows of overlooking buildings like my own, but a very relaxed air pervaded the place. Quite a few of the loitering football fans initially assumed the police were there because of them, but a few asked what the music was all about and seemed genuinely surprised, even annoyed, that the National Commemoration Ceremony, the one that the fuss was about, was taking place on the very morning of 'the Big Game'. I must say I was a bit surprised at this unseemly clash myself, but you can't blame the Government for everything. Those fans who'd read the front pages as well as the crucial back ones knew the story and passed on regardless. It was obvious the statue saga was not having a huge impact on the sport-going population or indeed on any of the population except those directly concerned. One man, seeing the black cars and hearing the mournful strains of the band, asked if there was a funeral going on. I felt tempted to answer not yet, my man, not yet.

The boys approached. I rested against the railings and read my programme.

'Watch me hats!' squawked the hawker when my shoulder shook his breadboard of crêpe creations.

'OK, OK' I said, moving aside. 'You know, if it rains those colours will run faster than the Kerry forwards.'

'Yeah, well, it won't rain and you won't run far with your money. The likes of you wouldn't know a forward from a backward.'

Thinks I'm a poshie. Here for the ceremony.

'I used to play in Croke Park.'

'Play, me arse. The only thing you play is the stock exchange.'

194

'Four All Ireland Finals I played in.'

'I'd say you did, all right – here, son, here's your change,' he said loudly for Daddy's benefit as he put coins in a nipper's fist.

'I played in my first All-Ireland at the age of ten, would you believe it? You see, I used to be an Artane boy. Blew my trumpet for Ireland. Blue-and-red uniform blowing in the – '

'This fellow giving you trouble?' Mellowes breezed in. Oisin behind.

'He's a weirdo. Show him some football.'

'Give him a good kicking, you mean?'

'Go on. Get out of here, the lot of you. I'm trying to do some business.'

'You'd have done more if you'd got up a few Easter lilies for this business across the road.'

'You mean red poppies,' said Oisin. 'You'd be getting into sticky turf if you sold the other.'

'And solid turf if you went for the pins.'

'Listen, lads,' he said contemptuously. 'I don't sell political garbage and I don't sell much to folk full of guff. Now, beat it.'

'Nice respect for the dead and the living. Come on, Shane. Let's go.'

Mellowes, eager to hear, prodded me on and pulled Oisin.

'Don't forget the Artane boys!' I shouted back at the hawker.

'Don't forget your invincible friends,' gritted Mellowes, dragging me towards the roadside. 'Come on, spill the story. What's the crack – did you meet him or not? I don't know which was worse, that dirty big grin you came out with or the cop-clean shirt you went in with.'

'Which nobody's noticed, so shut up. I can't talk here. I can talk across the road.' I could talk anywhere but I wanted to keep the atmosphere up. 'Over there! The Municipal Gallery – that's safe.'

'That's safe!? That's where the reception takes place when the ceremony's finished which is only minutes away. What the hell makes you want to go over there?'

'The huge head of Michael Collins – I'm only joking.' Collins's marble head is visible in the gallery window. 'OK, so let's go . . . across the road. Sure, why go further? The railings aren't bugged and there's a bit of a crowd over there watching the end of the ceremony. I wouldn't mind catching a last glimpse of Corny in his medals, standing for the flag. What do you say, boys? Come on, I bet you slipped down to see some of the show.'

'Yes, we did but mostly we kept watch to see how you'd get on, so kindly tell us how you did.'

'Corny's not there, Shane.'

'He didn't turn up, then? He's a fierce man for not turning up.'

'Nor was the Leader of the Opposition there. Or the Lord Mayor,' said Mellowes. 'So it wasn't a full show, as you'd call it. The band played, a plaque was laid and someone threw coins at the Taoiseach.'

'What, a contribution to the national debt?'

'You could say that. Some women did it. Republicans. There was more threat from them than there was from the other crowd. It's the plaque – honouring Irishmen who fell in *all* wars – that particularly has them upset. I can see why Corny didn't show up to see that unveiled. Did he mention the plaque last night?'

'Indeed he did. In fact, it may well have been our conversation that finally decided him not to come.'

'Oh oh, listen to him,' jeered Mellowes. 'So you put the fire in his belly?'

'Not yet, no. Last night, the wine did that. But I put the heart in his head.'

'What a catalyst you are. So tell us, did you put Samuelson's heart in his mouth or steady his head with reason?'

'A bit of both, actually.'

'So come on then. Tell us all.'

'I will. But let's first slip across here for the close of the show.'

'Ah, Shane!' Mellowes protested. 'We want to hear.'

'Listen!' A loud drum roll was sounding.

'It must be closing,' said Oisin. 'Look!'

We looked up and, high over the bushes and railings, at the other end of the garden, we saw the tricolour being hoisted from half-mast, jerking its way up the white flagpole with each pull of an invisible hand. The drums rumbled patiently.

'Come on!'

We rushed across the road and hustled in among the curious public standing on tiptoe to get a look over the railings at what was happening inside.

'Hey, don't push!' said a man with a child on his shoulders.

'Can't see anything. Can you?'

'The lady's foot, Shane. The lady's foot.'

'Oh. Sorry!' I sprang back and the lady glared at me ruefully. Mrs Gromyko in furs.

'Who's that next to the President – his wife?'

'Hardly. It's the Church of Ireland Primate. Look at the Taoiseach – will he ever get his hair cut?'

The drums rumbled to a quiet and stopped. The flag was at full mast, fluttering in the breeze. The reveille began. I hummed along. I knew these tunes.

'I used to play for their seconds,' I whispered.

'Scraped off their plates, you mean?'

'Shut up, boys. Here's the anthem.'

The National Anthem began and everyone stood still, absolutely quiet. Out of the corner of my eye I noticed that even the football fans on the corner were standing still. Rigidly still for this one. Later on they'll be singing it but on this occasion there was no singing. Mrs Gromyko's mouth tightened still further and the child on shoulders was told to hush. Inside the Garden, the rows of standing dignitaries assumed various forms of stern or contemplative erectness. Stiffest of all, in the front row, were what I thought were the veterans but in fact were the Government. The veterans were – blast it! – out of view beneath us and so I was denied the chance of seeing those of the Old IRA and British Legion who did attend standing together for a unique time. Unique because it won't happen after the next election and this government looks like they've had their day, even if they're standing up for themselves on this occasion. Even the Ministers of State, of which, second last in line and these days perhaps first to go, was our own TD, his Bulben chest out to its full Mitterrand concavity, trying to put a brave face on things. (What's he thinking? He's not here, the bastard, Vol. O'Shaughnessy. But I'll see he's in the Green – for ever.)

Behind the present incumbents were former ministers and assorted backbench members of the Dáil and Senate, and then, people who don't even have the prospect of office – representatives of the SDLP and Alliance parties from the North, followed by the advanced toads of the judiciary, senior paperkeepers of the Civil Service, the academic equivalent from the universities and, next to them, a line of rightly troubled countenances from the Garda Síochána. After that, a dozen rows of suits I couldn't make out but who I assume make up the semi-state bodies and the

197

health boards and, finally, the diplomatic corps, unless the local authorities are now in the hands of dark men in turbans with half a roll of sunburst-patterned Hickey's fabric hanging off their backs. They weren't exactly standing stiff and swollen but then neither was Mellowes. He had been at me since the anthem began.

'So you met him?' he confirmed through clenched teeth. We didn't look at each other.

'Yes.'

'Shush!' said a concerned lady behind us.

'Dangerous?' he whispered.

'No.'

'What did he say?'

'Cease-fire still on. Give me a week.'

'To do what?'

'Stop statue.'

'How?'

'Shush, please!' insisted the lady.

'Tell Government.' I spoke very softly. 'Too dangerous. Must put up Redmond as well. We'll pay for.'

Mellowes nodded. 'That it?'

'No . . .'

'Told him I could change Government mind. Threaten to release dirt on C.'

'What dirt?'

I smiled.

'You bastard.'

'Do you mind, please!' said the lady and she was joined by a chorus of outraged citizens. He'd said it loudly and they'd heard him.

'Really! Did you ever hear – ?'

'Language . . . in the middle of the National Anthem.'

'Disgrace,' said another woman.

'Sean, come back!'

Mellowes had taken to his heels and was walking away, piqued. Oisin and I ran after him.

'Sean!' He walked to the front of the Municipal Gallery and stood there shaking his head.

'Sean!' We caught up with him. 'Sean, what's wrong?'

'You told him, full stop.'

'Yeah, but – '

'You had no authority to tell him! That was strictly confidential –

198

do you understand the meaning of the word? No one was supposed to know anything about it. No one. Least of all them.'

'Yeah, but I had your clearance to do – well, to do a deal. Sort of plenipotentiary.' I shrugged.

'Sort of plenipotentiary – listen to him!' He looked at Oisin. Oisin shrugged. 'You're living in a dream world! Who do you think we are – Mephistop . . . Mephis – '

'Mephistophelean,' said Oisin.

'Mephistophelean traders in pacts and secrets? Eh? You go out and you link our little operation to your bloody statue and a statue of John Redmond. Guarantees and bargains and . . . blackmail! Jesus, what have you stitched us into?'

'Lads, lads, lads – quiet, quiet. We're in Parnell Square. Remember? Off to a match. Don't look now, Shane, but there are two blue strollers about four yards behind you.'

I looked around and saw two cops pass. People were mingling again after the anthem. The bank struck up 'A Nation Once Again.'

'We should have you arrested,' said Mellowes.

'My life depends on that statue,' I said, dropping my voice. 'I thought you might be willing to help me get off the hook. Obviously, I was wrong.'

'You weren't wrong,' sighed Mellowes. 'We do want to see you off the hook. You know we do. Anyway, you're not on a bloody hook. There's a cease-fire on. It's the Government's ball game. Ultimately it's they who have to ensure the safety of the statues and the Proclamation. OK, I thought if you could do something to help the situation it was worth a try. Something subtle, something discreet. But, Jesus, there was no need to drag the whole Booterstown operation into the picture. There was no need to risk all that. Shane, you had no right to tell them what we were up to. No right! What if they tell someone? They won't be interested in what we want to do with it.'

'No, because they won't know what we want to do with it. They know nothing about it. Nothing. And neither will anyone else until we decide when and how we're going to use our information.'

'But you told them you'd go to the Minister with the information, threatening to release it unless he capitulated.'

'Only with your permission.'

People were passing us. Mrs Gromyko – she again – gave me a severe look.

'No, but – '

'No, but nothing. As far as they're concerned you're off to the Minister as soon as you get this info.'

'That's if I get the info at all; I could say I didn't or I could say I did and I went to the Minister and he said, "No go, the statue goes ahead."'

'And they'll say so publicise.'

'And I'll say no, not just yet. The info will be published shortly. By Sean Mellowes, BA, perhaps, in a limited edition.'

'The whole scenario you describe is a nightmare.'

'Keep it down, Sean, keep it down.' Two gallery ushers came down the steps.

'It's a bloody nightmare – they'll publicly call upon the Minister to release the information about Mr O'Shaughnessy given to him recently by one Shane McArdle, the same Mr McArdle who is working on the statue. They'll call your bluff. It'll be devastating. You'll look a scheming idiot. You'll have betrayed everybody. You'll have ruined everything. The only person you'll have fooled will be yourself.'

I looked at him blankly.

'It's not as bad as you think,' I said. 'We're covered and I'm covered. There are escape clauses.'

'Escape clauses,' said Mellowes derisively. 'What escape clauses?'

'I can't really say . . .'

'Worse!' said Mellowes. 'Now he's not even telling us what we're stitched into.'

'You're not stitched into anything. That's the whole point.'

'Look, Mellowes. He's got a week,' said Oisin, to my rescue. 'Give him a chance. He's a wide berth. He can't consult with us on everything. I mean, he did get the key, he did go to the dinner. He did, with our encouragement, go and meet Samuelson. And he was encouraged by *us* to explore the means to a solution. Now he's on a sticky wicket and, Christ, he's the right to use what means we have.'

Mellowes pouted, not so convinced.

'And listen, if he was going to go to the Minister with the information – that's if we get any bloody information – then so what! We're going to be releasing it anyway so he might as well use it to save his own skin. If you ask me, it could be just the thing to sort out this mess. And, Jesus, it'll be some mess we'd have sorted out! Think about it: we might have enhanced one reputation and ruined another but, Mellowes, we'll have saved the Proclamation. Think about it! Men have fought for less.'

Mellowes thought about it. Oisin winked at me, confident he could bring him round.

'I'm trying not to think about it,' grimaced Mellowes. 'The whole sequence of events if things went wrong is too terrible to be imagined. The nobler option, to save one piece of paper with another, would appear to be the only option. We're stitched into this. Jesus, Shane, I could give you some stitching to do. Obviously you've the same respect for consulation that your mentor had.'

The back of whose marble head I could see at the moment in the gallery window.

'I'd hope to have the same respect for my comrades and that they'd try and bail me out as I would them. They sprang a man from Lincoln Jail.'

'Behind you, boys, behind you.'

At the top of the steps, two guards had emerged and were looking down, waiting for the guests to arrive. We nodded a mute hello and they smiled weakly.

'You'll have to move on from there,' one of them said. 'Some very important people will be arriving shortly.'

'Come on,' I said. 'We'll go around to No. 40. You haven't seen it yet.'

'We wouldn't want to be in anybody's way,' Oisin told the guards as we left.

We walked quietly around to my new abode and Mellowes cheered up a little.

'OK, we'll give it a try,' he said. 'We have to.'

When he got inside and had a cup of tea in his hand and heard the description of Mr Samuelson and his extraordinary room he cheered up some more. I could see they were relieved that he didn't seem as dangerous as he had once sounded and I was on the verge of telling Mellowes about Samuelson's other enquiries but then I thought it'd be better to withhold such information until . . . well, until after tonight.

Chapter 8

Moonlight Takes Over

A car horn sounded out in the street. Oisin. He obviously wasn't going to come in, given the way he'd insulted poor Delia and her dead cat on Thursday night. I raced downstairs, damn near killing myself at the bottom when I misjudged a step and slid against the wall, courtesy of a footloose wicker mat, obviously placed there by hands as blind as the Rathmines ones that made it. Steadying myself, I had to steady also a Ming vase which was going, quite literally, 'minnngg' on top of its precarious column.

Also going minnngg were the various bodies I had to say goodbye to strewn around the room and too far gone in pleasant inebriation to protest at my leaving. I shook a few hands. Jimmy and Maeliosa were so wrapped around each other on the sunken couch, swapping sunken dreams and booze-oozed nostalgia, that I had some difficulty determining whose head was whose, but they both gave me big kisses and hugs and Maeliosa told me to be careful out there. Does he know something? A littler kiss and no hug at all from Ariel, sitting perched and recomposed on her Cornelius-leathered chair. She, obviously, wasn't in agony about my leaving and when I said I'd ring her during the week she winced this little stoic smile and said OK.

The French au pair said nothing. She just sat there like Whistler's mother, in her bathrobe, hoping Nina Simone would get her through 'this facking town'. Robbie Thunder, it appeared, was doing exactly that in his relentless search for more whiskey. He had been out now for twenty minutes, four times the time it took him earlier to go out and seemingly just pick one from the tree.

Wendy had gone with him. Our hostess was upstairs, in reclusive mourning, trying baby clothes on the dog or some such distracted nonsense. I'd see her again, no doubt. Invite her to the unveiling. She'd raise a few eyebrows standing there in her Maud Gonne black and her fake-fur overcoat. Her boyfriend, the electronic sculptor, I couldn't say goodbye to for he had passed out, or should I say, plugged out, and lay slumped, thalidomide-like, in his armchair, dreaming of the day when he might be mothered like a cat or give birth to the same, for such are the shapes of dreams. And to any further shapes I might have missed in the whiskey-reeling darkness I muttered a general see you again and then made for the door, nearly killing myself again; this time on an empty Power's bottle, anxious to come with me. More than can be said for Ariel to whom a last smile and blown kiss merited nothing less than a tight little grin of thinly disguised bewilderment.

Sod her, I thought, stepping into the hall, for if I mourn one loss, here's the plaintive sound of another coming down the stairs. Muffled wailing. If it's not herself, the child has woken up or the dog's protesting at the imposition of a nappy. I didn't dally to discover. Distress signals of another sort were sounding: Oisin's finger on the car horn.

Clunked the big door shut and – careful this time – down the steps and narrow path.

'Come on, come on,' said Oisin, revving the engine and knocking the door open. I climbed in.

'Jesus, what a scene in there!'

'I don't want to hear about it. Was Maeliosa in there?'

'Yes, in Jimmy's arms, or vice versa.'

'The tinker. He didn't come to practise.' Oisin watched his mirror and let a line of slow suburban Sunday traffic pass him – kid-filled cars with grannies and nodding dogs – before pulling out with a screech for Ranelagh.

'The whiff off you!' he said, drawing up for the lights.

'Is it bad?'

'Bad enough to be noticed. And you're the one who gave out to us this morning for turning up with sore heads. Theobald Matthew indeed! Jesus, Shane, what's wrong? Did you need to tighten up for the big job?'

'Not at all. Quite the opposite.'

The bottle of whiskey on the Mountjoy table. After the Four Courts four.

'I've been in that house all afternoon. I had one or two. It can't be all that bad.'

'Well, I won't be lighting up for a while,' he said with a grin, pointing to the Major packet on the dashboard. 'But Mellowes might if he smells our breath.'

'Our's – why, did you . . .?'

'I had a few pints in the Docker's. What else could we do waiting for that Maeliosa to show up. He skied off to do a blessed cat's *caoine*, so the rest of the band took an amble on the quayside. Rockers for the Docker's!' he said, slapping my knee and spinning the steering wheel to take the Ranelagh triangle. 'Don't worry, McArdle, Meath got hammered so Mellowes might have felt tempted to follow suit. One pint down for every five his team lost by. Hammered, they were, sorely hammered.'

'I know, I saw the news. Nothing on the Proclamation. Only Corny's statement as to why he wasn't there today – wonder was he at home all day?'

'We'll soon find out. Here, take one of these.' Oisin fished a mint out of the glove department.

'How old is this?'

'Very old. Look at all the coaches bringing our rustic half back.'

All along Ranelagh Road big touring coaches with private company addresses in Letterkenny, Roscommon, Nenagh, were letting off young people laden with baggage. Back to the city for work tomorrow.

'You nervous?'

'Yeah, why?'

'You're fairly booting it.'

'Why not? I'm a good driver. You say it yourself.'

'True.' He was a very good driver.

'Are you not nervous?'

'A bit.'

'I mean, you know what we're up to. Whose house are we breaking into? Whose security are we violating?'

'Yeah, but you see, I don't think of it like that. I don't think of it as a raid on the deadly underground files of the great Mr O'Shaughnessy at a time when he is involved in a great national controversy and is in the limelight and is under watch and all the rest of it.'

'What do you think of it as?'

204

'I think of it as a foray into an old man's garden. We could be robbing his apples,' I added jauntily. 'Listen, I've been there. There are no cops, no alarms, no jungle nets in the bushes. I've been out to the coal cellar, there's nothing to worry about. There's him who's out tonight, there's Mrs Williams who goes at ten and there's Vanessa who generally keeps him "occupied" from thereon.'

'You're winding me up.' He braked for the lights and looked at me.

'I'm not,' I laughed. I was a little giddy, I'll admit. The whiskey, Ariel, and the idea that I was going off to Clonskeagh again tonight. 'I'm not. Really. She looks after him. Lovely girl. It's safe. For us, I mean.' I burped. 'Trust me.'

'We trusted you with the secret of the Operation Booterstown,' said Oisin, changing gear, 'and look who you told about it.'

'Don't bring that up again.'

We were approaching Milltown crossroads.

'As far as I'm concerned, I had a green light for that, something you don't have here, so don't plough through the way the 11 bus did when I was on it yesterday. Sheer panic, it caused. Some spud on a Honda 50 almost met his head on a lamppost. I had to close my eyes.'

'Unusual for you,' said Oisin, pulling up for the red light and fetching himself a cigarette. 'Given your taste for gore. How did that funeral go?'

'Freakish. You'd have enjoyed it. She in black, moping around telling us about the cat's personality and filling us with food. Loads of food, and wine and whiskey, courtesy of Robbie Thunder, who kept nipping out for fresh supplies.'

'Not paying for it, I assume.'

'Oh no, just organising. But listen, some of the gathering. Delia's boyfriend is an electronic sculptor who took very seriously my theory on the sexual sub-textual references of ballistic missiles, and there was a French au pair in a bathrobe who sat there sour-lipped and said nothing all afternoon.'

'Sounds nice,' said Oisin, blowing smoke and moving over to Clonskeagh Road.

'Ah, but listen, there was something nicer. A gorgeous little creature from Connecticut of Russo-Jewish extraction. And what extraction! Brown and soft-limbed in a sleeveless dress of two-tone green. It was amazing. She came out to sit in the garden with us and as soon as she sat down and heard me rattling on, she just started

205

giving me this really strong look. We said nothing until we were inside – and many hours later, after much chat by the fireside, she stared at me with these powerful eyes and her soft little pump was suddenly rubbing the inside of my calf. So I said, "Are you going to show me the house now?" and off we went.'

'No?' Oisin looked at me.

'Hey, watch the – !' The car screeched as it cut the dangerous bend by Ashton's pub.

'What happened?' he asked, spinning the wheel back.

'We went upstairs to her bedroom and fondled about a bit.'

'Did you . . .?'

'No, all but that. She stopped suddenly and mentioned her thirty-five-year-old boyfriend in New York.'

'Ah, sod that.'

'But she was gorgeous. A beauty. Ariel was her name. She was seventeen.'

'Seventeen – Jesus, Shane!'

'What? Sure, your man's thirty-five.'

'Yeah, but he's her boyfriend. And in the middle of a bleeding funeral, Shane, albeit only a run-down mog's one. What did the rest of them think?'

'Don't know, don't care. She was a little embarrassed returning downstairs.'

'But you, of course, weren't. Well, fair play to you. I'm glad to hear you defiled the occasion by your thoughtless lust. Good man. And she was lovely, was she?'

'A work of art. I'm meeting her next week.'

'Oh good, so we'll all get a chance to see her.'

'Maybe.' I smiled. We were going over the Dodder and I could smell her perfume on my hands. Had I drunk too much? Felt fine, alert, but giddy too. Ariel. The thought of her made me smile.

'Here we go,' said Oisin, revving the engine and leaning forward to climb the hill of Clonskeagh Road. He looked tense.

'Relax, Oisin.'

'I'm relaxed. Do you want another mint?'

'No thanks. I need my teeth. Ariel liked them, brushed them with her tongue. Get your enemy when he's teeth in his head. That's what Corny told us.'

'Jesus, thanks.'

'That's why he reckons no one's out for him. Physically, that is. Are you ready for his house?'

Roebuck House was coming up on the right-hand side.

'I don't even want to look.'

'Don't be silly. You'll be inside it shortly, and inside lengthily if we're caught. Five years for breaking and entering.'

We drove on in silence past the Phillips factory and the architectural faculty of the college, the neon lights, Isaac Butt's house and, across the road, deep in the trees, the shadowy outlines of Roebuck House, set well back from the road. There were refuse bins outside the gates and – were there lights on inside? Or were they just reflections? I couldn't see. Oisin didn't slow up for me to get a good look. He just drove on around the diamond and on to Bird Avenue, lowering the window to dispatch a half-smoked cigarette.

'Looked a bit dead, didn't it?'

Oisin swallowed hard and nodded.

'But then it probably looked like that last night and, I can tell you, it was anything but dead inside!' I started laughing. Oisin didn't. 'Cheer up, man, it'll be a bit of crack!'

He slowed up and pulled in along the kerb outside Loyola, parking perfectly.

Up the concrete slipway we went to the front door. Ding-dong. A shape approached the pimpled glass, long and vaguely greyish, its pale hand fidgeting with the mortice. Once freed, the door was pulled back by Greycoat Ryan, standing there in the coat he'll die in. Sooner, perhaps, than he thinks.

'Operators Booterstown reporting for action.' I clicked my heel.

'Ah . . .'

'Ah, he says. Can we come in?'

'Certainly, gentlemen.' Curtseying, he swiftly drew back the door and we filed in.

'They're down the back.'

On the way down the hall, I alerted Oisin's attention to the tattered Meath rosette hanging from the gilt frame of the O'Higgins painting. We both laughed.

'Well, Sean,' I said, coming into the back room and gesturing backwards, 'I see you've pinned your loser's colours to the right man.'

'Shut it, McArdle,' he snapped, looking up from his papers. 'At least my man consults the team before he sets them up.'

'Oh, touchy. And your analogy fails me. If it wasn't for me and my key we wouldn't be here tonight.'

'Sit down.'

Oisin pulled up chairs and we joined them around the table. As usual, it was cluttered with mugs, cups, maps and drawings. The drawings were a series of A3 sheets marked with a multitude of red, green and blue lines and dotted diagonal lines and 'x's and squares.

'Jesus, are we going to wire the gaff while we're in there?' I winked at the Goat.

'Comprehensive research means comprehensive planning,' explained the shirt-sleeved, serious Mellowes, running red pen along a National School ruler. 'Preparations and precautions. We need to have a complete picture of the place. I don't know if you deal in the complete picture, Shane, but we do.'

The Goat nodded.

'Tsk, tsk. Harsh words,' protested Oisin, leaning his long frame back and striking a match. 'It was McArdle filled us in, you know.'

'Thank you, Oisin,' I said, 'a sculptor's duty. Who poured your key? And cased the joint. And gave you a lot better information on the inside than old Joe Moran supplied us with when we poured coffee into him on his Bewley's stool. Pages and pages of tightly typed tremulous prose – Jesus, man, and here you are doing the same in a geometric way. In the name of God, Sean, what do we need all these diagrams for?'

Mellowes looked up and lifted his fag out of the ashtray to survey us.

'To find a way in.' He took a good clean pull, 'And to find a way out.'

'But I've been in there,' I protested. 'I don't need any plans.'

'You've been in the house,' explained Mellowes calmly, 'and you've done excellent reconnaissance work there. No doubt about it. But you haven't been all over the garden and let's face it, gentlemen, it's likely that we're going to be all over the garden, front and back. I'm going to do a briefing. It'll be short and sweet. Study these.'

He handed each of us a plan of the garden, front and back. Quite detailed, it included the vegetable patch at the very back, giving the vegetables grown (Mellowes got into an adjacent garden to look over the fence) and the grown-over pets' graveyard, a Victorian indulgence of Mother. The front garden was thick trees, trunk to trunk all the way up to – daylight – the pebbled driveway in front of the house. Just inside the front gate, Mellowes noted the old security hut dating from Corny's days as Minister when (OK, I was wrong) he did accept the presence of a cop or two during the night.

Mellowes also noted the size and type of fencing used around the perimeter of the garden: a high, broken-glass-topped grey wall along the west side, separating Corny from the clothes lines and bourgeois back gardens of Nutgrove Park. Then, at the very back, beyond the vegetable patch, there was a smaller wall, moss-felted and shielded by entangled shrubbery and small sycamore trees, including, would you believe, a tree hut. Corny's reversion to childhood, perhaps, or a tolerated Enid Blytonism of Mrs Brisket's next-door son. If so, let me tell you that how young Brisket got into the garden was how we would be getting in: over the wooden-cum-occasional bush fence that ran along the east side of the garden, keeping out, or trying to keep out, those apple – or document – thieving brats of the neighbourhood, who might come through the back gardens of Leinster Lawn or, better still, via the lane between the houses 18 and 20.

'We can't delay in this lane,' explained Mellowes. 'It stands to reason that we're more worried about the neighbours' eyes than we are about what's over the fence. We'll go straight over, making as little noise as possible. I've measured it for footholds, and once inside, we merge with the bushes.'

'Merge with the bushes.'

'All in, safely, we take stock, and begin to creep up the garden, one by one, behind cover of the pine trees.'

'Pine trees.'

'We come to the second-last pine tree before the back of the house. Careful here because the back porch is always lit.'

'Yeah, but you can't see anything from the porch – I mean, in the trees.'

'No, but between us and the steps down to the coal cellar there'll be about ten yards of open lawn. We'll have to cross it quickly.'

'Dodgy, we can't all race at once.'

'No. You'll go first.'

'Me?'

'You've got the key. You've got to get down those steps and have that coal door open before we can join you.'

'Really, I mean, Jesus, it would be me.'

'Yes, it would. You've been there before and you've opened the door. Now you've got to open it again.'

'When I get it open, how do I signal to you?'

'Come back up a step or two and put your hand in the air. We'll tiptoe over one by one. Greycoat will stay, remaining behind the tree for most of the time we're inside the cellar. At certain stages he may feel it necessary to leave his perch and check that things are OK out the front. It's up to him. The bushes around the east gable are an ideal jungle to roam in and connect with the thick trees out front. No better man than Greycoat to blend in with the undergrowth.'

He nodded gratefully and the Goat grinned.

'As for us' – Mellowes smiled, knocking his papers together – 'once we're inside that cellar, with the door locked behind us, we'll be getting down to the real business – the search for the red suitcase.'

'Red suitcase?'

'So, Joe came up with – '

'Yes, gentlemen, Joe came up with the goods. What were your smart remarks about him earlier on, Shane? Something about you giving us better information than old Joe Moran on his Bewley's stool?'

'I stand corrected,' I admitted.

'You certainly do. We're looking for a red-leather suitcase, gents. Joe has had this confirmed by his friend in Kensington. I was talking to him at about half-eight. He wished me luck.'

'We need it,' said Oisin.

'Maybe,' said Mellowes, 'we are relying on some elements of luck and I want you to be fully aware of that at the start, as I'm sure you are. Firstly, Joe's words on a red suitcase, though I believe him, can never be guaranteed. No more than any of our words can be guaranteed. We'll just have to put it to the test. We'll just have to take our chance.'

'That's what we're here for.'

'The other thing is that – ' Mellowes paused here. 'It's not absolutely certain that Corny has gone to this dinner, or that he may not come home early from it. He was certainly due to go to it. He was a guest of honour – but with the events of the week, and, more particularly, the events of the day, he may have decided to give it a skip. I say this because I rang the Hidden

Arms in Portlaoise earlier in the evening, as Justice Barrington's son, to ask if Mr O'Shaughnessy would definitely be coming, and I got an indefinite answer: "We hope he'll be coming, despite everything." This brings a small element of doubt into the equation although if I know Corny he'll be there in style. Unfortunately, I can't check it now because Justice Barrington's number is, not surprisingly, unlisted. I could try other means to check but there's no point in raising suspicions. What I'm saying is that we should be prepared for everything.'

We nodded our heads.

'Now take one of these,' he said and handed us another map; this time a detailed ground-floor plan of the house, my version supplanting Joe Moran's. But we had had enough of maps and were anxious to get on with it. Tension was setting in and Mellowes knew it. He fielded a few more hypothetical questions and then there was silence. Mellowes looked at Oisin. Oisin looked at the clock.

'How about getting down to the real business?'

'Let's go,' agreed Mellowes and we all rose from the table.

Each of us was to take a box of matches, as an emergency light. Greycoat would carry a pocket-size black-rubber torch. I had the key, Mellowes had his penknife. Nothing else was needed. Mellowes and Greycoat folded and tucked away the plans they'd be carrying.

Skin the Goat insisted we all shake hands. Ridiculous business but I willingly obliged. Oisin squeezed mine and grimaced at me bravely, assuming his best Walter Matthau expression.

'Let's do it,' he said.

'Wait,' said Mellowes, before we bundled out the door. 'Let's have no more holier-than-thou accusations about who comes on the job with a whiff of a drink the night before.' He walked over to the cabinet. 'Let's have a parting shot.'

'For which crime you'd have got just that from the movement in the old days.'

'We're answerable to no movement, old or new.' A Power's bottle was drawn out, followed by five glasses. 'We're not off to kill people – we're researching history, not making it,' said Mellowes, unscrewing the bottle and filling the glasses.

'Oh, well said,' said Oisin.

We lifted our glasses.

'Invincibles all,' he said.

'Invincibles all,' we chorused and clinked our glasses. Once whupped and savoured – burning the stomach nicely – we banged down our glasses and followed each other out into the hall.

Mellowes stopped in front of O'Higgins, himself stopped in a quizzical frown.

'We're off to find out, Kevin, who the bastards were that killed you.'

A mild summer's night, fragrant with the nutty scent of washed and dried grass and alive with the soft sounds of the summer suburbs. Insects making music with their little bones, grasshoppers playing castanets, a dog barking and the far-off sound of truant children squealing. Cars flew down Clonskeagh Road at their usual breakneck speed, heading for the city. Mostly taxis, otherwise the road was relatively quiet. The shops shut. The 11 terminus empty. A lone bicycle with a lump creaked its way up the hill towards Goatstown. We turned into Leinster Lawn, Oisin pushing away the drooping branches of pavement cherry trees. 'Caution Children' read a sign with a black silhouette of a boy chasing a ball or something. Across the road, behind the houses, loomed a more forbidding silhouette, the high dense trees surrounding Roebuck House, black and shifting against the moon-blued sky. It was a shock to realise how close he was. The branches slapped us as we walked along Leinster Lawn, but when we looked back we could catch occasional glimpses of the house behind the trees, a sickly bone-white colour, pale and frightening.

I could hardly believe it was the same house I was in last night. We walked on very quietly, past the front gardens and driveways with their two or even three cars. The gardens were full of gladioli and roses and those white installation sculptures they call lawn sheep. Lights still burned in some of the living-rooms. People going to bed or staying up. From the ceiling of one still illicitly lit loft bedroom, painted Airfix models of fighter planes could be seen splendidly suspended on invisible cat gut until a 'lights-out' extinguished our view. But after a few moments of parental-directed darkness, the white spot of a torchlight appeared and loopily roved the ceiling, picking out the planes. Some kid was reenacting the Battle of Britain, God bless him, and I thought of a world I never knew.

'OK,' said Mellowes, looking behind for the others. They had just come into Leinster Lawn.

A car door slammed suddenly and Mellowes drew us back. We slipped in behind a tree, a very thick cherry tree. Four doors away, a big man in a yellow jumper was rummaging in the boot of his Corolla. He took out a gear bag and a rugby ball. The Sunday 7-a-side was over for another week, followed by the customary 7-inside by the sound of his wet and hearty belch reverberating through the peaceful street. He stumbled heavily up to the door. The weight of the ball. Keys jangled, scraped the door, missed, try again, hope I've better luck, there, got it. He went in and sort of heeled the door shut behind him. Prop forward. The wife's about to be torn apart.

'Right, now, come on.'

We hurried across the street and slipped into the laneway between 18 and 20.

'Shite!' said Oisin walking into a dustbin.

'Shssshh!'

'Leg's gammy. Can't go on, men. Shoot me here.'

'Shsssh, will you – stop laughing, Shane.'

Mellowes stopped and waved us down.

'Incoming?' I asked.

'Shut it, will you.'

'Foot's fucked,' cursed Oisin, limping behind me. I couldn't stop laughing.

'Shane, will you be serious?' snapped Mellowes. But how could I be? Here I was, raiding O'Shaughnessy's house the night after I was in there for dinner. It was unbelievable. What was I up to? What were we up to?

'Right, now, there's the hedge ahead,' whispered Mellowes, crouched down in the big grass. 'Keep your heads down in case anyone's looking out. What you have to – Oisin, are you all right?'

'I'll make it. But if gangrene sets in – '

'Listen.' We huddled against the concrete side wall. 'You've got to get a foothold on the wooden laths. You see where they join the gorsh bushes. Yes, gorsh. Well, try and get on to the top of the fence and then down the other side in two swings. You know, like the gymnasts on the beam.'

'Like the gymnasts on the beam – are you crazy? With my leg? Sure, I'd be crippled hitting the ground from that height and walk thereon like a gymnast on the Jim Beam. You'll be shouldering me like McArdle on Thursday night.'

'Yeah, Nadia Cominatcha didn't have to rip her tights. There could be a bed of gooseberry bushes waiting for us.'

'Right. Well, you take that attitude, smart arses. I'm going on ahead. Good luck.'

With which, Mellowes rose out from the wall, did a little jiggy-run, got a foot in and went up and over the fence. Gone. Into the darkness his red head went.

We were astonished. Such a large man and not a bother on him. Or a bother for us, and the others behind us. Did they know the format, or were they supposed to fend for themselves?'

'Greycoat and Tommy,' I said to Oisin. 'They won't shift that.'

'Mellowes just cleared it,' he replied, almost with disappointment. 'We all can. We all had to. Come on, who's first?'

'You go.'

Oisin looked at me with surprise.

'Go on.'

He took a deep breath, unstooped himself and sprung up on the fence, long legs awry and arms clinging, a comical sprawling sight – eek, creak! – until a hooked elbow manoeuvred him up to the rim and he dropped lengthways over the other side. A grunt sounded and the rustling of bushes. Not anxious to hang around for the neighbours' response to all that noise, I bolted up, stuck a thin Winstanley tip between lower laths and hauled myself up until I got into a position where I could safely drop on to O'Shaughnessy's grass, instead of his entrapping bushes. Thud! I landed on the soft grass and crawled in to join Mellowes and Oisin crouched beneath a fir tree.

'We're in,' said Mellowes with a smile. Oisin looked more dubious.

'Incredible,' I said. 'I'm back in Corny's garden.'

'We're now trespassing,' Mellowes assured us.

'Think of it,' I said. 'Trespassing on the property of a former IRA Chief of Staff. In different days we'd have been shot on sight.'

'Don't speak too soon,' said Mellowes and Oisin looked at the ground.

'Amazing,' I sighed. 'Trespassing on the property of a man who trespassed on so many other people's with deadly intent.'

'To punish the ultimate trespasser?' Mellowes made an amused rise of the eyebrows.

'Ah yes – second-last member of Collins's Squad. The penultimate Apostle. Boland's Mills veteran. *Bête noire* of the establishment.'

'Shssh!'

'The man who didn't turn up today. The man they all wanted to see, for a change. In his garden we sit and plot.'

Greycoat and Skin came tumbling over the fence in rapid succession, the first crashing into the bushes, the second shouldering the earth.

'Shsssshh!' Mellowes sounded like he was going to produce Bewley's coffee and by the response to his cautioning the boys sounded like they were being forced to drink it.

And looking like they had, when, still cursing, they crawled towards our tree on all fours, Skin the Goat in a doggy position I saw him assume once at a party to woo some Spanish student who'd lost her contact lenses (when she found them and saw him, she shrieked) and Greycoat, a length behind, as they say in greyhound racing and gay night clubs, shuffling along in flapping coat and hair full of twigs like Jesus down from the cross and in need of a drink.

'What in the name of Jasus,' barked the Goat, coming in beside us, 'did you want us to do? Jump the effing thing and land without a sound on bloody air?'

'Sorry. It's just that the noise of the bushes might wake – '

'Wake, me arse. We're over, aren't we?'

'All right there, Greycoat?' I jovially enquired.

'F-f-fine,' he stammered, looking like someone had just squeezed his nuts.

'Right,' said Mellowes, 'let's move down tree to tree. I'll lead, Shane behind me.'

We went around the tree and nipped in behind another one, getting our first view of the house from the back. No lights on.

'Spooky,' said Oisin. He sounded nervous.

We went from tree to tree until we got to the second-last one. The big moment. Curiously, I didn't feel as frightened as I expected. I was emboldened by being in the garden, got this far,

215

come this close, and by the feeling that, hell, I've been in there, I've seen this fellow O'Shaughnessy and he's an old, wizened man. Ruthless once and famous but old now and manageable. Why should I be afraid? I who am going to sculpt him.

'The signs are good. Back porch light's right down.'

'The signs are very good,' he said. 'No point in delaying.'

'Good luck then.'

'Thanks.'

I raced across the open lawn and padded down the stone steps to the coal-blackened door. I put the key in and, fingers crossed, hoped for the best. Please, please, please. I turned the key and it came to something weighty in the chamber. I pushed. With all my strength, I pushed it and then – remembering an old maxim that goes for lovemaking as it does for burglary – I let the key fall back and turned it forward again slowly and, clunk! It worked. In near disbelief, and suppressed elation, I gently prodded the heavy wooden door and very, very slowly it gave, groaning open on its heavy hinges and letting a line of blue moonlight enter and travel across its pitch-black interior. Time to get the others. Key out of its socket and into pocket, I went back up a step or two and put my hand in the air.

Mellowes braked at the top of the steps and came trundling down in agonised silence.

'Not bad, eh?'

'I love you!' he said and he embraced me madly.

'Shsssh!'

'In, in, in,' he urged, looking up at the black windows of the house. We went into the cellar, hands out for protection in the darkness, the unseen coal crunching under our feet.

'It's cold.'

'A bit. I'm going to light a match.'

The matchlight threw our black limbs all over the inside of the curved brick ceiling and caught Oisin's psychotic wolfman features at their most wild and jagged as he came through the door. I brought the half-gone match across to the oil lamp hanging over our heads.

'Coal dust all over.'

'Will I light this then?'

'Shush!'

'Use the electric light, for God's sake,' said Oisin, his black silhouette not moving from the doorway.

'Don't use the electric light,' insisted Mellowes.

'Come on . . . make up your – it's gone.' I lit another match, flaming their faces yellow and haggard, their heads huge and moving on the mortared brickwork. I reached up and opened the glass door of the oil-lamp bird cage.

'Go on, then,' whispered Mellowes, barely audible. He was tense, looking around.

I opened the glass door and lit the wick. They waited. The wick took and grew into a warm yellow glow, weak but enough to make out gradually the huge coal box to the right of the door as you look out, the bags of something beyond them, the bench along the left wall, the crates, buckets and dustwebbed dark holes set back into the walls and shelved with indeterminate objects, tools and spirits. At the end of the cellar, there was what looked like another open doorway, an arch to another room. Oisin sat down on the bench.

'Where's Skin?' Mellowes turned around and back with a look of panic.

'Deserted us already. There had to be a Luttrel in the camp.'

'Seriously,' said Mellowes, but when he crept over to the doorway to check he nearly collided with the Goat, out of breath and coming down the steps like he'd seen a ghost.

'Seen a ghost?' I asked him.

'Jasus, man. We thought we saw a face at the window.' He shook his bony shoulders. 'At least, Greycoat thought he did. Something moving . . .'

'That's it then,' said Oisin, folding his arms. 'He's gone for his parabellum. Might as well join me for a decade.'

'Well, what was it?' demanded Mellowes. The Skin's mouth opened.

'It was only a bust – a statue of some fellow in the window.'

'Oh, that'd be a first draft,' I said. 'I left it with him last night.'

Oisin laughed and Mellowes looked at me. 'Sit down, Tommy.' He was getting edgy.

'Right,' he announced suddenly. 'I'm going to start looking down here.'

He took out his torch and pointed to the interior of the cellar. 'Shane, you look along here, by the coal bunker. Oisin, along there, around about where you are. The benches and alcoves.

Without causing a fire, please. Tommy, the same: the chests and boxes down there. OK? OK.'

And so the search commenced with people bumping into each other in the pointillistic darkness.

'But be very, very quiet,' said Mellowes. 'Absolutely quiet. Remember – one sound and we could be done for.'

Oisin gave me a very funny look. Rightly so, for anything we moved was going to make a noise. The Goat had no sooner put his hand to things but they squeaked, creaked or fell with a thump and an agonising clatter, as if protesting on their owner's behalf at this gross intrusion of their, and his, privacy. Our faces clenched with each scratch or scrape of a nail-bottomed box braked by a cog of coal. Torture. The sort of faces we'd repeat for real if Corny heard the trunk's cries and found out we were down here. Mellowes, needless to say, shushed after us at every squeak but at least we were trying our stiff-shouldered, restrained best to keep him unpanicked and the operation quiet, more than can be said for his second piece of advice: 'Put everything back where you found it.'

'What?' Oisin stood up, incredulous.

'Well, as close as poss.'

'Tall order,' I said. 'That's like Dev asking Corny to put the flour back in the sacks.'

Hands on hips, Oisin exhaled indignantly through red nostrils. All our faces were red-blooded from stooping but the Goat, who never stopped picking his nose in any situation, had added bits of black coal dust around the spittle-lined mouth and eyes. Gothic mascara.

'Thirsty work,' grunted Oisin, doubled over, braces stretched.

'This coal dust is everywhere. Shane, were you flinging it about in here last night?'

'What's her name?' said someone.

'Skin, you're in my way.'

'Ariel.'

'No, Corny's.'

'I can't see half the – ' The Goat, finally minus the coat, protested meekly at the darkness.

'Light a match,' said Mellowes. 'Or no, use your torch.'

Mellowes was getting confused in the excitement, a state we joined him in once the Goat's crazy torch got underway, shooting all over the gaff like the kid in the bedroom.

'Jesus, Skin,' said Oisin. 'Keep your torch to your own side. You've sent spiders over here running. They're as frightened as I am.'

Subdued laughter greeted Oisin's remark.

'Qu-i-et,' sang Mellowes like a teacher in a museum, and there was further tittering so he went back to shushing us and the Goat kept his emergency searchlight to himself.

'This is a junk yard,' snorted Oisin. 'I've pulled out nothing but gardening tools, paint brushes and about five million electricity bills. What's he doing up there – animal experiments?'

'The man's a vegetarian, Oisin, do you mind?'

'Some vegetarian. He must be running on some high-voltage transformer he hasn't told us about. Mellowes, what's the story, where's the papers?'

'I told you,' he insisted, ducking for the lamp. 'Only the most crucial of his papers are down here. The ultra-sensitive stuff. The O'Higgins stuff, for goodness sake. That's why we're here.' He clicked his fingers. 'A red suitcase, lads, a red suitcase. It's here and we're going to find it.' He paused and stared. 'If it takes all night.'

Oisin sighed and held up a pair of baggy twills to the lamplight.

'You'd get a few quid for them in Tobin's.'

'Nice scrap,' I said, kicking a box of fittings. 'You'd get a few quid for them off Wycherley.'

'Boys!' exclaimed the Goat.

'What?'

'I think I have it.'

We rushed over.

'Watch the lamp!' cursed Mellowes.

'Keep back!'

'Will you get to eff out of my light!' cried the Goat. He was down on all fours, pulling at a handle in the darkness.

'Will I light a match?' We stooped out of his corner, knocking into boxes. The weighing scales fell and Oisin darted his foot out to break their fall and potential clang. Bills spilled down from a spine-broken file.

'Good man! Bring it out,' said Mellowes, stating the obvious.

The Goat was still grunting. His corner was tightly packed.

'R-right,' he said, with a release of breath. 'I think I have it.' He got up and backed out, slowly dragging something. The Goat looked over his shoulder and, as he emerged like a coal miner into

219

the yellow lamplight, a dirty big grin broke out on his loose-fanged face. 'Ha-haaaa,' he drawled, eyes twinkling, and he hoisted, high over the clothes-filled tea chest, a dark, square blur which nearly put the lamp out. The light flickered, we shuffled, and he put his find flat down on the coal dust.

'Jes . . . us!' said Oisin. Mellowes was speechless.

We looked down at the dark-red suitcase, ox-blood red, Doc Marten red. There was a leather strap wrapped around it twice and a worn sticker that read, '265 1950 E. Window', whatever that means.

'Is it locked?' asked Mellowes.

'Yes,' said the Goat.

Mellowes drew out his Swiss penknife and told the Goat to get out of the way. Crouching down, he brought the case up on his knee and proceeded to jiggle the keyholes of the two silver flaps with the narrowest blade. Within minutes, he had, click! one, and then, click! the two flaps open.

'I practised for this,' he whispered up at us. He was pleased. Very pleased. He looked at the case for a moment, drumming his fingers on its sides, taking it in, its spots, scratches, and powder-ringed damp stains. Gently, with trembling fingers, he undid the strap hasp and lifted back the undulous hide belt, bringing it around twice until it slithered loosely off the body of the case. Slowly, tentatively, almost reverentially, he put out a tensed hand and ran soft fingertips across the surface of the case, collecting dirt. He was on his knees. The lamp shone on the back of his neck. He could have been in front of an altar, opening a vestibule or an icon, or the quilted lace knickers of his patient aunt, but that's another story.

'Here goes,' he whispered and with hidden fingers he began prising off the lid. Eaaakkk-clooka! It sprung open to reveal – a string vest. A couple of string vests.

We said nothing. This was no time for jokes. Shaping an 'O' with his disgruntled fingers, the nail of his thumb and index, Mellowes picked up the edge of one of the vests the way you'd pick up a dead rat by the tail, if you or your cat were hungry. Disdainfully, saying nothing, the back of his head not moving, he drew it back: this tattered remnant of another world. Andy Capp in a Brighton deckchair or morning Corny in his baggy Y-fronts searching for his teeth and gun. The military analogy is not unfitting, for the filament of the vests resembled the sort of webbing you see strewn over field guns or tank-carrying trucks rumbling through the Curragh night. And thus when Mellowes pulled off two or three more vests, revealed beneath was something as potentially deadly as any netted T52 – two neat piles of file folders at the bottom of the suitcase.

Oisin whistled. 'I got worried there for a moment.'

'I never lose faith,' answered Mellowes with tense drama. Continuing in this vein, Mellowes' hand went out and stopped mid-air, hovering over the files.

'What's wrong with you?' said Oisin, insensitive to the moment. 'Ghost got you by the wrist?'

'On the contrary,' replied Mellowes quietly. 'I feel as if I've got a ghost by the wrist.' His hand opened and closed. 'At long last.'

'Well, let's see who he is then.'

Mellowes took up the first folder on the right-hand side. He opened the flap and took out a sheaf of papers. Gestetner copies of Ordnance Survey maps.

'I'm passing these up to Shane and I want you to keep them in exactly the order I hand them to you in.'

'OK.'

The first map was of a wooded area. It turned out to be somewhere in Wicklow. Kilmacanogue.

'His orienteering schedules,' quipped Oisin.

'Maybe some of the orienteers didn't make it back,' said the Goat.

Other maps were of the same area. Killakee Arts Centre. The Hellfire Club, where Sir Jasper Wycherley, Bob's ancestor, allegedly burnt a cat's head in a chalice. Some of the maps had markings on them. Dotted lines. Obviously for training. The IRA used this area in the twenties and thirties.

'Check this out,' said Mellowes and he handed us up a map of a densely wooded area with crosses marked at certain spots. I looked at Oisin.

'They could be arms dumps,' he shrugged.

'Or the altars for open-air masses,' said Skin with a horrible chortle. God, he was ugly.

Fold-out greaseproofs followed, crudely marked and amended and quite soiled from thumbing and incorrect refolding. Localised maps again of the inner north Wicklow area.

One was of the mountainside around Luggala Lake at the bottom of the valley. Times were written – '5.30 p.m. . . . . K't in charge.'

'There's a hole in this one,' said Mellowes, solemnly passing it up.

Someone had burnt a cigarette hole in the map.

'Practising for their lips,' said the Gòat.

'This is amazing! Listen to this.' I read them a letter:

Cormac,

Amused by Kirwan's suggestion that he be put specifically in charge of bringing out the Dublin North graveyard vote on Thursday. This was my job for '18 election. But I was one of many then and so is he. Tell him to liaise with Fitzpatrick and get the lists from him. CJ is handling all the general Dublin area *vis-à-vis* final lists of emigrants, non-tenants and corpses. Multiples we leave to local o/cs. As you know there is no co-operation in some areas. For D Central, F. is working to Lemass in FF. Lemass was my o/c in B Company, Dublin Brigade. That was in the pre-slightly constitutional days before they, or we, became bad democrats. They say we, but here we are making sure that even the passed away have a vote!

Tiocfaidh ár lá,
C.

'Indeed it will,' I said. 'And come very shortly.'

'Shane. Don't be morbid. Here, give it back to me.'

He gave me the next item, a thick strip of paper like a piece of crumpled tickertape, bearing the inscription: 'The Thompsons are arriving from US. Tuesday. Eight.'

'Who the hell were the Thompsons?' asked Oisin. 'A dance band?'

'No, but they featured in a song or two,' I told him sagely. 'Don't you remember that hit of hits, the one that goes "when the bayonets flash and the rifles crash to the echo of a – "'

'"Thompson gun,"' finished Oisin. 'Jesus. But why would he keep something like that written down?'

'Who knows? Because he's a lawyer and he likes to keep things written down or because he was Chief of Staff and he wanted to make sure the books were kept in order. Remember the row over Russell and whether he was using the IRA's petrol. He was nearly shot for it.'

'Yeah, but now?'

'Like I said, who knows? He's a lawyer, he's his own historian,

222

or thinks he is, because he's lived so long. He likes keeping notes and thinks they're safe down here for ever. Maybe he keeps them for his own private enjoyment. To look back upon when he gets old. Or show his biographers so they can show he got stuck in and wasn't some rarefied chief of staff with a French accent who fled away to his mammy when the subject of bombing England came up. I mean, I don't know. Maybe he keeps notes on everything.'

'Obviously not everything,' said Mellowes in a low voice.

'Why, how are we?'

'One folder left and these,' he said, looking at the case and at what he had in his hands. He was getting worried. Dirty knuckles appeared at the back of his neck, scratching the ginger fur. Knees in the undergrowth. Auntie in the hay. Odd thoughts hit you at tense moments.

'Give us that back.' The knuckles on his lamp-lit neck opened for receipt.

'Ta,' he said and he brought his hand round over his head. Tidied into the remaining papers, he slipped the lot back into the pocket, tucked in its flap and placed the file neatly on the left set in the case.

'Our last chance,' he said calmly, without looking up. He was staring at the case. 'Here goes.'

He reached out, white-shirted arms gilded by the lamplight, and took the last folder from the suitcase, his nails scratching horribly for a grip at its cardboard bottom. Mellowes' calloused fingers, fingers that milk cows, do exams and fix us steaks, picked discreetly at the inside flap. Flipped open, it revealed the edge of some very old yellowed papers, or was that the light and they were all like that? He took the first document out.

'What is it?' we asked eagerly, crowding around.

'Well?'

'Lists of jurors.'

Mellowes took out the next one.

'Lists of jurors' addresses.'

He took out and held up to the light a faintly written-upon page, waxy yellow like a *bodhrán* skin.

'Jurors again. List of approved cases.'

'Eh? Cases for them to serve on?'

'List of approved cases for elimination,' said Mellowes calmly.

'Jesus!' the Goat gasped. 'It doesn't say that, does it?'

'No, it doesn't. It says "for engagement". How'd you like

223

to be "engaged", Tommy? Like, to two men with hoods and greased-down coats?'

'No, thanks.'

'It actually has here . . .' Mellowes read the faded small print. '"Beyond persuasion". There you are now, the ultimate shotgun wedding.'

He put it away. I felt queasy, chilled. In whose cellar are we?

'Mass cards,' said Mellowes matter-of-factly and into his hand slid four black-edged mass cards each with the traditional Silvikrin-haired Jesus tripping over the rocks in primary-coloured gown and clean sandals.

Another chill.

'Are they blank?' asked Oisin.

'They're blank.'

'That's sick.'

Mellowes put them away without comment and took another religious item: I could see the little black cross from here.

'The priest's calling card?' I guessed plumly, rallying myself, but Mellowes didn't answer.

'What is it?'

'Mass times in the Parish of Booterstown,' he said in a stunned voice. He looked around at us. O'Higgins coming from mass in Booterstown. He was shocked. We said nothing. He put it down and took out the next document: a hand-drawn map.

'No writing on this,' he said in a sort of choked whisper. He held the confused harp-shaped diagram up to the light.

'That's – that's Mount Merrion Avenue,' said Oisin without any hesitation.

'Are you sure?'

'I'm certain. That's where I live – look, Waltham Terrace.' His outstretched finger traced the lines of his street and then, at the left side of the harp, the long, long lines of Booterstown Avenue from high Stillorgan down to the sea, where Oisin and I walked in our greatcoats of a wintry Sunday.

'Keep it still.' The bruised harp, its blots now as grey as lichen spots, shook in Mellowes' hand as he held it up to the light, but Oisin's plectrum-stiff finger calmly continued to explain his neighbourhood, indicating the rugby fields of Blackrock College where de Valera played, moving his nail down to the Loreto Convent on the corner of Cross Avenue and then along the Avenue to the other corner where O'Higgins was 'engaged' on that sunny Sunday.

Mellowes put the map down and blew. It was nearly too much for him. To confirm Oisin's version of his neighbourhood, the next item out of the folder was an actual official district map of Sandymount-Booterstown-Blackrock coast and hinterland, in which could be clearly seen the harp with the single string of Cross Avenue across it.

'Whew! I'm nearly afraid to look at what else is in here,' said Mellowes, and fists on hips, he sighed heavily before resuming, as if pausing in some hard physical labour. He pulled out a very thin sheet of paper, almost membraneous.

Another map. Hand-drawn, neatly drawn, in a hand I thought I recognised. It was a map of a road and corner. *The* corner. A dotted line led from the corner to a house. *The* house.

'Dunamanse,' said Mellowes softly.

'Wow.'

'Jesus, Mellowes.'

'What does the writing say?' Oisin pointed to tiny inscriptions made with a fountain pen along the house's front. The ink had merged and faded.

'Can't really read it,' said Mellowes, squinting.

'Show us.' Oisin took the crumpled edge in his fingers and examined it nearer to the lamp glow.

'Says . . . it says, "Shout from here."'

Mellowes looked up with an industrious brow.

'Oh, hold on . . . it says, "Gannon shout from here."'

'Gannon!' repeated Mellowes savagely. 'So he was there. Bill Gannon. Oisin, are you sure it's not "start" – start from here?'

'No,' said Mellowes, reading it closely. 'It's "shout" and then there's a scribble and, hold on, "Approach for 8."'

'Eight?'

'What are they, house numbers?'

'Oh, they're far too high. No, it must be the time.'

'Eight? But he wasn't shot until a quarter to twelve – that means they must have been planning to kill him when he went out for his swim. He went out for his swim about eight, before breakfast.'

'I can't read any more of this,' he said. 'What else do we have?'

'I told you this stuff would be here. Listen, listen.' We fell quiet. There wasn't a sound in the cellar. '"7.30 to Boland's, Stillorgan."' Mellowes' voice trembled like the water-warped paper he read from. '"Bring personal." That means personal issue, I presume.

225

"Doyle car from Goatstown, Lower Kil." Archie Doyle, the bastard. So he bragged honestly to Harry White.'

Mellowes shook his head.

'Read on.'

Mellowes read on.

'"Take SW from Monks." Monkstown – I don't know what that means. "Gannon to Boland's, Fitzp. to Boland's." Who's Fitzpatrick, I wonder? "From Boland's clt." – collect, I suppose. "Knight at 6 Linden Lea." Knight – what a strange name.'

'These could be cover names,' I said.

'Well, Doyle and Gannon aren't. I don't see Bill Murphy's name here. He was the other one saddled with the honour. Knight,' said Mellowes again, 'what a strange name.'

'What else does it say?' asked Oisin.

'Listen to this! "3 options: corner, way to swim; beach, at swim; corner, way to mass. Doyle command first 2. If 3, leave to Knight."

'The third it was,' said Mellowes sadly. 'That's it.'

Oisin released a long soft whistle.

'Nothing else?'

'Nope. Can you be sure this is his handwriting, Shane?'

'Pretty sure. From what I've seen – yes, it's definitely his. Those are his crossed "o"s.'

'And would these be his "s"s?' he said, pointing to the word 'Knight' and staring at me over his shoulder.

'Eh . . . what?'

I was stunned, for a moment, because I thought in some confused, illogical way, he was referring to the AVNS: the way O'Shaughnessy was written with three 's's in one of their letters. Oisin laughed grimly.

'Shane?'

'What, oh, eh, I don't know.' What was wrong with me?

'That's what we have to find out.'

Have to sit down.

'How, though?'

Been standing too long.

'Find out some bloody way,' he promised the others. 'To come this far.'

'Enough to ruin him, as it is.'

'Yeah, but to clinch this . . . Knight – by Christ, I'll find out some bloody way.'

226

'Incredible.' Someone gave a whoop. Oisin or the Goat. Mellowes was saying, 'Told you, told you they'd be in here.' Over and over again he was saying it. 'You're all sickened,' and they clapped him on the shoulders. Nothing else in folder, only map.

'Could come all the way in here. The professors will dance for us . . . saved Shane's statue. Hey, Shane, listen. What do you – Shane? Shane, what's wrong?'

'Nothing.' I was on the shoe crate. 'I'm OK. Just been standing too long.'

'You all right?' Someone rushed over. Oisin or Skin. Oisin. 'Do you feel weak?'

'A bit.'

'It's the excitement. You're OK. Just relax. Take it easy.' Someone felt my forehead.

'We should be getting out of here anyway,' said Mellowes.

'Yeah, let's get the stuff back in order.'

Oisin moved me to the bench and there I sat listening to the squeaks and scratches of the cellar being put back together again. Gradually I got better but for a moment or two I felt terribly tired, sleepy. So much, so much. I heard Mellowes pick out the documents he was going to take and put the case back.

'Don't forget the belt,' said somebody. Mellowes started cursing O'Shaughnessy and they all laughed.

'I won't,' he said and they laughed again.

Boisterous, they worked with renewed energy. A lot less quiet now than they were earlier on. They kept shouting over was I OK and I said yes.

'This is, without doubt, the ultimate coup for the invincibles,' they were saying and after a few minutes I did begin to feel OK.

The frizziness lifted and the awful yellow haze of the lamplight focused into something I remembered to be the cellar. It suddenly felt cold. What time was it? I wondered. I was in here in this cellar and it felt like I'd been in here for a long, long time. Are you OK?

'I'm fine,' I said, coming to. Around my feet, spiked bundles of ESB and gas bills. They suddenly looked very sad.

'Move your legs.'

'No, really, I'm fine.'

'Yeah, but you're standing on his clothes,' said Oisin, laughing. 'I've to put them away.'

'Oh – right.' I moved my legs and got up. Tottered a bit but I was OK. 'Phew . . .'

'What happened to you?' said Mellowes, coming over.

'I don't know. I just felt weak.'

'You've been under a lot of pressure recently,' said Mellowes, putting his hand on my shoulder. 'All the statue stuff. The threats and deals and deadline. It's crazy. I mean, fair play to you, you come out then and get involved in this. Operation Booterstown, reporting for action.' He laughed. 'Good man.'

'It's nothing.'

'It's great,' said Mellowes. 'You get up at eight to make a key. We wouldn't do that. Well, I would but, you know, generally . . . you're ace, Shane, you're the business.'

'Fair balls to you,' threw in Oisin, his black hands around a beer box full of old toys and papers.

'Come on,' I said and I bounced to pick up the lead candlesticks.

'Let's get to hell out of here.'

'Good man!' shouted Mellowes and he flexed his milking arms to hoist the weighing scales up on the books where they originally sat. Or did they? Mellowes didn't seem to care, nor did he appear vastly concerned about the noise-level. It was all 'Corny the assassin' and the 'hot fate' that awaits him instead of the shushing he went on with earlier on.

'Shouldn't we be quieter?' I meekly suggested.

'What?' barked Mellowes, his fist throttling a headless lampshade.

'We're as quiet as we have to be. He's not in, the murderer. He's off plotting killings.'

The Goat laughed, his face blacker than ever.

'There's a few elderly Somme veterans he's still to get, the vengeful little cunt. Well, I can tell you, no one down here's afraid of him. He'd be scared stiff out of his little wits to come down here and check out a strange noise in the dead of night. Shivering inside his blankets or running to his deluded Ariel, the girl he stole from youth.'

'Vanessa.'

'Lads, lads,' said Oisin. 'Let's get this stuff back in order. With a bit of quiet.'

'Yeah, come on. Let's get moving.'

We got back to work, lifting boxes and restacking bundles.

I sidled up to Mellowes. 'What did you take, anyway?'

228

'Eh . . . what?' He looked at the wall. Thinking of something else, the papers' implications. 'Knight', 'at swim', 'the kill'.

'The papers, what papers did you take?'

'Oh, eh, I took the two maps,' he said quietly. 'The one of the area, the harp and all, and the one of the road – his road. And I took, of course, the instructions. They're in here.' He tapped the baton bulge in his trousers and smiled weakly. 'Gold dust.'

I smiled.

'They'll change the Minister's mind,' he said, 'and in time truth will out and everyone will know who shot him.'

'Don't lose them,' I said.

'Shane, I can't believe I have them. I mean, they were here, Shane! Instructions, maps. It's – oh, it's too much.' He looked into my eyes. 'They're burning a hole in my pocket.'

I nodded. It was incredible, I suppose.

'"Knight", Shane. Got to find out who "Knight" was. Corny? Corny sent them all, that's for sure.'

The Goat sat down, wearied from his work, the finder of the case. He looked like one of Mr Masterson's miners, up from the vault in Navan and wondering what time it was on the earth's surface. Good question. It was 1.30 a.m. Mellowes sat down beside him and took out a packet of Major.

'I don't think,' he said, looking around the cellar, 'that anyone with two eyes in their head could mistake the fact that someone was in here rummaging the place. But, sure, so what?'

'Exactly,' agreed the Goat, taking a Major.

'I mean, they discover someone's been in here. So what do they do – tell the guards? Tell them what? "Nothings been taken, Officer, only my instructions for the killing of a government minister fifty-nine years ago."' Mellowes shrugged and lit up his cigarette, and then the Goat's, with my gemstone zippo. They looked good in the lamplight. Black-faced, cheeky, triumphant. They exhaled and smiled and generally relaxed. Suddenly, out of the darkness, came Oisin's voice.

'You sure you want to take nothing else?'

I knew exactly what he meant. I don't know why but I was sort of waiting for this.

'No, why? You want that jacket?'

'Eh, yes,' he replied slowly, shuffling in the darkness. 'But I could live without it. I was thinking more of something that wouldn't be noticed gone.'

'Oisin, come out of there. What are you up to?'

'And how much are you up to?' came the reply and, grinning, he emerged out of the darkness holding a bottle of wine.

Mellowes put his face in his hands. 'Ahh . . . no.'

'Jesus Christ!' crowed the Goat. 'Where did you get that?'

'His cellar's back there. Shane, Mellowes, come on, what do you say? A celebratory slug. Let's toast the bastard now we've found him out. Mellowes, come on. Just a nip. We deserve it.'

Mellowes said nothing, only smiled. But Mellowes smiling, in itself, was an indication of how far his standards of discipline had waned since the discovery.

'Come on, Mellowes. We deserve it,' urged Oisin, pushing this weakness. He obviously felt that the Goat and I were already takers. We were.

'What is it, anyway?' I asked Oisin casually.

He blew the dust off the bottle. 'A fine bottle, I'd say.' He held it up against the lamplight and it flared red like chapel-stained glass.

'1974. Château de Nobel Fraude. Oh, a juicy number. His Nobel year. Shane, you were dead right about his wines. There's rakes of them back there.'

'Of course I was,' I said coolly. I was thirsty and I felt a little reckless but I was a trifle annoyed at the brusque intrusion into something I had shared with O'Shaughnessy. Inexplicable, maybe, but I felt something for last night when I was at his table on my own. I was his *sommelier*, his guest of honour. His toastmaker.

'Come on, Mellowes, are you on or what? Are you mice or men?'

'We should be leaving here. Greycoat's waiting.'

'We'll gulp this back and then we're off. Revive us, Mellowes, we're parched, dust in our throats. Come on. It'll be the invincibles' grand gesture: a drink on the site of the crime.'

Mellowes pulled on his cigarette.

'Come on, Mellowes. Give us your army knife.'

We looked at Mellowes. He said nothing but just sat there with a strange satisfied smile on his ruddy face. Then he tipped his cigarette free of ash and, as if recollecting, he slowly put his hand in his pocket and took out the Swiss army penknife. Oisin took the red penknife with a whoop. I was surprised at Mellowes but then I wasn't. A lot had changed in the last hour.

'Off you peel, you bastard!' said Oisin to the corkfoil as he struggled with bottle and blade between his legs. 'There!' He threw the ancient-looking lead foil into the dust but Mellowes scurried to put it in his pocket. 'Evidence'. What a joke.

'Watch your balance,' said Mellowes, concerned.

Oisin's greasy quiff-tails shook and fell and he grunted, twisting the corkscrew into the brown cork. 'This is damn old,' he warned. 'It might never open.'

'Push the screw right down,' said Mellowes.

'But not too far,' I cautioned, faking expertise, as usual.

Oisin stood for a breather and wriggle-fingered back on to his head the Frytex hair slices that were falling into his eyes. 'Here goes.' He put the bottle between his knees and pulled. His face went red and shook. Hair fell forward again and then – gooinnk! – out comes the cork with such energy that it, hand and penknife nearly flew up and hit the brickwork. 'Here.' He thrust it straight under my nose. 'Have a swig!'

'Me first?'

'You tasted for him. You can taste it for us.'

They all watched me. Granny-like, I put my fastidious lips to the rim and sipped. Sweet, very sweet. Venturesome, with their eyes upon me I took a swallow or two. Sweet, and pungent. And strong, very strong. Their eyes opening wider, I took a good solid gulp of the stuff. If I go down on this, what does it matter. I'm in Corny's cellar and he tricked us into it. Cheers.

'What's it like?' asked the Goat, the eyes nearly out of his head.

'Ahhh,' came my throaty response. It felt like a mixture of baking syrup, Tipp-Ex thinner and Romanian diesel was crawling down my throat in separate lanes. 'Like? It's gorgeous,' I said.

'Give us some.' The Goat's dirty great paw shot out like a wino at a Stephen's Green sit-in. Lie in, sleep in.

'Ta,' he rasped and he threw the neck towards his teeth.

'Good man, Skin,' applauded Oisin. 'You're fairly putting it away.'

Mellowes' appreciative gaze turned to one of mild horror as he watched the Goat's apple go up and down like a jammed lift or the blockage in a condom when it's picking up speed. Even in this half-light, one could see exposed below his ears that skinful of pre-cellar dirt that gave the corrugated collars of his nylon white shirts the special black-striped zebra effect the ladies appreciate.

'Come on, Skin,' said Oisin, 'leave some for us.'

231

And so the bottle was swiftly emptied of its contents. Even Mellowes, God bless him, managed to put rapid mouthfuls of the horrible stuff down without wincing.

'That was good,' declared Oisin, wiping purple rivulets from his chin.

'It was?' Mellowes was dubious.

'Oh, a splendid number. Wasn't it, Shane?'

'Another?' Oisin raised a wet finger, testing the wind. But at this Mellowes winced.

'Oisin, we should be on our way.'

'Sure we're on our way!' laughed the Goat.

'What are you afraid of? There's no one up there,' said Oisin dismissively. 'You're not going to be afraid even when he's not around – like everyone else.'

'Like who else?' I protested.

'Let's have a quiet little sip and then we're out of here,' said Oisin.

'We'll never be in here again. Come on, it'll be something we'll tell our children and our grandchildren about. We'd regret it if we didn't. Shane is always going on about Collins going back to an ambush to enquire about the casualties, or cycling round on a bike. Come on, the reckless gesture. The memento taken from the police files. Come on, where's your bottle? Let's drink up and be gone.'

'Hurry up, then,' said Mellowes and Oisin scrambled across the coal and escaped bills to fetch another.

'Sod it,' said Mellowes, flipping smoke out of his head. 'If he's out he's out, the bastard.'

'Aye,' said the Goat. 'Sure, haven't we a look-out man to keep us safe.'

'We came to collect the bad news and now we've got it. And it's as bad as we thought it was. So let's drink to our achievement and his come-uppance, at his expense.'

'Aye, his come-uppance at our expense,' said the Goat in a pseudo-posh accent.

I snickered and said nothing. Who did we think we were? I was beginning to get a little contemptuous of Mellowes' grief and our dare-devil drinking of Corny's wine in Corny's basement. I saw and met Samuelson. Play-acting. I'll do something that'll make them all sit up.

'Knight, Shane.'

'What?'

'Knight,' repeated Mellowes. He was doing a lot of repeating. 'In all my reading on the Independence period I can't remember ever coming across the name of Knight. Can you?'

'No.' I shook my head. 'Could be a code name, Sean. Or else an Englishman. A knight, maybe?'

'You're being funny.'

'Am I?'

'Ahh . . . Oinnk!' went a cork again and Oisin's arm did its mannequin jerk.

'That, was quick.'

'Jesus,' said the fuddled Goat, his spindly legs apart. 'What was in that wine? My eyes are narrowing together.'

'If you're lucky, it'll do the same for your teeth.'

Oisin looked at me in warning and the Goat did have a puzzled, hurt expression for a moment but it passed.

'Hold on now,' said Oisin, holding the bottle up to the lamplight.

'A '76 Prix de Paix de Lenin,' he read with relish. 'Here, get that down your neck!'

'Ta,' said the Goat. 'I need a good slug to shake the dust from my lungs.'

'Leave the empties here?'

'We've no option, have we? It'll be fine. Just leave them back where you found them. It'll be weeks, hopefully months, before they're discovered and investigated.'

'Fingerprints?'

'Our fingerprints are on everything. So what?' said Mellowes and he threw his hands in the air. 'Who knows us? By the time we come forward with these little beauties' – he tapped the pipe in the pocket – 'it won't matter how we got them, it'll be Corny's handwriting they'll be talking about.'

'Whose finger's on the pen, his finger's on the trigger,' I said, surprising myself.

'What?'

'Nothing.'

'Weehaoww,' whined the squinting Goat, recovering from a slug. 'God, that's brutal! But it get's you straight.'

'You shocked by what you saw tonight?' asked Oisin, changing the tone. Mellowes paused and held his mouth, like he was having trouble swallowing.

233

'Sort of,' he said in a breathy voice.

'You, Shane?'

'No,' I lied curtly. Oisin gave me a funny look. I was in a funny mood. 'I just didn't think those documents would be here,' I said.

'Well, they were and we've got them. And we can save you with them.'

'As well as the Proclamation –' began the Goat, with a pompous finger raised. 'The Procla – '

'Save myself?' I muttered, cutting him off.

'Don't be snotty,' said Oisin. 'You're in a snotty mood. Come on, what's wrong with you?'

'Nothing,' I snapped. 'I'm fine.' A mechanical smile went round to reassure them.

But they weren't reassured. 'He is, isn't he, lads?' said Oisin. 'He's in a snotty mood. Ah, what's wrong with you, Shane?' He came over and put his arm around me.

'Nothing – stop it, you're tickling me.' I was laughing. Jesus, was I in funny form.

'Tickle, tickle, tickle,' he said in a baby-sitter's voice and he started tickling me.

'Are you snotty because Ariel didn't tickle you?'

'No!'

'Was she a dandelion maiden, Shane?'

'Shut up,' I said and I pulled my box back. I had the giggles.

'Was she, Shane? A dandelion maiden.'

'What's a dandelion maiden?' asked the Goat, his face leering.

'Oh, a very bad thing, Skin, a very bad thing,' warned Oisin, still jabbing the occasional finger butt at my belly. 'Very bad. They have' – the Goat's mouth opened – 'long green hair.'

Mellowes rocked with laughter and Oisin, sitting bolt upright, widened his eyes in a demon smile.

'What the hokey?' said the Goat, confused. But he laughed anyway. Why wouldn't he?

'You can learn from a poem, Tómas,' said Oisin mincingly. 'Listen to this – ' He cleared his throat.

'"Ye dandelion maidens who are so fair,"' he began in a gentleman's double dactyl.

'"Why do ye dangle your long green hair."'

'Indeed,' said the Goat.

'"With us howling dogs won't you come to the fair."'

'Most assuredly,' came a mutter.

'"And then to drink wine in O'Shaughnessy's lair!"'

'"Ye dandelion maidens who are so fair."' The Goat stamped his feet and we all joined in, to no particular tune, just a makeshift football chant:

Why do ye dangle your long green hair
With us howling dogs won't you come to the fair
And then to drink wine in O'Shaughnessy's lair!

On 'lair!' Oisin and I raised our bottles and clinked and began the refrain once more but at this point, at this crucial point, I want to take you reluctantly away from the merry proceedings and bring you outside to poor old Greycoat, sitting behind his mulberry bush, tensely waiting. He's been there for quite a while so let's go back to the start. After twenty minutes keeping watch on the back of the house and the cellar, Greycoat decided to go around to the front of the house. Treading softly, careful not to break twig underfoot or branch under arm, he negotiated his way through the thick shrubbery along the interior of the outside wall and then, long-legging it over the briars and thorned tripwires, he slipped in among the barked columns that stood back from the inclined driveway and crouched. And watched. Still no light in the house, still no movement.

It was only when he looked to his right, to the end of the driveway, or its entrance, that Greycoat noticed a man's figure standing inside the front gate. Greycoat tried not to be shocked. It could be someone peeing. Or it could be a curiosity seeker. Passing students, on their way to or from the university, often stepped into the driveway to get a look at the great one's house. Corny said that after parties in the area whole groups of them would dare-devil each other up to his very windows. Greycoat now saw the shapes of two men inside the gate. Or even three. He wasn't sure because the sentry box was in the way.

He decided to get closer. His heart was thumping, thumping in the dark stillness of Corny's little forest. But he must be commended. Rather than panic and run back and alert us to the fact that there were people out front, he determined on sneaking up and trying to see who they were. Why not? We had enough bottle to come this far. We weren't, and he wasn't, going to skive off because some kids or something were hanging around down the

235

front gate. Sharp intake of breath and Greycoat got up off his knees and calmly, cleanly tiptoed along a line of trunks well camouflaged from the road. A cough. He stopped in behind a beech bark and clung to its peeling skin. They weren't students. They were three men. Fiftyish, sixtyish. Greycoat couldn't see faces, only shapes. God, no. Was it Corny's private protection, seeing as he didn't want the official version? But how could they be: Corny's out. Where were they last night, when Shane was here?

It was only when Greycoat got closer that he realised who these men could be. He went two more trees out, that's two in from the drive and only yards from where the men stood. In his exaggerated sense of complete stiffened silence, his heart took on a resounding volume. He listened very carefully. He heard one man tell another to keep in off the road and another say, 'They stopped before.' He heard mutters but he could only make out bits and pieces. Small talk, muffled laughter.

'We go back . . . time is it?' followed by, 'One-ten . . . not yet,' and then a pause.

And the conversation-opener, 'Wonder what'll happen to this place when he's gone?'

Greycoat strained to hear but he couldn't catch the replies, but when he heard 'keep the police away' it was confirmed for him. These men weren't protecting Corny, they were spying on him. Not waiting for us, waiting for him. AVNS. It's them. Greycoat wasted no time. Gathering his coat about him, he picked his way back through the trees, tiptoeing like a bathrobed adulterer from the scene of a husband-returned bedroom. Trunk to trunk, he slinked his way back to the briar-entangled shrubbery. Less professionally, it has to be said, than the way he approached, but drama was beating his heart out now. They were here. They were at the end of the driveway, waiting. Pushing through the bushes by the gable wall, breathless, Greycoat ducked under the sweeper bushes of the first of the fir trees and looked for a stone to throw at the cellar door. He stopped. He couldn't believe his ears. He heard singing coming from the cellar. Singing!

It was a sound even more strange and troubling to another quarter, a quarter neither you nor I expected to encounter. Picture the scene, if you will. After a long night of hard work on the papers for the Robert Williams extradition case, scratching and rescratching out schemes and points of law under the low, green-shaded desk lamp that can be sore on the eyes, Corny, for it is he, crouches over his desk for the last time and scrapes a few final marginal sentences on the brief before deciding to call it a night. He had the clincher. He was sure of it. If he could fix it on the argument (ironically, used also by the Unionists) that Articles 2 and 3 of the Irish Constitution oblige, and even compel, a committed nationalist to seek the reintegration of the national territory, by all means, *including the force of arms* . . . Ah yes.

And so he spells out 'constitutional' for what must be the millionth time in his life, the bony brown claw going back to run low crosses through the 't's. Done. He full-stops the sentence and unsquints himself from the paper. The scratching claw guides the quill over to the Georgian silver inkwell where it hovers for a moment before finding its ink-splashed thimble. His brown-spotted hand flaps on to the desk and drags, compasses its way back to his chest. Corny is tired, very tired. He rubs his eye in the way that frightens you to think the eyeball might pop out of its fleshy socket, that rim of scrotum-loose folds that hangs around the wet bulbs as the skin drags and tightens on the famous high cheekbones, tightening back to the bone. The mouth too tightens and the eyes fall half lidded into their midday lizard's glaze.

Corny considers the day's events. He didn't go the ceremony; he explained why. They weren't surprised. They knew it had nothing to do with what 'the other group' might pull off. They did nothing. Nobody was surprised. This week he'll help Mr Wycherley do the statue. It'll be finished soon. What a week. The Minister understood about today. We're all concerned but we're getting there. Busy week ahead. To get off. Save another from injustice. Corny eased up off the chair too quickly and felt the blood swirl in his head. He tottered a bit but he was fine. Time for bed. One hand on the wall and another on the great oak table, he made his way across the room to the hall, where a simple antler lamp was burning. He looked at the picture of his mother and smiled. Still fighting them, Mother, still fighting them. He smiled again and approached the staircase clutching the curled end of the banister. The periwinkle, they called it as children. He lifted a puppet's leg up on to the first step and then another. Creak. And then another. And then he stopped. What was that? He listened. Was he hearing things? He couldn't believe what he was hearing. He listened again. Someone was singing in his basement. In the name of . . . he listened again . . . a chant. Someone was chanting.

Corny steadied himself on the stairs and grabbed his mouth.

He'd drunk nothing tonight. De Valera said we all heard things as we got older but that he'd hear the most extravagant because of the life he had led. He had heard things, of course, but singing in his cellar. Singing? I'm not ill, he told himself bitterly. I'm not ill. They won't – I won't – Vanessa. I won't. Damn them all, I'll go down and find out. His tired puppet's frame was suddenly emboldened. He turned around carefully and went back down the steps he'd come up. Down the hall he eddied with a grim controlled fury. He was annoyed at this inviolable intrusion, be it by tricks to his imagination or by tricksters in his garden. The singing continued. There were people down there. Well, by Christ. Singing. No police. One thing was for sure, there'd never be police called to this house. Never. No way. Not that they didn't come uninvited and why wouldn't they, considering what was in his basement. Christ, no.

He went into the kitchen and his hand hissed and scraped the wall for a light switch. He was shaking, gibbering, white with an old man's baffled fury. Finally his fingers found the switch and the light came on just as Greycoat's fifth stone hit the door.

The first one we didn't hear but the second hit the door with a crack. In mid-swirling melody: '"With us howling dogs won't you come to the fair,"' and this my dear friends with our fists in the air, '"And then to drink wine without dangling your hair."'

Bang!

'What was that?' shouted Mellowes. The Goat dropped his imaginary fiddle. We, our mouths.

'The door!' shouted Mellowes. 'Scarper.'

'Jesus!' Mellowes stood up and knocked the light out.

'Shite!'

'Ah, for Christ's sake! My head!' cried Oisin. 'There's blood.'

'Lads, lads, lads, don't panic. Don't panic, lads,' said Mellowes, panicking. We were in complete darkness.

Crack! Another stone hit the door.

'Shane, turn on your torch.' The Goat switched his on.

Blood flashed on Oisin's forehead.

'Jesus!' he said, looking at his hand. I nearly laughed.

'Listen.' Mellowes grabbed the Goat's torch. 'Oisin, put the empty bottles back.'

'I'm bled, look at me.' He held out bloodied fingers and on to them Mellowes slapped a torch, saying, 'I know, but put the effing bottles back or we'll all be bled.'

238

Another stone hit the door.

'We know, we know,' grunted the Goat, shuffling around with his fingers spread to kill someone. Oisin, a torch in his mouth, shuffled to the back with the bottles.

'What'll we do?' Oisin asked me.

'Don't panic.'

'Go out in a rush?'

I looked at him. 'Yes.'

'OK.' He nodded and swallowed. 'Unlock us so.'

I went over to the cellar door and put the key in. I was going to be first out but so what. Time has come. If he sees me, I lose my job. Not my liberty, I'll go on the run. I couldn't care any more.

'Ready?' I looked back at them.

'No,' said Mellowes. 'Oisin's not – Oisin, come on.'

'Jesus, lads, look!' cried Oisin from the darkness, and with bloodied hands and forehead, he walked into our torches carrying a gun.

'Holy God!' gasped the Goat. Mellowes was speechless.

'Where did you get that?'

'There's loads of them back there.' Oisin flicked the torch along the steel black barrel. 'Antique, or what?'

'I'm ready,' smiled Oisin and he held up the gun.

'Oisin,' said Mellowes firmly. 'Put that back.'

'These'll clear us,' he said.

'Put it back!'

I couldn't believe what I was looking at.

Clack! Another stone hit the door.

'Come on,' I shouted. 'Are you ready?'

'But your papers won't save us.'

'Back, Oisin, back – you'll land us in jail, or worse,' cried Mellowes. 'Put it back.'

'Right, I'm leaving,' I warned.

'Wait! You cowards.' Oisin scurried to put the gun back.

I put my ear to the door. 'Ready?' I whispered back at them. They bunched up behind me.

'OK,' said Mellowes softly.

I turned the key – click – and pulled the handle. The heavy door opened to the night sky, cold air, stars and treetops. It seemed like ages away. Except, at the top of the steps, the furry edge of the lawn was whitened by a light. The kitchen light?

Here goes. I ran up the steps and was immediately hit by a stone that bounced off my forehead.

'Aow!' I stopped in my tracks and clasped my temple. It was only a pebble but it hurt. Flung by Greycoat, the blind bastard.

Hit or not, I ran on across the lit lawn and stumbled in behind his mulberry bush.

'What the hell's going on?' he asked incredulously.

'I might ask you the same.'

'I wasn't singing. What, are you drunk or something?'

Oisin came across the lawn, hand on head, and floundered in on top of us.

'Shush!' Greycoat flapped us in behind coat and bush. 'Get down . . . the light's on. Someone's coming.'

'Yeah – Mellowes,' I laughed. 'And the Goat.' Oisin gave me a dig.

'Get in. Get down! Get in,' pleaded Greycoat to the incoming pair.

Confusing signals but, despite Mellowes breaking heavily on the crunchy soil, they managed to gather in behind us and keep heads well down. The Goat belched and was shushed violently.

'There's someone at the door,' said Mellowes, head up like a weasel. I rose at his shoulder to take a look. A shape moved between the glass panels on the kitchen door, someone trying to free the lock. The door opened and there in the yellow kitchen light stood the figure of O'Shaughnessy.

'It's Corny!'

'Christ, no!' cursed Oisin behind me.

'Christ, yes,' I replied. Corny took a step out on to the kitchen porch and looked into his garden.

'Hey, where are you going?' cried Mellowes, grabbing hold of my arm.

'The fence. Come on!'

'Fuck the fence. He'll see us. Come on, out the front.'

'Shane, no!' said Greycoat. 'There's men out the front.'

'Men? What fucking men?'

We rounded on him.

'Why didn't you tell us?' I rubbed my head. Blood.

'Tell you? I told you,' he said, exasperated. 'You were singing, you were drunk.'

'Who's drunk?' slurred the Goat.

'. . . came in the front. Threw stones . . . the light came on and then he appeared.' He pointed through the bush. I looked over. Corny was on his way down the steps.

'But they're definitely not police,' he stressed. 'Definitely not.' Corny was down two steps. Time to move. He was agitated, moving quickly.

But Oisin was even quicker. Cursing us in whispers, he burst up and ducked under the sweeper branches of the first gable firs.

'Come on,' he cried, heading for the front.

Without further argument we followed and tore after him, ripping through the ivied shrubbery without a concern for vegetation or camouflage. It's not easy legging barbed bushes in brisk silence when you've a bellyful of fright and wine to carry. Fight: we might have to shortly. The Goat cut his knuckles on a sprung-back blackberry whip but he didn't cry out, the brave man. We reached the wall.

'Straight ahead!' said Greycoat and Oisin pushed on through the thick shrubbery. But the shrubbery got very thick. I felt like I was going through a carwash. Oisin had veered to the left in his haste and suddenly we found ourselves thrown out on to the gravelled driveway in front of the house.

'Whoah, there!' I said, recoiling and tiptoeing, as if it was hot coals or Murphy's Monday weld ash I was treading.

'Come on,' said Oisin sternly and he led us, feet gently crunching, around the corner and into the main driveway at the end of which three men were waiting.

'Oh God.' We stopped in our tracks.

'Come on,' gritted Oisin with remarkable confidence. He walked on, swaggered even. The men heard his approach and spun around to see us. They looked as startled as we were and stepped back, on to the road, to try and see who we were. But this tunnel of trees was too dark for them to see us or us them. Who knows the dark better? They were older and less frisky and if need be we would take them on. Turf them into the bushes and scarper. We're close by. Come on, Reddies. A thump for the man who had a hand in my letter and gave my friends the runaround. It's time for action.

'Are you all right?' I urged on the rest as Oisin urged me on, strolling ahead, quite far ahead. Very far ahead.

I flexed my fists, my metal-pouring, bone-breaking fists, and the lads joined me. Albeit reluctantly, being students. We strode to catch up with Oisin. The men at the end shuffled and stepped

241

back. But they didn't go away. One of them rubbed his hands. Watch out, Oisin.

'Come on,' I said, hurrying the rest. Suddenly the man with the hands skipped as if to make a grab at Oisin. We ran at them. The Goat tripped and fell on me, the bastard, so that I had to palm a drop to the hard dust and struggle like a flank-attacked scrum-half to gain ground. Straightening up, I tasted blood and headed for the confusion of dust and voices.

'Watch out!' a voice suddenly shouted. 'They've got guns!'

'What the – ? The voice wasn't ours. I looked behind me and when I looked forward again the men had taken to their heels and scarpered.

Oisin ran after them. I ran after Oisin to get a look. Down Clonskeagh Road ran three retreating jackets, big and stocky. They slipped into Wynnsward Drive and headed for the darkness of the UCD playing fields.

'That's them gone,' said Oisin and when he turned around he was brandishing a revolver and a bloody smile.

'You bastard!' I said.

Mellowes ran straight into his path. 'What the – ?' He put his hands in the air.

'It saved us, so shut up.'

Mellowes nodded and took his hands down. He looked shocked. We all looked shocked. Except the Goat who wobbled out through the gate blubbering some rubbish about taking them all on.

'Shut your mouth,' he was told.

'Come on, let's get out of here. Drag him, Greycoat.'

'He's drunk,' said Greycoat. 'How could you?'

'Shut up,' said Oisin, pointing his gun at him. 'We don't want to hear it.'

'Did you even get what we – ?'

'We got them.'

'Did those guys know?'

'Shane, what did you tell them?'

'Nothing about coming here tonight, and you know it.'

'Redmondites, old boy,' said Oisin. 'Checking the old boy out. Why not? He's no cops, no personal guard; they can case the gaff as they wish.'

'Except for himself out in the garden. Come on, let's get out of here.'

We bundled up the Clonskeagh Road, past Leinster Lawn and

the diamond. There was no traffic. Greycoat pulled the Goat until we got to the corner of Bird Avenue after which he was told to walk for himself or be left behind. Or else . . . click, click. Filthy, bloodied, weary and frightened, no one said anything but just walked quietly and quickly until we got to within a few yards of Loyola.

Oisin turned and shouted back to the Goat, 'Do you want to be put out of your misery?'

After this, everyone laughed and recovered themselves and when we got inside the house, Mellowes let out a whoop of delight and put the papers down on the back-room table. There was a cheer. Oisin added his gun. I threw in my key for good measure. Another cheer. A conversation of great excitement ensued but I was fading fast, fast, fast, and the last thing I heard before I crashed out on the couch in the front room was Oisin saying, 'But how much of this is my blood and how much is from that cunt inside?'

Chapter 9

The Coalman Returns

I woke up with the cold edge of a zip on my cheek and clean sunlight coming through the window. Someone had thrown a sleeping bag over me during the night. Over my head, in fact, and when I clawed it back and rubbed my eyes, dried blood flaked off my forehead. Maybe they couldn't stand looking at me and who could blame them if the ghastly apparition across the room was anything to go by. Flat on his back, half covered by a searchlight blanket, the snoring Goat lay open-mouthed to the morning sun, the bloodied hand bent back in an apellant gesture and a sock on a shoeless foot coming loose like a spent condom. His face was a mannequin's mixture of sickly white, black coal spots and purple-stained mouth, mucus-stained fangs included, and the sounds emanating from therein reminded me of blowholes on the lunar surface of the Burren and the throttling noises the sea would throw up to give us schoolkids a good laugh as we danced in the Atlantic wind. How did he feel, the Goat?

I must say I felt fine. Grand. The immensity of what we'd done last night was coming to me and I felt excited. We'd come through all that drama so well, so far. We took risks. Fair play to us, we took big risks. I rose and put on my shoes and went into the kitchen. To my surprise, Mellowes was sitting there, drinking a cup of tea and reading the papers.

'Ah, the dead awaken!' he said, a big smile on his sleep-ruddied face. 'You just missed the news.'

'Anything on it?'

'Not a thing. Government TDs criticise Leader of Opposition

for not attending ceremony yesterday. No one criticises Corny for the same, needless to say. His action is only 'regretted'. All parties relieved that no stunt was pulled by the anti-statue people. Grab yourself a cup of tea, Shane. Kettle's boiled.'

'Yeah, well, we saw three of the anti-statue heads,' I said, walking to the kettle. 'There was nothing about that, I hope.'

'Not a mention,' said Mellowes joyfully. 'Incredible, isn't it? Corny can't tell the cops there was someone in his cellar because he has an arms dump down there. What a conundrum. Jesus, he must be raging. Outfoxed, Shane. Outfoxed, the bastard.'

'Stroke of luck we came across that arms dump.'

'Sure thing. Now we can back up our sweet documents with revelations about the sort of equipment he keeps to back them up, if you get me.'

'I was thinking more of the stroke of luck it was to get us out of there,' I said, stirring my boiling coffee. 'And *you* were going to stop him taking a gun.'

'Listen,' said Mellowes. 'Did I know there were three men at his gate? I also tried to stop him taking a wine bottle and look where that led to. A bloody sing-song. If I'd been listened to on that score the old boy wouldn't have heard and there'd have been no bleeding panic. But I'm not going to go on about it.'

'OK, OK, OK.' I sipped my coffee.

'We got what we wanted.'

'Where is the gunman, anyway?'

'They're all still asleep. We were up till four.'

'What about the gun?'

'I told him to bury it. Anywhere. The Dodder banks, his own back garden. Just to get it out of here. Out of this house. Do you want milk?'

'Thanks. What about the papers?'

'Oh, just descriptions of the ceremony. Who was there, etc. Ecumenical triumph. Controversy but success in the end. Meanwhile, no leads on the Proclamation.'

'No, I meant our papers.'

'Oh,' he said. 'Eh . . . they're here.' Out from under the morning papers he pulled a brown A4 envelope, one of his own. 'Do you want to see them again?'

'Please.'

His beaked fingers drew out the three pieces of paper: the hand-drawn map of Booterstown Avenue, the Ordnance Survey

245

map of the area, and the sheet of written instructions. I read them again with fevered eyes.

'Incredible,' I said. 'How did Joe Moran know these existed?'

'Corny must have let it slip once. Someone told someone else.'

'Do you really think Knight is – '

'I don't know but I'm going to find out. I'm going to 6 Linden Lea this afternoon.'

'Mellowes, be careful.'

'Shane, these papers are sixty years old. There's probably an old granny there now. With, I hope, a long memory.'

'It's a long shot.'

'It's been a long shot from the start and look where we've got to.' The morning sunlight on his face. He'd washed since last night. 'The hard part's over, Shane.' He smiled up at me. 'We did well.'

'We did.' I pulled out a chair and sat down beside him. He tidied away the papers.

'Now you've got to convince the Minister.'

'When can I have them?'

'I'll give them to you in a day or two. Make an appointment now to see the Minister. There's no hurry. You have till Friday and you can fob them off. Who's afraid of them, anyway. They ran away from us. Ran like rabbits. You just want to get them off your back so you can get that statue finished.'

'Yeah, I'd better get back to work. What time is it?'

'Eleven-ten. Wash yourself, there's blood on your mug and your clothes are filthy. You can tell them you were scrapping to defend Corny's honour. When's he coming to the studio?'

'Wednesday. Jesus, I hope to Christ he doesn't have a vague recollection when he sees me.'

'Don't be silly. You're his dinner guest, his prized young toast. What he saw last night was a blur in the dark, a thief in the trees.'

'It was fullish moon and he heard us sing.'

'Your voice among many distorted by wine and, under the moon, sure we couldn't even make out the guys at the gate and we were as near as about to kill the bastards.'

'Should have too. What the hell were they doing hanging around like that? Jesus, you know, I'm going to ring Samuelson.' I stood up.

'What?'

'Ring Samuelson and give out to him for it. Those cunts nearly ruined us.'

'Is that wise?' Mellowes followed me into the hall.

'Of course it is. I've got a pact with the man.' I lifted the receiver. 'He gave me a promise to lay off and leave us alone. He'll listen to me. By Jasus, he'll listen. Four . . . five . . . shut the door there, Sean.'

Mellowes shut the door on the Goat's snores and watched tensely as I dialled the five digits. It rang at the other end. After a long time, about forty seconds, a voice answered. 'Hello,' it said sharply.

'Samuelson!'

'Who . . . who's that?'

'Samuelson, you bastard! Your mates nearly paid for your blood last night. What's the fucking story? Hanging about to kidnap Corny. Wait till Hurley hears that's your number – you'll do ten years added for conspiracy.'

'I can explain everything.'

'You'll be explaining in the Bridewell very shortly, with the oniony breath of Hurley wetting your thick neck.'

'Those men had no idea you or your friends would be in that vicinity. They rendezvous about there once every so often just to check. They have their own reasons for doing so.'

'How come they didn't scarper when we came down the drive?'

'They saw you very late. That driveway is pitch black. Once they heard you they wanted to see what they were dealing with. For future reference. Those men, are, after all, trained conspirators. They have a cause in mind.'

'Bollocks! They ran like rabbits.'

'You had guns.'

'We had the toy replica of a pistol. Can't you guys tell the difference between reality and the make-believe?' I winked at Mellowes.

'In dealing with you, Shane, we were afraid of the latter but now we know you're up to more than the make-believe. We caught you in the act. You're genuine. We're pleasantly surprised. You were serious about what you said.'

'I'm serious about this too – get off our backs or you'll get no documents and no co-operation, understand? I'll shop you to the police. Hurley was cracking his fingers yesterday in the stands. He's keen to get his hands around a Redmondite's neck.'

'Tsk, tsk. Let's not lose the run of ourselves or we could all end up losing a lot else besides. We have an agreement, remember.'

'I remember. The agreement was for you to leave us alone. No spying, no trailing us about.'

'Last night was an accident, Shane. It was pure coincidence.'

'There's no such thing. Ask Corny.'

'It won't happen again.'

'You realise you've set us back – '

'We're patient people. We're prepared to wait.'

'You'd want to be.'

'The end of the week?'

'Perhaps.'

'The end of the week it has to be, Shane. I can't keep the reins on the men for ever.'

'You can't keep the reins on them at all, it looks like.'

'I can guarantee you there will be no more accidents such as last night. We'll be sitting peacefully on the Proclamation until we next hear from you.'

'Good. I'll ring you on Wednesday.'

'Good luck, now, Shane and thank you.'

'Thank you, I'll need it and so will you.'

I put the phone down.

'That's him tied up for a week,' I said, laughing.

'Brilliant,' said Mellowes, in a shock of admiration. 'I hadn't realised you had that sort of relationship with him.'

'He thinks I'm crazy.'

'He's not the only one!'

'He needs me, Sean, that's the thing. They're running out of steam. They need our co-operation. They know that stealing the Proclamation is not going to get them their statue, and they're running out of time.'

'Be careful though, all the same.'

'Oh, I will. I'd better get to work, so I can shorten their time even further.'

'OK, listen, I'll be in touch. I'm going to work on those instructions but not here. I think I'd be safer in my aunt's house, perhaps, after last night's fracas. Away from this area.' He paused.

'God, did you give that Samuelson a talking to. Confident man, Shane; is it infectious?'

'Ring me later,' I said, stepping out. 'And give my regards to the others. How come you've no head?'

'I drank two and a half pints of water before hitting the sack. Besides, when you've got documents like those under the mattress, you don't hang about in the morning.'

'Good man.' I stepped down off his porch and he watched me go.

'Be careful down there.' He nodded towards the terminus.

'After last night, Sean,' I said, looking back from the gate which my clever fingers were unclanking, 'I don't think we've any great need to be careful.'

I don't know what this meant but I let him think about it, with a bemused frown, closing the door. I walked on down Bird Avenue, briskly, inhaling the morning air. A job well done. Four doors down, the ball of yelping fluff that I converted on Saturday morning emerged pop-eyed through its zinc-leaved gate but retreated mutely at my brazen gaze. Not this time, Bingo.

Across the diamond, a No. 11 was standing at the terminus, the driver and the conductor reading newspapers, the sports pages, Meath's defeat. I clamped upstairs and toddled down the back to take out my own newspaper:

CEREMONY PASSES OFF PEACEFULLY – THE FALLEN SONS OF IRELAND ARE REMEMBERED

The First National Day of Commemoration to honour all Irish people who died in past wars or on UN duty took place yesterday in Dublin. The President unveiled a plaque and laid a wreath in the Garden of Remembrance, watched by invited VIPs and several hundred curious Dubliners. There was tight security before and during the ceremony due to the possibility of a disruption by the AVNS, a neo-Redmondite group who, though not opposed to the ceremony, regard it as a sop to former Unionists rather than themselves – the 'heirs of constitutional nationalists'. The AVNS are seeking 'the proper, specific' honouring of their tradition, namely in the form of an official statue of the Home Rule leader, John Redmond. This is to 'replace' or 'balance' the one the Government have proposed of the former IRA leader, Cornelius O'Shaughnessy. On Saturday, the AVNS stole the original copy of the 1916 Proclamation

249

from the Civic Museum in Dublin to hold as ransom against Mr O'Shaughnessy's statue.

Ironically, Mr O'Shaughnessy was among those Republicans who had criticised yesterday's historic ceremony as being 'a sell-out to the memory of Irish freedom' and his absence was not unexpected. The Leader of the Opposition was also absent and Fine Gael and Labour politicians have accused him of 'insulting the minority community' and 'playing party politics with the dead'.

As it happens, the only incident of protest at the ceremony occurred as the Taoiseach approached the Garden on foot and accompanied by an escort of army officers. An unidentified woman threw a fistful of 10p coins on the ground behind him. It was understood that thirty silver coins were used. The crowd became silent, but the Taoiseach ignored the incident and the ceremony continued without interruption.

The ceremony brought together, for the first time, under state auspices, men such as Old IRA standard bearer Andy Lord (85) of E Company, 3rd Battalion, Dublin Brigade and Lt.-Col. Brian Clark wearing his George Cross and Military Cross medals, attending as chairman of the Royal British Legion in the Republic. Mr Lord described it as a wonderful occasion. 'We should do more for unity,' he said. 'If we had more of this, we might have less trouble in the North.' Mr Andrew Gibson, 85-year-old veteran of the War of Independence, said he was 'very proud' to be there and held a stiff salute as the sombre notes of the last post and the jauntier tones of the reveille echoed over the Garden.

The bus was pulling out. Not Dan Breen? Revving gently; not Dan Breen.

'I was more interested in saying my prayers for the dead,' said Mr Gibson. 'Talk is no use, prayer is worth far more.' Proudly wearing War of Independence and 1939–45 service medals, Mr Gibson, from Dublin's Marlborough Street, recalled the Custom House battle, being taken prisoner by the British and being told he would be the first to be shot if their lorry was ambushed. He had no comment to make on the absence of Mr O'Shaughnessy or on the possibility that the AVNS might disrupt the ceremony.

The lights changed and I sat back. The bus left the diamond and moved out on to Roebuck Road, driving down past the house. I must say, it didn't look that frightening any more.

When I came into the yard, Murphy was hosing away at the underside of a Willoughby horse, whistling as he probed. As soon as he saw me, he thumb-tightened the hose's mouth and threw a high loop of sun-sparkled water over towards the gates. It landed with a clatter on the corrugated iron.

'Do you mind?' I shouted, jumping back a couple of steps.

'Not at all,' said Murphy. 'I thought you might need a shower if you'd slept it in.'

He turned off the tap and I approached safely.

'There we are now. Day's work done.' He began coiling the hose around his arm. 'Nice of you to come in at all. Were you on the razzle with O'Shaughnessy again last night?'

'Don't be silly,' I said but I had to smile at the suggestion.

'Heard you skulled a couple of bottles on Saturday night.'

'Yes, it turned into quite a session. We were there till well after twelve.'

'No kidnappers? No M.I.5 agents?'

'No, we were left in peace. Any news inside?'

'No, we've been left in peace as well. That is, until you stepped in. Here!' He flicked the hose end and the last of its water shot up at me.

'Murphy!'

I came through the plastic curtains to see Wycherley and Tess standing over a dwarf's scaffold of wood and plaster.

'Good morning,' said Wycherley, holding two propped planks steady as Tess, on her knees, filled the trench between with sloppy wet plaster. It looked like someone had sprinkled Johnson's baby powder on their heads, or baking powder. An idea there for Wednesday.

'Sorry. I slept it out.'

'Out rough, by the look of your clothes,' he said swiftly. 'Whoa, Tess. That's enough now. That'll do.' Tess lifted the bucket and straightened up.

'Well, I thought with the work we'd be doing today, and all.'

They started laughing.

'Leave it now,' said Wycherley, standing back. 'It'll set with the

251

stones against the wood.' Tess came away wiping wet hands on her overalls.

'First foundations?' I asked them.

'Yep and last cremations,' said Wycherley. 'That's where his feet will end.'

'You'll do separate reliefs of his legs, I take it?'

'We'll do separate reliefs of everything,' said Wycherley in a distant voice. 'This'll serve for the main body when it's built up. The chest and trunk. He'll have to step into it for a while, but it won't kill him.'

'Nah, sure he's all for it,' said Tess with near heart-rending innocence. '"Participating in his own statue", remember. He loves the idea.'

'Of course he does.'

'And' – she poked at me with a wet finger – 'his favourite little boy Shane will be here to help him.'

I shrugged and smiled.

'Unless he's snoozing in bed after a rough weekend.'

'Listen,' I said, stiffening up, 'I've no clock in my new place, and it was a rough bloody weekend. I had to move to Parnell Square in the first place, because some madmen were after me for working in this place.'

'No one forces you to work here, young man, or even to come in in the morning.' He mock-smiled. 'But make damn sure you don't sleep it out on Wednesday morning.'

'I'll be there.'

'You'd better be,' he warned. 'No problem at the weekend, it seems. I hear you were casting in here yesterday?'

'Eh, that's right.'

'Something about a present for a friend? Ramsey said it was a little stick man to symbolise your discovery of each other. What the hell was that all about?'

'Oh, that was just a story for Ramsey,' I explained, sweating – the studio was hot. 'It's for the girlfriend. Memento. Her birthday. Didn't want to tell him the full story. You know the way.'

'No, I don't.'

'I suppose not.'

'Don't get wise, Shane. And stay the right side of me in the coming days. They could be tough and I don't want you getting up to any monkey business on the side.'

'What the – ?' I played incredulous, hurt.

'Ah, don't,' said Tess. 'He misses his girlfriend.'

'Well, just as long as that little stick man is being sent to her and not to some Captain Moonlight joker as some sort of revenge gesture. You started out like me ignoring these people but, now that they're on the run, I don't know – it's become a bit of an intrigue to you. A game, perhaps?'

'Don't be ridiculous,' I said. 'You're just sensitive because of a near court case. Because you didn't ignore them but went and blamed Forbes for it all.'

'Exactly, and I don't want any more trouble like that. I shouldn't have suspected him to so many mouths. I was nervy.'

'Forget it. I'm not like that.' I smiled slyly at him. 'I'm discreet. Even in love.'

'You must have money to be able to send solid bronze through the post.'

'No, not on your wages but I starve if necessary. After all, what is money, compared to – ' I touched his elbow coquettishly.

'Come on,' he said brusquely. 'Let's have tea.'

We followed him out of the workshop and into the kitchen. Tess held the plastic curtain open for me. 'So where did you have dinner in the end?' she asked. She had offered me Sunday dinner with her family.

'Rathmines,' I said, dipping through. 'The cat's funeral. You'd have loved it. Roast Siamese and kitten stew.'

'Ah Shane, please.'

'Seriously, you'd have loved it. It was a weird gothic scene altogether. I'll tell you about it.'

We came from the kitchen and Wycherley sat down to read the paper.

'So, no news from Hurley?' I asked, plugging in the kettle.

'No, nothing came up. He rang this morning. Hurley is of the opinion that the recovery of the Proclamation was not a priority for the authorities but the safe completion of the statue was.'

'Well, we've always known that.'

'Yes, but it's nice to hear it confirmed. The Minister was on to me at eleven this morning with the message that we were to work as quietly and quickly as possible in the next few days.'

'Days?' exclaimed Tess.

'Days,' repeated Wycherley. 'If we get successful reliefs from O'Shaughnessy's body on Wednesday and we have everything else ready I see no reason not to fire ahead straight away. The Minister's strategy was quite clear and I agree with him. We were to avail of these people's so-called cease-fire to get the job done before they had time to reactivate. By the time they realised the tactical error they made in relying on the captured Proclamation for results, rather than on their previous momentum of poison letters and threats, the statue would be completed and ready for erection.'

'Exactly!' I said, slamming the table. 'Let's go for it. Days – it'll have to be days. These people are probably realising the error of their tactics already.'

'Perhaps, and God knows what they plan to fall back on.'

'God only knows,' I shrugged and let slip a sly smile I couldn't disguise. How could I? Here was Wycherley taking in Tess, as he took in the Government, who thought in turn they were taking in the AVNS and here was I taking them all in.

'The Government have agreed to make a financial arrangement by which we will earn a certain percentage more for each day we can take off the deadline. Believe me, it is a necessary arrangement, for the less time we spend on this blasted contract the better,' he said, raising his eyebrows and drumming his fingers. 'He's ringing me today.'

'I look forward to it,' said Tess brightly.

'We'll work quickly. We don't want the man to be hanging around here all day.'

'No, the quicker the better,' I agreed.

'I explained the process to Tess again earlier on – you've both worked on one before: the split moulds, the setting, the stiffened clothes, no movement, etc. Anyway, I'll be going through it all before then, so you needn't worry.'

The phone rang in the hall.

'It's for you,' said Ramsey, putting his head in the door. 'It's Mr O'Donovan.'

'Ah.' Wycherley sprang up and put down his cup. He had acquired unusual energy of late. Must be nervous. Although Mr O'Donovan had settled one thing for him. Forbes: the slander threat was off, sweetened by a small commission from the Minister.

'Listen, then,' said Wycherley, turning around. 'I'll see you kids later. Go and have lunch. We'll talk when you get back.'

Tess drained her cup.

'What are you up to now, Shane? Do you want to come with me to Marks Brothers?'

'Yeah, sure.'

'Wait here.'

Ramsey ambled into the kitchen.

'Ah, I am thirsty,' he sighed. 'I've been trying to clean the Willoughby horse.' He filled himself a glass of water at the sink.

He too was covered in white dust but then he was always covered in white dust and scorched holes and broken drippings of wax. Those baggy blue overalls, torn at the arse and riveted where they should have been stitched (Murphy's idea), protected nothing more immediate on himself than another pair of blue overalls, but they'd stood over, scraped and washed and seen into the world God knows how many creations in this studio over the last twenty years. Icicle birds and bicycle trees, businessmen's busts and Biafran legs: these singed and torn midwife's overalls have seen them in. Pity they won't see our greatest creation off, but that's another matter.

'Come on.' Tess dragged me by the sleeve.

'I'm coming. Bye, bye, Ramsey,' I said, flapping my free one.

'Sure, we'll see you later,' he said softly. The royal we, I note, for the other one on the phone, the unfree one. Still tied up.

'Hey, do some work in the afternoon!' shouted Murphy out in the yard. He was halfway up a hill of scrap with an accusative welding rod in his hand.

'I will, of course.'

'There's an Oldcastle's lorry coming in at three with sixty bags of coal. You'd want to get your shoulder ready.'

'They'll bring them in, that's their job. They're delivery men.'

'Not to the kennels they won't, that's yours. And they'll want their bags back so I wouldn't change your clothes.' Laughing, he came down the shingle of metal trailing a flex of some sort. What's he at? Always at something, this handyman for wily Wycherley. Magician, electrician. Spoon in the meter or wires rerouted from over the wall. The defunct Academy Cinema: someone's still paying for the last picture show.

'Do we get danger money for delivering down here now?' asked the fat gaffer standing on the end of his truck. He was admiring the lads below him breaking their backs lugging sacks to the coalshed, our coalshed.

'You should be paying us royalties,' said Murphy, spitting between pulls.

'Are you not glad to be involved? Think of it – all that coal

255

going to burn a statue of a famous man.' He gestured to the back of a panting youth. 'Sure you'll be able to take your grandchildren up to Stephen's Green and tell them, '"There you are, kids – I delivered the stuff that put that fellow where he is."'

'Yeah, well, you can give me a bullet-proof vest for the ceremony,' said the gaffer. 'I'm risking my life coming down here keeping you people supplied. And I reckon you're wasting your time too. What comes out of here won't be long-standing.'

'Same goes for what comes in,' I told him. 'And you're a standing target up there. No bullet-proof vest would cover you.'

The gaffer looked a bit upset.

'But our man will be well covered, won't he, Shane?' said Murphy.

'Well covered. Constant surveillance, the sort he didn't want when he was alive. Where it goes up in the Green is right across from the Departments of Justice and Foreign Affairs. There are cops on duty there twenty-four hours a day, every day of the year. It'll be a long time before anyone gets to tamper with the statue we're putting inside those railings. A long time . . . You all right, son?'

One of the youths had stopped for a breather. He nodded dumbly.

'You're not scared, sure you're not? Here, have one of these.' Murphy thrust an open Major packet before him and a finger obliged. Blacker than the Goat's.

'The sums now, Murphy,' said the gaffer, leaning down to hand him a crushed pink docket from the backside of his sagging denims.

'Shane,' said Murphy, handing me the dockets. 'Run in there and get Bob's scrawl on that. Go on, you're the man for paperwork.'

I looked at him. Closer to the bone than he thinks.

'Bob?' I burst through the plastic curtains and, to tell the truth, I wouldn't care what chocolate castle of a waxed arrangement was being hoisted aloft on the other side. If it's hit by a blind shoe that's not my problem.

'Is there a fire somewhere?' They looked up, Tess and Wycherley, from the mould.

'No, but there soon will be by the rate that Ramsey's working at over there.' The said man was bricking up the back wall of the main oven as if his life depended on it.

'What time are we cooking at?'

'Shane, please.' Wycherley checked me with his lowered eyes. He had his hands around a funnel that Tess was pouring plaster into.

'Sorry.'

'What's your problem?'

'Docket here for you to sign. Receipt of coal, sixty sacks.'

He whipped out his Sheaffer and signed the meat-heated docket with his usual flourish of loops: a concertina of barbed-wire 'e's and 'w's, like pairs of boobs, swinging as heavily as the loo doors we graffitied them on in distant Artane.

'Here.' He gave me the docket.

'You're going well here,' I said, looking at how much of the mould they'd built.

'Don't step on the lath!' warned Tess, rummaging on her knees with wet plaster and a trowel.

'Tess,' said Wycherley. 'We're going to move it over there when it dries so we can get it on to that slide I was telling you about.' He gave me a significant look.

'Sounds great,' said Tess, looking up.

'Yeah . . . great idea.'

'We'll build the rest of the main mould on that when we take fittings from O'Shaughnessy so the whole thing can be slotted together and slid along the tracks into the oven. Otherwise we couldn't move as quickly and the thing would break up. Understand?' Wycherley eyed me keenly.

'Right.' I exchanged the glance.

The phone rang. I went to get it.

'If that's for me, Shane, it'd better be important. Otherwise, I'm busy. You can take their number and I might call them back. And no journalists!' he shouted.

'OK,' I shouted back and lifted the receiver.

'Hello. Mr Wycherley?' A clipped voice.

'No, this isn't Mr Wycherley. Who's that?'

'Can I speak to Mr Wycherley?'

'I'm afraid he's tied up at the moment. Who's this?'

'This is' – pause – 'Nigel Smith of the BBC. I wonder could I – ?'

'No, you couldn't. He's not talking to journalists. I'm sorry. Doctor's orders. Any news on the statue you'll have to get from the Garda Press Office or Government Information Services or Major Vinny Byrne who has more than the Proclamation under his bed.

'Oh . . . eh, well, it's not news I'm looking for, actually. We are hoping to do a feature on Mr Wycherley: his recent work, his past commissions, development of his style and so on.'

'Sounds like a ruse to me.'

'The . . . I'm sorry? Well, you see, the O'Shaughnessy sculpture would only be the tie-in.'

'Exactly, but tied into what? You guys come in here, pan the cameras round and the next thing there's more than sunshine coming through our windows.'

'I'm afraid I don't understand.'

'No, but spend more time in this country and you will. I'm sorry, sir, but we're not falling for your tricks. There'll be no cameras in here to violate the tranquillity of our working atmosphere and set the mob on our back. We want to stay out of this. Call O'Shaughnessy if you want a couple of shots of a man's last days on earth.'

'Well, I really don't understand. I mean, maybe, after the O'Shaughnessy commission is finished, if it is finished.'

'Yeah, maybe then. We'll be in Mountjoy. You can give us a shout from the roadside. Thank you, Mr Smith, I'll tell Mr Wycherley you called.'

I put the phone down and went inside, happy enough with having sent him packing. Wycherley, however, wasn't so happy. Some of the laths had broken and the plaster was coming through like a trench in a mudslide. Bob and nurse were on their knees tending to the wounded. The phone was ringing again.

'Get that Shane, will you, for God's sake.'

'OK, OK,' I said and, in a leap and a bound, I was through the curtains and grabbing the receiver. A croaky voice.

'I can't hear you.'

'. . . speak to Mr Wycherley.'

Oo now. Pompous little voice. Friend of his from the club?

'What about?'

'Private matter.'

'Private Mater Nursing Home, maybe? No, he's not into subscribing and I'm afraid he's wrapped up at the moment in his father's loincloth. Get the picture? Or should it be winding sheet. Can I get your shoe size and get him to give you a buzz?'

'. . . can please get . . .'

Yeah, yeah, croak on, my friend – Jesus, it's O'Shaughnessy! I dropped the phone.

'Excuse me.' I fumbled with it. Quick, quick, quick. Calm yourself.

'Sorry. Mr O'Shaughnessy – still there? Good. Listen, I'm sorry about that. The gentleman here who answers the phone can be a little rude at times. Our apologies. He had no idea. He thought it was another journalist. I really am sorry. H-H-How are you anyway?'

'Fine.'

'Good. You' – Jesus, I was shaking – 'you didn't go to the ceremony yesterday?' What else could I ask him?

'No . . . could you get Mr Wycherley for me, please?'

'Certainly! Hold on for a moment.'

I put the receiver down with agonised gentleness, as if it was a fragile sea shell or a bit of delft or Corny himself I was placing on the shelf.

'Bob.' I put my head through the curtains. 'It's O'Shaughnessy.'

'Ah, good.' He took his gloves off and came to the phone. We passed at the curtains but he ignored my meaningful grin.

'Shane!' shouted Murphy, his head suddenly bursting through the curtains. 'Come on! Are you getting that thing sketched or something? We like to chat but these guys can't be hanging around here all day, like you, doing shag all.' He winked at Tess and she agreed with him.

'I'm coming, I'm coming.'

'They could be shot too' he said, parting the curtains for me. 'They're planking it out here, the poor lads. Come on.'

He followed me down the corridor and we passed Wycherley shouting very patiently into the mouthpiece. 'OK . . . OK, I've got that, I've got that.'

'Sounds remedial,' said Murphy under his breath. 'Is it long-distance or what?'

'It's O'Shaughnessy.'

'Oh,' said Murphy, laughing, as we came out into the sun. 'Well, that's long-distance enough! Here give us that docket.' Murphy was quite oblivious to the old boy.

'Don't fret yet, men,' he shouted, as he ran across the yard. 'There could be a cancellation.'

He handed the docket to the fat gaffer who was leaning out of his cab window, with his engines revved. The two boys were beside him. They looked like they were anxious to leave.

'OK!'

259

Murphy stepped back and they pulled out, big tyres rattling over loose scaffolding, and sacks of coal bulging out over the side in a way that coalmen always stack them and I always wonder why. Is it to frighten suburbanites into buying them before they litter their streets?

'So,' said Murphy, coming back, rubbing his hands. 'That's them gone.'

'Wycherley was asking about who was counting the sacks, i.e. why didn't we get the docket signed after they'd finished.'

'Well now,' said Murphy, smiling broadly and putting one foot up on the veranda. 'Wycherley's not as wise as he thinks he is, is he? We get the docket signed during delivery because the boys were counting themselves. Unfortunately, as often happens when two people count, they get confused and have to ask the opinion of the third – me.' He pointed to his heart. 'You have to get up early in the morning, Shane.'

Obviously. He had me confused now. Wycherley came out on to the veranda.

'O'Shaughnessy will be here on Wednesday morning,' he said quietly, his face quite white. '11 a.m.'

We nodded. Murphy rubbed his hands. 'Good stuff, then.'

Wycherley smiled mutely and retreated inside.

'So.' Murphy frisked his pockets for his cigarettes. 'You're all set, Shane. You didn't think you'd go through with it, maybe. What? All ready and no one to stop you, eh?'

I was on another planet. Corny here in two days; it was incredible.

'Yeah,' I repeated dumbly. 'We're all set.'

'Shane!' Tessa's voice came out the window. 'Phone!'

'Who is it?' I asked, jumping up on the veranda.

'Your friend Sean,' she shouted. 'I think.'

I ran in and picked up the receiver.

'Sean?'

'Hello, sir, how are you? How's the head?'

'Grand.'

'Did you enjoy that party last night?'

Party? What's he . . .? 'Oh, great party, yeah! Good crack. How did the others get on? Oisin, Tómas and the Goat came back to Clonskeagh to stay with me. We got a taxi at the end of Westminster Road, and weren't home till about three. Oisin was fierce excited about the woman he'd snipped, but not too excited

260

to tell us to keep quiet about it or otherwise someone will hear about it and tell his girlfriend. Do you know what I mean?'

'I know exactly what you mean.'

'And we'd be blamed for it as well. You know we would. For putting him up to it. As far as anyone's concerned, no mention of the party. You sat at home last night studying, Tómas was in Leeson Street, Oisin was practising and Greycoat was reading magazines in someone's flat. Those are our alibis, right?'

'Right.' It was brilliant: telling our alibis to whoever's listening. What a joke. 'So listen, I went down to Linden Lea to check on the friend of your great-aunt's who was selling the bicycle, but she wasn't in. No trace of her but I might try and get the bike I want through other channels. You were saying hers would be a bit rusty. It's many years since it was brought out for a spin and it could be hard to put it in contact with the sort of life it first had when it was an active machine. The chain could be broken.'

'Right.' The chain could be broken. I got it. 'Right, I see what you mean.'

'So listen, I'll meet you later on, maybe.'

'Yeah, say the . . . say, the place of the yellowing light and the yellowing paperback in the back pocket. At nine.'

'Right. Tobin's.'

'Oh, listen, that light Oisin took from their living-room. What did he do with it?'

Mellowes paused. 'The cigarette papers?'

'No, the cigarette lighter. You know, the one that was shaped like an antique musket.'

I could hear Mellowes' sharp intake of breath and then the forced jollity.

'Oh I don't know, Shane. I don't know.' But he was annoyed. 'Listen, I'll see you at nine.'

'Cheers then, Sean.' I put the phone down. That was a bit cheeky. He wasn't pleased. But sure, what the hell. By Wednesday, the taking of a gun will be a crime of little importance. We might as well enjoy ourselves in our intrigue.

Corny on Wednesday – yahow! I was most excited and went into the workshop to get details.

'So, Bob' – he was actually working on the wax body of the man – 'he's coming in at eleven?'

'Yes – ' But before Wycherley had a chance to expand Murphy walked in.

261

'There's some weirdo outside,' he said, wrinkling his nose.

'Who?' said Wycherley, ruffled. 'A reporter?'

'Don't think so. He looks like the something you'd see collecting for Fianna Fáil. The kind of guy who carries pictures of aborted babies in his pocket.'

'Murphy, who is he?' Wycherley asked impatiently.

'I don't know. He says he's looking for Michael Collins.'

'Michael Collins?' said Tess, laughing nervously.

'Hey, what's going on here?' Wycherley dropped his wax scalpel.

'It's OK,' I said, stepping forward cheerily. 'That's my former landlord, Mick Pigott.'

Wycherley looked at me incredulously.

'Or should I say my former non-landlord, because he always denied he was the actual landlord.'

'Shane!' shouted Wycherley. He rarely shouts. Nerves getting to him. Wednesday and all that. 'Just what is going on?'

'Do you want me to explain?' I said, swallowing.

'Please!' He put his face forward.

'Well, before I started working here I wanted to apply for rent allowance because I was broke but the landlord wouldn't sign my application form because he wanted to avoid tax and didn't want to reveal to anyone how many tenants he had in his house. Of course, he didn't tell me that. He told me that, first of all, he wasn't the landlord, his brother was the landlord and he was just the agent but he knew his brother made a policy of not signing rent-allowance forms. So I told Social Welfare this and they said we understand, there are lots of landlords like him. Go and get a receipt for rent. That'll suffice. We need some more proof of how much rent you're paying. But the cunt wouldn't give me a receipt. He said his brother's policy was not to issue receipts. So I thought maybe I could give Welfare my original receipt for one week's deposit which he had signed and they said OK, but it needs to be signed by the landlord which it isn't. So I said no, but he's the agent and he said it was OK for him to sign for his brother, which he didn't say, of course, but I didn't care because if he's not the landlord, I'm not Michael Collins.'

They looked at me dumbfounded. Wycherley's mouth was open.

'How, pray,' said Wycherley, with his face like he had a toothache, 'did you become Michael Collins?'

'Ah, that's a different story. You see, I wanted to – '

'No, please.' Wycherley put his hand up. 'We don't want to hear it. To hear is to become aware. It has to involve fraud and duplicity of some sort.'

'I beg your pardon,' I said, offended.

'You certainly should, bringing your corrupt landlords in here. It's bad enough that you've brought yourself in here, with your past of fraud and impersonation, "Michael Collins". I could turn you in for the amount of impersonation and petty fraud I'm sure you've been up to in this city and now you bring your corrupt landlords on to my premises, as if we hadn't got enough trouble already. Aren't you lucky, young man, that I'm not an informer.'

'Aren't you lucky, old man, that neither am I?'

'Go on,' he said, laughing. How nervously he laughed. 'Tell that fellow out there to get out of my yard.'

'With pleasure,' I declared, turning on my heel.

'Oh, and Shane!'

I paused before the curtains.

'Can you imagine what Detective Sergeant Hurley would think if he found out that you called yourself Michael Collins. Regardless of whether it was for the purpose of rent allowance or getting around a landlord, can you imagine in what direction his mind would run?' He looked at me keenly, the others behind him. A trio.

'I can,' I said calmly, 'but I wouldn't care, because two years ago I was Michael Collins.'

They looked at me blankly and I went out. That's left them with something to think about. Now, to confront this rack-renter. What's brought him down here? Can't be to give me the deposit, can it? I thought I'd have to fight for weeks for that. Maybe he's found out that I'm not Michael Collins at all but Shane McArdle of the missing packages and the police enquiries. Maybe he's a very angry man. Maybe I'm going to enjoy this very much. Very much indeed, now that I've entered the realm of the real conspiratorial and people like him are of no consequence to us. Thinks he can fool me when here I am pulling off one of the biggest stunts the city has ever seen. Where is he, the skinflint, till I tell him what's what?

I came out into the sun and there he was standing beside the oil drums with his hands behind his back as if he was waiting for communion. Anything for free. Jesus, well, he doesn't look very angry, that's for sure. Indeed he greeted my emergence with the sort of anticipatory smile a priest or a child-molester reserves for a child on its First Communion.

'Mr Pigott,' I said, hopping down off the veranda. 'I didn't expect to see you again so soon.'

'Ah, well. I thought I'd drop down the deposit.'

'I hope that you mean that figuratively, by which I mean not in figures.'

This confused him for about three seconds.

'Ah,' he said. 'The penny drops.'

'But not the deposit.'

'No, no, goodness no. Here it is.' He drew out an envelope and opened it with fidgety fingers to indicate nineteen pounds inside. Now this surprised me. Pigott giving me my deposit back within four days. Pigott giving me my deposit back at all. There had to be a catch somewhere and the catch came.

'Ah em,' he said, but it sounded more like 'Amen'. He was clearing his throat. 'You didn't happen to take a blanket from the flat?' He looked at me from under one eyebrow. 'A green blanket with a pattern on it?'

'A green blanket – let me see.' I tensed my face to remember. 'Green blanket, green blanket,' I murmured, as if invoking its name would yield the damn thing up to my tortured memory when it was, in fact, sitting there, stolen and clearly visualised, on an orange crate in Parnell Square. 'Oh, that old thing.' I snapped my fingers. 'Sorry, yes, I have that. I took it as a kind of memento.'

'A memento of the flat?' he said, agreeably surprised.

'Good God, no. That flat doesn't deserve a memento. No, it was a memento of my girlfriend and the loss of her virginity. The night left a large blob of blood stained into the blanket and I thought I'd keep it for that reason. But if you want it back.'

Pigott was shocked. He was sorry he'd come. He was certainly sorry he'd given me £19.

'I'll tell you what,' I told him. 'I'll bring it in here and you can come and collect it tomorrow, or the next day, or whenever you can tear yourself away from the absorbing pastime of converting cupboards into apartments and tenants into victims and fixing holes in the roof with Quinnsworth bags. OK?'

He looked at me as if I had three heads.

'Wha-wha-wha-what time?'

264

'A-a-a-a any time,' I said, gleefully imitating him. 'But afternoon's best, Mick. Toddle down in the afternoon. You can spare the time and the shoe leather, I'm sure. Is that OK? Great. Goodbye and thanks for the cash.'

'Good-good-goodbye,' he said, starting to back off.

'Oh, by the way, Mick – '

He looked over at me.

'Did you ever find out who that Shane McArdle was?'

'No.'

'Strange, isn't it? You seem to be keeping a haunted house up there. Maybe you should ask the phantom landlord had he seen the phantom tenant.'

'G-g-goodbye,' he stuttered on, stumbling as he turned, for in his confused haste to leave, the aforementioned shoe leather slid on a roll of copper piping. He recovered himself but he didn't look back. Serves him right for not resoling his shoes or taking buses more often.

'Shane!'

The kitchen window was opened and Wycherley appeared as if he'd been watching all along and waiting for Pigott to go.

'Come on in here, Shane. I want to talk to you about something.'

About Corny, surely, not 'Michael Collins', or does that little ruse still annoy him? How did I know Pigott would turn up here? And with my money too. There's a shock.

'Don't look so forlorn,' said Wycherley. 'I want to talk to you about an actual Irish hero, still with us, and not a dead one.'

'Oh, I wouldn't be so sure about that,' I said and so I went in out of the sun and sat down with him to work out the strategies for Wednesday morning. We drank about five cups of tea and didn't go for a drink. We had a lot to think about.

Chapter 10

The Setting Up

It felt funny going back to Parnell Square tonight. I hadn't been there since yesterday morning and so many things had happened, so many things since I left the house and bumped into those two guards planting traffic cones for the commemoration ceremony. I got my key made, I met Samuelson and did a deal with him. We got into the cellar, we got the papers, unbelievably more clean and murderous than we ever expected. We had a scrap with Samuelson's men and almost, God forbid, with the great man himself after rousing him from his bed. What a night. It's funny though, how when the hard part is over I feel more nervous and on edge. Why now, when I am least under threat from the AVNS and they tied up for a week and, in fact, relying on me, their buddy, do I feel most scared, most spooked, walking back here to the badly lit square at the end of O'Connell Street?

It was the immensity of things to come, obviously, and the square deserted now when it was full of the nation's elite and old soldiers yesterday. God, yesterday – it seems so long ago. And Corny not among them. And he's not to get a second chance. Jesus. Just think. But it was more than that. It was the O'Higgins instructions. 'At swim'. 'Bring personal'. 'Brought'. 'The parabellum'. These scared me and the way we sneaked in there to get them. Rummaging through his old papers when he was upstairs. God, were we playing dangerous. The intrigue of sixty years ago and our intrigue fused in my mind to create a confused and shameful picture. Exhilarating, yes, but less than one expects. Wooden too, unreal, cruel and cold-blooded, a giddy mixture of real death and the comic make-believe.

I had abstracted O'Shaughnessy beyond humanity, a mental preparation for the actual denudement of his flesh and blood, and something of the same I'd done to myself and those around me. Who was I conning? I was conning everyone. My own invincibles, hugely and crucially, and my friends, Tess, and even – God credit me for balancing this one – my accomplice and master, dear old Wycherley.

And of course, over there, across the square in the Belvedere Hotel, I conned, in glorious fashion, the man who was out to kill me a week ago. Or said he was. We're all saying things but here I am telling nobody the full story. What you tell one, you withhold from the other. Darling Wycherley, with whom I had entered into the most diabolic pact, the deadliest intrigue of all, not even he could hear of my other activities, related though they were to him and me and salvation. Let's hope it works. Let's hope the trickery holds together. I had to hope it did. After all, in years to come, in the way of the best stories, all can be told safely or almost safely to those with an unprejudiced ear.

I pushed up the big red door of No. 40 and went up the long stairs. Someone was in the kitchen below, cooking and listening to classical music on Radio 3. Inside the door of the main room on the second floor another radio was playing as I passed. The nine o'clock news. But I couldn't be bothered trying to eavesdrop. Around the elbow of the upper staircase, I was hit by the urinous whiff of the outside loo, hanging to the back of the building until it rots and drops. How could you bring someone in here? How could I bring Ariel here if I got lucky again. Ariel: I'd sort of forgotten about her. Goes to show how absorbed I've become if the memory of such a delightful creature passes so easily to the back of my consciousness. Weeks they should live for, even years. Why, I still smile about the girls I got off with when I first left Artane. Northside girls, seaside girls, nutcase girls, girls with Snoopy quilts on their beds and girls who went hang-gliding off Clontarf Beach. But I've given up on Niamh. She appears to have given up on me. She's not privy to any of this. How can I relate to her when she comes home. I'm a changed man. I'm a changed man since I last saw her. The steps get hollower as you get to the top of the house, and the floorboards rattle as if the house was decaying from the top down: slates missing, windows broken, draughts everywhere. I must make sure I'm not here in winter, which means beyond next month.

I pulled back the curtain and stepped into the darkness of my big room. The lights of the traffic were playing on the broken plasterwork of the ceiling, enough light for me to see myself safely past the pot-holes in the floorboards and the upended broken telly and across to the window so I could look out into the street. A few cars passed below, taking up speed to make the climb up the square to Granby Row, and a wailing bus lugging behind. People going home. There were no people in the streets, except for a group of young fellows on their way back to Dominick Street flats. Whistles that sound so lonely in the empty streets.

The Garden of Remembrance was dark now, empty, the flag down and the water in the cross-shaped pond calmed by the night breeze. Does anyone sneak in there at night? Winos or homeless people or glue kids. Probably not. Nowhere to sleep in there. No big bushes or huts with bits of the *Evening Press* to wrap around you. The hullabaloo there yesterday, and it's all quiet now. Until the next time. Will there be a ceremony there next year? Probably not, if Fianna Fáil are in power. Corny's one and only chance is gone. These well-meant attempts to bridge our past. No hope. Slave to history. It's too late to change the course of things now.

I went over to my bed and switched on the lamp. I was tired. Tired, tired, I've been tired for ages. The way I felt last night in the cellar. That's never happened to me before. Never. It's a new life I'm leading. I'm caught up in something. Tension and wine and excitement. I haven't had a proper night's sleep for ages. Up early on Saturday to go to Loyola and then the long dinner in Corny's. And then the Pink, and then up again to cast the key and then Samuelson and then the cat's funeral, wine and wit and then the Operation. The garden, the coalshed, the gates, the couch.

My God, but it was worth it. We pulled it off. Against all odds. To get inside and then actually to find the suitcase and then the papers. And what papers. And then to escape after making a merry mess of ourselves with his high potent wine. Where's he now? In bed? Working? Tomorrow's extradition case, maybe. Or new statements on the statue saga. How frightened is he, I wonder, sitting at his desk out there in Clonskeagh? Deep down does he feel any fear? The sound of footsteps in his garden, the threats, the English agents, the people who are out to get him. The life of earned revenge. Is he ever scared at all out there, unprotected in that big house, or is he, as Mellowes says, too old to be bothered to care now? Oblivious. Above them. Taunting them. Glad of their attention even. You have to get your enemy when he's a tooth in his head, he said, but if he has that treasury of guns in his cellar what does he have upstairs? A revolver still, under his pillow.

I hit my own pillow, cool and soft, and thought how useful such a thing could be. If anything came through those upstairs curtains – cold black parabellum like that. Snug, snub-nosed, handily fist-sized. Did you see it? They say if you keep a gun by once or twice, you'll keep one by for the rest of your life. It never leaves you, and creates the reason for its staying. Attracts other guns, sits burning in your desk and its heat transmits. I am a gun, use me, try me. Like a dog on heat. What am I saying? I'm tired, very tired. No prayers for me, no siree. I watched the lights of the traffic on the plasterwork of the ceiling and then surprised myself by drifting slowly but heavily into sleep.

Reconnaissance had me in here, at the back of a large, carpeted and velvet-curtained room with three senior judges on a high wood stage and a bench at the back for the public to sit on. The Supreme Court. Corny was speaking and all was hushed. There was no room and I had to stand. The atmosphere was very serious. An extradition was being challenged. Gardaí chewed their fingernails and listened. Classroom benches of lawyers leaned forward, shoulder to shoulder, and whispered in each other's ears, discreetly, so that the only sound to be heard in the sumptuous room was the minute scratching of pen on paper and Corny's low phlegmatic delivery, monotonous and unchanging, spoken to no one in particular but upwards, perhaps, to the golden harp of the State, quoting its constitution. But not quoting it in support. Quoting it against the State, forcing it to live up to its expectations.

He read stooped, with only half a gown draped over his narrow shoulders and a wig pushed to the back of his head as if struggling out of these ill-fitted raiments, these costumes of the law. Or they out of him. How has he managed to continue practising for so long? OK, he's obviously not as active as he was but he comes back month after month, session after session. What keeps him going? On all fronts. What keeps him writing tracts, addressing meetings, chairing committees, joining protests? What keeps him doing the things that has the State tapping his phone at the age of ninety?

Cases like this, I suppose. Kenneth Williams. Latest in a long

269

line. Williams, a native of Belfast, took part in the mass breakout from HM Maze Prison in September 1983, fled to the South and was arrested. An order for his extradition was granted. He is wanted in the North on foot of eighteen warrants, some relating to his escape, one relating to the attempted murder of an RUC superintendent. While held in Portlaoise Prison, Williams tried to escape in August 1985, and is now serving a two-year sentence.

Corny read patiently. Now and then, he looked up to finish a sentence, lengthening the final few words as if to savour the wary familiarity, the bleak integrity of the quarrel. Williams had been discriminated against over employment in the North because he was a Catholic. From the outset of the present troubles in the North the authorities there, and the British army, failed to protect the Catholic minority, and as a result they had to defend themselves. Williams later joined the IRA which had as its primary objective the ending of British rule in the North and the reintegration of the national territory, if necessary by force of arms. He did not have any part in the shooting of the superintendent and the offence had been investigated by the RUC as a political one. He took part in the Maze escape, which was organised by the IRA, because he considered he was wrongfully imprisoned and that this was because of his Catholic beliefs, his well-known Republican politics and the failure of the Northern authorities to give a fair and proper trial.

Corny went on for a long while, going into the usual details on discrimination, torture, revenge and murder. Then he paused suddenly and put his knotted hand to his head. Was he tired? No, he was finished. He put down the document and took up another one. A row of wigs in the back row tensed their shoulders and the guard beside me ran his tongue along his gums. Corny was talking to the judges. It was barely audible but Corny was nodding his head. The three judges conferred. All was hushed in the courtroom. A few of the Anti-Extradition people, straining their necks on the back bench, never wore such peaceful expectant faces, and it struck me how small our case might be compared to what was going on in here and the sort of people O'Shaughnessy was defending and attacking. It struck me too, how important he was to these defendants and how bloody dangerous it was for us to be entertaining the sort of ideas we were. The AVNS were risking their thick necks coming out the way they did against his statue in public, but what we were planning in private was so catastrophic, in comparison, that its effects upon these sort of people didn't bear thinking about. To many he may be a wizened old fraud, droning on about sovereignty and nuclear power and his great and checkered career, but to the people who still have their fingers on triggers, he means a lot, quite a lot, and I just hope no one pays the price for his disappearance.

The judges signalled Corny to proceed. He took up another document. It was time to go.

'Excuse me,' I said but before I moved I felt a hand on my shoulder.

When I turned around Detective Hurley was smiling. He indicated the door. 'Let's go for a chat, will we?'

'Eh . . . sure,' I said and I started making my way to the door with him following. My heart was thumping. Judges, guards, people on the jury looked up and watched our exit.

'And, your honour, I believe that if this was the case, then . . .'

We came down the steps and the guards and people collected by the door parted quickly for our passage.

'Hello, Mr Hurley,' they stood aside and whispered.

'Hello, lads,' he whispered back as he came through and a crowd held the door open for us.

'Thank you,' said Hurley in a surprised voice and he stepped out. I opened the second. He said nothing but came down the step after me, with a strange grin. Is this it, then?

'Let's go over here,' he said and he pointed at a bench at the far side of the hall. Our heels tapped loudly. The sunlight streamed down. For the first time in my life I didn't know what lies to prepare.

'Sit down,' he said and he pulled up the creases in his trousers.

'Ahh,' he said, landing his bulk on the seat. 'That's some business in there, eh? Some business altogether.'

'It is,' I said. We were outside Court 2. Sunlight was streaming down from the cone of the dome. Corny was up there in '22, dodging flames and gunfire. Did he ever think it was the end? How often did he think he was facing his end?

Hurley took out a packet of mints. 'Would you take a mint?'

'No, thanks.'

'OK,' he said and he popped a mint into his head. 'I'm off the pipe.'

'Oh, did it show up?' He had lost it.

271

'No, but I want to talk to you,' he said, chewing the mint, 'about something that did.'

'Oh.' Here we go.

'It's about . . .' He looked at me slantways. 'It's about a man called Harrington.'

'Oh.'

'Is there something wrong?'

'No.' He looked at me keenly, his fleshy jowls moving on the mint as if it was a wad of cabbage.

'I think I'll have a mint after all,' I said, changing my mind.

'Sure.' Before I die.

'So about Harrington.' This is it then: why did you meet him? Who's Samuelson? What are you up to? 'Tell me what you know about him.'

'You mean Harrington who works here? The barrister – '

'Yeah.'

'Jesus, I don't know much about him. He's a barrister. He's single. I see him in night clubs. He lives in . . .?'

'You don't know anything else?'

'No – not that I can think of.'

'Come, come,' he said, laughing. 'You do, of course.'

'I do?' My voice was nearly broken.

'Sure. You've known him for years.'

'Oh . . .'

'The two of you have been known to have a fierce spar the odd time over a pint. Big political discussions. You first met him when you were a young fellow on Grafton Street. You used to sit with him in Bewley's.'

'I did?' I did and this mock surprise at my own past was getting stupid.

'College friends of yours introduced you. They knew him from college debating where he was something of a big figure. A group of you used to sit around and listen to him, debate with him and a couple of other big fellows.'

'How do you know all this?'

'You needn't worry, Shane,' he said, putting his hand on my knee, laughing. 'Don't look so alarmed. I've been doing a bit of research on this fellow. I interviewed a Mr Humphreys and he mentioned that he knew you.'

'He did, did he?'

'He did, which I thought was interesting.'

'Oh.' I looked at the floor as if annoyed but, in fact, I was relieved for if he spoke to Humphreys he didn't know about our deal.

'I'm interested in him, Shane,' said Hurley, crossing his legs. 'Tell me more about him. He's been doing a Ph.D. on that John Dillon for almost ten years now. He's involved in the Ivy Day Committee. He writes letters to papers. A few years ago he wrote urging support for a statue of John Redmond in Dublin.'

'He did? I didn't know that.' I didn't.

'Oh indeed he did. Before your time. We do our research, Shane.'

'I don't doubt it.'

'But his character, Shane – what's he like?'

It was time to shop Harrington. It was time to set up my alibi.

'Well, he's a funny sort of chap. Very articulate. Intelligent. A bit foppish.'

'Snobbish?'

'That as well, perhaps. He's passionately interested in history. Irish history, particularly the Home Rule period. The old IPP and all that. The Redmond letters wouldn't surprise me.'

'Right.'

'He's an old debating figure, as you say. He was auditor of one of the societies out in Belfield. And like all those debating figures he can be quite mischievous. Oh, in a harmless sort of way. Pranks and stunts.'

'I see,' said Hurley, very interested.

'That's really it,' I said. 'I'm sorry. That's all I know.'

'It's enough,' said Hurley.

'Why do you want to know, if you don't mind me asking. He's not under suspicion, is he?'

'You may say he takes this Home Rule thing seriously. He and a bunch of others. So seriously do they take it, Shane, that they bought a house a number of years ago in Clonskeagh. The house is in his name. Do you know whose house it was? Isaac Butt's. There's a blue plaque outside.'

'Isaac Butt's. Jesus, that's – '

'Directly across the road from O'Shaughnessy's residence.'

'He owns that. That's amazing.'

'Not really,' said Hurley. 'It explains why he seemingly hasn't any property of his own and still lives at home. It explains where his money as a criminal lawyer goes. He's investing in history. He and a number of others. Since 1979, they've been going around Ireland trying to buy up, cheaply, properties once associated with the Irish Parliamentary Party and Home Rule. They bought the back part of an old hotel on North Great Georges Street because John Dillon lived there. A prime investment if it was renovated, but dilapidated as it is. The greatest prize of all, Aughavanagh or Avoca House in Wicklow, they missed. The State sold it to Án Oige and now it's full of German tourists and French backpackers walking around where Redmond did his shooting. Their plan is to open museums simultaneously in all these properties.'

'How did you find out all this?'

'Harrington was seen leaving Isaac Butt's house on Thursday evening.'

I was dumbfounded.

'He was seen by one of our lads on duty outside Mr O'Shaughnessy's residence until Friday evening when Mr O'Shaughnessy had them removed. The report was that at six on Thursday evening the garda saw a man leave the house in what could only be regarded as a very suspicious manner. The man reacted badly to the looks given to him by the garda and when the garda prepared to cross the road to talk to the man, the man walked away quickly. The description was of a stout man with a black beard and a pin-striped waistcoat. I did some research on the property. I found out it was owned by a company called Renaissance Ltd, in the name of one Finbar Harrington. I made a few further enquiries and I discovered that Finbar Harrington was a barrister-at-law and man about town and that this Renaissance Ltd had a few other people involved and a few other properties involved. It didn't take long to discover that all the properties were connected by this Home Rule thing. It all began to sound familiar. Wouldn't you agree?'

I was dumbfounded. What could I say? It did. It certainly did, I told him. So he's on to Harrington – now it's a race against Hurley as well as them. If he knows all this now how long would it take him to find out about Samuelson and our deal? Longer than tomorrow, that's for sure. And then it won't matter. I'll have my man, he'll have his man. Harrington will be hauled up and what can he say? That I made a deal with him and implicate himself further. I'll say, yes, I did, and for what good? To save us all. And if Harrington says I took part in the theft of documents, what will it matter when people are concentrating on the immensity of

Corny's revealed crimes and the fact that he isn't around to face the charges.

'You're taking it in, I see.'

'Do you think Harrington is actually . . . involved?'

'What does "involved" mean with these people? They don't sign their letters, they don't give their names, they don't appear on television. I think our friend inside must be as involved as anyone.'

'Wow. A barrister and all. It's incredible.' The bastard, it's perfectly credible. I should have known he was further in.

'What? Sure this is where the real rogues are. I think the "and all" bit captures him. This history lark is very suspicious, going around buying up houses.'

'What are you going to do about it?'

'I can't move until I have proof. The cease-fire runs until Friday and I'll see what happens then.'

'Right.'

'But we have to watch them, Shane. They're just biding their time and any opportunity they get to put pressure on the Government they'll take it. They stole the Proclamation on Saturday, remember. An easy target, to say the least, and in my opinion, an ineffectual one. God knows what they hope to achieve by that. But they can turn nasty again. We have to be careful. Be on your guard tomorrow morning. Always be on your guard but particularly over the next few days when your work down there gets going. I don't care what Mr O'Shaughnessy thinks, I'll have two boys down there keeping their distance. There'll be one on Pearse Street and Lombard Street corner and another at the other end of St Mark's Lane.'

'I appreciate your telling me that.'

'If you see anything at all you think suspicious, don't hesitate to contact them. Or ring Pearse Street and have them radioed. Or 999. Either way, ring me as well, and I'll be down there straight away. OK?'

'OK.'

'Cheer up, man,' he said and smiled. 'Come on. Let's go back in there.' We walked across the hall floor.

'Have you told Mr Wycherley about this?'

'God, no. I won't tell him about this until his work is over or nearly over. He'd only start throwing around some more wild allegations. You've got to watch your tongue, you see. You've

275

got to keep your suspicions to yourself until you're in a position to prove them totally. There's Mr O'Shaughnessy now and he's going to go on TV tonight and slander the British Secret Service. Well, that's a different thing. They're not going to sue. He's a famous man. He says those things all the time.'

'Is that what he's going to say tonight?'

'So I believe. He has new information, he says. Why doesn't he come to us, if he's new information? But, oh no, he's Mr O'Shaughnessy. He'd rather go on TV than go to a garda station. Tell the world. We won't help him, he says. We're part of the establishment, bugging his phones, passing info on to the British, harassing his clients like that young fellow inside.'

'Do you bug his phones?'

'Of course we do,' he said, opening the door. 'Sure, wouldn't he be a very sore man if we didn't.'

We went into the courtroom and stood among the guards and people at the back. Hurley was immediately ear-filled in by a young cop as to what had happened. I stood in front of them and let it all sink in. Harrington. Jesus! I mean, what's up with me that I didn't latch on to him as our main man? Why did I insist on thinking of him as someone on the sidelines, relaying messages, being mischievously helpful. Hurley's right; how 'involved' are any of these people? I told him in the Pink he could have written that statement. He smiled. He probably did. I asked him, when he said he'd arrange for me to meet Samuelson, when we were going to meet someone who was actually in the AVNS and he smiled again. And no wonder: he's probably Captain Moonlight. He owns that house across the road from Corny's. He probably saw me go in and then come out and then . . . and then followed me into the Pink. How often has he been watching me? How long has he prepared for this? Harrington, old Harrington with his Charles II face. Jesus, you had to half admire him. We, in our small ways, live out the lives of our heroes but here is a man who is going around buying up their houses. To wrestle Avoca back from the State, or Aughavanagh or whatever it was. What a plan. And now this, a plan on a grander scale. Presence or patience be blessed. He may well be the one who is ultimately behind all this, who wrote those letters, threatened our lives, but, you know, I sort of admired him for it. He meant no real harm to me, to Wycherley, or even to O'Shaughnessy. He told me so, that drunken night in Risk and in the Pink and in the letters and statements he may have co-authored.

And yet, brother Harrington, I've got a much greater plan than yours in mind. It is the perfect artistic and political crime and a much more radical recasting of things historical. And the sad thing is you are going to pay for it. You mean no harm perhaps but I do and for it you are going to take the chop. Poor fool, and you think that I am going to get you the documents on O'Shaughnessy and go to the Minister to save your statue and ours. When in fact, instead, you've let Captain Moonlight take over and you, the redundant constitutionalist, are going to be blamed for one of the most damning revisions our history has seen.

Why dally any longer? It was time to seal Harrington's fate. I left my space at the back and pushed through the irritated guards to reach Hurley.

'Let's go out for a little chat, will we?'

'Sure . . .' he said, frowning, but not displeased, and we squeezed through the narrow doorway out into the sonorous hall. There was no one about except the usual wigged lawyer passing to and fro. I led the puzzled Hurley over to a nearer bench than the one we'd been on earlier.

'Eh, Mr Hurley, there's something I feel I should tell you.'

'Go on.'

'I just thought of it while I was in there. One thing Mr Harrington said to me – oh, when I met him that time in the Pink Elephant night club, he said – now this mightn't mean much or anything . . .'

'Go on.' His lips were licked.

'He said, "Wouldn't it be funny if Mr O'Shaughnessy was kidnapped and ransomed against his own statue."'

Hurley nodded his head very slowly and very quietly. 'I see,' he said.

'Now he meant it . . . like, as a joke and all,' I stressed.

Hurley licked a bit of loose skin on his lower lip.

'You don't think,' I said, 'that anyone would ever – '

'Jokes,' said Hurley grimly. 'A lot of this affair has been a series of jokes; a self-declared cease-fire, the theft and ransoming of the Proclamation, poems that don't rhyme. This whole campaign began with an ill joke; there's no reason why it wouldn't end with an even iller one.'

I said nothing.

'Thank you for telling me about this,' he said.

'Not at all,' I said. 'I felt I should.'

'You might be called as a witness yet,' he said, smiling.

'God, I hope it won't be necessary.'

'Who knows what might happen.'

'Who knows indeed,' I agreed.

'OK, come on.' He put his hand on my shoulder. 'Let's . . . eh
. . . let's go inside.'

We got up off the seat.

'You don't think,' I asked him, 'you'll need more protection for
Mr O'Shaughnessy.'

'Not until Thursday.'

'Good.'

Very good. But after the requisite few moments of having my
palms sweat on the benches where many have sweated before, I
thought it was time to depart quietly the courtroom and head
back to the studio to tell Wycherley the news. For good or ill, he
had more than he bargained for. Whether I was a plenipotentiary
or not did not matter. Get off that gangplank, I've work to do.

Naturally, when I got back to the studio, Wycherley was very
anxious to see me. It seemed that Hurley had decided to talk to him
after all and called him while I was walking back; given what I told
Hurley about Harrington I supposed he'd have had to. Wycherley
was very tense and wanted to talk to me immediately, upstairs,
in private. So up the spiral staircase we went. Dink, donk, dink,
donk on the metal steps. Time was running out. We went into his
eyrie and Wycherley went over and sat down at his desk beneath
the skylight. He pointed to the chair.

'I was talking to Detective Hurley,' he said, linking his
fingertips.

'Oh.'

'Who says he was talking to you.'

I nodded. Wycherley pursed his lips.

'I was quite shocked, as you can imagine, to hear that this man,
Finbar Harrington, almost employed as legal counsel by Forbes,
is, in fact, a prime suspect in the campaign against our statue. You
know him, I believe. You spoke to him about the controversy. He
gave you clues about who was behind the campaign. Why didn't
you tell me any of this?'

'You wouldn't have wanted to know,' I said frankly. 'You told

278

us to ignore this campaign and concentrate on the statue. What I knew about Harrington last week wouldn't have merited passing on. I didn't know he was a prime suspect until this morning. I thought he was someone who just knew something about who or what was behind the campaign. I never suspected he may have been behind it himself. I was still sort of going along with your ideas about Forbes. I was quite shocked myself when Hurley told me all that stuff about the houses and all.'

'Oh, come now, Shane. You argued history with this man in night clubs.'

'So. I argue history with lots of people in lots of places.'

'You knew he was big into Parnell.'

'So are lots of people. How are we to apportion blame here? I'm big into Collins. I didn't like the sort of films Cimino and Co. were going to make about him. It doesn't mean I'd set out to intimidate them out of the country.'

'According to Hurley, this man Harrington appears to have an obsession with the old Parliamentary Party. He and a bunch of others buy up properties.'

'According to Hurley. I knew none of this until he told me. What I knew about Harrington up until this morning you wouldn't have been interested in. You told me to ignore the AVNS row and concentrate on our statue. If I came to and told you about this guy I knew called Harrington, who's a barrister, who writes books on the IPP, who's involved in the Ivy Day Memorial Committee, and who drunkenly buttonholed me, you'd have told me to fuck off and do some casting.'

'I wouldn't have used such firm language.'

'No, but that'd be the gist of it.'

'Hurley tells me that you were led to believe that Harrington knew of, or was in contact with, the people who were behind the AVNS.'

'That's true. That's the impression he gave me. But, big deal, it's a small town. I'm in contact with people who are next to bank-robbing for the IRA.'

'And Hurley told me that from what he had heard there as a proposal within the AVNS, albeit a light-hearted one, that if this didn't work out with the letters and the Proclamation, as they haven't, they could go for the really big number and kidnap O'Shaughnessy to ransom him against his own statue.'

'That's right.'

'Shane, that's an incredible thing to tell Hurley.'

'It certainly is.'

'Why?' He was staggered.

'Because it's not even true.'

'What?'

'It's not true. I made it up.'

Bob stared at me, white-faced.

'What the fuck are you up to?!'

'You're annoyed, aren't you? Because this means there'll be cops watching him now, whether the old boy likes it or not.'

'Annoyed is not the word, Shane,' he said, putting his spread hands up as if he was keeping his control at bay. 'You've invited the cops in unwittingly to witness a murder. There was going to be police anyway but you've ensured a bloody vigil!'

'Exactly, and we were always going to be doing this job under the noses of the police, regardless of what that man said about the law on his trail. So, once Hurley told me that Harrington was a suspect I thought – bingo! – an alibi. I'll tell Hurley that Harrington told me this and then tomorrow when O'Shaughnessy disappears, who'll immediately get the blame?'

Wycherley looked at the table.

'I mean, they can't pin anything on him, the way they can't pin anything on us. But he *is* the prime suspect. Credit to the guards where credit is due. And if you weren't getting anywhere writing threats and kidnapping Proclamations to ransom against an old man's statue what better way to up the ante than kidnap the old man himself. And the beauty of it is it's exactly what the old man himself is predicting.'

Wycherley linked his hands and stared at me for a long time.

'It's just a pity that, for once, he won't be around to see his predictions realised,' I said, smiling, and, showing a considerably more detailed knowledge of Harrington's background than I perhaps should have, I explained why the Redmondite would be the ideal fall-guy.

'Shane, I don't know,' he said and he shook his head. 'I just don't know.'

'What?'

'I don't know if you're a genius or a madman.'

'Let future generations decide.'

'You're certainly a gambler.'

'Fortune favours the risktaker.'

280

'Christ, Shane, you've increased the odds against us no end. Harrington will be under close watch from hereon and so will Corny. Do you realise how difficult this makes things for you?'

'I do.'

'You've got to leave here with his clothes and get them into the river by eleven-forty-five without being seen.'

'I'll walk to the end of the docks if necessary.'

'You've got to get back here by twelve.'

'No problem.'

'What about the church?'

'I've checked and double-checked. You know that. It can work, it will work. All it needs is my legs, the bottom of my legs. I have his "sitting on the jakes" posture to a tee.'

'The mould has to be closed by one. Murphy's away until two-thirty. Tess and I will slide it in around two if necessary. You know all this. Do you want me to write it down?'

'Don't write anything down.'

'You've got half an hour max to and from Neligan's. You'll go looking for the police at two. It's all very changeable, you know that.'

'I know that. Don't you worry. The schedule can change at any time. But absolute cool at all times. If something goes wrong, not a tremor of panic . . . because no one could possibly suspect what it is we are up to.' I rattled it off by rote. It was all in my head. I'd worked tomorrow morning out about a million times. What could go wrong, what will go right.

Wycherley smiled softly.

'It's great that you're confident,' he said.

'Confidence is easy when you know you can fool people. I've been fooling people all my life.'

He smiled sadly.

'I've got nothing to lose,' he said and shrugged. He shrugged in the sad sort of way that convinced me we had to go through with this; for him, for me, for all of us.

'Do you want to come and stay with me tonight?'

'Thanks, but I've got to be on my own. I have to be on my own keeping my head together. Thanks anyway.'

'We can watch his nibs on the box. He's on at nine-thirty. The big revelations.'

'Christ, no.'

'You sure?'

281

'I'm certain.'

'Right so.'

'Do you want to come out for a few drinks then?'

'I'd prefer to go out for a few drinks tomorrow night. Whiskey on the table in Mountjoy. After the deed is done.'

He looked a bit uncomfortable.

'I ought to give you a ring later on,' he said. 'You'll be at home?'

'Where else would I be?'

It's ten minutes past eight and I'm sitting in here in the basement kitchen of 40 Parnell Square drinking a cup of coffee and trying to read the newspapers. But the sentences aren't sinking in and my eyes are straying to the pictures, my pictures. When I get to the start of a sentence, I've forgotten the first part of it. I can't concentrate. The words are just collections of letters, sounds, strung together to create a huge hollow feeling. I can't eat. I can only take sips of coffee. I'm running out of time, they say, but, God knows, I could do with less time now. Run out, time, run out. But I went for a walk instead.

Up Parnell Square I walk again. I put the key in my pocket and it jangles with the other fellow. Still in there, my talisman, key to a great discovery and a deal that was never to be. Just off this square, on the other side, he sits and waits, old Samuelson. I wonder how often he'd be in there, up in that extraordinary room on the forgotten fifth floor or whatever it was. Not now, surely. Not at the end of a summer's day with the sun going down on first loves and old memories. The heart that sets in Dublin. God love them, their aims were noble.

It's so quiet here now where two days ago the inclined square was a hive of activity with the guards milling about stopping traffic, and the Government, lining up with religious leaders, Old IRA, Old British Legion, their people, our people, all in the Garden for the country's first National Commemoration Ceremony – a brave idea of the Taoiseach's that ironically may have given them the idea of going a step further and taking him on. You've tried to balance us in the ephemera of a ceremony, now give us the relative permanence of a statue. What a demand; give us Redmond or we'll destroy Corny. And, God bless them, they're not going to get it. Or are they not? Not ever? Maybe later rather than sooner but maybe then, when the whole thing's blown over. Maybe then.

We all have to lose something. Corny's going to get the statue but he's going to lose the funeral. Poor old Corny, he's going to be denied one of the great honours of Irish Republicanism, an honour for which men dream all their lives and for which he more than anybody else, with his long and illustrious life, must have dreamt about to a degree of near dress-rehearsal lucidity (what's that word 'hearse' doing in there?). He who has lived so long and accumulated so many honours, he, the embodiment of the cause, the last of the big fellows to be buried. There's few enough chances these days for an old-style burial of a chieftain and his is a funeral that even now the speeches are being written for, the flowers picked. Save them for the unveiling, gentlemen. It's to Glasnevin he'd be sent. God, he must have looked forward to that journey all his life, the journey he'd have to trust to posterity. To Phibsborough and up the Prospect Road, generations of crowds have lined the streets to the final resting place. Children held high to see O'Connell on his way in 1828 brought their own grandchildren and lined the same footpaths to see Collins, Griffith, Brugha pass by in the twenties. The dead Collins.

I came to the gates of Glasnevin Cemetery and put my head between the railings. Full moon. I looked in at the darkened graveyard. O'Connell's tower black against the warm blue sky, Casement's slab hidden in the near grass, Griffith amongst the multitude. And I thought to myself – hardly an original thought – while we hold these graves, will we ever be at peace? Maybe it's better to abandon them altogether and let snow and time fall on the living and the dead. Not the most unusual of solutions but at least, in my seemingly paradoxical combination of the original and conventional, nobody can say that I didn't take an unusual way out.

Chapter 11

Day of Action

I didn't as much sleep last night as go in and out of sleep. Cat naps in between periods of wakefulness, fragments of dream and staring at the ceiling. It's incredible how quick the night passes when you're not partying or twisting limbs with a female of our species. Or male, or whatever takes your fancy. It seemed like I'd only been lying here an hour or so when the day started to blue in and the birds began their twittering outside and I knew it'd soon be time to get up. I heard the little electric engines of the milk lorries moan as they went up the square. I got out of bed and went to the window. The dawn sky. So beautiful. Clean blue and draining away golds, a new day breaking through. Childer's last wish. How many down the years have gone to look at the dawn because it will be their last sight? Casement. The sixteen at Easter. Major Tom O'Shaughnessy in the stonebreaker's yard, his son left behind. Barry on the morning of an eighteenth summer. Dunne and O'Sullivan on the morning of Griffith's funeral. O'Connor, Mellowes, Barrett, McKelvey being led from their cells in Mountjoy. Thousands of other Irishmen being led like lambs to the slaughter in Belguim.

I put on my shoes quickly, and my trousers, shirt and jacket. Had I everything? I had. I went down the stairs quietly. The house was asleep and would be for hours to come. I twisted the inside key and pulled the door back and stepped out into the warm morning. Ascension Wednesday. A new day!

Down the street I went, greeting the few people I encountered. 'Lovely morning,' I told them.

'Oh, lovely morning,' they replied.

284

Lovely morning, indeed, my friends. *Carpe diem.*

Past the shell of Beaslaí's house, past the Kingfisher chipper and over to Moore Street.

'Lovely day,' I told an old lady.

'Ah, God, lovely,' she enthused.

Breathe it in. Breathe it bloody well in, while your breath's still with you. Down Moore Street I went and straight over to that old bat who sells the newspapers. I looked at her stall and there it was, in large bold letters on the front of the *Irish Press*, 'BRITISH ARE OUT TO GET ME'. Well, I nearly jumped with joy. 'O'Shaughnessy claims British intelligence out to settle old score,' read the *Independent*. And the more sober *Times*? 'O'Shaughnessy claims M.I.5 involvement in campaign against statue.' Well, stone the crows and sculpt them while you're at it!

Speaking on the RTE programme *Today, Tonight* last night, Mr Cornelius O'Shaughnessy claimed once again that British intelligence services were involved in the campaign against his statue and further alleged that British agents had actually infiltrated his garden over the weekend.

'Are you going to buy one or what?'

'I'm not sure,' I said, without looking at her.

'Well, clear off so – '

'Clear off yourself, you wrinkled old bat.'

'How dare ye! Jesus, wait till I get me husband.'

'Get him. Before I incinerate you and put him out of his misery.' With which I strode off with a smile upon my lips.

Corny, Corny, Corny. You have written my alibi and prepared your own death warrant. Why, it reminds me of the old saying, just because you're paranoid doesn't mean they're not out to get you.

Around the Collins side of the GPO I came and laced across O'Connell Street. Sure why not risk your life now you're about to take somebody else's? No one harms you in the hours before a murder; it's fictional truth and a factual expectation and you've only got the two to choose from.

Statues on either side of me and Redmond could join them if he plays his cards right. On reaching the island I chose William Smith O'Brien to pass under, and he was still getting a root up the arse. Symbolic, in a way, since he died on a scaffold cut from a tree. That's Oisin's wish when he's feeling dodgy at the wheel of his Renault, 'to be buried in the tree that killed me'. Meaning cut down the aforesaid and plane it for the box. Corny wouldn't approve.

Now look at that. Some battered horse was trundling a cart of gutted cookers and fridges across O'Connell Street, nodding at the ground like something that'd sooner be a vat of glue if it was the choice of the rest of us. The driver, a raw-faced tinker who thought he was Ben Hur, was standing up with legs outstretched, slapping the straps on the moving side of his clattering nag. Is this as far as we've come? Jesus Christ. Modernity, how are you? And down the main thoroughfare of the capital. I wouldn't mind if it was some back boreen or a part of the city where you'd almost welcome such sights as a touristic diversion, but O'Connell Street? They should put on a barring order: 'No horses on O'Connell Street except for state funerals'. Now, there's class. An empty saddle with the stirrups reversed. Fallen leader. I'm telling you, it was better in the old days. But then I thought of Michael Collins as a young emigrant in London and the story he told of walking along Shepherd's Bush one morning with his mates. A donkey and cart suddenly came around a corner and they broke into a cheer. Horray! Home. Childhood. Part of your blood and past and you can't deny it. The further away we get, and I don't mean in space but in time, the more we've got to rescue these things from sentiment. Seriously, folks. Your memories could end up in a Bunratty folk park.

Are the mullets . . .? They are. I had a look down over the parapet and their big, green doleful backs were breaking the water, swimming slowly to stay still in the current. It's early morning but they're rising. They're rising, all right. And two nippers with rods were heading down the near steps. I'll be joining them later but on different steps. Ah yes, a lovely morning to get close to the water.

Or at least I will be shortly. I checked on the Church of the Immaculate Heart of Mary when I passed it. Everything looks OK. There were no cars parked in the forecourt and the doors were open. Here's hoping. Here, indeed. I must be the first man to pray for a church rather than in one. Michelangelo and Henry VIII excepted. You're in good company, Shane.

When you've been through the hoops like I have you can tackle a ring of fire and I'm so vivid now that I could jump from my silver skin. But I'm afraid I'd prefer to see someone else do that first, so here goes.

I saw the first cop as I passed the terrace of red-brick corporation houses at the end of Princes Street. He was on Townsend Street in front of the shop's entrance to the flats. That's good. Because if that entrance is directly opposite the entrance that leads to our gate, for anyone going to the church, it would be the entrance further down they would use, the entrance directly opposite that one that I'm about to go through. Some kids were talking to the cop. Banter, careless talk. Lives cost talk. Too much talk. I didn't recognise him with his back turned to me, arms folded, and I passed in under the flats unnoticed and walked across the enclosed square.

Squabbling kids were playing football, using heaps of shed jackets for the goalposts. 'House! House!' the oldest one shouted. Corny, watch your house. Around the sides of the concrete pitch, bits of bright white clothes were dripping from Victorian washing lines, slung between chipped poles and flapping occasionally like trapped seagulls. Some small children were hanging out of the bigger poles on ropes and swinging around, like they were going to hurt themselves. The whole scene seemed so stagey and old-fashioned that it could have been a film set for *Strumpet City* or one of those gur cakes-and-coal-blocks *Boys' Own* stories from Dublin in the forties. But it wasn't. It was Dublin in the here and now and it was only eight minutes from O'Connell Bridge.

And this, this gate in front of me as I come out from under the flats on to St Mark's Lane, this sculptor's gate is exactly four minutes from the Church of the Immaculate Heart of Mary but for a ninety-year-old man it's approximately fifteen minutes, and one can only be approximate when one looks into the future. Very approximate. Who knows what steps he'll take to examine how the past has changed.

Look right, look left, look right again. The guards posted at both ends of St Mark's Lane were the same guards who were posted there last Wednesday. Garda Larkin was accompanied by another guard. And Garda Allen? Yes, he had a buddy as well, chatting away with his foot up on the wall. That makes four and one at the shops – five. And there are probably a few others hanging around at a distance. Four's risky but five's a crowd. Keep chatting, lads, keep enjoying the sun. It's going to be risky but that's what we want.

I went in the studio gates with my heartlines crossed and my

287

fingers straight. Murphy's van's not here. He's out on his first round already. Later, he'll be delivering the Willoughby piece to their house in Cabinteely and he'll be the best part of the day installing it. It's finished now and there's no need for any further delay, as the artist said to the gunman. Wycherley promised them that Murphy would start on the placement today and Bob himself will head out there tomorrow to check.

I went into the kitchen and there was the man himself, sitting with a mug of tea. He looked like he hadn't slept the best, with red-rimmed eyes, but he was dressed resplendently: mustard tie, oversized white cotton shirt and a blacker than black suit.

'Good morning,' he said without emotion.

'Good morning.'

'Have you seen these?' He indicated the papers.

'I caught a glance at them on the way over.'

'There are cops at both ends of the lane, Shane. Pairs of them. That's meant to be, Shane, but things could be tricky.'

'That's as meant to be.'

Wycherley looked at his hand quietly.

'Sleep well?' he asked.

'Eh . . . in and out, but not in the happy sense.'

Wycherley frowned and smiled.

'No jokes today, Shane.'

'Not even one?'

'Not in front of the kids.'

I smiled at him.

'We're taking enough risks as it is.'

'Oh, I don't know. Gratuitous risks, or what I'd rather call stylistic risks, are the key to confidence and confidence is the key to everything. Collins riding around on his bicycle or going back to a party searching his house to ask them did they get their man.'

'Yeah, well, we all know where Collins's bravado led him. They got their man.'

'And we got our state, Bob. And you got your contract from its government. And now you've got the chance to get your man. So don't knock my MC,' I said in a black American accent. 'He's my main man.'

'Heroes, Shane. I thought you said you were giving them up.'

'I said I was working on it.'

Wycherley smiled and nodded his head.

'You can read these so,' he said and he took some letters from

288

the table and gave them to me. They were from Old IRA rebels. God bless them. The handwriting was tense and crabbed, like a child's.

Keep up the good work . . . God damn the blackguards. Stand firm by the flame of the Republic . . . I hope you do a good sculpture and may he stand to your credit.

Is mise le meas,
Roibard O'Driscoil (Vol.)

It's disgraceful the abuse the men are getting that freed this country. What have we come to! Thank God there are people like you who have the courage and imagination to honour those who fought for us so bravely.

Yours, *a chara,*
Donail O'Reagain,
Tipperary, North Riding Brigade

It is with profound distress and regret that I witness the attempts being made to intimidate those who have, at last, succeeded in committing the Government to honour the outstanding contribution made to this country by Mr Cornelius O'Shaughnessy. I have long been an admirer.

Yours sincerely,
Charles J. Haughey TD

'Wow! The Leader of the Opposition. The no-show man – '
'They're right behind us,' said Wycherley.
'Great, isn't it?' I said, laughing. 'Jesus, it's incredible. Even Charlie's been taken in.' I started laughing hilariously.
'It'll be all action today, Shane,' said Bob, making a serious face.
'We'll have to move quickly.'
'Very quickly.'
'Do you want to run through it again?'
'No.'
'Mr Wycherley.' Ramsey stuck his head through the door. 'Phone, Mr Wycherley.'
Who is it?'
'It's not a journalist.'
'Excuse me,' said Wycherley, getting up.

289

'Good morning, Shane,' said Ramsey.

'Good morning, Ramsey.'

'Ramsey!' called Wycherley from the hall. 'Would you get me my phone book. It's on the wax desk inside.'

The kettle boiled. I made a cup of coffee and sat down to read the papers.

'Man in my garden', said the *Irish Independent*, inside. 'O'Shaughnessy alleges British involvement in statue plot'. Underneath was a photo of Corny leaving the Four Courts, accompanied by half of Detective Hurley's arm.

'Intruders at the home of O'Shaughnessy', shouted the *Irish Press*, in a subheadline. 'Sensational TV claims'.

On RTE television last night [read the *Indo*] Mr Cornelius O'Shaughnessy made new and dramatic allegations to add to his claims that British intelligence are behind the campaign to have his statue replaced by one of the Home Rule Leaders, John Redmond. He also claimed that intruders in his garden last Sunday night may have been an advance party sent to harass him or test him after his non-appearance at the controversial National Commemoration Ceremony in the Garden of Remembrance. Apparently the intruders were singing when they were encountered by Mr O'Shaughnessy and had to be chased off the premises.

Mr O'Shaughnessy's sensational claims were made in the course of an interview on the *Today, Tonight* programme last night, in which Mr O'Shaughnessy was filmed in his garden indicating the probable movements of the alleged intruders. They appeared to have entered the garden over a side fence having gained access from Bird Avenue, and proceeded to hide in the vegetable patch at the end of the garden where they could be heard singing. They left via the pine trees at the side of the garden. They did not try to enter the house, Mr O'Shaughnessy said. From what he saw, the intruders were young men and appeared to be pretending to be intoxicated, singing and cursing at each other in the dark. Mr O'Shaughnessy dismissed suggestions that the intruders could have been ordinary high-spirited youths who were not politically connected and entered his garden out of mischief or mistake, or that they could have been students from the nearby university.

'There is a concerted, if unsuccessful, campaign being waged against my statue and it is directed by forces more powerful

290

and sinister than those of a few people masquerading as neo-Redmondites,' Mr O'Shaughnessy said. 'I know what it's like to have students coming on to my property. There are many of them living around here in flats and digs and during Rag week or after exams they can stray into the gardens and side streets. However, these men were far too brazen and too cunning to be up to this kind of thing. Their sheer neck was extraordinary.'

Mr O'Shaughnessy did not elaborate on how brazen they had been. The gardaí refused to comment on the former Nobel Prize winner's claims. Mr O'Shaughnessy has persistently refused to allow gardaí protection to be placed on his home.

It is understood however that the gardaí have been following certain leads in the case and that these leads may in fact centre around the historical nature of the campaign and its backers. Little has been heard of the AVNS since their statement at the weekend claiming responsibility for the theft of the Proclamation and disassociating themselves from any possible disruption of the Government's National Commemoration Ceremony.

The controversy over the statue revolved around the demands of the Anti-Violent Nationalist Society to have a statue of the former constitutional Home Rule Leader John Redmond erected in Dublin, as a balance to what they claimed was a surfeit of memorials to revolutionary or Republican figures. Initially the AVNS were opposed to the statue of Cornelius O'Shaughnessy outright, as yet another 'violent Republican', but they have since conceded to accept a statue of Mr O'Shaughnessy if one of John Redmond is erected in O'Connell Street. If this is not done, the AVNS claim they will destroy the statue of O'Shaughnessy and the copy of the 1916 Proclamation they stole from the Dublin Civic Museum on Saturday afternoon.

The sculptor, Mr Wycherley, continues not to talk to journalists about the case or about the commission in general but it is understood that the project is going ahead and that the first stages of the sculpture are nearly completed. Speaking on the steps of the courthouse, where he had been acting in the Robert Williams extradition case (see separate story, page 5), Mr O'Shaughnessy said that as far as he was concerned . . .

'Hi,' said Tess, coming in in a lumberjack shirt.
'He'll be very upset when he sees that,' I told her gravely.
'Why?'

'You know how he feels about trees.' Afforestation was one of O'Shaughnessy's recent obsessions.

'Ah, Shane.' She threw her keys on the table and started rinsing a cup.

'I don't see your photo in the papers.'

'No, but I'm being quoted for a round of drinks,' she said and she bit her lower lip.

'Much more dangerous.'

'Shane, I'm a bit . . .' She paused.

'What?'

'Bit scared. If they do anything they're going to do it this morning.'

'Nothing's going to happen, Tess. This thing is almost fixed up.'

'There was no need for the paper to say that we're almost finished "the first stages".'

'That means nothing,' I said, putting my hands on the table. 'Listen, no one knows he's coming down here. And there are cops outside. Hurley's got a line on these guys now and there's no way they're going to break their cover to try anything precipitous.'

Tessa squeezed her tea bag slowly.

'Besides,' I muttered, 'those guys will still be too busy scratching their heads over what Corny saw in his garden.'

'Shane!' said Wycherley. 'Murphy wants you outside.'

I went out to the yard and the sun.

'Grab a hold of the other end of that,' said Murphy and we lifted one of the Willoughbys' dancers into the back of the Hi Ace.

'Push it up, push it up,' he said and on bits of carpet it slid up the floor to make room for her mate.

'Say goodbye, girls,' said Murphy, slapping his hands together, and taking out a cigarette. 'Well, are you all set?'

'All set to let it all set.'

'You weren't in that garden last night?'

'Yeah, I was the one with the camera.'

'Off the wall,' said Murphy and he shook his match and his head.

'Well, I didn't see it but it sounds pretty wild – M.I.5 agents singing in the vegetable patch.'

'Honest to Jasus,' he said and in the sun his smoke smelt nice. 'It's time *he* was given a little patch somewhere.'

'Ah, that'll come,' I told him softly.

'I don't know what RTE are at. And a bloke with a big bleeding microphone going around the garden after him. It was something else.'

'Well, you have to admit it's a story.'

'I tell you what, though, it's not Brits or Redmondites I'd be looking out for this morning, it's Sam bleeding Forbes. God, that man must be sore by now, dead bleeding green. He must be so sore that he'd be half tempted to do some of the things that he was accused of in the first place.'

'That's an interesting one,' I granted. 'Like the bloke who gets accused of cheating so much by his girlfriend that eventually he feels obliged to cheat.'

'Well, Shane, that's one way of looking at it. Or two ways,' he said with a puff of smoke. 'I'd be thinking more of the man who does fifteen years in prison for bombs he didn't plant and the first thing he want to do when he comes out is plant those bloody bombs.'

'Well, we live up to our expectations.'

'He's done good work, Wycherley, hasn't he? Did you see how much he did last night?'

'No, I haven't been in the – '

'Ah, the things nearly finished,' said Murphy. 'Jacket's on the figure and everything. I mean, I know he's pissed off because he's not what he calls an "ultra realist" and he's been forced to do a glorified golf trophy but, Jasus, it'll be one of the fastest statues I ever saw put together. All it needs now is his hands and face and bingo, that's it.'

'Not before time,' I sighed. 'It'll be good to get it out of the way.'

'Jesus,' said Murphy. 'Is that him?'

I turned around and there was the chocolate beetle at the gates. His daughter was at the steering wheel and Corny's lizard's head was looking out like a child arriving for his first day of school.

'Murphy, get Bob!' I shouted and I went down towards the car. Corny's daughter smiled as she twisted the steering wheel. Corny looked at me and smiled sweetly. Until his head was thrown back like a dummy in a road-safety ad. God forbid, how did I set myself up to do a thing like this.

'Right back, back,' I said, flapping my hand. 'Whoa whoah! Back again.' I directed them into the sand-pit and away from any metal. We don't want you getting any punctures and getting in our way. 'That's right, that's right, that's fine now. Fine.'

The engine revved – wrong turn of the key – and then wound down, and then hiccuped and died.

Christ, they're here.

She got out of the car quickly. I went to Corny's door.

'It's OK,' she said, coming after me. No hellos or anything. She grabbed the door handle but it was jammed. Corny pursed his lips and smiled: cheated you.

'Child proof?'

'No,' she said, pulling. 'It just needs . . .' Her tendons tensed. Corny twinkled. 'There!' And the door opened.

'Mr O'Shaughnessy, how are you!?' I shouted. Best to be on the loud side.

'Good morning,' he said in a German accent. What's happening?

'Well, look who's here!' cried the Walton family behind me. Bob and Tess. You'd think it was long-lost Uncle Joe who was coming.

One slim shod foot emerged and dangled.

'Easy now, easy,' said the daughter, quite unnecessarily. It's not as if he was going to make a bolt for it.

'OK, Dad? Are you OK?' she interrogated, and then ducked into the car to scoop him out.

Distendedly, a mottled grey claw appeared on her neck, offering an epidermal comparison that, believe me, did justice to his ninety-year-old skin. The hand stiffened. Dubious clucking noises sounded and the hand stiffened again. Wycherley and I did a sort of Charleston, offering help but standing back. Murphy and Tess kept a watch-out. This is the moment when we might be denied by a sniper. Unfortunately for one horrible moment it looked like we would be denied even without a sniper. The clucking noises increased and suddenly his familiar coffee percolator broke into a heavy wheeze. Talk about whispering sweet nothings into her ear. Maybe her breath smelt and he didn't want any assistance. With alarm we looked at each other and then at the shaking claw. Jesus, not now – not on our own doorstep.

But her shoulders rippled and once the other foot was out, reaching earth, she was able to pull him out and stand him up blinking in the morning sunlight. Phew.

'There you are now,' roared the daughter, locking the door.

'Yes, here we are,' said Corny, smoothing the trousers I'll be wearing in an hour's time. You could see he was embarrassed, as well as half shocked by her rushed assistance. It was hardly necessary.

Wycherley stepped forward and extended his hand. 'Welcome to our studio, Mr O'Shaughnessy.'

'I'm glad to be here,' he said, shaking Wycherley's and then my hand.

'Shane: your trusted lieutenant.' He looked at me keenly.

'That's right,' said Wycherley proudly. 'And Tess is the other one.'

'Ah, Tess,' he said, tottering forward. Was it my imagination, or had he aged another ten years in the last few days?

'Lovely to meet you again, Mr O'Shaughnessy,' declared Tess, going down on one knee. Ludicrous gentility ideas she gets from Bob.

'Yes, lovely . . . lovely,' he repeated, with a prolonged squeeze of her hand. He could have been gaining a life force from it, for he was beginning to perk up a bit.

'My daughter, Biddy,' he said, signalling over his shoulder in a dismissive way.

'How do you do?'

'How do you do?'

'This is Mr Murphy, my assistant,' said Wycherley, with an expansive wave behind him.

'Pleased to meet you,' said Murphy and he grinned as he grabbed.

'And Mr Ramsey, my assistant, who looks after the ovens.'

Ramsey scuttled forward and apron-wiped his hand before offering it.

'Nice to meet you all,' his daughter agreed and looked at her watch.

'So this is your studio,' said O'Shaughnessy, stepping forward and looking up at the high walls.

'Yes, I've been here for eleven years now.'

'What's this?' Corny indicated the rump of a young nymph sticking out of a box.

'Oh. That's a series of sculptures I've been doing for a family in Carrickmines, the Willoughbys. The series is based on the theme of the Three Fates.'

'I see,' said Corny. 'And this curious sight?'

'Oh, that's a piece I did for a – careful, watch your foot.'

Wycherley pulled a flex out of Corny's way. 'I did for Aughrim Memorial Committee commemorating the great battle there in 1691 – it's an earlier version: the headless horseman. The later version, eh, gained a head.'

'I see,' said Corny, unamused.

'Let's go inside, shall we?' Wycherley pushed a stepladder out of the way and Murphy kicked a drum.

'I'll take your arm, if you don't mind,' Tess kindly offered.

'Yes, if you don't take anything else,' he said with a chortle.

Wycherley and I looked at each other.

'And you do all your work here, Mr Wycherley?' asked the daughter.

'Yes, casting, cleaning, everything. Watch the step there.'

'It's grand,' said Corny, mounting the steps without a bother, but didn't the daughter have to lunge forward and give him a hoist that nearly sent him into the plaster sacks. That comes later, Daughter, relax. It was hard to know how much assistance this guy actually required. He was light-footed enough in his house and in the courts, whatever about her being over-cautious because he was in our yard, and we needed him in one solid piece to fulfil our contract. We didn't want to see him damaged before the job was done.

'Here we are now,' said Wycherley as he led Corny and the rest of us through the half-door and down the corridor towards the plastic curtains.

'That's the kitchen in there,' said Bob as he passed. 'That's where we do our most important planning.'

'Like what's for dinner,' I said and Wycherley looked behind to catch my eye sharply.

'Thank you, Shane. This, Mr O'Shaughnessy, is the bathroom, where you'll be changing your clothes. Our apologies that we can't provide anything a little more civilised.'

'I've seen worse,' said Corny and he squeezed Tessa's arm.

'OK then.' Wycherley stopped and stood at the end of the corridor to face us. 'In here,' he said and his hand burst a sudden hole in the plastic curtain, 'is the workshop.'

'Ah,' said Corny, 'so this is where it's all done.'

'This is where it's all done,' said Wycherley and he waved us forward. 'Please.'

We filed in, with heads bowed, and shuffled over broken planks, plaster, wax drippings and flattened cigarette packets.

'Very warm,' said the daughter, looking up at the roof.

'It gets warmer,' I told her.

'What's up there?' She pointed to the top of the spiral staircase.

'My eyrie,' smiled Wycherley. 'A little office where I plot my little schemes.'

'It would have been a nice sort of place in the old days,' said Corny and we all laughed.

'Ah, the little fishies,' said Corny, catching sight of the tank. 'What are their names?'

'Names?' asked Ramsey, stepping forward. 'Oh, eh, they've no names. I call them the blinkies.'

'You should give them names,' said Corny. 'All animals in your house should have names. Everything should have a name.'

'Now,' said Wycherley, raising his voice and stepping forward. 'That big iron pot with the chimney and the sliding top' – he pointed to the left – 'that's the furnace where we melt the metal for pouring. Those tea chests beside it contain the scrap metal that's melted.'

'Worked by electricity?' asked Corny.

'Yes. Now, that brickwork chamber over there' – he pointed to the far-right corner – 'is the oven. The fourth wall is closed off once the mould is placed inside, and at the side you can see where the coke is fed through continuously until such time as the figure inside the mould has melted out and left the empty core for the metal to go into. This floor slide,' and he tapped his foot on the stolen tracks, 'enables us to build a mould out here. And this here is my mould of you, Mr O'Shaughnessy.'

He pulled off the white sheet and there was the slender wax effigy of Mr O'Shaughnessy, minus a face and hands.

'Ah,' he laughed and he turned to his daughter. He was pleased. Why wouldn't he be?

'And thus when it is complete, we can slide the mould across the floor into the oven.'

'Ah, very interesting,' said Corny, and he gazed down at the tracks.

Wycherley looked at me. I gave him a squinted look back. You're doing fine, Bob, you're doing fine.

'How long would a mould be left in the oven?' asked Corny.

'A day, a night, a couple of hours. It depends on its size. Over here on this chair, Mr O'Shaughnessy, you'll sit while we take reliefs of your arms and legs. Some of the joints we may wish

297

to use, depending on the final position of the statue. However, given that the statue is a standing one, the priority is to take reliefs of your arms and particularly your legs in an upright posture. These we'll do here on this pallet.' Wycherley's shoe tapped a wooden structure. 'You'll be standing up here for some time, unfortunately.'

'That's no problem,' said Corny. 'I'm used to standing. If I'd gone to the Garden on Sunday I'd have been standing for the bus to arrive.'

We all laughed at this.

'Right,' said Wycherley, catching my eye again. 'Well, the idea is to get the divisions of your trunk and chest, and a shell-halved mould' – Wycherley cupped and clasped his hands – 'would do that. As you can see, to make things easier for us all, we've already built much of the base and structure of this mould.'

'How long will the whole operation take?' asked the daughter.

'You mean, getting the reliefs? Depends on when we start,' said Wycherley. 'If we begin at nine-thirty we could be finished by about two.'

Corny looked at me. 'Sure, that's grand.'

'OK,' said the daughter. 'Well, listen, I'll' – she looked around – 'leave you to it.'

'Grand,' said Corny.

'I'll pop back in about – oh, I suppose about two.'

'Or a bit earlier if you want to catch some of the show.'

What are you saying, Wycherley?

'Sure, eh, I might do that,' she said. Jesus, Wycherley.

'OK,' she said, backing towards the door. 'Well, I'll see you all later then.'

'I'll show you out,' said Tess and they went through the plastic curtains.

'So.' Wycherley clasped his hands and looked at Corny and then at me.

'That's it then.'

'That's it,' said the lizard. Alone in our studio. Small and vulnerable in his huge suit. At last.

'Do you want a cup of tea before we begin?'

'Oh, I don't see the need.'

'You sure?' asked Wycherley.

'We'll be having one as we go, won't we? You take a break?'

'Of course,' said Wycherley, laughing nervously. 'Of course.'

298

Corny looked around the workshop, eyeing up the oven, the furnace, the hanging chains, the heat and dust. It was extraordinary to see him here, standing in our studio. His huge pin-stripe suit was dusty already. It was dark brown and shiny at the elbows. I hadn't taken my eyes off that suit since he came in. He looked around again and smiled at us. Then, as if he was reading our thoughts, he suddenly turned to me and said, 'I'm here, aren't I?'

'I'm sorry?' Wycherley didn't know what he meant.

'I'm here,' he said sharply. 'No one's going to stop my statue, not if I've to come and participate in it myself, they won't.'

'Oh, right, of course,' said Wycherley. 'No, no one.'

'You're here and we're going to make it,' I said.

'Well, Mr O'Shaughnessy, as you well know, I never had any reason to hesitate.'

'I'm grateful for that.'

'I'm grateful to you for inspiring me. Last Saturday brought it home to me. Once I saw how you never flustered once during this affair I realised what I was being the sculptor of.'

'Ah, never mind that,' said Corny and he flapped his hand dismissively. 'Englishmen posing as Redmondites posing as I don't know what. These arguments never scared me. Not then, not now. Did you see the programme last night?'

'I did.'

'It's a game they're playing with me. Trying to frighten the Government, trying to frighten me. Singing in my garden. It's a game. I'm too old for them now. It's my statue they want, my reputation. But they won't scare me. Not a bit of it.'

'You're a brave man,' said Wycherley and I murmured consent.

'It takes little to be brave at my age. Come on,' he said, rubbing his hands. 'Let's make this statue and defy them.'

'OK,' said Wycherley. 'Well, Shane, will you bring Mr O'Shaughnessy to the bathroom? Good man. I'll get the oils ready.'

I put my arm out and he spurned my assistance.

'I know where I'm going,' he said as Tess returned through the curtains.

'Oh,' she said, stepping back to hold the flaps, 'I've left your clothes in the bathroom, Mr O'Shaughnessy.'

'That's lovely,' he declared, ducking through the held shape in the curtains. 'Grand.' His foot crunched some glassy grit in the hall.

'Be careful,' whispered Tess as I passed. I was looming up behind him.

'I am being careful. OK, Mr O'Shaughnessy, the door to your left.' But he already had his mottled claw on the bathroom handle and was turning.

'If you need anything just give us a call.'

'It's not a shower I'm going for,' he replied with a grin and he closed the door.

My God. I stood in the hall and sighed.

'Shane!' Wycherley calling.

I burst through the curtains. 'Yes?'

'Tess, go out and get me two scoops more, will you?'

'Right so,' she said and she flew past me.

'What is it?'

Wycherley smiled. He was standing with a bucket of oil in one hand, a brush in the other.

'Are you ready?' he said.

'I'm ready.'

He looked at me and smiled. 'Good man.'

'Stop asking me am I ready. I'm ready.'

'Good man. You'd better go out and wait for him.'

'I was doing that,' I stressed and I returned to the hall.

After about ten minutes, the door handle rattled, horror-movie-like, and out from the bathroom emerges Corny in another huge pin-stripe suit. Maltese falcon, how are you.

'I'm dressed for a statue,' he chuckled. 'Most men get dressed to be painted.'

'True.'

'That's your job,' he said with another chuckle. Jesus, don't do this to me. Don't joke all the way into the tomb.

'Very nice!' declared Tess as Corny appeared.

'Very stylish.'

'He looks so cute,' she said, getting carried away.

'What's that?' asked Corny, clearly interested, and why not.

'You look very impressive,' Wycherley put in.

'Well,' he said, looking at his shoes. 'It's much the same as the other suit but a bit stiffer material which is what you said you wanted.'

'It's ideal.'

'You told me to wear an old suit as it'd be ruined, yet I wanted to be sculpted in one of my best so I went halfway.'

'It makes no difference in the end,' said Wycherley and he looked at me and at this stage I had to look at the floor.

'Come on,' said Corny. 'Let's get started.'

'OK, well, Shane, hold that, will you.' He gave me the oily wax bucket.

'Mr O'Shaughnessy, sit up here.'

'No problem,' he said and he slowly sat up in the wooden armchair.

'Stretch your arms out.' He stretched his arms out. Abe Lincoln without a beard. Wycherley began to brush the oil on to his trouser bottoms.

'This won't take long,' promised Wycherley, flopping the heavy oil on to his trousers, around his socks, over his shoes. 'Here, Shane.' He handed me a brush. 'You start doing the other side.'

We worked from the legs up as planned, quickly brushing oil over his arms, his legs, his jacket.

'What kind of oil's this?' he asked.

'It's not really oil,' said Wycherley. 'It's wax, with a mixture of oil.'

'I hope no one lights a match,' chuckled Corny.

Wycherley looked at me through his legs.

'No, no, no. You're quite safe.'

Tess came back in with the first of the mould halves, hardening on the outside, soft on the inside. Like Corny himself? Give it over. I'm not for changing now. Wycherley clamped the first two mould halves on to his left foot, the second on to his right.

'Don't move your feet now,' said Wycherley. 'You can't move anything at all.'

'I'm being still,' he said and he winked at Tess, who was standing behind Wycherley with the moulds for the arms. Wycherley took them from her.

'You ready?'

'Fire ahead, as the man said.'

From under a white eyebrow, Wycherley looked up at me. I smiled and brushed on, oiling Corny's bony shoulders.

'This is a bit like being strapped into the electric chair.'

Wycherley clamped the moulds around the left arm and then the right. And no jokes, he says.

'You're pleased anyway with the way the Government have held firm?'

'Oh, indeed I am,' he said.

301

'Right,' said Wycherley and he stood up and wiped his brow with his sleeve. 'That's the arms and feet. You'll be like that for a few moments.'

'Fine, fine,' said Corny. We stood and looked at him.

'Tess', said Wycherley. 'What time are you meeting those buyers from the Ulster Bank?' Bob had set up the appointment.

'9.40 a.m.,' she replied. 'I suppose I'd – '

'You'd better be going,' admitted Wycherley. 'Mr Thompson will be expecting you. He's to sit in on it.'

'OK,' she said and she wiped her hands on her hips. 'Eh . . .' She bopped her head from side to side. 'See you, Mr O'Shaughnessy.'

'Ahh,' he sighed. 'Are you off?'

'Have to. Sure I'll see you later.'

'Please God.'

'All right then.' She smiled and she headed for the curtains.

'I'm afraid I can't shake your hand, Tess,' laughed O'Shaughnessy.

'Oh, that doesn't matter,' she said coyly and she shrugged and paused strangely before going through the curtains. It was the last time she would see O'Shaughnessy.

We let the moulds set for a few minutes. Wycherley went out to give Murphy a message to bring with him. I was left with O'Shaughnessy. I looked at him. Now, at this final moment, I was going to ask him about 'Knight' but I couldn't. The tongue was stuck to the roof of my mouth. He stared back at me without blinking with watery eyes, and then he smiled weakly.

The curtains opened and in came Wycherley.

'OK,' he announced. 'We can take the moulds off now.' He stooped down to the feet first. 'Shane, put your finger to where the instep would be. Very carefully . . . careful! That's it. Right. Do you have it?'

'Yep.' We prised off the first one and then the second foot mould and then did the same with the arms.

'Right,' said Wycherley, taking the last mould away carefully. 'You can stand up now.'

'Ahh.' He took to his feet. I gave him an immediate hand which he again declined, and steadying himself, he got down off the chair and on to the dust. No stiff plaster dimmed his energies. Not yet anyway.

'I feel like I'm getting out of a dentist's chair,' he revealed.

'Sure you wouldn't be going to a dentist's now,' said Wycherley with familiarity.

'I might,' he grinned.

'Get your enemy when he's a tooth in his head,' I blurted. 'Isn't that what you said once?'

'God, you remember the strangest things.'

'I do.' I remember everything.

'OK, eh, let's be getting on now.' Wycherley looked at me harshly. 'Shane, would you move the main mould structure over here now. Mr O'Shaughnessy, if you're ready and not too stiff after the last one, we'll go straight on to the standing-up cast.'

'I'm ready.'

'OK. Well, this involves you standing up there on the wooden platform.' The foot accordingly tapped the wooden frame. 'And we'll push the halves of the trunk around you.'

'No problem,' he said and he stood up on the platform.

'Feet just slightly apart,' said Wycherley.

Corny moved his feet so they were just about a foot apart. Wycherley swung around the moulds and clamped them on this legs, up as far as his small waist. 'Grand.' said Corny and together we sealed shut the leg moulds with iron clips.

'Putting the mummy in his box,' he said, trying to look down at his legs.

'Ah, ah. Don't stir now, don't stir,' advised Wycherley. 'Keep your chin up. Shane.' He flicked his head and I grabbed the bucket of molten plaster.

'Shane's going to pour plaster into the legs so that the gaps between your legs and the interior surface of the mould can be filled. This means that when the plaster dries we'll have the perfect plaster relief of your limbs, right down to the creases in your trousers.'

Bucket held upended, I started to pour the porridge-white substance into the channels. It slushed its way down around his crotch and fell to his calves where it began to build up quickly.

'OK. Now how does that feel?'

'It feels like I'm standing in wet cement.'

'Well, you are in a way. But it's plaster which is a lighter substance. It dries very quickly.'

'Very quickly,' I said. 'It won't be long now.'

'OK. We'll put on the upper mould now.' Wycherley looked at me. I looked at him.

'Now,' he resumed, 'these are two very heavy pieces so be careful not to move too much or you could knock one of them over and then we'd be rightly schnoozled. The break in this mould is at the front, not at the side. Buttoned-up, if you like.'

Corny smiled but he looked a little puzzled.

'So when we lift it towards you, you put your arm through here.'

Corny nodded but he looked dubious.

Wycherley pulled in the wheeled scaffolding with the two big halves of the upper mould. He pulled them in as close as he could to the oily worsted of Corny's waist.

'Right, Shane. Lift!' he said and we lifted the first mould and placed it gently on top of the leg mould, pressing it into his side.

'Arm in, arm in!' said Wycherley and Corny's long shaking arm shook into its appointed cavity. 'OK?'

'I'm in,' he said and we let the mould gently rest on top of the leg mould below.

'How's that?'

'Cold,' said Corny, 'but I'm all right.'

'Won't be long now,' promised Wycherley. 'Come on, we'll do the other side.' We grabbed the mould for the right-hand side and lifted it towards him. 'Keep your arm to your stomach,' said Wycherley. 'Like Napoleon. That's right, like Napoleon,' and we fitted the mould on to the right side of his torso.

'That's grand,' said Wycherley and we stood back to take a look. Corny was now up to his neck in plaster.

'You look like a snowman,' said Wycherley.

'I'm not surprised. I don't feel on the warm side.'

'Don't worry. We'll warm you up again very soon. We'll just pour the plaster around your chest and arms to get the correct relief. This is an important part. This is the part of a statue people look at. Right, Shane. Plaster.'

I picked up the garden watering can and put the tip of the funnel to one of the three big holes in the mould, where his nipples would be. I poked in the spout, tipped it and the plaster started to pour in, glug, glug, glug, down around his chest and resting arm and seeping out of the joints and cracks between the moulds.

'My goodness,' said O'Shaughnessy. 'What an operation.'

'Yes, like I told you, Mr O'Shaughnessy. You have to move fast. And *you* have to not move at all.'

I moved to the back and poured through the slanted holes beneath the shoulder blades, and, when they were solidly full, at the bottom of his back. Then to the plaster protrusion that

304

was his arm, I poured in plaster until the channels started filling.

'Don't move your finger,' said Wycherley and Corny looked at him. It was as if he was silently pleading now.

'Keep them still. It won't be long now. Keep them absolutely still. Otherwise the plaster will set loosely around them and the relief will come out all twisted.'

'Done,' I said and I stood back with Wycherley to watch.

'That's great. Smile, Mr O'Shaughnessy. It's all for posterity, all for the future.'

Corny gave a very weak smile.

'Keep that sort of expression,' said Wycherley and stepped back to fetch a plaster mask. 'But make it more determined, more noble, heroic. That's what I want to catch in the face. Do you understand?'

Corny nodded that he did. I stepped behind him and picked up the plaster helmet.

'This will take only half a minute, on and off very quickly. And then you'll be completely finished.'

Behind Corny, I stood poised with the helmet. I looked at the flaky bits of skin in his hair.

'OK? Now look as if you're looking into the distance. That's it, grimly determined. That's it . . . now . . . deep breath – on we go!'

And Wycherley pressed over his face a soft plaster mask while I hooded his head with the helmet. We held them there. We were both shaking and so, horribly, was the mould itself. It rocked to and fro for about fifteen seconds and then it subsided.

'It won't be long now, Mr O'Shaughnessy.'

But there were no more answers.

We stood back. Wycherley looked at the mould.

'Right now, Shane, go,' he said softly.

'Hold on,' I said and I picked up a stick. 'Mine's the difficult part and if I deserve one wish I deserve this.'

'Go ahead,' he said.

I lifted the stick and smashed the wax figure of O'Shaughnessy to smithereens. Bits and pieces flew around the workshop but the back of it buckled and crumbled before us. A black skeleton was left and Wycherley smiled and took it and lifted it straight into the warm cauldron of molten wax. He turned up the gas and quickly picked some of the bigger giveaway shards of wax and added them to the pot. Then he stopped smiling and stood up to stroke my head.

'Good luck, Shane. I hope you can do it.' He was almost crying. He squeezed my hand tightly and leaned forward to give me a kiss on the cheek.

'I can do it,' I said.

I left the workshop and went into the bathroom. His sad old suit was lying neatly over the chair. I took it up in my arms, folded it and put the shirt inside the jacket and stuffed the lot into the Liverpool FC bag left hanging on the back of the door for this purpose. Down the corridor I went. I was frightened but I was exalted. I went out into the yard. The sun hit me like it was someone else's sun. Out of the yard I went, turned to the right and down Mark's Lane to Lombard Street.

Women were starting to put out washing on the balconies above me. I'd nearly forgotten it was morning, still before eleven. The guard was standing on the corner watching me approach. I switched to the other side of the lane so I could meet him.

'Well,' he asked nicely, his hands behind his back. 'How's it going?'

'Well so far. We've done all our moulds. I've to drop down to Heiton's to get more setting agent.'

'Beautiful,' he said, looking up at the true blue sky. 'Peaceful morning.'

'Thank God,' I said, and made to leave him. 'See you later.'

'Good luck now.'

I waited for a break in the traffic and ran across Lombard Street, jumping the kerb at the Registry Office for Births and Deaths. I've one to register. Down Lombard Street East and stopped at the corner by the Windjammer doors, waiting for the traffic to halt. Red lights; I crossed Townsend Street, past the big Volvo garage on the corner and the children playing on the lawns of the new corporation housing. My heart was thumping so much I thought it would lift me off the ground. The boys were playing football on the big circular lawn. Why weren't they at school? Because it's July. I was coming past them when the ball tumbled out on the road, yards from me. What could I do? I cantered out on to the hot asphalt and kicked it back to them. They cheered. But when I went on a few yards, some kid shouted, 'Liverpool are killers.' Jesus, Heysel. They'd remembered. I'd forgotten. I turned the corner at the river and quickly went the few yards up to Neligan's on

Creighton Street, off City Quay. Their garage door was open and I went around the back to the office. Some fellow was whistling and looking down a ladder.

'Alan,' I shouted. 'How are you? We need about twenty pounds more of setting agent.'

'Oh no,' he laughed, 'look at what we have here – a marked man.'

Two other guys came out to have a look.

'Oh, I don't think we can do the business with you,' said Alan, and reiterated the point by shaking his head and sucking air through his teeth.

'Come on, for Jasus' sake, we need the stuff right away.'

'And would I be what they call a legitimate target for supplying you?'

'Give it over.'

'When do you want it for?'

'Soon as poss. I have to drop out for something.' I didn't say what. 'I'll be back shortly.'

'Leave it with me,' he said and folded a piece of paper not mine.

'Fifteen – twenty minutes. Go on, away with you.'

'Thanks,' I said and I went back out on to the quays.

That's that set up. Now for the hard part. Walking quickly and keeping close in to the doorways I walked the two hundred yards to Immaculate Heart Church. My heart was pounding now, I'll have to admit. I took a check. Nobody about. I slipped quietly into the little churchyard and hoped to my last hope that the church was empty as it usually is at this time of the morning when there's no service on. I nearly bleeding prayed, that's how much I hoped. I went in through the swing door to the vestibule and then into the church proper and it was. Apart from the red lights on the altar and the morning sunlight streaming through the stained-glass windows the small church was completely deserted. Tiptoeing with my feet creaking on the tiles, I sneaked around the corner behind the painted plaster statue of our blessed virgin standing on a snake and immediately began to undress. I kicked off the shoes and dropped my trousers. Into the satchel bag they went. I took out Corny's trousers and put them on. I leave to another time the extraordinary feeling that went through me when I did this. I had visualised it so hard over the last few days that it seemed as if by sheer force of imagination it was happening. Braces were altered. A vow to myself that I said I would keep – if I'm cured of this, I'll be cured of everything – I *didn't* go through his trousers. I looped the braces up on to my shoulders and buttoned up the flies. Christ. There was an empty hole in my stomach. Christ, I thought, and there he was but he's only a bleeding statue to me. I slipped into his shoes and my toes winkled inside, trying them for size. I zipped up the satchel bag and stuffed it well in behind a statue of St Martin de Porres, where it wouldn't be seen, and then I went and took my place in the confessional. I drew the curtain across so no chink of a sight could possibly be revealed of me above my waist. The grille was dark. My heart was beating so hard I could hear it thumping. Thumping solidly. I was almost afraid someone else, some old priest's housekeeper, might hear it. I sat still, composing myself, and I waited.

Tess returned to the studio at 11.10 a.m. and walked in on Wycherley picking up the last stray bits of wax around the workshop. The model of the original figure was melted in the basin beside him.

'Oh great,' she shouted. 'You got it done.'

'Told you I'd be quick, didn't I?'

'Damn right, and you've closed the mould and all,' she said, coming over to rest a hand on Corny in his plaster overcoat.

'Well, like I said. For the type of statue the Government wanted, everything was done. Once I got the reliefs of hands and feet and whatnot I was able to attach them to the figure right away and then put the figure back in its mould and close it.'

'Wow,' said Tess, admiring the plaster. 'Almost as quick as the Foster House job.'

'Well, like I said, the fewer distractions the more I'm in action and, God knows, this contract needs action.'

'Where's Mr O'Shaughnessy?'

'He's gone for a walk.'

'Is that wise?'

'I couldn't stop him,' said Wycherley, drying his hands. 'Sitting up there really took it out of him. He was determined to go down the riverfront and get some air. He said he hadn't been around this area in years and he had this bright idea of going to check out the little church and get confession.'

'Confession?' Tess was puzzled.

'I know. Confession, of all things. You Catholics – you're really something.'

'Well, I suppose that's sweet – at this stage of his life.'

'I don't know,' said Wycherley, not sure.

'But . . .' Tess wasn't sure either.

'Anyway, the police are out there, keeping a close eye on him. Even if they've to keep their distance. You can be sure Mr O'Shaughnessy would lose his temper if he thought they were following him to confession.'

'Mmm.'

'You know' – Wycherley had a thought – 'maybe you might go down there and check. Like, just to be on the safe side. Don't for God's sake let him see you. God, no. Just take a peep into the church. He's not gone long. He'd only be arriving there now, if even that. I'll tell you what to do. Nip into the church and very quickly take a peep under the curtains in the confessional boxes. They're the old sort of confessionals where you see the people's legs. Don't, for God's sake, let him see you or hear you. Just take a glance from the distance. You'll recognise his trousers. Sure you can't miss them. And don't hang about. Report straight back to me.'

I was sitting in the confessional for about six minutes when I heard footsteps. I sucked in my breath and sat perfectly still. If it's the priest and he sees me I'm fucked. This is the risk we had to take. The footsteps paused, then started again and slowed up and then a bench creaked. Someone had come in to pray. It was a quickie. After about a minute the bench creaked again and there was a wheeze of breath (an old woman?) and then there were footsteps again down the aisle to the back of the church. Money went into a collection box and the footsteps grew fainter on the church porch and she was gone. About two minutes later there were more footsteps and I could tell immediately they were Tessa's. The quick soft squeak of her Doc soles. She walked up the aisle and kept stopping, checking the confessionals. She'll wonder how come Corny's sitting in a confessional if there's no confessions. Let her wonder. We'll sort out that one later on. He's an old man. She stopped when she drew level with my confessional, and got into the bench. I imagine her head is stooping down lower just to make sure. Satisfied. The bench creaked. She got up and walked out of the church.

Two minutes later I very discreetly drew the curtain and peeped out. You'd never know who and what might have spirited its way in during the last ten minutes. All clear. I got out of the confessional quickly and went down to the statue of the Blessed Virgin Mary standing on a snake. I pulled out the Liverpool bag from behind the statue of St Martin de Porres, unzipped it and took out my trousers and shoes. I knocked off Corny's shoes, wriggled out of his braces and dropped his trousers. I put on my own trousers and shoes and put his back in the bag and got ready to leave the church. No one in the vestibule? Good. And no one in the yard? I took a peep over the retreat posters on the glass swing doors. No one. Good. I left the church, turned to the right and headed back down the quays, keeping close to the houses. An old tramp asked me for money. Go and raid the church, I felt like telling him; it's empty but its coffers ain't, or here's a pair of trousers . . . In fact, there's an idea: wear these and you'll be blamed for killing him. 'Tramp held for O'Shaughnessy disappearance!'

I crossed the Gloucester Road quickly and walked along the river road to the quayside, and then along the riverfront, past the unloading pylons and warehouse sheds where Corny held out against the Black and Tans in the twenties. I walked along another thirty yards, in behind the shipping containers, and came to my chosen spot.

I had to make sure absolutely no one saw me, which is not difficult down here at this time of the morning. People were busily working on the other side of the river but over here, the quays were quiet and litter-strewn. Good. No one even strolling.

I went down the green scummy steps, careful not to slip or I'll die with shame to my name. Shame, my eye, it's glory. I came to the step lapped last by the knocking waters of the river. Opaque green water. Shifting marble water. The Liffey. Mother, hee, hee. I looked at the water. I'm twenty-two. I'm a free man now. I pulled the shoes out of the satchel and threw them into the water. They sank without a trace. I pulled out the trousers and threw them into the water. The water soaked them but they floated. Thought so. I picked up a stick and prodded the trousers until they were good and wet. Float away, my friends – you'll be found in a day or two. But before they could float too far I pulled an arranged brick out of the satchel, wrapped the shirt and jacket round it, and threw it on to the trousers to sink the lot.

I closed the satchel and, quickly but carefully, I went back up the steps and on to the quayside. Shielded by parked cars from the footpath, I walked along until I was level with Heiton's and I crossed the road and went in.

'Ah, our marked man,' said Alan.

'Have you got it?'

'Here you are.' He came forward with a bundle. I put it in the satchel.

'Will it fit in there?'

'No problem. There's room in there now. There's room for all of us now.'

Warning: say nothing strange.

'That's great. Listen, put it on the bill, will you?'

'No problem. Hey, are you guys still doing that statue of your man?'

'Yep.'

'Fair play to you.'

'Sail close to the wind,' I said with a wink. 'And I'd better get back. I'll see you.'

'Good luck,' he said and he stood there watching me depart. He admired us. Why wouldn't he?

I went out and turned the corner up Lombard Street. The kids playing football cheered when I passed. I waited for the traffic on Townsend Street and crossed over to the Windjammer. In there later on, I hope, if not in the slammer. I continued on up Lombard Street East and crossed over to Mark's Lane. The guard greeted me.

'You're back?'

'I am. Anything strange?'

'Nope,' he said crisply and he whistled as I passed him.

'See you later.'

'All the best.'

As I came down the lane, I saw Tess running out through the flats and into our yard. Coming back for the second time. Jesus, she moves fast. That dead pigeon in the gutter. Will someone please remove the damn thing. Lazy underclass. Children playing here as well.

In the gates and across the yard into the studio. I went down the corridor and burst through the plastic curtains into the workshop. Tessa and Wycherley looked at me with concerned faces.

'What's up?'

'Have you seen Mr O'Shaughnessy on your travels?'

'No. Why?'

'He went out for a walk.'

'Out for a walk? On his own?'

'Of course, on his own. He insisted on it. Down to the church. He said he wanted to get confession.'

'Confession? Jesus, at long last! I hope he booked the priest for the week.'

'Shane, this is serious,' said Wycherley. 'I sent Tess down to check on him.'

'I saw his legs under the curtain.'

'Well, that's all right then.'

'Yeah, but she went down again and he wasn't there.'

'Where could he be?' asked Tess.

'He can't have gone far. There are cops out there. You don't think they'd let him stray far, do you? Not on a day like today. Look at those bleeding papers, for Christ's sake.' I pointed to the 'Out to get me' headlines on the floor.

'This is quite worrying,' said Wycherley.

'You got the mould into the oven, I see. That was quick.'

'Yes,' said Wycherley, in an act-distracted way. 'Tessa . . . helped me push it in.'

'Listen, will I go out and check with the guards?' said Tess.

'No!' said Wycherley. 'There's no need to alert the guards just yet. Give it a few moments. He has to come back.'

'No harm in asking the guards,' suggested Tess.

'No . . . wait,' said Wycherley, and he did a very good act of chewing his nails.

'He'd throw a wobbler if he thought we were getting the guards on to him,' I said.

'We're not getting him on to them. Or them on to him, I mean.'

'I know that but . . . but you know what I mean, just telling them. On the other hand, what's the loss of his temper compared to the loss of – well, you know.'

'Right, Tessa, you go and check with Garda Allen – down here.' He indicated Lombard Street. 'Shane, you go and have a word with Garda Larkin up here at Princes Street. I don't . . .' There was a rustling at the plastic curtains and we all looked around hopefully. In came Ramsey, a shaker of fish food in his hand.

'Ramsey,' said Wycherley. 'Have you seen Mr O'Shaughnessy?'

'I did, thanks.'

'No! I mean recently.'

'Oh, eh, no. He was in here, wasn't he?'

'He was in here but he went. Did you not see him pass you?'

312

'I was very busy, Mr Wycherley, shining those bronze plates. My back was to the gate.'

'You shouldn't have let him out, boss.'

'How could I stop him?' protested Wycherley. 'He said he was going out for a walk and that's that. "I do not need to be accompanied," he said. He wouldn't hear of it!'

'Is he gone?' asked Ramsey, but when no one answered him he went to feed the fish.

'He said no one is going to stop me going for a walk in my city.'

'He's right,' I said. 'I'm going down to the river,' he said. 'You go on fixing up that statue and I'll go down the riverfront. I haven't been down there in years.'

'Let's hope he's not down there for years.'

'Look, maybe we're panicking,' said Tess. 'He's only gone for a walk. He goes on strolls quite regularly around the grounds of Belfield.'

'He likes walks,' I confirmed. 'You saw how fit he was on Saturday.'

'Well, I don't quite like being restless. He's been gone a good twenty-five minutes.'

'What's twenty-five minutes? I said he was fit but I didn't say he was that fit. Give him a chance. He's going on ninety not doing it.'

'Shane, do you mind!' said Wycherley, frowning.

'Hey, I know, he could have left the church and then gone over to the quayside to have a look at the river, like he told you he would. Will I go down and have a check?'

'We could do that or we could go and alert the police, which I'm very reluctant to do.'

'We should really tell them,' said Tess. 'It's no big deal. We can just ask them have they seen Mr O'Shaughnessy. That's what they're there for.'

'Let's face it, Bob. They'll wonder why they weren't told when he was going out for a walk in the first place so it'd certainly look bad if we didn't tell them now, when he's late coming back.'

'Right.' Wycherley was decided. 'Tessa, you go and check with Garda Larkin down on Lombard Street and Shane, you go up to the other guy, Garda Allen. Just ask them did they see Mr O'Shaughnessy.'

Neither Garda Larkin nor Allen had seen Mr O'Shaughnessy

leave the premises and they got quite panicky when they realised he had. Garda Larkin said that he had kept his eyes on the studio at almost all times but he had to admit he was keeping his eye on what was 'going into' the studio, not 'coming out'. Spot the difference. Barring those times when he would have had to pace some of the street as instructed and would have lost sight of the studio doors for short intervals, he nevertheless felt that he had the lane under watch. But he hadn't seen O'Shaughnessy emerge and he hadn't even seen me emerge, a fact that boosted ourselves and reflected badly on their vigilance. Having greeted me but not had the pleasure with Mr O'Shaughnessy, Garda O'Brien, he of the 'peaceful morning' and winning smile earlier on, now fumbled with his radio to call in reinforcements from Pearse Street.

The reinforcements arrived within minutes. A squad car, and then a second squad car, screeched up outside the studio and out got four, five, six, eight burly guards. Another car pulled up and headed off immediately for the riverfront. A Sierra detective car pulled in and, after consultation with Wycherley, in got Tessa with two garda sergeants. They tore off down to the church where Tess was going to show them where O'Shaughnessy was last sighted.

Events were moving quickly now. Inside, the questions started. The questions that wouldn't end for three days, the questions which, on certain days and nights, in pubs and student restaurants, are still being asked and pored over. What time did he leave the studio? What time did Tess see his legs? Why did he want confession just after posing for his statue? Was he making terms? Did he think it was all over? How did he know of the route he took?

Surprisingly, the guards didn't dwell on the propriety of Wycherley's letting him go for a walk. It was accepted that Mr O'Shaughnessy was a difficult man, that he would have been stubborn to the last, and that when he demanded that he be let go on a walk without any assistance or surveillance it would be well nigh impossible to stop him. More than anything else, the guards themselves knew how difficult he could be about protection and what he saw as restrictions on his personal freedom.

In reply to the question of why Wycherley didn't alert the guards to the fact of Mr O'Shaughnessy's going for a walk, Wycherley not unreasonably pointed out that he assumed that the guards, keeping watch on the studio, would automatically see him emerge. He thought Mr O'Shaughnessy would go for a little walk and come straight back, with the guards watching him. Sergeant Tobin narrowed his eyes. One half of them hadn't even seen Mr McArdle emerge. Someone was going to answer for this.

'OK, let's move it!' shouted a big-jawed officer at the curtains, clapping his hands, and some of the guards left the workshop. Garda Sergeant Tobin gathered a crew of ten men and issued instructions. They were to fan out in all directions from the studio doors in two-man foot patrols. A patrol would set out down Mark's Lane to the left and right and thence to the seafront and three two-man patrols would comb the flats on their way to the river.

'Ah, Detective Hurley, thank God you're here!' cried Wycherley when the plastic curtains opened.

'Yeah, but we're not all here, are we?' he said with barely concealed anger. His face was red and beating.

'What happened?'

'Detective Johnston, come here for a moment.'

'Bravo, six, bravo, nice,' a radio crackled. 'Come in . . . this is Ringsend, out . . .'

'We can use your phone, Mr Wycherley?' asked a rookie garda with a notebook in his hand.

'By all means, it's in the hall. Now, Mr Hurley, as I was saying, I came – '

'Detective Hurley,' said another big cop and whispered in his ear.

'In a minute.' His hand flicked up. 'Look,' he told Wycherley, 'I want to establish . . .'

Guards were milling all over the studio and I was beginning to get scared. None of them looked in the oven, but, in time, you can expect them to look everywhere.

A fat head burst through the curtains. 'Shane McArdle?'

'Yes?'

'Come with us.'

The head vanished and I followed it out into the yard. Three cops in a squad car were waiting for me. Fathead hopped into the front and a back door swung open for me.

'Bring us to where you went,' said a voice at the wheel.

'Wh . . . what do you mean?' I asked. My heart sank. I almost got sick.

'To where you went,' the driver said, turning round. He had

a young face and neat white teeth. The sun was on his face. 'To where you went to that time you went out. We want to retrace your route.'

'Oh, right,' I said, which he took to be the direction, and spun the steering wheel to reverse.

'Eh . . . why?' I asked. 'Why': it sounded so hollow.

'Because it's another path back,' said the young guard. 'He might have lost his way.'

'But where I went wasn't near the church. It was down on Feighron Street. And the traffic doesn't go left here!'

'It does now,' said the guard as he veered a sharp left out of the lane and down Lombard Street. We met a guard on a motor cycle coming the other way. Greetings were exchanged. I never realised there would be so many guards on the scene so quickly. They drove like that until we reached the river.

'Unbelievable,' muttered Fathead. 'Un–fucking–believable.'

The driver shook his head, his face gripped tight.

'The man says people are after him and the next morning he goes for a walk on his own.'

'Ah, he's always been like that.'

'He's a born victim.'

I said nothing.

The car swung on to the rough cobbles of Feighron Street and took the corner slowly.

'I went in there,' I explained as the car drew up outside Heiton's.

'And what way did you go back?'

'The way I came.'

They looked at each other.

'Sorry,' said the Guard driving. 'We thought you were further away.'

We drove on up the Liffey. I never knew what this journey was for. Later on, much later on, enquiries were made about the times I called to Heiton's and Alan filled them in, not without a few imponderables (the coincidence between my sitting on the quays taking air and Corny appearing to be disappearing into it was something I was going to have to live with), but as for my being taken down here like this this morning, I never found out why. It was either genuinely to work out another path of return for Corny or else it was a way of psyching me out early on. Either could be standard police practice for all I knew. If I was being psyched out,

I held my nerve. I had to, we were on our way to the church. Perhaps it was standard practice in the immediate aftermath of an event such as this but I find it difficult to believe that local guards wouldn't know where Heiton's on Creighton Street was in relation to the rest of the neighbourhood.

More gardaí were standing around outside the church. Two or three of them were pacing back and forth peering at the gravel. Tess was inside, answering questions. There was a priest outside, looking quite shocked.

'Extraordinary thing is,' he was telling two garda sergeants, 'why would he have thought there were confessions on a Wednesday morning.'

'Let's go in,' said our driver and in we went to the church.

'Not moving at all, no,' said Tess, standing beside the confessional. She was explaining again what she saw, this time to Hurley, who was standing with his hand on his hips concentrating on the wooden door of the confessional. He was enraged. He obviously couldn't believe what he was experiencing.

'You see, I didn't want him to hear me, obviously. I wouldn't want to give him a start.'

Hurley looked at her as if he was about to cry.

'So I crept through the benches like this,' explained Tess, acting out her role exactly as I told you she would. 'And came along – '

'Woa! Step back,' said Hurley, putting out his big hand. 'Don't touch those.'

'Tom!' he shouted and he snapped his fingers. 'I want forensic to go over all this area. Confessional, both sides, benches, tiles, the lot.'

'Right so,' said Tom and he took note of it all with quick eyes.

'Tess, could you identify over here . . .' Another guard was calling her.

'Let's go outside,' said Hurley, and he put his hand on my back. When he came level with me I noticed his eyes were going everywhere: behind statues, behind doors, across the well-thumbed glass panels on the vestry doors.

On seeing Hurley emerge the priest came forward.

'Mr Hurley, I checked again with the housekeeper and the sexton and none of them saw anyone in or around the church, unfortunately. Some of the ladies from the sodality were in earlier, of course, to fix the altar flowers and some children – '

'What flowers?' asked Hurley with great irritation.

317

'For the altar,' stressed the priest.

'Look, we'll need to interview them,' said Hurley, looking all around him.

'Who, the sodality?'

'The housekeeper and the' – he jerked his thumb – 'thewhatdo-youcallit, the sexton. Garda Reynolds, will you arrange the taking of statements, as soon as possible.'

'I will, indeed, Mr Hurley.'

'Sergeant Leahy,' said one garda down on his haunches, examining the gravel. 'I think this is worth a look.'

Sergeant Leahy crunched over quickly and peered down.

'Yes, indeed. Blood, Mr Hurley.'

'Where?' he said and he walked over quickly. We all peered down at the small blobs of cherry-coloured blood.

'Sergeant Leahy, get on this immediately.'

'Looks like animal's.'

'It could be pigeon's,' I said.

Hurley nodded and walked towards the church gate. His brow was deeply furrowed. He was thinking.

'What are those men doing over there?' There were some guards crossing Sherwin Bridge.

'They're checking the other side, Mr Hurley. They're from Sheriff Street.'

'I see. That's good. Jimmy, I want Sergeant McDowell and Sergeant Deale to co-ordinate over there.'

'Right so, sir.'

'Let's go back to the studio,' said Hurley. 'Shane, come on with me. Sergeant Leahy, radio for Lyons and Purcell to return to the studio.'

I got into the back of the Sierra with Hurley and two young guards drove us back up Moss Street towards the studio. On the way we saw guards moving down lanes and back lanes, combing the place out. Slowing up to turn right at the lights in Townsend Street, we met a stream of shirt-sleeved gardaí emerging out of Back Row, beating the nettles around the steel picket fence. It was impressive stuff. Keep it up, lads.

'Shane.' Hurley turned to me. 'I want to thank you for coming forward with that information.'

'Oh, it was nothing. God, it was my duty.'

'Thank you. Others might have passed it off as a joke but you were vigilant. Good man.'

'But is it . . . is it not a bit late?' I said gently.

'Oh no. By God, no. We might have lost our man, for the moment, but we've got our men, if you follow?'

'I do.' I do, I do.

Hurley looked out the window and then back at me.

'What did he have against police?'

'It's terrible. I don't know, I really don't.'

'It's always been the same. Back in the fifties when he was Minister he could hardly be prevailed upon to accept a garda on the grounds of his house. He'd been shooting at us a decade earlier but so what, weren't they all at some stage.'

I said nothing. All?

'There he was last night crying out to the country about being a hunted man and any protection we offer him is spurned. Spurned! Not just declined or gently discouraged but spurned! Jesus Christ, I ask you. Pull in here, Jim.'

We drew in for two sergeants, their backs to us, walking back to the studio. Hurley rolled down his window.

'Get me O'Rourke on the blower. I'm moving on this.'

'Right so,' said Sergeant Quigley.

We drove out on to Pearse Street, again in defiance of one-way traffic, and around the church and down the lane to the studio. Two squad cars were parked outside and a rather unseemly row was going on in the yard. Biddy O'Shaughnessy had returned and was understandably distressed. She said the gardaí had done nothing for her father and was surrounded by a response of soft cooing words to calm her down.

'Now, now, please, Ms O'Shaughnessy,' said Hurley.

'O'Sha*u*nessy,' she corrected, amid sniffs.

'Oh, sorry, Ms O' . . . Sha*u*nessy, you mustn't get upset and you mustn't attack people who are trying to help your father and help find him. He'll turn up. Don't be alarmed. He went for a walk and he hasn't come back yet. There's no need to be upset.'

'Mr Hurley, Mr O'Rourke wants you on the line, urgently.'

'I'm coming. Really, Ms O'Sha*u*nessy.'

'Why was he allowed to go for a walk in the first place,' she sniffed and looked at Hurley with recrimination.

'Now, Ms O'Shaunessy,' said Hurley, with great patience. 'You know what your father's like. You know how obstinate he is about his personal freedom. You and I have spoken about this before.'

She sniffed and said nothing. She knew Hurley was right.

'Mr Hurley, he says it's very urgent.'

'Coming!' he said and he jogged towards the telephone, jiggling the veranda-floor planks.

'Come inside to the kitchen,' said the ban gharda. 'They're making a pot of tea. Come on.'

She got up reluctantly. Wycherley looked over at me.

'Why don't they leave my father alone?' she cried. 'He's an old man. What's wrong with them? Jesus, what's wrong with a statue?'

'Come on, Bid,' said the ban gharda, taking her by the arm.

'They'll never leave him alone, never. Jesus, what's the country coming to?

'Come on, now, through here.' The ban gharda held the half-door back and Biddy could be heard complaining into the kitchen.

Wycherley sidled over to talk to me.

'How do?'

'OK, so far. I was taken to – '

'I know.' He nodded. 'It went OK?'

'Fine.'

'Where's Tess?'

'She's down there still. The guards are taking statements. She's, eh, the most crucial witness so far.'

Wycherley blew through his thin lips.

'Rough on the nerves, what?'

'Sure is,' I said, 'but it's getting better.'

'One of us should always be in there, Shane,' said Wycherley through gritted teeth, 'if any of them are in here.'

'OK, but . . . gift horse and all that.'

'Mr Wycherley, can I talk to you for a moment?' asked a plainclothes detective, standing by the plaster buckets.

'Sure,' said Wycherley and he went over smiling.

'It's about the arrival,' said the detective.

I stood and watched the guards as they moved in and out of the workshop. I watched them nervously, very nervously, but not without growing confidence. Absorbed in directions and questions, they circled quickly but carefully with the equipment and materials, stepping over half-figures and broken moulds and paying no attention to the large sealed moulds that stood by the oven on makeshift tracks. Why should they?

By now, some guards were beginning to return to the studio.

Nobody had seen anything untoward, as far as their first tentative enquiries were concerned, but Mrs Maguire of Flat 15a and Mrs Finnerty of Flat 18c were fairly sure they had seen 'that Mr O'Shaughnessy' walk through the flats below them. And so had another woman who was with them, they said. The children playing in the Gloucester diamond said that yes, definitely, they had seen an old man in a baggy suit earlier on and when they were shown a photo of Mr O'Shaughnessy, they chorused, 'Yes, that's him!' Detective Sergeant Hurley wanted a thorough questioning of the residents of the St Martin's flats complex started immediately. The children also said they had seen me go down Lombard Street and they'd seen me go back up. I'd kicked their ball. Detective Sergeant Hurley wanted the children brought in for questioning. Eh, approached, he added, wiggling his fingers and correcting himself.

Chapter 12

Disturbances in Dublin

A t 3 p.m., Hurley decided to call a meeting in the studio kitchen. He was about to return to Pearse Street from where, after this meeting, the search would henceforward be directed. Wycherley and I looked at each other. That was a relief. Hurley wanted to make a few crucial arrangements before he left. By now a number of theories were emerging. The main possibility and, in a sense, the most hopeful one, was that Mr O'Shaughnessy had got lost. This took a number of options. Sergeant Tobin took us through them. O'Shaughnessy could have come back from the church via Lombard Street and turned accidentally left and gone into a building of flats very like the one in front of the studio.

'Have we men down there?' asked Hurley quickly.

'We've men everywhere, sir.'

He could have walked up Lombard Street and easily missed the narrow entrance to Mark's Lane.

'Pearse Street's very busy,' said Quigley. 'He'd have been seen by now.'

'Yeah, well, he hasn't been,' chortled Hurley. 'Has he?'

A noise sounded over the roof. Chukka-chukka-chukka. I couldn't believe it. A helicopter.

'What's that?' I asked excitedly.

'Helicopters,' said Hurley and he went back to the map.

He could have walked back via Moss Street and then taken a wrong turn into Townsend Street, or continued up Shaw Street and on to Pearse Street. In both cases an easy thing to do.

'Not if he knew the area.'

'The area's changed since he was here.'

322

'That's why he wanted to check it out,' I said.

'What?'

'Eh . . . check it out. That's what he said he'd love to do sometime.'

Hurley stared at me.

'Tell us what he said.' He practically grabbed me by the throat.

'Getting out of the car, he remarked that this was his old IRA combat area in 1919–21 and he'd love to check it out some time. See how it's changed, or whatever.'

'Jimmy, get me Sergeant Leahy on the radio. Thank you, Shane. Thank you very much.'

'As far as I know, that's what he said. Isn't it, Wycherley?'

'That's what he said.'

Biddy was brought in to confirm this. 'Yes, he did say something about how he would love to look it over. You know, he really did love the city and I don't see why people think that just because – '

'Thank you, Ms O'Shaunessy.' And she was ushered back out.

'Don't push me!'

'But, Mr Wycherley,' said another sergeant, 'you told us he told you he'd be straight back.'

'He did tell me that,' said Wycherley.

'Yeah, but sure,' said Hurley, 'once he got walking.'

'Exactly,' I said. 'I mean, we saw him on Saturday. He's a nostalgic old man and once the old legs got moving . . .'

The guards looked at me.

'Stirred by recent events he may have decided to walk his old combat area to remind and embolden himself. Stir the blood.' This was my offering and the guards looked at it with disdain. No imagination.

'Shane, please,' cautioned Wycherley. 'You and your walks.'

'We'll need to get exact definitions of his old combat area,' said Hurley.

'I can give you them,' I said.

'Shane!'

'It's OK, Mr Wycherley. Any help I can give on this, the better. We'll need to move quickly.'

'You've covered most of all his combat area by now. It's approximately from here' – my finger drew a line from Merrion Square to the quays – 'to here.'

'We have,' said Hurley. 'But it's good to know. John, radio panda nine to cover Merrion Square – fast! – and Lower Mount Street, and get panda four to run over the back of Holles Street again and Lower Grand Canal, as soon as possible.'

'And Boland's Mills,' I said.

'What?'

'Boland's Mills. Where he was in 1916. Surely the most nostalgic spot of all?'

'Yeah, right. You hear that, John. Take in Boland's Mills.'

Wycherley looked at me, and for the first time, permitted himself a nervous smirk. Hurley looked grimly at the map before him.

'Gentlemen, gentlemen, gentlemen.' He linked his fingers together and kissed the knuckles. 'Let's hope he's lost, let's hope he's lost. Because' – he looked behind him, mindful of the daughter – 'because, because the other possibility is, gentlemen, that the man has been' – he look at us frankly – 'abducted.'

We all nodded our heads sorrowfully.

'It would have been an unfortunately very easy thing to do, if he insisted on walking to the church or beyond without any protection or even company.'

We nodded our heads again.

'He could have been abducted from inside or outside the church. The priest said he heard nothing. But he wouldn't need to. O'Shaughnessy's an old man and he wouldn't have put up much of a struggle. I'm having the church and churchyard and surrounding area checked for signs of a struggle.'

'He could have been abducted on his way back, on Gloucester Street. It would have been very easy to jump out and bundle him into a car or van. The ground is being checked for any signs. Given the abductors' speed and probable amateurishness, there could be skidmarks. Abducted' – he rubbed an eye – 'on the quayside, if he went for a walk on the quays. At Custom House, if he went over there. Indeed, we're having all the areas he was in or could have been in checked for signs of struggle,' said Hurley, and he said it sadly and for once I felt very sorry for him. How was he going to explain this to the Minister? How was the Minister going to explain this to the country?

'Right, that's enough,' said Hurley. 'The base of all operations is now moving to Pearse Street and I'm contactable there. Jim, Pat, Liam, liaise on the ground with Sergeants Purcell and Lyons on this side of the quay, with Deale and McDowell on the other. Let's go then.'

A young guard came in.

'There are some journalists outside, sir. Do you want to make a statement?'

'No, for Christ's sake! A man goes for a walk and the vultures are down on the quayside. Not yet. Tell them to be at Pearse Street Station in an hour's time and there might be a statement then. Mr Wycherley, you'd better come with me to the station.'

'Right, so. Shane, will you stay here?'

'Sure.'

Wycherley gave me a discreet parting smile and they all left the studio. How strange. I could hear their voices in the yard, car doors slamming. Retreating. Quiet. I could hear the helicopter in the distance. The sun was streaming through our perspex roof. I will never be the same again. I don't want to reflect. I don't want to reflect just yet. I looked at the mould quite coolly. It was a mould now, nothing more.

The phone rang. I went through the curtains to answer it. The voice was faint.

'Is Detective Hurley there?'

'He's just left.'

'Oh, has he gone back to the station, do you know?'

'Yes, Pearse Street Station.'

As soon as I put the phone down it rang again. Another caller for Hurley.

'He's gone,' I said. 'Very gone.'

'Thank you very much.'

'You're welcome.'

I put the phone down and looked into the yard. They were all gone. What if Corny returned now? Again. I could hear something – something I never thought I'd hear – the helicopter blades whirring around in the blue sky. He had them brought in quickly. Of course, the Government would be on to it now. He'd have any resources he wanted. I went back towards the workshop and as I passed, it rang. Someone watching me?

'Hello.' I picked up the heavy receiver and looked at the bits of food and oil gathered in the speaker.

'Oh hello – is it true that Mr O'Shaughnessy has gone missing?'

'Look, fuck off, will you?' I shouted and I slammed down the phone.

325

The next thing Mellowes and Oisin walk through the door. Mellowes and Oisin. Familiar, aren't they? Think they can just walk into the studio. Believe it or not, I was glad to see them. Of course I was.

'We were outside. We met Wycherley in the lane. He said it was OK for us to come in.'

'What happened?' asked Mellowes.

'He's gone.'

'Gone?'

'Gone.'

'He just went . . . missing. He went to the church down on the quays. He wouldn't let anyone come with him, on any account. You know how he can be?'

Their heads eddied. They knew.

'He went out and he didn't come back.'

They were silent, stunned.

'Wycherley knew he was going to the confessional so he sent Tess down to sneak a look. He was there all right. She saw his legs under the confessional curtain, but when she went down to check a second time, he was gone.'

'He could have gone for a walk,' said Mellowes dubiously.

'He could, yeah, but you saw the bleeding police operation out there!'

'It's incredible,' said Oisin. 'It's like a Mountjoy break-out. We saw the helicopters from Nassau Street. There are cops all along Pearse Street. People are going bananas out there. "They've got him, they've got him," some old biddy told us outside the Dart Station. She didn't sound displeased.'

'Heads will fucking roll for this.'

'It'll bring down the Government.'

'Do you think?'

'Well, Christ, they'd better find him. Jesus, Shane, can you imagine – and him having warned about this on the TV last night. Everyone knows the threat he said he was under and the next thing he's gone. Jesus, that minister – he'll be shot, Shane! He'll be strung up. And the big T, who's regarded as soft on the Brits and is blind to the activities of their intelligence service. Now Corny goes missing! Sure, how could you trust a government that would allow that to happen.'

'He could turn up,' I told them.

'You won't be seeing the Minister today, that's for sure.'

'Nor ever again, probably.'

'Probably . . . unless you get involved to secure his release.'

'I doubt it. It looks like Hurley's going to move on Harrington and Co.'

'Really?'

'To be taken in for questioning.'

'Proper order.'

'Yeah, and about time.'

'Jesus, I hope we're OK.'

'Yeah.' We all grudged ourselves a smile.

'Is that the mould for the statue?'

'Yeah.'

'That was quick.'

'It needed to be,' I said slyly.

'Ah, stop it.'

'Will Samuelson be lifted, Shane?'

'I'd say so.'

'Wow.'

'Do you want a cup of tea?'

We went into the kitchen where the table was strewn with damp, lipstick-marked hankies. The daughter's. I filled the kettle and plugged it in. Ramsey in the yard.

'Jesus, we're living dangerously,' said Mellowes.

'At least we're living,' said Oisin.

'Don't worry,' I told them, looking at the worn soap bar in the sink.

'What if those big boys say they saw us at his home?'

'We'll say why we were there and produce the papers. Straight up.'

'It'll be very embarrassing for you,' said Mellowes. 'The man who's working on his statue trying to break into his house to steal top-secret documents.'

'It's an embarrassment I can live with. Relative to everything else.'

'Well, yeah,' said Mellowes, looking ruefully at the floor.

'Compared to him vanishing from your studio, I suppose it is.'

'It's not my studio and I wasn't here,' I snapped. 'If I was here he wouldn't have gone. Quite frankly, this is not the hour to talk rashly or apportion blame and I, as you know, am the last one not to stand solidly with my master in a time of crisis, but the fact is that if I was here I would not have let that fool Wycherley let that man go for his deluded walk.'

'Don't upset yourself, Shane,' said Oisin with a shrug. 'It's too late now.'

Mellowes and Oisin looked glumly at the table and the littered hankies.

'Anyway,' I said, going back to what the big boys might say when they're lifted, 'we can say we saw them at O'Shaughnessy's and then they'd be rightly nobbled.'

Mellowes narrowed his eyes at this plainly obvious statement.

'True,' said Oisin, with a tilt of the head. 'In fact, Samuelson might try and get in contact with you so that you'll say nothing – that's if he's time or chance and is desperate.'

'He also might think I double-crossed him, and being desperate, he'll flail wildly and try to pin some of it on us.'

'Our word against theirs.'

'Yeah,' I said sourly. 'And the only witness is missing.'

'Mad,' said Oisin in a soft voice, and shaking our heads we listened to the kettle boiling and the far-off sound of the helicopter blades and thought about what had happened, the ludicrous immensity of it all. They never reckoned on this, they never thought I'd bring them so close to it. And, when it's all over, they'll never know, God bless them. They'll never know it again.

'I mean . . . it's a terrible thing to say,' said Mellowes, breaking the sun-filled silence, 'but I kind of hope, even for the sake of what we fought so hard to get, even for the sake of the documents, that he's still sort of alive.'

'Ah, Jasus, Sean, what a bloody attitude!' said Oisin. 'Don't tell me you hate him that much. You vengeful cunt, you sound like Skin the Goat. Do you know that?'

'Hate him?' shouted Mellowes. 'Did you not hear me? I said I hope he's still alive. That's a charitable thing to ask for, isn't it? It's more charitable than wishing someone were dead, isn't it?'

'Well, in this country, yes, I suppose it is, but what a perspective to take.' He shook his head.

'Perspectives have changed,' I told them both and unplugged the kettle. Sage in the eye of the steam.

'I mean, I want the man to be given the chance to answer the charges,' said Mellowes sadly, 'to answer the new evidence. Otherwise, they'll never be fully confirmed, never fully confessed to when there was such a chance. Otherwise, God knows, he could draw some sympathy and support from the fact that they suspiciously seem to emerge just after he goes missing.'

'Ah lads, lads, give it over,' said the cryptic one. 'Nothing's missing yet and there'll be plenty of time to answer the charges.'

'It's madness out there!' said Tess, bursting through the plastic curtains and disturbing my unwanted peace.

'What have you been up to?'

'All over the place,' she shouted, chest heaving with the excitement.

'My God, we were up in Pearse Street Garda Station; it's like a madhouse with people coming and going and God, there was . . .' She smoothed her hair back 'Emmm . . .'

'God?'

Her hand flapped. 'The what-do-you-call-it? The bloody Minister or whatever, trying to get through to Hurley who's taken off to Ballsbridge or somewhere. Have you been here all the time?'

'Yep,' I said sadly.

'Shane, we'll see you later,' said Mellowes, leaving with Oisin. 'See you later, boys.'

'I had to give them a statement,' said Tess, after they'd gone. 'And then go back over the – '

'What did the statement say?'

She shrugged. 'Just what happened. The stuff in the church is obviously the most important – seeing his feet and all that.' She looked at me sort of oddly. 'You'll have to give one as well.'

'I know.'

'Shane – ' Huge eyes protruded at me.

'What?'

'I . . .' She bit her lower lip. 'I . . . did see him.'

'I know you did.' Her lip released and my heart beat again.

'I mean, I really did.'

I looked at her big brown eyes. I loved the girl.

'I know you did,' I told her softly. 'You saw his shoes.'

'Exactly,' she cried. 'As clear as you're standing there, I saw them.'

'Is someone expressing doubts?'

'I don't know,' she sulked. 'I think some of them do. They keep asking if I was sure they were his shoes – or if they were shoes at all. There were no confessions on when he was there and that has them mystified.'

'They were going to be on at half-one.'

'So why would he get into the confession box early?' Her full, frank eyes looked at me.

'Search me,' I said coolly. 'Private meditation. A rest. A little prayer. A big man who doesn't need a priest and goes straight to God . . . I don't know.' I shrugged. 'He's a very old man.'

Tess had an anguished face. 'Well, what I saw, I saw,' she said and she hunched her shoulders. 'I can't do any better than that.'

'Exactly.'

'Ms Masterson,' crowed Ramsey, coming through the curtains with a fish-food canister in his hand. 'There was a call from home for you. You've to contact them as soon as you can.'

'Thanks, Ramsey,' she said and she headed for the hall.

'Look at Ramsey,' I started, 'feeding the bleeding fish. In the midst of all this he feeds the dayglo mutants, the stunted sci-fi rejects as docile as he in the face of the storm.'

'You leave me alone,' he whined. 'I haven't harmed anyone.'

'What's going on?' said Wycherley. He was back.

'You tell us.'

'They have a few sightings,' he said gravely, and frowning deeply he looked around the workshop with rehearsed concern. At everything except that, 'it', the mould. That needed no rehearsing and he averted his eyes.

'You mean, other than the children and the two ladies in the flats?'

'Yes,' he said with seriousness and he nodded firmly. 'Some other ladies think they may have seen him around Lombard Street.'

'Great.'

He gave me a sudden frown.

'I mean, good – they may be able to find him.'

'One old man,' he said, relenting with a glint, 'thinks he may even have seen him around Ladbroke's bookies.'

I held my breath.

'But,' added Robert with a most withering expression, 'apparently he wasn't a very reliable witness.'

'No, nor our man, a gambler,' I mumbled. 'At least not on the horses.'

A Wycherleyan eyebrow told me to get serious.

'Whoa, boy.'

'So how have things been here?' he asked softly and, linking his fingertips, he looked at the floor like as if he was a guilty priest about to – let's be honest – about to hear confession.

'Fine, Father. We can't complain. Ramsey's been in and out. He wants to know can we shift the moulds out of the way. His usual impatience.'

'Excellent. We can't complain.'

'A few phone calls. A few cops putting their heads in and heading back to the station.'

'No frights?'

'None at all. And out there?'

'Hectic. They're thinking of sending in a sub-aqua team to check the river.'

'You're joking.'

'I certainly am not.'

'Already?'

'Well,' he shrugged, 'some people are optimistic but some people fear the worst.'

'Jesus, I've got to see that.'

Ramsey appeared at the curtain.

'Don't mean to be hasty,' he muttered as he hobbled towards us, 'but the moulds are close to finished now. Should we not – ?'

'Ramsey!' exclaimed Wycherley. 'You're being hasty. There's a man missing. Now would you relax.'

'I have to go home,' announced Tess, coming in from the hall.

'Fair enough,' nodded Wycherley.

'It's only for a short time,' she said, sucking a finger. 'The parents are getting . . . anxious, very anxious.' She looked filthy, tired. They'd drilled her in the station. 'United for once – in anxiety,' she said as an afterthought.

'Of course,' said Bob softly and he gave her a sweet look. She'd taken the brunt of it. 'You should take a rest.'

The phone was ringing. 'Ramsey,' said Bob and he went for it.

'Don't bother coming back, Tess. For God's sake – there's no need.'

'I don't know.' She hunched her shoulders. 'I mean, I . . . I just wished things hadn't turned out like this.' She grimaced. Was she close to tears?

'Oh no, listen,' appealed Wycherley and he put his hand around her neck. 'Things are going to turn out fine. No really, every-thing's going to be OK.' He gave her a little hug. 'Don't worry.'

331

'It's for you,' shouted Ramsey, meaning me. 'It's urgent.'

Over Tessa's shoulder, Bob's eye lit open.

'Coming,' I said and I threw the boss a slow wink of reassurance.

As soon as I touched the plastic curtains they burst open: Murphy. He was back.

'What the fuck is going on?'

But I let the curtains fall between him, me and my phone call. Let Bob explain this one.

'Hello?' I said, holding the receiver at a distance. Oily bits of food.

'Shane.' It was Mellowes. 'We've just heard.'

'What?'

'They've been lifted.'

'Who?'

'Harrington – at his mother's house in Waterloo Lane; they took him away for questioning. Isn't it incredible?'

I tried not to react. 'It was only a matter of time.'

'And your old friend Samuelson. Apparently he was arrested at a guesthouse in Dun Laoghaire.'

'Old friend?' We could be tapped, the fool.

'Yeah, only a short while ago. He'd been sitting in the sun watching the yachts in the bay when along come three men from the Special Branch to take him away. He was brought to Dun Laoghaire and then to Pearse Street. Jesus, Shane, what do you think? They're fairly closing in.'

'How did you hear this?'

'We're up here outside the station in Pearse Street with all the journalists. It's crazy up here. There are all kinds of rumours flying about.'

'Who else was taken in?'

'Some guy called Knowlson who I've never heard of and . . . hold on' – he was checking with Oisin – 'a man called P.J. Ferriter. Ring a bell? A solicitor from Cork – arrested at his Mountjoy Square offices.'

'Never heard of him.'

'Well, you will from now on.' Pips sounded. 'Listen, money's running out here; do you want to call us back?'

'No, I'd better go.' Spread the news. 'Thanks for calling us.'

'Come on up,' said Mellowes.

'I can't. Really, not yet.'

'Well, look, we'll call you if we hear any more.'

'Thanks.' The pips were sounding again. 'Thanks a lot.'

'No problem. And keep firm, man. Chin up.'

'I am firm,' I said and the line died. How dare he suggest otherwise. Very bloody firm. I burst back through the curtains and Murphy was sitting on a beer crate shaking his head.

'And what in the name of Jasus did he want to get confession for?'

'Well, perhaps only the good Jasus can tell us that,' I said, rejoining their mournful company.

Murphy looked at me with a sneer. 'And I can see you're taking your usual constructive attitude.'

'Well, with my constructive attitude, I can give you some news.'

'What news?' he snorted. But Bob looked more hopeful. Tess perked up.

'They've lifted Harrington and the boys.'

'Wow!' They all went quiet.

'For what?' asked Murphy.

'I presume for the general campaign – the letters, the threats and now the disappearance.'

'Who else has been . . . lifted?' asked Wycherley. 'Who are they?'

'Samuelson, Knowlson, I don't know. They sound like a solicitor's old boys' club.'

'The fucking lawyers,' said Murphy, flipping his head. 'Wouldn't you fucking know it!'

'But is there no word?' pleaded Tess. God love her, her face was all eager.

'Still no sign,' I sadly reassured her.

'Well, they'll soon get answers out of those bleeding lawyers, I can tell you.' Murphy was sure of that. 'A wet towel across the chest and a couple of clatters. That'll have them lawyers talking. They do enough of it the rest of the bleeding time.'

'God, they asked us enough questions,' said Tess, staring at the dust.

'I think we've done all we can,' agreed Wycherley sadly.

'Did they give out to you for letting him out?' Murphy asked him frankly.

'A few of them tried to,' he admitted. 'But they know they haven't a leg to stand on.'

333

'You can't stop a guy like that,' said Murphy. 'No way.' Murphy, the rebel expert.

'It's their job to watch him,' sniffed Tess, her head in her hands. 'They were supposed to guard him . . . the bloody fools.'

'Shsh.' Wycherley counselled caution, respect.

'Well, at least – ' said Murphy after a pause. But he thought better of it.

'What?'

'Well, at least, at least, you got your statue done, or the bones of it.'

'Jesus, Murphy!' I scolded, falsely shocked.

'Well, come on,' he insisted. 'I don't think you'd get him to do it again! You know what I mean, I don't think he'd be let do it again.'

'Gentlemen, gentlemen,' said Wycherley and he dropped his head as if he'd a sudden attack of migraine. 'Let's forget about it, please. There's nothing more we can do.'

'But what about the moulds?' said Ramsey, coming forward with beautiful timing. 'Will we not get them out of the way?'

Wycherley looked at him as if he was a persistent child.

'You got it sealed and all,' said Murphy, nodding towards O'Shaughnessy.

'This is certainly a rush job – or at least' – he grinned horribly – 'it was up to now.'

'Look, Ramsey,' said Wycherley, with forced patience. 'You want to move the moulds tonight, we'll move the bloody moulds tonight.'

'There's no reason why not,' he shrugged.

'Fair enough,' he said and he folded his arms and nodded.

'I've got to go home,' said Tess with a pained expression of apology. 'Family and all that.'

'I'm breaking too for a while,' I told him. 'I've been here all day.'

'And where the hell are you off to?' said sensitive Murphy. 'You've no home or family.'

'Down to the river,' I told him through a smile of clenched teeth. 'I've a couple of mortalers on me mind.'

'You'll need to give him air, John! Even now.'

On the quay in front of the Immaculate Heart Church a bunch

334

of frogmen were walking around as if they were treading glue. Flap, flap, flap, their flippers were saying as they stomped around, clumsily getting pipes and bottles together for the descent into the Liffey. I can tell you, there was little else being said. Entering the river was a recognition of the worst and the atmosphere was very quiet and sombre. Just a few clipped instructions from the sergeant and the far-off drone of the helicopter over Merrion Square.

'I hope the water's warm,' I told two of them and they looked at me blankly.

'Mind you.' I shrugged and smiled. 'For some of us it's good to cool off.'

Their faces twisted under tightened masks.

'Go about your business now,' said a gruff garda attaching a snorkle to his neck.

'You're a cast-iron plunger, I'd say. What? At swim, two buckos.'

'John, who the hell is this?' said one froggie to another and he nodded in my direction with such aggression that his blow pipe shook. But John took him aside and whispered in his ear. He's one of us, he was obviously saying, he works for the sculptor.

'Ah.' The frogman understood. And his look was plain: the boy's not well.

'Full fathom five.'

'Yeah . . . listen, step back there, son, because we're going in. Go and have a rest. There's a good fellow.'

There was a splash shortly afterwards.

I'm sure the water settled. Everything does. And the way one would want to after a bracing swim, Wycherley and I were sitting in the back snug of the Windjammer at 9.40 p.m. Pints and short ones were in front of us and the hard part behind. Murphy and he had pushed the moulds into the oven and left reliable Ramsey to brick up the last of the doorway. Ramsey had thrust in the requisite amount of coke and, if he had been as reliable as his part had always deemed him to be (an occasional shudder of 'what if' still cut through this peaceful moment), he had lit the oven at 8.20 p.m.

It was a moment we'd have liked to have been there for but you can't have everything. You can't risk your innocence for the sake of a moment – not any more than we have done. We're more permanent folk than that and the last ones – give us credit – to look a gift sculpture in the mouth.

Murphy was with us earlier on but he's gone home now. In a squad car: the neighbours will talk. Bewildered was he, by the events of the day. But not too put out. He wasn't a big fan of old Corny's anyway and he thought the old man had asked for it by going off like that. Confession, my eye. He was play-acting, just looking for attention. Maybe even half hoping something like that might happen. Cry wolf, said Murphy, more on our side than we could hope. It'd suit the martyr in him. Harsh words. But then Murphy wasn't convinced that O'Shaughnessy wouldn't turn up yet so he felt he could afford to be harsh.

Hopes were still high. We'd been out in the main bar earlier watching the nine o'clock news, with the regulars pretending not to watch us. Sensational treatment, to say the least. Pictures of the church and the quays and the ominous river and groups of gardaí walking up and down, poking at bushes and questioning old ladies, were damningly spliced with extracts from last night's interview.

'They're out to get me,' he told the camera. 'They are testing their nerve . . . I heard them with my own ears! They are getting ready to strike.'

I hadn't seen these pictures yet and God, it was awful. Awful to watch him now that he'd gone. Awful to know that he was right and his words were going to come all too horribly true. There he was warning of future kidnapping from the hitherto safety of his garden and his warnings – or rantings, as they then were – were now cruelly cut with blithe shots of helicopters hovering hopelessly over Lombard Street flats.

Horrible too to see the studio in all of this. Our studio. *Our* studio – up there in hyper-colour! There were pictures of it from one end of St Mark's Lane, pictures of it from the other, pictures of it from inside the flats with two squad cars outside, as if a drugs raid was in progress or someone had split an uncle over a will. Can we take shots of inside the workshop? they had been asking earlier on. No, said Wycherley in one of his better lines of the day, I'm upset enough as it is.

Instead they were granted a *pièce de camera* against the studio gates which featured, of course, for one blurred moment, none other than my good self. Less of me than I thought but at least I was there, shuffling across the yard with as purposeful a working gait as any I faked in that lousy joint until destiny took hold. Little wonder, then, my putative boss didn't see me when I shuffled

336

across, live and more lively this time, to order another. He was concentrating instead on the dramatically intoned words of the reporter, Charlie Bird, and transmission of the Minister's reaction. Public reaction, of course; Wycherley, among others, had been in constant contact with the poor man during the afternoon and each time found himself being more and more energetically consoled.

But as far as the nation was concerned no one was to panic. The Government were continuing to monitor the situation and were keeping all options under control. The Gardaí were making strenuous efforts to have Mr O'Shaughnessy 'recovered'. In an earlier statement, he actually said come forward, as if poor old Corny was, as ever, deliberately withholding himself, or worse still, had already acquired the Lazurus-like qualities Bob and I plan to invest him with.

But come forward, Minister, more like. For there was no sign of him in Charlie Bird's report nor of any other minister or government representative. They were staying in the background and who could blame them. The unbelievable had happened and the Minister was not as yet available for interview. Not the time or the place. Keep our senses. Gardaí making vigorous enquiries and pleased with initial results. No need to give these people the credibility they do not deserve. The Redmondites, that is, not the Government. They'd decided to do what Corny had always told them to do and, taking a leaf out of his now never-to-be-written book, they were lying low to see how 'events developed'. And you could see that that wasn't going down at all well with the Opposition, the media and some of the old codgers who had been wheeled on to the quays.

'Are we down here for real?' sputtered old Vinny Byrne and he was shouldered on by two gardaí as if, this time, it was his long overdue arrest he was re-enacting and not some unfortunate's 'plugging'.

'Or what kind of cod acting is this whole thing?' he asked and the camera could have been on MacNeill in the week before the Week. 'It's absolutely terrible! How can the Government allow this to happen?' He pointed vaguely at the Custom House. 'How? From the very start of this bloody campaign . . . with their letters and everything.' He shook his mottled fist. 'Where are the culprits?'

Not on film, unfortunately. The shots I was most anxious to see – of Harrington, Samuelson and the intriguing others being led handcuffed into Dun Laoghaire Garda Station and thence to Pearse

Street – were unrecorded by the cameras. They'd been picked up too quickly with insufficient notice to the studios and none at all for themselves. Otherwise they might have had their historical recorders out, the way Parnell had the London sketchmen tipped off to catch his haughty arrest at Mallow, as innocent as he was then. More so. At least Harrington and the boys only wrote the notes. Ah well, not to worry. There'll be plenty of time yet. Plenty of time, indeed, and no better men than he and they to do it.

The RTE report concluded, as the BBC's had opened (we switched over briefly), with shots of the house. Yes, that house. Roebuck House. The house from which he set out that Wednesday morn. We were informed, sadly, of the family's plight as they awaited news and we were shown some earlier pictures of Biddy O'Shaughnessy running up that gravelled path where we had the scrap with the Redmondites. How long ago it seems. We were also told, to be fair, of Mr O'Shaughnessy's complete distrust of official protection and of his extraordinary refusal – for a man with such a 'controversial career' – to accept the generous security the State could offer him. (No mention of the fact that they also tapped his phone.) 'He was known as a man of mystery for most of his career,' said the smug-voiced BBC reporter. 'Now his whereabouts are the ultimate mystery. In the Old IRA, one of his specific responsibilities was allegedly' (careful – he's also a lawyer and he may not be gone yet) 'to look after the "disappeared", but tonight, under the Dublin summer sky, bizarre circumstances have taken hold and he appears to be among them.'

'Among whom,' said Wycherley drily, 'the bizarre circumstances or the disappeared?'

'Bastard,' I hissed, meaning the Beeb not Bob. 'They're a bit bloody smug.' Which is not to say we weren't among them ourselves.

'Isn't it a strange thing,' said Wycherley, sitting back with the weird *gravitas* he had assumed when he took us aside that night and told us we were in. 'A strange thing . . . that these people have been forced to try and stop him in his tracks, or appear to stop him, the real man, as if' – he paused with an air of discovery – 'acknowledging that they cannot stop his statue.'

'What?'

'No siree,' he said and he hit the table with his rigid fingers. 'They can't stop his statue! They can stop the man, but they can't stop the sculpture of him. Isn't that something? Isn't that something to be proud of?'

'He'll be very pleased,' I told him.

Back in the studio the ovens burned. And so too did our faces – all our faces – when we sat around and consumed the two bottles of whiskey we had brought back from the Windjammer's hatch. Ramsey, his job done, joined us and so did the returned Tess, now somewhat cheered up by her father's conviction that the men they'd got today were the 'right men' and O'Shaughnessy would soon be free. Old leadhead, as if he knew or cared. Tess, though; it was good to see Tess again. She was cleaned up with a new white blouse and her hair in a ponytail and her eyes still burning, only ember-keen now, after the day's excitement. She'd come back to give us, and herself, moral support. We, the bedraggled crew at the coalface; I, who hadn't eaten a scrap all day. Have you noticed? I couldn't have passed a morsel. Not a chance. Not until tomorrow.

For the moment we were OK, though. We'd gotten over the shock and we were getting through. Against the humming of the oven we consoled each other that there was nothing we could do. We'd just have to hope for the best. Out of our hands now, the big political stuff. But our job had to go on – the Minister said that – and we would cast by the end of the week. God damn it, we were still a bit bloody proud that, despite everything, despite all the threats and stress and uncertainly, *we*, at least, were still on schedule.

'What's that?' said Tess and her big eyes bulged.

'What?'

'A cracking noise . . . I thought I heard – She stopped to listen.

'The oven, I think.'

Wycherley and I looked at each other but we were too tired to care.

'It's probably just the wind now,' said Wycherley and he risked a smile. 'Just the wind and nothing more.'

After the others went home, I stayed the night in the studio. My choice. I wanted to. I was thanked profusely but, in truth, I couldn't have slept anywhere else. No, I didn't feel scared or spooked. Not at all. I didn't even feel guilty. On the contrary I lay there in my sleeping bag on the oratory floor and I listened to

339

the humming of the oven downstairs and the louder it hummed the happier I felt. Sad too, of course. Immensely sad. But happy. Or, more precisely, relieved. Greatly relieved. It was all over, it was almost all over. On the streets outside I could hear the far-off sirens moving about the city. Not for Corny, no, but for life going on regardless.

Thursday, 17 July: I woke at eight-thirty, vivid, still vigilant, and went for breakfast. I was starving. But I'd slept soundly on the whiskey and the achieved fatigue and I was up like a shot. Not a trace of a head and the heart still beating strongly. Wish I could say the same for our friend. I threw him in some coke before I left and got a look at the three moulds standing there in the burning red embers. Bone white, dead white, sepulchral white in the intense orange cavern. God Almighty. A child's vision of hell. Torture condensed and designed to its maximum. For ever and ever. But in the real world, dear God and devil, nothing lasts for ever. And yet do I see his tail or foot in the flames? Visions, ladies, visions. Seductive kinetic effects can be traced in the luminous breathing embers. No smells, though. Only the sweet whiff of the coke's escaped gases. I'll miss him, the old bastard, I'll miss him.

On the way up to the café, I passed more gardaí on their way to the riverfront. They'd been down there since early morning and apparently at the crack of dawn they were back in the water. Ah, the healthy life. There were a lot of forensic people too coming into the area, checking out suspicious skidmarks and requestioning people who thought they might have seen someone like him, but they couldn't be sure. Put me on the news, mister. Tess was going to take them back over the route yet again, but, most crucially, Ramsey and Wycherley, whom I'd left back in the studio (the latter looking pale and wan after three hours' sleep) were to prepare to receive some of the detective investigation squad in the workshop. They wanted to make an examination of the place. ('If you don't mind. It has to be done.') They didn't mind but Bob was shaky. The cops had been all over the gaff yesterday and we were used to it but still it's not a nice prospect to have a bunch of hawk-eyed police in your house when you've a patriot cooking in the corner.

Rashers, sausages and a runny egg – I had a delicious breakfast and I read the papers. Well, I'm not even going to give you the front pages. God above me, they were too much. The immensity of what I'd done was coming home to me. It seemed like the whole country was up in arms. The Taoiseach was urged to return from holidays abroad. The Minister was being called upon to explain how the greatest living Irish rebel could publicly claim he was about to be got at and then the Government allow it to happen in broad daylight in the middle of the city.

Fianna Fáil wanted the Dáil recalled to debate the matter. The 1916–1921 Club vowed to emulate O'Shaughnessy and never again attend a state commemoration ceremony unless something was done immediately to recover this 'unfortunate friend of ours and of the whole nation'. The gardaí were asked why, if they had the information to apprehend some of these 'notional Redmondites', they waited until Mr O'Shaughnessy went missing to do so. 'Were these even the right men?' asked one high-pitched editorial, jumping freely into *sub judice* but voicing what many were saying. 'Maybe now Mr O'Shaughnessy's claims about M.I.5 will be seriously listened to,' was the suggestion of Lorcan Walshe, Fianna Fáil backbencher, and he announced that, along with other TDs, he was launching straight away a campaign to have the Anglo-Irish Agreement suspended until a government investigation be carried out into the activities of British intelligence in this country – North and South. And until Mr O'Shaughnessy is freed, he said, giving Corny an anti-collaborationist role he might have appreciated.

Even Provisional Sinn Fein, hitherto seeing the whole thing as a ludicrous piece of small-town posturing, a satisfyingly embarrassing spectacle for the Free State Government as well as a pathetic example of the West Briton, Empire-loving sentiment still prevalent in the South, now castigated the 'collaborationist authorities' for allowing one of the country's foremost Republicans (and one of 'our' foremost lawyers) to be snatched from a Dublin street on his way to church. 'The long-suffering nationalist people of the Six Counties are used to such goon-squad activities by British intelligence and their lackeys. Now perhaps the people of the South will wake up to what is being done to them. Vol. O'Shaughnessy has called attention repeatedly to the dirty tricks of the British and for this he seems to have paid a price. If the Free State authorities are not prepared to defend the people of Ireland, and those who fought on the people's behalf, they should leave the job to those who can.' It is just as well perhaps, that old Samuelson and the boys were in the safety of custody rather than abroad on the Free State streets.

Whiter still was Wycherley when the detectives came to check out the workshop. They asked a lot of questions but nothing that seemed to cause them, or Bob, any suspicion. They were friendly enough and, like the Minister, sympathised with Wycherley's predicament and the attendant publicity it had caused. It should soon be over, they told him confidently. As might be expected, they expressed great interest in the whole casting process, which was something of which they knew little. Wycherley, however, was learning fast.

He offered to show them the inside of the oven but said that to do so would involve shutting it off for a while, so they weren't to tell the Minister or anyone else that that had been done because the Government were anxious to have the cast completed as quickly as possible. Oh no, in that case, don't, said the detective, we don't want that kind of trouble gone to.

'Sure an oven is an oven,' they said, chewing their lips. 'It's enough to see what goes inside it.'

'True enough,' said Wycherley and he was recovering his colour.

One matter he did sweat for, however, and it was one he'd sweat for again, was the tortuous question of whether he was right to abide by Mr O'Shaughnessy's strict instructions not to follow him or try to tip off the police as to where he was going. Some gardaí, and the odd journalist, tried in the early days of the case to accuse Wycherley of negligence and blame him for the disappearance of his subject but, in the end, the prevailing opinion was that O'Shaughnessy was 'an impossible character'. He was as irrationally suspicious of the police as he appeared to be about British agents and their associates, and he was an impossible man to disobey or argue with. In Wycherley's favour it had also been reasonable to assume that once O'Shaughnessy was outside the studio the guards would have seen him. It was also reasonable to assume that had O'Shaughnessy spotted Wycherley trying to follow him or alert the police to his departure, O'Shaughnessy's reaction would be so severe as to put in jeopardy any co-operation O'Shaughnessy might have offered in regard to his statue. At least that's what Wycherley said and everyone believed it. Like him, how were they to believe all that stuff about spies in the garden waiting to get him? He didn't. And neither did anyone else. And that's half the point: the whole country had egg on its face.

And speaking of yoke on the dewlap, where was Hurley in all of this, I hear you ask. Well, we were asking the same. Officially, he was still directing the operation from Pearse Street Station and there was no necessity for him to go running about like so many other senior officers were. However, it was becoming quickly apparent that Detective Sergeant Hurley was not playing the central role in the investigation that he played yesterday, that he was, in fact, receiving the co-operation of his overseeing officers, only he was being not so much helped out as baled out, you might say, or 'gradually disengaged'. There was no need for us to go directly to Detective Hurley, Sergeant Leahy told us, we could go to Superintendents Mulready or King or to Leahy himself.

'Ah, and how is Detective Hurley?' asked Tess, as if she'd just heard the name of a long-disappeared uncle.

'He's fine,' said a young garda behind the sergeant, and vague expressions of painful dismay appeared on the faces of him and a younger colleague.

'Did he ever find his pipe?'

'No,' said the young garda, staring at her. 'He never found . . . his pipe.'

They found Mr O'Shaughnessy's clothes, though. At eleven-thirty the news came through. His suit had been found near the riverbed, a hundred yards down from the church, which was quite far away, and begged all sorts of new questions. Encouraging as the discovery was in terms of breaking the mystery, it was extremely disheartening in human terms. It meant that O'Shaughnessy very likely was kidnapped. Or worse. There was no question now that he was sitting in a house somewhere impishly sipping a cup of tea, and laughing at the world to prove a point. No siree, this was his suit with his belongings in the pockets. (No inventory was as yet available. Having kept to my promise I'd have been curious to find out.) Unless of course, the man of fathomless cunning did a John Stonehouse or a Reginald Perrin on it and dumped his clothes to fake a fateful exit. And I'm afraid to say, and it really is typical of people's minds and their insistence on finding conspiracies, that some people were imputing such an appalling and elaborate ruse to Mr O'Shaughnessy. Just like his vanity, they said, to find out if people really cared for him, and what they really thought of him when he didn't show up.

It'd be like he was getting a look-in at his own funeral. But worse than this was the suggestion of quite a few other people, many of them people whose opinion I would respect, that, well, maybe, the whole thing did become too much for him. Man of ninety, watching his ideals and principles mocked and threatened, watching the commemoration of his reputation being cruelly put at stake, listening to the taunts and threats of people singing in his garden – maybe it really did get to him. Maybe he felt enough was enough and he didn't deserve the indignity of it any longer. Maybe – and here the craftiness comes in – he felt that only by the ultimate act of self-sacrifice could he ensure that his statue was erected, could he embolden the Government to erect the bronze image of a man whose lonely exit they would have felt in some way responsible for. And it was clear from some of O'Shaughnessy's earlier comments on the campaign that his image, or his statue, had now become more important to him than his transitory and declining body. Well, maybe.

The sub-aqua team were told to widen their search and the media – that battery of bedraggled cameramen and notebooks collected on the quayside since early morning – were told to keep back and show some sensitivity. This from a garda sergeant in a rubber dinghy who had earlier flung the great man's trousers unceremoniously on to the quayside and enquired of his colleague if he had a hat. (I knew those boys were OK to joke with.) Mind you, I think that even the invincibles, Mellowes and Oisin, were surprised by my mirth when they nervously joined me on the quayside to observe the search. So disturbed were they that they departed quite early, well before waiting to see whether the shoes turned up. Not that they would have expected shoes. They didn't make any excuses either. They candidly admitted that they were scared stiff. Having been in his garden they felt they were in danger of being dreadfully compromised. If identified by the men in custody it could cause them serious trouble and they would have had a lot of explaining to do. I told them they were losing their bottle and they should be glad of their involvement. I had noticed their frightened attitude yesterday and I didn't like it. What were they – mice or men or play-actors? If that was their attitude, how was I to feel? They couldn't answer that. Did they want to put the papers back? Undo the courage they summoned up to get the things in the first place? The more guilty you act over something you didn't do, the more likely they'll get you for something you did, I told them and they thought about that for a while. Chin up, I told Mellowes with a smile of fine irony, you're either able for this game or you're not. Now go on, out of that. I might see you later in Tobin's. If not, send along the Goat and Greycoat, they're men

344

who are crazy enough to sail close to the wind and laugh about it afterwards.

And that was them off my back for a while. Damn frauds. Posturing invincibles and fake soldiers. I'm finished with them. Yes, with them too I'm finished. Finished with them all. Paper Collinses and modern emulators and men who ape the fables of others. I want to live from now on. Live for the day and the future. Live for the moment, which is why, when I went back to the studio, I called someone who I wouldn't mind having on my back, or hers, for a while. Ariel. For it is she! And today's my day to call her. But when she finally answered she was whingeing about her thirty-five-year-old boyfriend in New York, or wherever, and 'it' not being such a good idea. And perhaps we shouldn't have 'done' what we 'did' the other evening and . . . so she was losing her bottle as well. Copping out.

'Ariel,' I told her.

'What?'

'You shouldn't cry over spilt milk.'

Click. That was enough for her to put the phone down.

'Watch your foot, Tess. Tess – watch your foot!'

The mould was out of the oven and standing slantways on Murphy's tracks. Baked a yellow brown, it was very cracked and braces had to be applied as reinforcements. With the existing channels and handles, they gave the thing a spiky appearance like the leg of a giant crayfish or a rocket in a children's playground. Tess and I had opposite ends of the tongs and were about to pour in our eighth bucket of molten metal.

'Right. Come, on, come on!'

Through great heat and sulphurous smoke, Wycherley was shouting instructions. Behind us, the furnace was humming furiously.

'Over, over, over.'

We brought the cup over the opening of the mould where the head was supposed to be. Will be, was. Who cares, we were getting there.

'Now, tip, tip . . . tip, for Christ's sake!'

We tipped the bucket and out poured the fluorescent orange metal, coagulant and viscous. Plop, plop, fallop. It fell into the channel's opening and down the channel. Down, baby, down.

'Right, up – up. Up!' shouted Wycherley, his gas mask around his neck. He stepped forward with large iron pinchers and shook the mould to get the metal down.

Stiff-fingered, we twisted the tongs until the bucket was practically upended, draining the dregs of the metal. The last bulbous bits of black and orange dropped out reluctantly, as if unwilling to join the process, even at this late stage.

'Right, that's it! Come back. Come on – come back!'

We put down the tongs and bucket and Wycherley upped his mask and went in to shake the mould again. The entrances to the channels at the top and sides were messed with grey metal. Unreal looking: like drying mud or spattered pâté with smoking holes that threatened to vomit back all they had taken, as if this mould (or all moulds), with its cracks and braces, really did have something that was trying to get out. Ah reality, I lose my – But the metal was in to stay and that was the main thing. When the first bucket flowed, slowly but freely, down the main channel where his head was, we knew we were in business. Bob gave me a nervous smile from beneath his gas mask and I shut my eyes in return. Chin up.

The only difficulty was on the left arm, where the twist meant that the metal had no momentum and would get stuck. Welding and metal surgery would yet be needed, of course, but so much metal had gone in that we were confident that no bone fragments would be sticking out and, if they were, they would be so charred and broken as to be unrecognisable for what they were. Last night the heat in the oven had been dramatically increased, probably to the highest it's ever been. All vestiges of the man were to be absolutely carbonised. No traces, or at least no more than there would always be. Perhaps I'm being fanciful but at one stage, as I got closer to Tess in the sleeping bag, I could have sworn I heard a loud crack in the workshop below. My goodness, his skull exploding? A warning. Like Dylan Thomas's father in the crematorium. Or maybe it was just a spark, an errant spark on the brick? No matter. I pulled my bag closer to Tessa's bag and fell asleep with only the sound of our zips snagging. Cosy. Yes, there was a fire escape outside.

The agreement was that we would break the mould later that afternoon, at three, but when Tess got conveniently called away at around two, that agreement went under the hammer and Bob and I attacked the plaster an hour early. We had to see the metal before she did and make sure the basic cast was OK. We couldn't have any bits that would give the horrific game away and Bob

346

pulled up his cutters and welding rod so he could immediately get to work on any if there were.

The baked quality of the plaster assisted our haste and whole chunks of the stuff fell away with gleeful ease, giving off exciting spumes of steam and dust. The plaster was still warm, luxuriously, horribly warm, and the metal inside would still be hot, very hot, hot enough to burn our fingers. But it was too late for that now. Chewing his nether lip, Tess-style, Wycherley had his chisel out and was working into the head. Head first and the rest will follow. The head was where the game lay. Secure that and we're halfway there. He hit the chisel with a wallop and a wedge the size of an iceberg fell to the floor. A bit rough? I looked at him but I said nothing. His hands were shaking, he was already losing patience. Big lumps came off the side of the neck. He grunted and hacked and the lumps kept coming. How far in would he go? He was getting down to slices. The chisel skidded. Another slice and then – clink! – he hit metal. He smiled helplessly. It was a thin neck. But it would be. As thin as it should be. We had been relying on a wider neck to hold the fragments of what had fallen but maybe it was even better and the intense heat had carbonised anything that fell.

Bob's sweaty twitching fingers continued their explorative taps. Chink! Chink! Good, he kept hitting something solid and it was bronze. Solid bronze. Hard to tell what shape it was – a lopsided egg, or a distorted munchhead, smaller than we expected – but whatever it was, it was bronze. Bronze, bloody bronze!

Like a rescue worker in an earthquake, Wycherley dropped his chisel and fingered feverishly at what would have been the plaster-covered face. Vein-popping hands broke off dusty chunks and clawed for features. Feverish, desperate. He surprised me. Show me your face – where is your face? He picked up the sweat-stained chisel and tapped, gouged at the huge eye holes filled with . . . plaster? No. Below the plaster was bronze, unyielding but malleable bronze, thank God. Air-pocket sockets: that would be an effect too post-realist for realism. Morbid literalism, you could say. No, thank God. My heart fell back and Bob's hands resumed their faith healer's massage, their graveside routine of the policeman's widow, the clawing feel for human features. And the features were coming, they were coming all right, and they looked . . . God, I don't know what they looked like. Blunted, beaten, distorted, a shut mouth, podded eyes, plucked, in need of

347

filing . . . God, it looked horrible. In need of lots of filing. Lots. Horrible. I could hardly –

'But it looks wonderful!' said Tess behind us. She was back.

'Doesn't it? The dimensions are exactly what we wanted.'

'Get me a bucket of water,' growled Wycherley.

'At least something's working out,' she said excitedly looking for the pail.

His cheekbones, however: they had come out. High, sharp. They'd never gone away. Be with us for some time, I'd say. Long time. But when I thought of the other features now gone, gone for ever, the glassy eyes, the red rims, the diaphanous ears, the mottled mouth, I felt desperate, awful. I felt a sadness so overwhelming I had to leave the workshop.

Chapter 13

Commemoration

From Pearse Street Station, the story was that the Redmondites, as they had become known, were not behaving in a very co-operative fashion. Indeed they were taking their detention very badly. The Parnellite coolness we might have expected of them from their bold declarations in the Pink Elephant and the Belvedere Hotel, not to mention their firm and measured public statement, was sadly not to be. Mr Harrington protested loudly his innocence and said he would sue the authorities for wrongful arrest and the damage done to his reputation as a member of the Bar.

'It's outrageous,' he was shouting to all who would listen. 'When was the last time a member of the Bar was arrested in this fashion?'

To which the answer was O'Shaughnessy, believe it or not. Arrested in 1942 on possession of illegal weapons. And wrongfully acquitted, I – and only I – might add. Unfortunately, however, the learned acquitted was not now in a position to give his accused kidnapper the sort of advice the latter might have profited from. Neither, it seemed, was the beleaguered Mr Samuelson receiving any profitable advice from the one lawyer he was incarcerated with, for apparently the plum-voiced, bouffant-haired Parnellite was denouncing, with animation, the conspiracy behind his arrest, the Machiavellian anti-constitutional nationalist forces at work to do down the Parnellites for once and for all by making them appear responsible for the disappearance of the country's most persistent Oral Republican. Poor Mr Samuelson. The coil of his whole life's experience of frustration had come loose, and God love him, his paranoia now knew no bounds.

349

'They are killing all sorts of birds with the one stone,' he shouted from his police cell, but the comparative silence of Mr Harrington bore testament to the fact that not even his younger colleague was prepared to stop him.

The other legal gentleman, P.J. Ferriter, a hitherto unknown solicitor from Cork, behaved in a manner no less worldly, claiming in a low, sad monotone that once again the constitutionalists had been crushed between the forces of Irish terror and British conspiracy. Or was it the other way round? I can't exactly be sure because I was relying on Sergeants Purcell and McDowell for untutored accounts of the men's claims as soon as they were decently uttered, it being of crucial importance that I be ready to come to the defence of my comrades and myself, as soon as any attempt was made to drag us into the picture. Cutely though, Harrington was holding his tongue. As I thought he might. Otherwise, I had the absolute truth primed and ready to go off. Nothing less. We agreed on that. Fireworks it would have to be. If need be.

Of course the difficult behaviour of the Redmondites could, from another perspective, assist their case, for there was no doubt that many people now believed – gardaí and politicians among them – that the real responsibility for O'Shaughnessy's disappearance lay beyond this bunch of eccentrics in their Pearse Street cells, all of whom had good alibis for being otherwise engaged when the abduction took place, if abduction it was.

Who was really behind this strange collection of animated gentlemen? Or, more inevitably, who had led them to this? Who did the actual taking of O'Shaughnessy and where is his person being held? ('Person' took care of whether he was alive or not.) What did they really want apart from this idea of a statue? These were the questions being asked up and down the land and the failure to gain any answers from the men in Pearse Street Station increased the pressure on the Government to take up the initiative in other areas. There were demands that the Government should 'act on what it knows', it being assumed, as always, that the Government knew more than it was letting on. Ah yes, it was a field day for the conspiracy theorists and armchair detectives. None of the usual suspects should be omitted, they cried. A full-scale man-hunt should be launched, as well as a full-depth inquiry. Full fathom five.

That the search should be widened to new areas was a constant

350

refrain, which struck me as a bit unreasonable for already the gardaí had been lighting out for the oddest of places. Pictures of them appeared, walking with difficulty, up and down sand dunes on Dollymount Strand and furiously chopping shrubbery around the cavernous woods of the Glen of Imaal – both, incidentally, old stomping grounds of Vol. O'Shaughnessy. Did they think he might have gone back to check these out as well? Or did they credit his captors with the irony of taking him where he had taken so many?

The most earnest of conspiracy theories, however, were focused on the political level and here events were moving with extraordinary swiftness and drama. Indeed, for my liking, the political dimension had gone wonderfully, deliciously, out of control. Why wouldn't it? Here was a man, or rather *not here* was a man, who had claimed on national TV the night before his disappearance that the British intelligence services were out to get him. And now he was gone. Without a trace. In the most suspicious circumstances. After a lifetime of suffering plausibly recounted British harassment. Could you blame people for getting excited? And in this the summer of revelations about dirty tricks in Northern Ireland and Clockwork Orange – a plot to de-stabilise the British Government by its own secret service – and TV pictures of O'Shaughnessy's garden where contemptuous intruders had felt confident enough to sing. Sing!

In Dublin, the Dáil was in recess and the clamour was growing for its recall. The 1916–21 Club mounted a picket outside an empty Leinster House which, given its historic rejection of the usual inhabitants' legitimacy as a legislature, I thought was entirely appropriate. The *Herald* typically seized upon the details of some unseemly row that ensued between gardaí and the protestors at the gates over the lack of wheelchair facilities. Whether the Dáil was recalled or not hardly mattered for the airwaves and newsprint were a free-for-all of accusation and counter-accusation. All sorts of politically thrown dirt was being flung about. The Minister was being called up to resign by Fianna Fáil backbenchers but incredibly the Labour Party (playing the green card) said the Minister shouldn't be allowed to resign until Mr O'Shaughnessy's safety was ensured. Sinn Fein protesters mounted their own picket outside the Garden of Remembrance and claimed that the Government had blood on its hands.

Strong stuff. But the Government weren't taking it all standing

351

up, as Corny might say. Asked to explain how O'Shaughnessy was allowed to go out on the quays unattended or why there was no follow up to O'Shaughnessy's claims about the men in his garden, the Minister for Justice described robustly, and in some detail, just how completely averse Mr O'Shaughnessy was to all protection and bodyguards and monitoring of any sort, and revealed the subterfuge the gardaí had to go to to try and keep watch on him from a distance. (So ludicrous and paradoxical had the recriminating atmosphere become that the Workers' Party seized on this 'subterfuge' as damning evidence of the Government's sinister attitude to O'Shaughnessy whom they clearly regarded as nothing more than a subversive conspirator!) Of course, I could have piped up and revealed how slack that 'monitoring' actually was but my impish desire to do so had more to do with the tantalising possibilities offered by the Minister's other big refutation – which was that, when the gardaí had suggested coming into this garden on Friday to check the allegations referred to, O'Shaughnessy refused to allow them to do so, while he wasn't there. And even now his daughter was reluctant to allow the gardaí to come in until her father had returned to give permission. Why? Why the protectiveness, the lack of trust?

Let's face it, a lot of questions were now being asked about O'Shaughnessy's character. About what kind of person he was. Why was he so conspiratorial? What kind of life did he lead – did he have enemies we never knew about, people whom he had fallen foul of but whom we cannot find? What exactly did he mean in that interview? Was there a cry for help in there or even, God forbid, a coded farewell, a nodded goodbye? Like, was he . . . was he really – yes, it was still being asked – was he really missing? Did he, maybe . . . want to disappear? Take off down the pier and escape from it all – who knows? Would we ever find out? (Mellowes and a coalshed would eventually provide many of the answers.)

That night, as Biddy O'Shaughnessy made an emotional appeal on television for the captors of her father to please, please in the name of basic humanitarianism, in the name of our common bonds, release him, a number of things were, to use Detective Sergeant Hurley's phrase, turning up. The first were his shoes, pulled from the mud of the river bank at approximately 9.15 p.m., amidst a whole pile of other rubbish that included car registration plates, a crate of well-cooled beer, six thousand 'God Says No to Divorce' leaflets in a sealed carton and yet another upended pram, empty of its grown or abandoned infant. The shoes were his all right. Size 8 black Winstanleys, scuffed a little but only recently resoled and looking like they were hurriedly unlaced. Their discovery tended to confirm the public's darkest fears and people began to settle on abduction and worse. At the station, only money turned up in his pockets and an 'ould key ring with a horse's head on it'. Present from a prisoner, sniffed Biddy; souvenir of the 'disturbances', though which 'disturbances' she didn't say.

Brighter news from Clonskeagh, however. The Proclamation turned up. It was in good condition, removed from its glass frame and rolled up inside the attic ceiling of No. 85 Clonskeagh Road, birthplace of Isaac Butt. The Redmondites were in trouble. Also found on the premises, stuffed in a coalshed, no less, and wrapped in a Dunne's Stores bag, was a Royal .32 Carbon Special typewriter, matching exactly the typeface used in the threatening letters and the Statement of Revelation. The gardaí also removed from the premises for further examination the proofs of a silhouette of C.S. Parnell for an as yet unissued publicity flyer, along with the original plates of an Irish Volunteers World War I recruiting poster depicting an unfortunate village in ravaged Belgium you could have mistaken for something from peacetime Connaught, if it wasn't for the less than benign air of the Paul Henryesque smoke bubbling up from the broken cottages.

But the greatest turn-up of the evening occurred back on the quayside a short time later. The gardaí sub-aqua team shouted muffled instructions to the men on the shore: a body was going to be pulled from the river. There was great excitement and the guards had practically to fight with journalists to keep them, and the other ragbag of curious gawkers, back from the edge. Two anxious onlookers actually fell into the river in the rush to get behind police lines to witness the scene. To spare (deny?) the assembled mob the spectacle of Ireland's greatest living patriot being pulled feet first from the River Liffey in his vest and longjohns, a plastic screen was erected and some netting and more plastic was prepared for draping around the drenched corpse once it broke the surface. However, once it did, with a laborious splash and then an awful creaking noise, it was quite apparent that the body was not that of Mr O'Shaughnessy at all but of a large man with a badly decomposed stomach and an unsightly collection of tattoos. His relatives were surprised to identify him, on being quietly informed, for they had thought him working as a happy London tube driver these past four months, and it was plain to see that, in a different sort of way, the children on the quayside were almost as disappointed.

In the air, meanwhile, somewhere above Greece, the Taoiseach was also being quietly informed. He had cut short his summer holidays in Cyprus and the government jet had gone out to bring him back. By phone and by fax, the front pages plopping out of his machine almost as quickly as they appeared on the news stands, he was being kept up to date on the bizarre, unprecedented, even grotesque saga that was unfolding at home. He was mindful, no doubt, that even at that very moment, in the VIP section of the arrivals lounge of Dublin Airport, bemused workers were wearily lining up chairs and rigging for what was expected to be one of the most bitter, testing press conferences of his political career.

Wobbling over Paris, some good news came with the third Bacardi. The gardaí had 'raided' Isaac Butt's house in Clonskeagh [sic] and found there the 1916 Proclamation and the typewriter on which the anti-O'Shaughnessy threats were allegedly written. Four men being held in Pearse Street Station – the four men in custody since Wednesday – were about to be charged under the Offences Against the State Act, with the theft of state property and the unlawful intimidation of persons carrying out work for the Government (one was to be charged with being ringleader of an unlawful organisation known as the Anti-Violent Nationalist Society).

The Taoiseach shook his woolly head at the references to John Redmond and Isaac Butt. The Taoiseach was a historian, a politician, a man with a past: he thought he understood the effects of history on his fellow countrymen, but when he looked out at the marshmallow land of luminous white clouds below him he wondered if he had understood anything about it at all. Maybe it wasn't the effects of history but history *itself*; the very thing, the very story that had marked his benighted land and its entranced, trapped and remembering occupants. At least, later on, at the press conference when he dramatically and perhaps unwisely announced that they'd got their man, he was a lot closer to the mark than he ever could have known.

Saturday, 26 July: Sunny Saturday, sunny Saturday. At 2 p.m., Mr O'Shaughnessy, boxed at last, was taken by Peugeot truck to St Stephen's Green, escorted by Murphy and three surly men from the Office of Public Works. When Tess and I arrived on foot, Murphy had had a row with the men from the OPW, who

354

insisted on a bit of demarcation over a hammer, and losing the toss, proceeded to slip into a bit of a go-slow which involved, amongst other things that annoyed Murphy, using the lowest speed on their battery-operated turnscrews. But time waits for no man and by forklift and ball and tackle, O'Shaughnessy was lowered on to his plinth and temporary scaffolding was erected around the marble base and statue. The base was screwed down with heavy iron rivets and spot-welded with bolts of solid bronze.

It was an uncanny likeness. Even the OPW people commented on it. Even, God forbid, the guards commented on it when they strolled over from doing boring picket duty outside the Departments of Justice and Foreign Affairs.

'Cornelius O'Shaughnessy – Patriot and Republican', read the inscription in raised bronze letters. 'Selflessly he fought for his country's freedom and no sacrifice was too great a sacrifice. Erected in 1986 to commemorate the ninetieth birthday of Mr O'Shaughnessy and the Seventieth Anniversary of the 1916 Rising.'

The unveiling took place two weeks later on another sunny if overcast Saturday. Quite a large crowd gathered behind the makeshift crash barriers and the police took up unobtrusive positions beneath the trees. Curiosity, sympathy and a lot of lock-jaw-determined loyalty had brought Corny a bigger reception than he might have expected. The Cabinet were all there as were the Opposition, despite their threats to stay away as a protest against – well, against O'Shaughnessy's staying away. But they relented, if he didn't, and took their sober place alongside friends, ex-convicts, academics, corpulent clerics, European ambassadors (not the British, who was advised for his own safety to stay away) and a haggle of other political types including Sinn Fein representatives who couldn't be kept away and threatened their own Republican ceremony later on.

Friends and relatives of O'Shaughnessy stood near the front, their faces torn between muted expressions of pride, sadness and utter bewilderment. The past three weeks had been a severe trial and it was showing. Despite protestations from other more optimistic relatives, Biddy dressed completely in black and hid her worn face in a veil. She would continue to wear black, she said, and only black until her father returned. Vanessa, sniffing beside her, didn't wear black. A pity, for she would have looked quite interesting in black lace and stockings with her Rossetti curls tied back and her soft hands folded over his 'flying column'

355

rosary beads carved from the oak of captured rifle butts, but I was day-dreaming . . . and day-dreaming too were those perennial men in black beside her: tottered members of the 1916–21 Club – and members of 'the Committee' – leaning on sticks or each other, their medals jangling, their grey faces shaking with the anger and sadness of eight hundred years and three confused weeks. I couldn't put names to them, nor did I care to, nor did it matter to me what they did or didn't do with Michael Collins any more. Vinny Byrne, though, he was there, grinning without teeth and telling everyone to look on the bright side. He'd come to collect his bounty (he'd told Corny he'd be the last Squad member to live) and his shoes fairly tapped with the delight. So too did the shoes of the invincibles, happy that I had finally secured a deal with Harrington that would keep his mouth shut and us out of the picture. Oisin was particularly relieved. He had enough on his plate already and stood away from Mellowes with some of his coalshed weeds, who made a colourful and near Eastern picture in the sequined shirts and scarves they had begun to abandon their forties suits for.

No one was standing on protocol today; not for O'Shaughnessy, that most unstuffy 'man of the people'. Behind the politicians and priests, the crowd took on a motley democratic appearance with shoppers next to painters and Mohawks next to civil servants from the Department of the Taoiseach keeping well out of harm's way. Here and there among the mumbling heads, I could see artisans and artists young and old, academicians from the Royal Hibernian and all of the Apollo crew, Robbie Thunder and Jimmy Cinders, along for the free drink afterwards, and other hip and haggard *habitués* of Grogan's, Tobin's and the Bailey for whom the walk was not too far. The Foetus hovered at the back licking his froggy lips and Delia Stewart showed up in black leotard and fake fur coat, which was thoughtful of her. She was still a little down but her sculptor boyfriend was happy now that their house was free: Ariel had gone back to America. Even Tessa's father put in an appearance for those ten or fifteen minutes that her mother wasn't there ('Word in your ear – never marry,' he told me), as did Murphy's wife Jacinta and Ramsey's friends, Joseph Pembroke and Peter 'Bahrain' Moriarty, and other bearded men from Ballsbridge, who noisily locked their big black bikes to the crash barriers at the start of the ceremony and mingled near the journalists and the small army band (no colour party, no full military honours – family's orders).

The Taoiseach cleared his throat – to let people know he was going to say a few words. He never looked more solemn, or determined, and some people even thought his hair had become a little whiter. The last few weeks had taken their toll, and not even the Government's apology or the resignation of the Minister of State had been enough to satisfy his critics who were still calling for a full inquiry and for the matter to be raised at the highest level with the British Government.

The Taoiseach spoke for some time about the heroic sacrifice of 1916 and of its symbolic significance in Irish history, as well as its positive implications for other colonial struggles throughout the world. It was clear he was playing for the green card; he even criticised those misguided Irishmen of the time who thought they could achieve their country's freedom abroad – a clear swipe at the Redmondites. He then spoke about Cornelius O'Shaughnessy and his role in the Rising and he told an amusing story about Old Con (he surely meant Young Con) walking around Boland's Mills with flour on his back, so his comrades would see him at night and he wouldn't get lost. The story didn't go down that well, and without further ado, he said he would say some more about Mr O'Shaughnessy in a few minutes but that he wanted to introduce the guest of honour, Ms O'Shaughnessy, to unveil the statue.

Everyone waited. With a shaking hand, Biddy pulled the cord and the white sheet fell from the blackened bronze. 'Oohs' and 'Aahs' and cries of admiration reverberated through the crowd: 'magnificent', 'beautiful', 'noble', 'so lifelike', 'really catches him', were the epithets that echoed from the gathering as they shuffled and stood on tippy-toes to get a better look. I have to say now that this was Wycherley's greatest moment. Though the morning's papers praised him in the most glowing terms as an outstanding neo-realist, as a brave and imaginative artist who didn't go for the cosmetically dressed-up public statuary his contract might have obliged, but who boldly sculpted a craggy and aged figure, stooped, wrinkled and truly heroic (though the papers, the critics, his fellow artists and academicians were forced to eat their words in the days and weeks following), it was yet this moment that truly made him and freed him as an artist and a human being. I hugged him. Tess kissed him. The Taoiseach smiled at him and clapped along with everyone else. Good old Bob, I could see he was clearly touched. Why, Jasus, I think there was even an ould tear or two in there.

The band struck up 'The Bold Fenian Men'. It was very moving. I may be changing but I hadn't changed that much. It was still a fine air that could put a lump in the throat when you heard people hum it with their heads held high. The National Anthem followed and here the lumps were broken. Many sang along loudly and lustily but many others couldn't take it and broke down terribly. Biddy was doubled over and had to be comforted by the relatives and Vanessa kept wiping her reddened cheeks as she sang out the choruses. Some of the 1916–21 Club didn't appear too impressed by this unseemly display of emotion during the National Anthem and shook their medals stiffly. Hard men. Vinny Byrne looked like he had a fly in his ear.

Neither were they impressed with the Taoiseach's concluding 'few words'. Taking on and off his glasses, the Taoiseach praised the bravery of the sculptor, and his assistants, and of the Government in seeing the project through. He agreed with the obvious admiration for the statue and believed – he gestured to the bent and grimacing figure – that it captured the agony and indomitable spirit of Irish Republicanism: 'that spirit that was the spirit of Old Con O'Shaughnessy'. We have all come through a terrible saga, he said, and let us hope that it will have its resolution some day soon. After describing the famous heroic and difficult aspects of Mr O'Shaughnessy's career – no sacrifice was too great a sacrifice, he said, reading the inscription – the Taoiseach took off his glasses and vowed that, in the same spirit, the Government would not rest until a satisfactory outcome to the matter of Mr O'Shaughnessy's disappearance had been achieved.

'We will continue to search high and low and pursue all channels of enquiry,' he stressed, in different figures of speech, but his words sounded somewhat hollow and defeatist and it was a tribute to the artistic sensibilities of the audience that more than one person was heard to remark on the contrast between the shabby ineffectual figure of the Taoiseach and the old but bold figure standing in craggy bronze above him.

Six months later, the trial of the 'Redmondite Four' took place under heavy security in the Four Courts and they were sentenced to two years' imprisonment for the issuing of threatening letters, the theft of a state document, breaking and entry and an assortment of other charges. All the defendants pleaded guilty to the charges and their co-operation with the police, considerably improved since their outraged reaction when first arrested, was taken into account by the court. Another interesting fact to emerge was that they knew we were going ahead with O'Shaughnessy, because they could hear our conversation before we went in for dinner with him. They were in Butt's house across the road. That open window; I remember it struck me as odd at the time.

At the trial, they were skilfully defended by Mr Hartigan with his customary style of the halting tongue and the ping-pong ball balanced on his nose. Eloquent speeches were made by the defendants, speeches that drew sympathetic appreciation from many people not connected to the trial. A feeling had grown up that these men, however misguided their principles, were at least committed to them and brave enough to risk their necks in trying to rectify what they, and many others, saw as the wrongs and imbalances of Irish history.

The Government's inability to link the Four directly to the disappearance of O'Shaughnessy strengthened public sympathy for them and contributed to the idea that they were hapless romantics whose campaign provided the unwitting cover for 'others' to come in and capture O'Shaughnessy for their own foul ends (whether these 'others' were British agents, criminal elements or old O'Shaughnessy enemies was of little consequence now). Many letters of support for their innocence of at least this charge appeared in the newspapers. But of course there were many people who were very angry with them, especially Republicans, who although still convinced that the British or someone else was involved in O'Shaughnessy's disappearance, still understandably blamed the Redmondites for creating the climate in which it might happen.

The IRA vowed, in no uncertain terms, to 'get' the culprits who caused the abduction of 'Vol. O'Shaughnessy'. Chilling stuff but thankfully for us, the IRA – through An Phoblacht – also took the opportunity to praise the sculptor and his assistants for persisting in the completion of the statue, compared to the foot-draggers and cowardly appeasers in other areas. Wycherley's IRA memorial in Hackballscross was favourably referred to as were his 'independent' credentials. (Quite a contrast to the Old IRA's suspicion of Wycherley at the outset, which hadn't, I should say, lessened. One Old IRA man from Cork wrote to the *Independent* suggesting that none of this would have happened if a decent nationalist artist had got the job. He didn't elaborate.)

The Government were unable to sustain the charge of conspiring to abduct O'Shaughnessy against Harrington and company after the principal witness, Shane McArdle, refused to participate in the trial and denied any knowledge of a plot on Harrington's part to kidnap O'Shaughnessy. I even denied that I had told Hurley what Harrington had allegedly told me for a joke, further damaging the credibility of Hurley who had already been removed from the case. This was my part of the deal: to have heard or seen nothing. And since I didn't see Harrington outside O'Shaughnessy's house on that Sunday night, how could he have seen me? This was his part of the deal, and between the two of us we strengthened the idea that 'others' had been in O'Shaughnessy's garden, unwittingly assisting O'Shaughnessy in his crazy desire to think that the British had been rustling in his bushes.

As a further favour to Harrington who, let's face it, had taken a hard fall from the whole thing, I promised that the aforesaid documents, which he of course had known nothing about, would be released to the world before the year was out. This was done in October when Mellowes delivered the evidence to a bunch of unsuspecting undergraduates at the Irish History Students' Congress in Galway. It caused much more of a stir than I thought and, in fact, gave fresh life to the mystery of O'Shaughnessy's disappearance. All kinds of conspiracy theories were forwarded and considerable embarrassment was brought not just to the Government and to O'Shaughnessy's family and friends but to the O'Higgins family as well, given the reckless speculation that inevitably developed over O'Shaughnessy's disappearance possibly being a belated revenge for the killing of him; this presuming that the 'revengers' had a prior knowledge of the released documents, of course.

Mellowes is now writing a short book for Phoenix Press that will give meat to the allegations, including the addition of some lively speculations of his own which should be interesting. He is basking in the fame of his revelations and I am happy for him. Just to keep the pot boiling he is even thinking of abandoning the embarrassing story of how he got the papers ('anonymous gift of a terminally ill Old IRA messenger boy') and simply revealing to the world that he and his friends were the men in the garden, and further telling that on our way to discovering the incriminating document we also came across another interesting item – a large stockpile of illegally held weapons. This would really set the cat among the greyhounds. But others are not so enthusiastic, even with Mellowes' guarantee of an anonymity for us equal to that bestowed on his earlier bedridden 'source'. Will the world, regardless, eventually link Mellowes to the men in the garden and the singing in the shed? Who knows? Who cares? Who can stop the flow of history now? My name can't be mentioned for the moment. God, no. But in the future . . .

I have visited Harrington in prison to keep him informed. Not too often, of course; I don't want people to make any more of a connection between the two of us than there is already. They might start thinking. He's in good form, all things considered, and expects to be out within a year or less on good behaviour. Going back to the Bar will be difficult; he recognises that. O'Shaughnessy SC was popular down there. Harrington sees himself as having suffered for a good cause which had nothing to do with O'Shaughnessy.

Others see it too and Harrington gets his fan mail: old Redmondites, neo-Redmondites, constitutionalists, people who abhor the cult of violence. I told him he should have appealed to the people over the heads of the politicians or some such Parnellite reference but he got sore with the joke. He's writing a book about this ordeal; it's already commissioned. Another book. Speaking of which, if jail will do one good thing for him it might get him to finish that damn thesis on John Dillon. He admits he'll have fewer distractions and is going to give it a go, although he didn't like my suggestion of changing the title to 'The Lost Years of John Dillon'. He thought I was having a crack at his own time inside, as well as at the years it took him to get the thesis finished. I don't know, people read too much into things.

I saw Samuelson once but he didn't encourage visits. I don't think he likes me. I think he thinks I was up to something. He flatters me, so he does. These old men always do.

Well, life goes on. The Government is not expected to survive beyond the spring. The Minister of State is concentrating on constituency work and has gone back to compiling books on national election patterns and swings in key marginals. Unfortunately his own is one he'll have to study most carefully for his is one of the seats considered to be in big danger in the forthcoming election. As good as gone, in fact, according to some pundits. The Government is stalling on holding a poll but the Goat tells me that the Opposition have their campaign already organised.

361

'Who lost O'Shaughnessy?' will be one of the catchries, similar to the cry of the US Republicans in the fifties – 'Who lost China?'. Fianna Fáil plan to hammer home the point that not only can Fine Gael not be trusted to protect the Republic but it can't even be trusted to protect the Republic's aged founders. There will be a sly tie-in with the controversial issue of extradition with slogans such as, 'If O'Shaughnessy was extradited, at least we'd know where he went.'

As it is, the stories about O'Shaughnessy grow and grow. Only the other day, I heard again the extraordinary story of his struggle on the quayside during those last few minutes; of how he held off three grown men and nearly put one in the water, of how his jacket was well torn at the shoulders but the Government covered it up because it would show how the poor man was left abandoned, alone, to fight for himself in broad daylight on the city quays, and of how his last guttural breaths in the green water were tragically drowned out by the roaring seagulls.

And yet there are those who have seen him on a wet night at Bray amusement arcade, of all places, shuffling along in a big blue coat. Or on the upper deck of the Holyhead car ferry from where he quickly vanished when his spotters went to get the police. He vanished too from that wall in Coolock where three children became transfixed by his flickering image trying to say something to them. The local bishop came out strongly against such phenomena, cautioning against unconfirmed supernatural visitations, but the children got the day off school nevertheless.

Me, I'm still among the living. And still ensconced in Parnell Square despite my celebrity status. I'm well known now, with many offers of work and a considerable status among the town's artistic elite, not to mention my visibility on the political and media scene. But I'm tired of the fuss and have resolved upon a number of character improvements; the usual stuff – drinking less, becoming more healthy, being even nicer to old people and stray dogs and finding a steady girlfriend. I have taken a number of women up to the Green at midnight and introduced them to my grand old man, my captive spirit. He takes a dim view of most of my punters. He could even be disappointed I missed my chance with Vanessa and overdid my attempt to exploit her grief. She's leaving Dublin after Christmas and Mrs Williams is also being let go for the moment; I have no idea what has happened to Bingo.

Ah, but I'm being modest. I have changed. Changed utterly.

The Collins pictures are down from my wall, the books have been sold off cheaply. In August, for the first time that I can remember, I didn't go the Griffith-Collins Commemorative Mass in Phibsborough. What a relief was lifted from my shoulders. Mass is always a burden but for me it was a double burden. To escape from the slavery of having someone die for me in the abstract, I had to have someone die in the real. Strange, that. Hard, perhaps. But how real is real, as I've said before.

One day recently after the TCD garden party, a boozy pre-ball affair where people dress in boaters or turn-of-the-century costumes, I and my fetching partner were lying under the statue, kissing and delving. The intoxication of the Campari and the perspiration and perfume was such that as my hand was working through the antique drawers of her grandmother, now bequeathed and sheathed over her brown and still-virginal nether regions, I didn't notice an old leaf-gatherer approach.

'You did it, didn't you?' he croaked.

Eh? I was perplexed. Young girl even more perplexed, as you can imagine.

He shuffled closer. 'Did it . . . did him, then.'

Him? Her? Me? The girl's face was a flurry and her skirts were up. Was he blind?

'Him – there!' He pointed to the statue.

'Oh, O'Shaughnessy . . . why, yes, indeed,' I said, pleased to be recognised. 'I worked on that statue.'

'You really caught him, didn't you?' His mouth was open and he had about two teeth.

'Yes, I suppose we did.'

'He deserves it, God bless him. You gave him a stern gaze.'

'Yeah, and now he's giving me one.'

He stopped and nodded towards us.

'He's seen worse,' he said and laughed.

'Yes . . . I suppose he has,' I said and we laughed and thanked him.

He shuffled off, oblivious to the spilled breasts hanging red-tipped and cooled by the early spring air. He looked back at us from some distance and laughed again.

I told you it was a gruesome story.

A NOTE ON THE AUTHOR

Eamon Delaney lives in Dublin. *The Casting of Mr O'Shaughnessy* is his first novel.